The Pirates of Sol:
Book 1
The Black Swan

Lee Crystal

Published by Lee Crystal, 2024.

I0680224

THE PIRATES OF SOL:
BOOK 1
THE BLACK SWAN

First edition. August 1, 2024.
Copyright © 2024 Lee Crystal.
ISBN: 979-8991173216
Written by Lee Crystal.
Book cover
Jupiter/Io Public Domain image courtesy NASA/JPL.
The Black Swan and Moon Hopper model by Lee Crystal.
Character images were AI-generated.

Table of Contents

I want to give special thanks to my late wife, Sue. She was the best person in my life, always encouraging me and very helpful with all my writing.

I also want to thank my wife, Cindy, for all her help with this Novel.

To see Images related to the book, including layouts of the Black Swan, check out www.outpost13.com.

I will also be posting updates on Book 2 there.

Prologue

Mars
Several years after the Pirate War

"Everything ok?" Asked a man's concerned voice over the radio in the helmet of a young woman.

The woman was wearing a light gray pressure suit with her helmet and sitting on a backless seat on the right side of a beat-up small brown truck. The crude four-wheeled surface vehicle was open to the cold night of the thin Martian atmosphere.

She leaned back from her chair onto a small metal box sitting close to her in the back of the truck's flatbed.

She looked into a little window that was emitting a dull light from the inside on the top of the box. Below it was a small lit-up control screen and readout. She tapped the control panel and viewed the results.

"Fine." She replied over the radio in her helmet as she looked at the man sitting at the truck's controls wearing similar gear to her left.

The woman rose off the box and sat up to look behind them.

She could see the red dust the tires were kicking up behind them from the glow of the starlight in the Martian night sky. This soft light also illuminated the flat Martian surface all around her. Seeing nothing else, she let out a sigh of relief.

She then looked through the windshield toward where they were heading and saw lights emanating from a large white dome and several towers in the distance.

Their odd vehicle's dim lights illuminated the rough road before them as they sped along. It was alone on a crudely man-made, drivable surface made of only packed Martian soil with rocks and boulders moved over to the side.

Looking at the man, she asked. "How much further?"

"Not too far. I think I can even see a shuttle just leaving the spaceport." He replied, still staring straight ahead, focused on the road before them.

She looked out the windshield and could just make out the glow of thrusters on a craft rising up into the sky.

Turning slightly in her seat to face the man, she placed her left gloved hand on the metal box behind her and gently patted it.

Suddenly, she stopped and cried, "They're here!"

The man glanced nervously at her and asked, "Where?"

"I don't know!" she barked as she franticly scanned the horizon around the truck.

Then she nudged the man with her left hand, pointed with her right towards the dome's left side ahead of them, and said, "THERE!."

While watching the road, the man briefly looked up to see a light approaching them.

As it got closer, smaller lights on the object lit it up enough for them to see it was a white craft flying just above the surface and kicking up a trail of dust behind it.

The craft stopped just ahead of them, hovering near the road, slightly turned to its right, showing part of its left side.

In response, the man touched the control panel, causing the vehicle to speed up.

They were close enough now to see the craft was much bigger than the truck they were in and shaped like a 3-dimensional parallelogram with tiny wings on each side.

As they drew closer, they saw two figures backlit in a front window. A door could also be seen on the side of the craft just in front of its left wing.

From below the craft came a blinding spotlight that lit up the truck.

Over the radio, the couple heard a loud, gruff male voice say, "STOP!"

The man and woman looked at each other. She nodded her head, and he did as well. The man franticly touched the control panel again. The truck flew faster down the road, kicking up even more dust.

The truck quickly passed under the craft and flew on down the road past it.

Slowly, the hovering craft turned and started following them, retraining their spotlight back on the truck.

Over the radio, the loud, gruff voice demanded, "Stop, you are wanted for questioning!"

The man leaned into the steering wheel and focused on the road while the woman nervously watched the craft follow them.

Soon, the craft was directly over them, shining their spotlight on the truck. It was stirring up large amounts of Martian dust on the ground. Making it hard for the man to see the road.

The woman yelled over the radio, "Back off, damn it!"

Suddenly, the man exclaimed, "OH CRAP," When he realized he was too far off the road.

He tried to swerve back, but the truck's right front tire hit a large rock along the road's edge. The vehicle flipped over, tumbled violently down the road, and finally stopped in a smoldering pile.

The craft hovered over the crash, shining its light on the wreckage. It was clear the couple were dead and mangled in the debris.

There was a glint of something nearby along the side of the road. The ship lowered its landing gear and landed near the object.

Two men in black pressure suits exited a door from the right side of the craft and walked over to the object. They could tell it was some kind of metal box.

They saw a display panel flashing red below a small window on the top of the box.

The light coming from inside the box through the window was flickering.

The men got closer and looked through the window. In a webbed restraint and wrapped in a blanket was a crying baby.

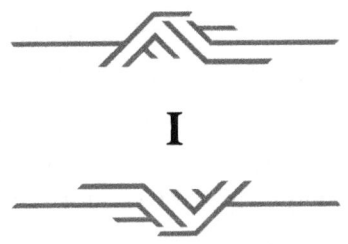

I

Many Years Later
Somewhere Along The Outer Asteroid Belt

In the dim light of the far-off sun, a small, pale, white, cylindrical spacecraft was decelerating backward towards a much larger, dark vessel awaiting it in the cold blackness of space. As the ship's speed slowed, its large ion engine diminished its output.

A long window glowed faintly on the blunt, rounded-off nose of the front of the ship. Tiny dark figures could be clearly seen inside. Two of them disappeared just as the ship came to a stop as its ion engine flamed out. The motionless craft was now only a few hundred kilometers away from the more massive vessel.

Two large doors along the length and in the middle of the smaller ship swung open. Inside was a small bay with a little boxy white shuttle pod that barely fit inside. It lit up, and through its sizeable front window, two dark, short-haired, chubby men in dark jumpsuits and silver boots could be seen moving inside.

Using hand grips, they pulled themselves along until they floated over to two of the pod's three seats. One took the center seat, and the other took the one on the left and strapped themselves in. The interior lights faded, and only the glow of the ship's instrumentation illuminated them.

With a click, the pod's bottom magnetic lock was deactivated. Separating the small craft from the airlock and docking bay. A small noiseless spurt of the shuttle's bottom thrusters popped it out of the bay and away from its mother ship. The pod's rear engines roared silently to life, pushing the small craft toward the bigger vessel.

The passenger in the left seat quietly looked at his reflection in the window. He stared at his green eyes that had thin dark eyebrows above them. He saw a man with a golden brown, long oval face closing in on thirty, looking back at him. His delicate features, long Roman nose, and thin lips gave his face a lot of character. He reached up and watched himself rub his jaw, feeling several day's worth of growth.

He turned to look at his pilot in the center seat. The pale-skinned man also had green eyes but had a thick, dark pair of eyebrows over them. At least his thin, narrow nose and thick lips seemed to suit his face.

The shuttle's motors stopped their silent roar. Ever so slowly, the pod made its way toward the stern of the large vessel that lay quietly before it. The tiny shuttle pod's mother ship grew smaller as the other craft became more prominent. Only starlight and the dim sunlight from behind them illuminated the dark vessel.

With a Scottish accent, the pilot leaned to his left and asked, "First time in deep space, Mr. Rush?"

"Brian," the passenger replied, then added, "Yes, I've never been out this far before." He then pressed his face up to the window to get a better look at the large ship.

The pilot looked over at Brian and was about to ask him another question but realized his passenger was far more interested in where they were going than talking.

Brian's eyes had finally adjusted to the darkness, and he could make out some details of his new, temporary home. Being so close to the window, his breath started to fog it. He was annoyed that he had to back away so it would clear.

The unusual ship had a large central section and two wing-like structures extending from its top and bottom. Their ends tapered toward their tips. The main hull was cylindrical and tapered out slightly from its center. Two large tanks were attached to the side of each wing and the ship's hull. The eight tanks created a circle pattern around the ship's center. Its hull was dark and appeared to be an unusual-looking heavy plating.

He frowned once he realized the ship had the typical old class C explorer craft characteristics with hydrogen propellant tanks and low-thrust plasma drive.

It was his own fault for signing on without checking all the fine print. His contract was rather vague about exactly what kind of ship he would be working on. He knew you can't be too picky when you need a job.

Odd though, he thought, why was there a 1 G stress ability requirement in the contract? At best, the old-style plasma drives for C-class ships typically only got the thrust up to create about half a G?

Brian saw a small navigation array with a dish and antennas on the blunt, tapered rear end.

The shuttle pod was close now and started to swing out and around the strange ship's starboard side, just slightly above the top of its primary cylindrical structure.

Brian spotted two large, long, closed hangar doors on the top rear end of the ship. It was clear to Brian that the shuttle pod was not heading for it, but he wondered what could be inside.

Above the large hangar were two closed, smaller ones side by side. Together, they were as wide as the big hangar but not nearly as tall. It became clear they were for EVA operations when Brian could distinguish the words EVA 2 and EVA 1 on them.

A row of large glowing vents was along the side of the ship, just past a few darkened windows about a third of the way from the ship's rear. They had Brian puzzled.

Halfway along, both wings were the ship's main drives. Each wing had two parallel connected engines that extended slightly past the wing's front and rear edge.

Brian was surprised not to see any powder burns on the drive exhaust. The ship had to have used its hydrogen propellant to get here unless it was towed all the way out here. Then, he recognized the electron injectors extending from the drives. This explained the purpose of the vents on the ship's side to Brian.

There was no obvious sign of a radiator system to disperse the heat buildup on the ship. Brian surmised that it was probably being bled off using a liquid circulation system along sections of the wing.

Above the top wing's starboard engines was an unusual boxy extension. Mounted firmly to a strut just above that was a rather big rocket. It reminded Brian of a long-range probe design he had seen somewhere before.

Brian couldn't distinguish what was protruding from the opposite side of the wing, where the probe was.

Towards the very top of the wing was a sensor array that wrapped entirely around it.

On the top edge of the wing was a short tower with some type of unusual pivotable sensor atop it.

Ah, thought Brian, the wings not only disperse excess heat but are also used to mount operational platforms for the ship.

The shuttle pod dropped downward and was now halfway along the starboard side of the massive ship. Brian could see a few rows of small, mostly dark, windows along the main structure. Two-thirds of the way from the ship's rear was a standard circular universal dock, but they passed it by.

Brian could see that it was not the best place for the shuttle pod to dock. The tanks from the top and bottom were a little too close to make for a safe docking. A dock like this is more likely to be used with a docking arm from a more massive ship or space station.

Brian scanned the vessel's hull for the ship's name but didn't see one. There was not even a registration number. He thought it odd.

Brian could now see part of the lower wing and noticed below its drives was a boxy extension similar to the one he saw on the top wing. Below that were fixed sophisticated sensors at the front and rear. On the side, he could see an extended rotating sensor dish and assumed there was probably a matching one on the other side of the wing.

Towards the bottom of the wing was another sensor array wrapped entirely around it like the one on the top wing.

A large rod-like antenna was below the array. It extended from the wing and was parallel to the ship. It was so large Brian could see part of its twin on the other side of the wing.

A combination laser and high-gain dish communication tower was mounted on the very bottom of this wing.

Brian was perplexed to see such a high-end device retrofitted onto an old explorer-class craft.

The shuttle pod fired its thrusters. It turned and swung out in front of the large dark ship with a slight jerk. The shuttle was now facing it.

Brian could see a long window just below the top wing, set back on the front of the main structure. Even though it was lit up, Brian could not see any figures inside.

However, he thought he saw a person in one of a smaller set of windows towards the tapered front end of the ship. Brian believed this may be the ship's command deck.

The flattened bow of the ship had another navigation dish and two antennas, just like the one Brian saw on the vessel's stern, but these were slightly larger.

The very front tampered section of the ship appeared to be a large command module. There was an obvious point along the hull where it could separate from the rest of the vessel. In an emergency, it could be used as a lifeboat.

At least that is not all that unusual in modern spaceship design, thought Brian.

The shuttle pod's thrusters fired again. It slowly rolled and headed for the bottom front end of the massive ship.

During this, a bright light from the pod lit up the underside of the ship's command module. Brian could see they were now heading for a dock. One that was much easier to access.

Brian nearly forgot about the strange object that extended from the other side of the top wing where the probe was. He attempted to get a good look at it before the shuttle's rotation took it entirely out of sight.

It was strange. A long pod-like object with an open tube...

Armed! Brian almost exclaimed out loud.

This souped-up old-time explorer was equipped with a sizable military-grade Direct Energy Weapon.

Brian looked over at the pilot and was going to ask him what he thought but decided not to. The pilot was far too busy docking the shuttle pod.

He heard the loud click, and the shuttle shook slightly as it docked with the larger craft.

"All right, laddy, everyone off. Last stop," Chuckled the lively Scottish shuttle pilot.

Quickly, the tall, husky man unbuckled himself from his seat. Using hand grips along the wall, he gently eased his way to the shuttle's floor airlock hatch. Brian unbuckled and followed closely behind. The pilot floated near the round hatch and punched a few buttons on a nearby wall panel. Slowly, the hinged hatch opened upward.

Brian looked at his friendly pilot and said, "Thanks for the ride."

Gracefully, he swooped through the mouth of the lock but soon realized the other hatch on the other end was still closed! Frantically, he tried to stop himself by grabbing the hand grips along the hatchway.

Fortunately, he was able to swivel his body and put his legs in front of him. He smacked heavily into the closed hatch, recoiling his legs to take most of the shock. Then, grabbing the hand grips inside the docking tunnel prevented him from bouncing off the door.

A few seconds later, the hatch in front of him started to open, and the one to the shuttle closed behind him.

Brian was a bit shaken up from his close call. After a quick check, he realized it had not caused any severe injury. This was the closest he had ever come to hurting himself in the six years he's been an aero-engineer.

He could smell something odd yet familiar among the usual human odors inside the ship.

Once the hatch was completely open, Brian stuck his head out from the hatchway and exclaimed, "What the hell are you trying to do? Kill m...."

Brian suddenly stopped ranting when he saw a very young, tall lady. She was wearing a dark gray, somewhat tight jumpsuit with silver magnetic boots standing before him. This was when Brian realized the lock was parallel to the deck.

Her pale face and dark eyebrows had lovely, subtle oriental features partly covered by a long dark ponytail. It floated freely around her in zero gravity, like a clump of seaweed in a gentle ocean current.

"Darn door, I could never get the thing to work right," She explained in a harsh but soft feminine voice.

"Uh... "Brian stammered, looking at the woman.

"Hello, I'm Val Elderman, the tech specialist, well, one of them." She said with a broad smile, extending her thin arm and small hand to the young man.

"Uahhhh...yea. I'm B, Bria...." He stuttered while staring at her fiery amber eyes and thin pink lips.

"Brian Rush," she interrupted.

He nodded, then said, "You can just call me Brian."

"Ok, Brian. You are our engineer for this mission?" She asked, shaking the man's right hand with hers.

He awkwardly replied, "Yeah."

No doubt about it, Brian told himself, her hand is as soft as it looks.

He was unwilling to let go of the woman's hand, which seemed to make little difference to her. She appeared content to let Brian shake her hand for as long as he wanted.

Brushing her flowing ponytail away from her face with her left hand, she asked, "Do you need any help?"

"No, that's ok, thanks," Brian replied.

Brian let go of her hand, pushed himself off the hand grip he was holding, and floated out of the lock. Once clear of the open hinged hatch, he remotely activated his boots from a control velcroed on the lower arm of his dark jumpsuit.

He stood beside her and quickly noticed she was a few inches taller than his six foot two inches.

Looking around the square docking room, he noticed it was almost as big as the shuttle he was just in. The entire room was pale gray and well-lit from some square panels above. A small window was on each side of the dock of the outer hull wall. Through them, Brian could see the bottom of the shuttle.

Still staring out the window, Brian said, "I hope my luggage and equipment I sent have already arrived."

"Yes. Your luggage is in your quarters, and your equipment has been stowed away. It will be released to you after inspection," Val responded.

Brian turned and frowned at her and asked, "Inspection?"

Val replied, "Sorry, those are the rules for all of us."

"Well, can you show me the way to my quarters then? I would like to freshen up," asked Brian.

Val answered, "Sorry, but we only have about thirty minutes until our briefing on the control deck. Everyone should already be there."

Val walked over to a nearby wall panel with her ponytail in tow. After touching it, the hinged hatch slowly shut and locked. Once, the air in the dock was vented, and after a loud click, Brian saw the shuttle depart.

She looked at Brian and said, "Oh, by the way, here is your C&PC."

She pulled a small, thin, five by five centimeter square device attached to a wristband from her jumpsuit pocket and handed it to Brian.

"What's this?" He inquired, holding it in his hand.

"Your Communicator and Personal Computer. We all have one encoded with our ID, and you will be required to wear it at all times," explained Val.

Brian began saying, "I am familiar with them, but why...."

Val interrupted and said, "You will also find several specialized jumpsuits like mine in your cabin closet. You will be required to wear them while on duty."

Brian asked, "Uh, does it have a velcro patch on the arm? I use mine to control my boots?"

"No, however, you can link your boots to your C&PC to control them," Val replied.

Before Brian could ask another question, Val explained, "I'm sure any further questions you may still have will be covered at the briefing. If not, you can bring them up after."

"Ok," Brian replied with some confusion as he stretched the flexible ban over his hand, making sure the black square of the device was on the top of his left wrist. It lit up briefly to automatically adjust its orientation, setting which end was the bottom.

She strolled over to a large open door opposite the hatch on the other side of the room. Her long ponytail flowed gently along behind her.

"Come along, Mr. Rush," she said as she went through the door.

Brian followed closely behind.

Passing through the open doorway, he realized it was a bulkhead door. Designed to protect the ship from decompression. If the dock was compromised and started venting air out into space, it would automatically slide down from above and close off the room.

They entered a circular gray hallway that was lit with square panels from above. Brian assumed this must be the method used for lighting on the entire ship.

Opposite the bulkhead doorway, Brian saw a closed door on the curved wall before him. A little sign above it read, "Maintenance Duct, ladder access to all levels," in several languages.

This door was of standard design for most access ways on any sizable spacecraft. It was shaped to match the wall it was part of so it would recess into it when opened.

Brian saw Val turn to the left and start walking down the hallway. Quickly, he followed.

They passed a chute on the wall to his right with an image of a trashcan above its flap.

As he walked by, he stuck his hand in out of curiosity. As soon as he did, he immediately took it out when he felt suction.

So that's how it works in zero-G, he thought.

They came to a closed, dull gray metallic airtight door on the left. There was a similar color-toned elevator door on the right with a sign above it that simply had the number 1 on it.

Brian looked at the lift and asked, "Electromagnetic, so they can be used all the time?"

"Of course, but in zero-G, it's always a good idea to hold onto the railing," Val said.

She walked over to the elevator and pushed the up call button.

Out of curiosity, Brian walked a little further down the circular hallway. On the right was another closed door. A sign on it said "Stairwell" in several languages.

Past that was a different standard spacecraft airtight door on the left. On the right was another elevator with a sign above it with the number 2.

As Brian returned to the first elevator, he surmised that the circular hallway he was in must be part of a large, long cylinder that made up the ship's central core that ran the ship's length.

Realizing Brian saw the stairwell, Val said, "The command deck is only one flight up. We could take the stairs."

Frowning, Brian replied, "That's not much fun in magnetic boots."

The elevator door opened to reveal a well-lit, gray oval room with handrails along the walls. Another sign in different languages on the wall said, "Secure Cargo in Lift, especially while in zero-G."

They both stepped into the elevator, turned, and faced the open lift door. Brian grabbed the railing firmly while Val looked at him, grinning.

Brian smiled back and asked, "By the way, I noticed a large bay at the ship's rear. Since we didn't dock there, I can only assume something is inside?"

"That has our Moon Hopper in it if we need to do more detailed investigation work," replied Val.

"I thought the ship was only doing some simple survey work?" inquired Brian.

"That Mr. Rush is what we all have been told," Val replied as she pressed the elevator controls and the door closed.

Slowly, they rose up to the next level. Brian felt a little silly and loosened his tight grip on the railing.

They exited the lift into another circular hallway and walked straight up to the door on the opposite wall. After a second, it automatically opened. They entered the large gray room of the command deck. The gray metallic door closed behind them once they passed the threshold.

They stood in a semicircle-shaped gray room that was half of the ship's top level. Several gray consoles with gray seats lined the outer hull wall. Like most spacecraft, all standard seats are fixed, usually can swivel, and have retractable straps to secure the user in zero-G.

There was another console with a seat near the door they had just entered. It faced away from the wall behind it. Halfway along this wall, near this console, was a closed door. It had a sign on it that read "Situation Room," but only in English. Near where this wall intersected, the outer hull wall was a large window to space.

Brian examined the consoles. He could tell they were all the same top-of-the-line, generic, all-purpose models. Any of them could be used for almost any ship operation. Along with their flat displays and physical keyboard, they could create interactive programmable 3D holographic ones.

At the top center section of the outer hull were the four windows Brian saw earlier on his way in. The two center windows were side by side, and each had a gray pilot seat with an attached screen and controls. These seats could tilt back so the pilots could physically look out the window into space to see where the ship was going.

A gray center console with unique controls was between the pilot seats. A matching keypad and a small display screen were fixed on each side of this console. Both sides also had a physical keyboard with an attached screen on a flexible armature so the pilot could use it in any position.

Opposite the pilot stations along the curved inner wall was a large, unusual gray console with a seat. It was not like the other consoles on the command deck.

Brian thought, could this one have something to do with the ship's energy weapon?

Between this console and the pilot stations at the center of the room was a sizeable gray hexagon-shaped table with two gray chairs. One is on the port side of the table, and the other is on the starboard side.

It was clear that the table was part of the ship's interface. It displayed a holographic image of where the ship was in space and everything its sensors could pick up around it. From this, Brian could tell the shuttle pod had already docked with its mother ship and started moving away.

Several people were in the room. He observed that most were thin and tall due to Earth's colonist's progeny living in lower gravity. Most of them were milling around, talking to each other, while one was sitting at a control console. They all had on their C&PCs and wore the same tight gray jumpsuit Val had. He looked out of place since he was still in his baggy dark jumpsuit.

Before Brian knew it, a strange hand grabbed his.

"Mark Linol is the name. Captaining is my game," said a chubby, jolly man shaking Brian's hand. "I'm also the ship's primary pilot and navigator. Three for the price of one."

Mark Linol was an older husky guy. Not really fat, just a big guy. His dark-toned skin made his bald head seem very shiny. His bushy gray eyebrows and trim gray beard on his chin stuck out. He had dark eyes and a broad nose but a tiny mouth with thin lips. His gray jumpsuit had pilot wings and two white bars on the chest's left side.

Before Brian knew it, Captain Linol quickly turned towards the others in the room.

17

"Ladies and Gentlemen, this is our young engineer, Brian Rush," said the captain, introducing Brian to the people he would be working with for some time.

Most of his fellow crew members all replied with a very hallow hello.

"Don't worry, son," Captain Linol whispered to Brian, "soon, you'll get used to them." Then, in a lower mumble to himself, "I hope."

"Yeah, they look really friendly," Brian replied softly, seeing their somewhat gloomy faces.

"Well, let's meet as many as we can before the briefing starts, shall we?" The captain asked.

"Ok," replied Brian with a shrug of his shoulders.

"If you will excuse us, Ms. Elderman," Captain Linol said to the young lady.

The jolly man grabbed Brian by the arm and pulled him toward a tall, light-brown woman.

"This is Zala Teka. She is our ship doctor," the captain said with a broad smile.

She was an attractive, tall, voluptuous older woman. Her short, curly brown hair, thin brownish eyebrows, soft brown eyes, small flat nose, and plump lips were arranged nicely on her smooth, round face.

"This is Brian Rush, our engineer," Captain Linol said, looking at Zala while gesturing at Brian.

"It's nice to meet you," Brian said, shaking her hand while staring at all her assets.

"Are you from Earth?" She asked.

Catching Brian off guard, he replied, "Um, what?" before looking up at the tall lady and refocusing his eyes on her face.

"I'm from a long line who migrated from Ethiopia to Mars in the earliest days of colonization," she explained while smiling.

Brian kept his eyes on her face, saying, "Oh, I'm from Earth. Texas, to be exact. It's where I was born and grew up."

"That explains your warm brown skin tones," She replied, looking over Brian.

"Well, there will be more time for further conversation later. I need to move on," The captain interrupted, dragging Brian away.

As they walked away, Brian glanced back to see she was still staring at him.

"Just to warn you, Brian, that lady will wear you down. Trust me, I know," said Captain Linol with a strange smile.

After a few steps, they came up to a short, stout, and muscular dark brown woman. She was older than the doctor and not as shapely. She had a tiny button nose and thick lips. Her stubbly blond hair, thin eyebrows, and light blue eyes stood out against her dark, almost leathery skin.

"This is our Extravehicular Activity or EVA, specialist LaNutza Teodoresco," said the captain, introducing the woman.

"You can call me Nutzie," she said with a slight Slavic accent.

"This is Brian Rush, our engineer." The captain said, glancing at Brian.

"You can just call me Brian. Would you happen to be Romanian?" asked Brian, looking down at the woman.

"Yes, how did you know?" She, in turn, asked him.

"I heard the accent a lot when I went to the Technical University of Cluj-Napoca for about a year," Brian replied.

Nutzie nodded while saying, "Oh, I see."

Brian looked at her skin and said, "From your dark skin tone, I bet you are on your class three license now."

"You seem to know quite a lot about me," Nutzie inquired, squinting at Brian.

"I just took an educated guess. You see, my father was an EVA guy. Even though EVA suits provide lots of protection, repeated

19

exposure can't stop all the ultraviolet radiation. He went from a class two license down to a class three. His skin is almost as dark as yours."

"So, did he stay in like me and be limited to EVA work at and past Mars orbit?" Nutzie asked.

"No. Dad didn't want to ship us all to Mars. When he got the class change, he took a good consultant job on Earth."

"I don't think I could do that. I can't see myself working at a desk. I got to be free in the vacuum of space with all the stars of creation surrounding me. When I'm finally forced to retire, I'm going to miss it," said Nutzie with a frown.

Brian was about to make a comment but stopped. Out of the corner of his eye, he saw a man standing beside the starboard side of the pilot station who looked familiar.

"Excuse me, I think I recognize someone," he said to Captain Linol and Nutzie as he quickly stepped away.

It couldn't be. Not all the way out here, Brian told himself.

He made his way over to a thin, tall, slightly tan man in a gray jumpsuit beside the starboard pilot seat, looking over its controls.

Brian stood behind him and, in a deep voice, said, "Hello there, sailor."

The man at the pilot station turned around, puzzled, and stared at Brian.

Brian noticed that he also had white pilot wings on the left chest of his jumpsuit, just like the captains.

"Brian Rush!" shouted the man as he stared at Brian.

"Robert Callen, it is you!" replied Brian, utterly amazed as he stepped back to look at him.

Rob had more color than the old Canadian pale pink skin he used to have. He was still four inches taller than Brian and had the same square face, hazel eyes, short brown hair, and eyebrows. But wait, there was something new. A light brown mustache was below his prominent nose, just above his thin-lipped mouth.

"So, you decided to grow one, after all?" Brian inquired.

"Grow What?" Rob asked, staring at the engineer oddly.

"That crumb catcher," laughed Brian.

"Oh yeah, I've had it for a while now," Rob replied, twirling it with his right hand's thumb and index finger.

"Ah, I see you already know my co-pilot and assistant navigator, Mr. Callen," Captain Linol said once he caught up to Brian.

"Yes, sir. I know him, "Brian told the captain.

"After studying abroad, I ended up at the Carl Sagan Aero Space Institute, where Rob and I were roommates for a while," he said, looking at his old friend's face. It had a few more wrinkles since he last saw it.

"What are you doing here, Brian?" Rob asked, smiling.

"Me? I needed a job, so now I'm the ship's engineer. What about you? I thought you landed a sweet pilot job with some big Earth-Mars space cruise company?"

"I did, but.... well, it's a long story," responded Rob with a frown.

"You will have to tell me sometime," Brian told his old friend.

"Maybe later, Brian, when I have the time," Rob replied, looking down at the floor.

After a slight pause, Rob looked back up at Brian and added. "I'm here just like you. I needed a job, too."

"I see," Brian said, noticing the sadness in his friend's eyes.

"It's great to see you again. We will have to get together later and talk about old times," Rob said as he grabbed Brian's hand and shook it.

Suddenly, Rob looked at his hand, then stared back up at Brian and said, "I'm sorry, I have to do something. I'll see you later."

Robert was off. Quickly, he made his way to the port side of the command deck and exited through the port door and out into the circular hallway.

While watching him leave, Captain Linol said, "He heads to the bathroom every time he shakes hands. I think he's germaphobic?"

With a curious look, Brian asks, "germaphobic?"

The captain replied, "It's odd. I guess he only shakes people's hands out of some kind of professional courtesy. "

Turning towards the engineer, Captain Linol asks Brian, "Has he always been that way?"

"No, that's new," replied Brian.

After a brief pause, the captain grabbed Brian by the arm and said, "Let's meet our communications specialist since we are close to him."

They turned around and took a few steps to the starboard side of the deck, just past a window to the first console. A pale-toned, tall, thin, frail man was strapped into the seat facing the crowd but paying little attention to anyone.

His egg-shaped head had just a sparse amount of short, brownish-red hair. He had thin, reddish eyebrows over green eyes, a long, bulbous nose, and thin pale lips.

"This is our communications specialist, Ralph Milsom," the captain said, introducing the man to the engineer.

Gesturing at Brian, Captain Linol said, "And this is our engineer, Brian Rush."

Brian shook the man's hand. It felt odd, kind of like wet sandpaper.

Ralph stated, "I hope we go into flight soon. I hate using the zero-G adapters in the bathroom."

"Oh," was all Brian got out before he realized there was a sudden silence in the room.

Brian turned to see that the door labeled situation room was now open. A woman slowly made her way out onto the command deck.

Those who could not see what was going on moved around the deck so they could.

The woman was short, stout, and very muscular. She had a warm medium brown skin tone and curly, short black hair. Her long oval face had bushy black eyebrows over deep-set hazel eyes, a round nose, and thin red lips.

Her curvy shape appeared to barely fit into her tight gray jumpsuit. A single white bar was adorned on the left chest of her suit. She wore a black belt with a few small gray pouches in the front and a large one on her left hip.

Brian heard a soft motor noise grow louder as the woman stepped to her left, away from the door.

An old, short, thin, gray-haired man walked up and stopped in the doorway. He wore a gray jumpsuit with a white star on his left chest. His body was strapped into a powered black exoskeleton frame from his feet up to his back. It seemed to be designed to give him the ability to walk.

A big gray pouch was attached to the right side of his Exosuit near the hip.

He was wearing soft shoes, not magnetic boots. His feet were strapped to the top of the foot pads of the suit. These pads seem to have the same magnetic abilities as everyone's boots to keep him on the floor.

The old man had a well-worn tan, wrinkled round face, milky gray eyes, and thin white eyebrows. His long, crooked nose looked like it had been broken many times. While his long mouth and thick lips seemed locked into a constant sneer.

Slowly, the gray-haired man made his way out onto the command deck. His Exosuit's magnetic foot pads made a slight cluck as he walked, louder than the clicking noise of most magnetic boots.

Suddenly, a crew member Brian had not yet met of what Brian thought was Chinese origins jumps out in front of the old man. She was a light tan, thin, tall lady with short dark hair. Brian was not close enough to her to make out any other details.

She yells, "Damn you, Thatorn! I would have never signed up if I knew you were running this!" Then she runs to the nearby starboard entrance. When it opened, she almost collided with Rob, who was about to enter the room. As soon as Rob saw her, he quickly got out of her way.

Brian asked the captain, "Who was that?"

"Fa Ming, our IT tech," Captain Linol replied.

The old man sighed and then walked toward the center of the room. The young woman who was with him followed. His robotic legs' soft, rhythmic noises stopped once he was at the table. The young lady walked over and stood beside the console on the inner wall.

Rob was close behind them. He quickly passed them and made his way back to stand near the co-pilot console.

The old man turns towards the woman. He gestures towards her and says, "For those who don't already know, this is Lieutenant Caroline Rocha. She is the security, tactical, and operations officer."

Turning towards the crew, gesturing at the captain, he states, "This is the ship's primary pilot and navigator, Captain Mark Linol."

He then looks over the crew, saying, "I am Admiral Ivan Thatorn. I am the mission commander and will also be our Science expert on this mission. Please take note you are to address all Unified Earth Alliance officers on this ship by their rank or sir."

After seeing several nods from the crew, Thatorn said, "I understand that most of us know several languages. Please only use the international Unified Earth Alliance Standard English while on the ship to avoid confusion."

"Before anyone asks, Yes, we are technically an armed military vessel if you were not already aware of this. For security reasons, your contracts only stated you could be working with the military on this mission."

The old man suddenly grunted while looking over the crew. He then focused on the captain and asked, "I see we are one short."

Captain Linol replied, "Ah, yes, sir, technician Lee Smith was not well and went to the infirmary a few hours ago."

Thatorn turns to glare at the doctor.

Zala replied, "He was complaining of motion sickness. I gave him something to help, and he was still asleep when I left him less than an hour ago."

Thatorn let out a huff and looked back at the captain.

"I will fill him in later, sir," Captain Linol said.

"Very well then," Thatorn scowled.

Staring back at the crew, he said, "This briefing will cover everything you need to know. Some of you may already be familiar with some of the items I will be going over. Nonetheless, everyone needs to listen carefully to ensure comprehension."

Thatorn then held up his left arm and touched the black device on his left wrist using his right hand. This caused the small square device to activate and light up briefly. Then, a 3D image of a 2D document appears in front of him just above the device.

While looking over the document, he said, "You should all now have your ship's communications and personal computer. C&PC for short. When given this device, you should have also been informed that you must keep it on at all times for the duration of the mission. This is also a stipulation in your contract. The devices are shockproof, staticproof, and waterproof. They are encoded with your personal ID and tied into the ship systems. Your health and other biometric data will be monitored. Most of you are already aware security uses this, along with your location and work schedule, to grant needed access to areas of the ship. The galley, command deck, and medical bays are always automatically available for everyone to access. The map system on your C&PC can display the areas you do and do not have access to at any given time. These devices can also access any needed data on the ship's mainframe. Information you have access to can also be stored on your personal C&PC for easier use. You can also link the C&PC to your cabin's work computer to upload any specialized items you create or have for your own use."

After taking a deep breath, he continued, "You all were issued several unique protective gray jumpsuits of your size. Your contract specifically states that you are required to wear them while on duty. You are responsible for cleaning them yourselves. On each of the three cabin levels is a laundry room. Use it to clean your uniforms and any other personal clothing. Please use your bathroom laundry bag to store your dirty clothes until you are ready to clean them. You will find it velcroed to the lower wall beside the sink."

He looked up for a moment and looked around. He stopped and gazed at Brian, frowned, and added, "I see almost all of you are wearing them."

Thatorn looked back at the document and continued, "Those with your own spacesuits have been checked to ensure they are all up to code. We have stored them in lockers designated for them in the EVA control room. We also have a few extra ones of different sizes for those who don't have any if needed."

While still looking at the document, Thatorn reached up and tapped the screen on his C&PC to turn the page. Then he started again, saying, "All external communication is restricted. You will not be able to use your C&PC for external communication. Your personal communication device will not work while on the ship. If you need to contact anyone, you can submit text messages for transmission to the security officer. They will redact anything deemed inappropriate that could risk our mission."

"This is a clean ship. Keep it that way. Vacuum chutes for waste can be found around the ship and in your cabins. Use them!" He exclaimed.

After glancing around the crew, he continued, "Except for the doctor. Contractors on board were not given any duties until the morning of the 3rd for pre-flight and system checks. That was to make the ship ready for full ship operations. As salaried contractors, you will be expected to work a minimum number of hours per day, determined by your classification. You are always on call in case your particular skill sets are needed. Starting tonight, my officers and I will handle all the ship's key night operations."

Thatorn tapped his C&PC and deactivated it. The 2D image he was looking at disappeared. He lowered his left arm and walked around the table behind him. Once it was between him and the crew, he reached out and activated some holographic controls over the tabletop. He stepped back, and the 3D image changed.

The image shrunk so you could see more that was further away. You could now see the ship's location just past most of the asteroid belt. A curved blue line extended outward from the asteroid belt towards the orbit of a gas giant.

Thatorn said, "Ship time is set to Earth Greenwich Mean Time with the current date of 4 APR 2272, and the current time is 20:35 hours. Your C&PCs are already set to this. We will be leaving shortly at 21:00 hours for Jupiter and its moons. We will be operating thrust levels to give us about .4 Gs. This should be no problem since you all have been rated for 1 G according to your contract agreements."

Thatorn paused to check the crew's reaction. After a few seconds, he continued, "Lieutenant Rocha will send out all your updated work assignments and the maintenance schedules over your wrist C&PC and cabin computer. This will also include your meal times and breaks. Those not on duty tonight should take this time to get some sleep and be prepared for their busy day tomorrow. That is all for now."

Before anyone had the chance to leave, Brian spoke up and asked, "Why are we not using the full potential of the ion drive? From the looks of our course and speed, we are going rather slow."

The captain stared at Brian and asked, "How do you know that?"

Brian replied, "As an engineer, I'm familiar with various ship propulsions. At first, it looked like an old hydrogen plasma-propelled craft. However, I noticed the drives were advanced Ion in nature once I got closer. I could also tell the ship uses an H3 reactor for power due to the hot waste gas vents."

"In fact, two H3 reactors, Mister....?" Thatorn asked, squinting his gray eyes at Brian.

"Rush," Brian replied.

Thatorn raised his left arm again and activated his C&PC. Quickly, he scanned through a few holographic 2D pages. He stopped at one and looked at it for a few seconds.

After deactivating his C&PC and lowering his arm, Thatorn looked at Brian with a smirk and said, Not bad for an engineer with only a B-class standing."

Brian asked, "So there is no hydrogen propellant in those eight large tanks. Just Ion fuel for the drives, H3, and deuterium for the reactors?"

"Yes, even extra water and oxygen. We also have several backup storage tanks of those items for redundancy all over the ship," replied Thatorn, still smirking.

"But why?" inquired Brian.

Thatorn replied, "You see, Mr. Rush, a requirement for this mission is to maintain the illusion of being a slow hydrogen propellant craft. Using a low-thrust plasma drive. Even you had assumed as much yourself."

Brian nodded in agreement.

Thatorn explained, "The reactor's byproducts, heated hydrogen and helium, are usually expelled through the ship's side vents.

However, an alternate specialized venting system can dump these gases into the ship's ion thrust. A scan or a spectral analyst will make our exhaust look like a dirty plasma thrust from a distance. Adding to the illusion of what kind of ship we are."

Brian asked, "Is this masquerade also why the ship is unmarked and has no name on it?"

"Precisely," Thatorn responded.

"All of this just to do a survey of Jupiter and its moons? Besides, that's got to have been done hundreds of times already? What is the real mission?" asked Brian.

With a snort, Thatorn said, "I had hoped some of you might have recognized me. If you had, it would have been quite obvious."

"I know who you are, sir," Nutzie spoke up.

All but the EA officers cast their eyes on her.

Nutzie looked back at the crew.

After a deep sigh, she said, "We're all going Pirate hunting!"

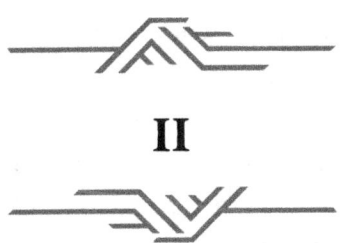

II

Brian hit the call button of elevator 1 on level 7 as he let out a long yawn. He had a restless night because of his new bed and not being used to the lower gravity caused by the ship's minimal thrust. At least the long, warm shower and shave he just had helped wake him up this morning.

While waiting, he took a moment to look around the hallway. At first, he thought the ship's core design was odd. He realized the ringed hall around its core was the final protection from possible decompression throughout the vessel. Especially if a bulkhead door had failed.

He took a look down at his tight jumpsuit and thought. It's far more comfortable than it looks and even makes me appear slimmer.

The lift opened, and he entered. Once inside, he turned to face the door just as it closed. Before touching the lift controls, Brian raised his arm and activated his C&PC on his wrist. It showed the ship's time was currently 6:17 hours, his mag boots were inactive, and he had a notice about his work schedule for the day from Lieutenant Rocha. Brian scrolled through the 3D menu options and brought up the ship layout to find the galley level. Seeing it was on level 4, he selected the appropriate button on the lift controls. When he dropped his arm, the hologram of information vanished.

When the doors opened on the selected floor, he stepped out of the lift into the gray circular hallway. He went through the starboard door across from the elevator and into a gray square room.

Still needing to find the galley, Brian raised up his left arm. His C&PC displayed the same holographic information it was last on.

He selected the fourth-floor layout, and a 3D representation of the level appeared.

The square room had four hallways that extended out from its corners in both the port and starboard directions. The ends of these hallways are connected to perpendicular ones on both sides. The four points where they joined were open bulkhead doors. Brian noticed this part of the floor layout was the same as most other decks, except for the smaller levels in the command module and those below the reactor level that houses the cargo holds, EVA bays, and the main hangar.

Looking at his map, Brian saw the galley was on the other side of the wall before him. Two entrances were at each end of this wall. Additional openings to the room are near the top of the intersecting perpendicular hallways.

Just as he was about to turn off his C&PC and drop his arm, he noticed one of the rooms he did not have access to on this level was marked "Restricted Officers Only" in red.

He shrugged his shoulders, turned off his C&PC, and lowered his arm.

Brian went down the short gray hallway to his left.

He passed a single-user bathroom on his left before seeing the door to the galley on his right. A sign above the door read "Galley" in several languages.

Brian was about to step close enough to activate the door and enter, but his curiosity got the better of him.

He looked down at his wrist and turned his C&PC back on. He took a moment and stared at the map.

Turning it off, he looked back up and walked through the bulkhead doorway into the starboard perpendicular hallway.

He could see the other entrance to the galley just before the dead-end at the outer hull to his right.

Brian turned to his left and saw two doors along the right side of the hallway. Another was on the left just after a connecting hallway, parallel to the one Brian was just in, and before the hallway's other outer hull dead-end.

"That's the restricted door?" Brian asked himself in a whisper.

Slowly, he made his way down the dull gray hall and past the lower intersecting hallway. As he approached the door, he noticed it was red.

Brian thought. Now, that is odd. There is a red door in a sea of gray everywhere inside the ship.

Brian gingerly stepped up to the door, sure it shouldn't automatically open for him. He found it was cold to the touch. Slowly, he leaned up to it and pressed his ear against it.

After a few seconds, he whispered to himself, "Nothing."

Suddenly, Brian heard a door open and close, followed by footfalls. It sounded like someone leaving the galley.

Quickly, Brian pushed himself off the red door.

He stepped away from the door. He stopped when he believed he heard a faint groan over the steps. Brian was sure it came from the red door.

Then, another door opened and closed. Possibly one to the circular hallway.

Brian leaned back towards the red door again to listen.

It was quiet.

He stood there silently for a moment.

Finally giving up, he returned to the other end of the hallway. He passed both corridors that ran perpendicular to the one he was in and stood close to the galley entrance near the dead end. Just far enough away from the door to prevent it from automatically opening.

He looked back down the hall and still heard nothing.

With a deep breath, he stepped up to the door. It opened, and he entered the galley.

The gray room was large. Four big gray tables with four gray chairs on each side were on Brian's left. Two tables in the center were parallel to the room's six big windows. The other tables were placed along the curvature of the outer hull.

To Brian's right, just past the door he almost entered earlier, was a large gray metallic box. It went from the floor to the ceiling and extended several meters from the wall. This box stretched down the wall almost to the port side entrance.

Someone was standing with their back to him at the center of the room beside the large, odd metallic box.

Once he saw the dark crop of long hair halfway down their back, he was sure who it was.

Brian casually walked up behind them and said, "Hello, Val."

With surprise, she turned and faced him.

"Did someone just leave?" inquired Brian.

"It was Rob. He just left right after chatting with me. He's such a nice person," Val replied.

Brian looked at Val, a little puzzled, and thought. I never heard anyone call him that before.

Val asked, "Didn't you see him?"

Brian started saying, "No, I...."

"You were checking out the red door, weren't you," Val interrupted.

With a bit of embarrassment, Brian replied, "Yeah."

"You're not the only one," Val stated.

"What is with that room?" asked Brian.

Val replied, "I only know what the layout says about it and that I don't have access to it."

"Hum," mumbled Brian.

Squinting at Brian, Val asked, "So you've not partaken in the fine cuisine the galley has to offer yet, have you?"

"No, and I've not eaten since I came aboard. It's been a while since I had anything good," Brian said with a smile.

Gesturing at the silver box before them, Val said. "It will not be exactly what you might have hoped for. You see, since we don't have a cook on the ship. All of the food preparation and distribution is handled mechanically."

Brian looked at the big box before them and saw only a row of touchscreen interfaces with tall tray-sized dispensers below them.

Since he started taking work off Earth, Brian had noticed that the mechanical preparation of food was becoming the modern standard for spaceflight. It can safely store food ingredients and utilize preparation methods that work at various gravity levels. Except in no gravity, that's when prepackaged food items are usually used.

"It's the price we pay for progress," Brian groaned.

"I think it's just a way to cut costs," Val replied.

They both made some selections and waited. Brian quickly skipped over the energy bar options and picked something hot to eat. Val got her tray within a few moments, made her way to the table by the windows on the port side, and sat at the closest end of the table on the window side.

While waiting for his food, Brian noticed an opening with a trash chute beside it at both ends of the big box. Above the opening were the words "Tray, Utensils, Plates, and Leftovers Return" in several languages. He grimaced, speculating if the machine was recycling the leftovers.

Brian quickly made his way over to Val after getting his tray.

"May I join you?" he asked.

"Sure," she replied with a grin.

Brian sat down across from Val. He soon noticed the chairs were not very comfortable. He had once been told that this is done intentionally at restaurants to get you to leave quicker so more people can get served. Perhaps this is even more so on a military vessel.

He looked at his food and frowned. He was sure he had ordered a western omelet with toast and orange juice to wash it all down with. A metal fork and plate with a little white bag that had an attached straw were on his tray. A flat yellow lump with odd things stuck in it was on the plate. Beside it was a square-looking piece of sandpaper.

Brian leaned over his plate and apprehensively took a whiff of his food. It did not have much of an odor, but it did not smell too bad.

He picked up the little white bag, and in black lettering, it read, "orange juice."

He saw a cap on the straw and realized it was attached and could be used to recap it. This was especially useful in zero-G.

With a sigh, he popped it open and took a drink.

"Wow," he exclaimed, "that's no kind of orange juice I ever had before."

Val giggled while nibbling on a yellow lump of her own and then said, "At least the food tastes better than it looks."

Brian looked up at her and smiled.

He noticed behind her, just out the windows, he could see the bottom front of the ship's top wing's Ion drive and not much else.

Val saw him. Grabbing her hair, she asked, "Is my hair that bad? I can't seem to do much with it since we went to gravity. I guess I should consider shortening it to make it easier for space travel."

Brian replied, "Oh no, I was looking at the view behind you. I just thought it was odd to have a window with such a terrible view."

Val let go of her hair, briefly turned to look, and said, "Refit, I bet," then returned to eating.

Brian responded, "Yeah, that makes sense. I bet the original plasma drives were shorter, and that would have made for a much better view."

Taking a second to survey the galley, Brian remarked," Funny, this ship is relatively large. It's designed for way more people than are aboard."

Val replied, "I think the original ship was meant for research. On the ship's schematics, I noticed designated research, lab space, and lots of cabins."

Brian looked at Val and asked, "I guess we don't have much need for research personnel. You would think we at least have enough crew to staff two rotating operational shifts? Could it be because of cutbacks, or maybe the military does not have much stock in Thatorn's mission?"

Val responded, "There's not much out there anyway. The Unified Earth Alliance, or U.E.A. for short, banned ice mining on Jupiter's moons until they could rule out any possible contamination of living microbes. After they did that, no company was willing to waste any investment on the off chance they discovered life. Since then, no one has been interested in living there, much less going."

"Asteroid colonies don't have much of their own water, so most of the water out here comes from the ice in Saturn's rings. The U.E.A. tightly regulates all that. Do you think the U.E.A. took Jupiter's moons off the market to ensure control of the water out here?" Inquired Brian.

"Or is the U.E.A. really afraid of something out around Jupiter," Val added.

Brian stared at Val, contemplating what she meant.

"What was it the U.E.A. used to always say about water?" Val asked while looking up at the ceiling to think.

Brian was caught off guard by the question. He was still thinking about what Val had previously said.

"Ah, yes! We must ration for our future!" She scoffed.

Brian stared blankly at her for a moment. Once he realized what she was talking about, he replied, "Yeah, I remember that."

Val put down her fork and took a drink from the straw of her white bag. She leaned close to Brian and asked softly, "Since we are alone, Can I ask you something."

Brian's eyes widened. Cautiously, he set his drink bag down.

"Um, sure," he stuttered as a bead of sweat formed on his brow.

She leaned closer and looked around the galley to ensure no one else had come in.

Brian gulped ever so softly.

"I think someone was in my cabin," Val said.

Brian fluttered his eyelashes and opened his mouth in both surprise and disappointment.

"Oh?" was all he could get out.

She explained, "I don't know when it might have happened. I just noticed some things were moved around in my room."

"I've not noticed anything, but I just came aboard and have just been in my cabin once so far," Brian said, rubbing his smooth chin.

Then Brian asked, "Should we tell security?"

After several facial expressions ranging from surprise to concern, Val replied, "No, no, I think we should just keep this to ourselves. At least until I know if there is anything to it."

Looking into Brian's eyes, she asks him, "Is that alright with you?"

"Sure, no problem," he said, looking back into her amber eyes.

They both picked up their forks and went back to eating.

After a few bites, Val asked, "So Brian, how did a class 2 engineer wind up here anyway?"

Brian laughed and said, "Yeah, that's a story."

Putting down his fork, he clasped his hands together, then continued," I was doing well working at the Solarian Corporation on Earth for years. Out of nowhere, I got my rating changed. Some government bureaucrat came along and decided my education and work experience no longer rated a class one status. I was out of a job and had to find work. I soon found out there were few jobs for a class two engineer. I knew I would have to return to school to up my class again, but that took money. In the end, I was finally able to find this job. They needed someone with knowledge of hydrogen plasma and ion drives. I'm not sure why there is a need for plasma drive knowledge on this mission."

"That's easy," Val interrupted.

"Why," asked Brian.

With a wink, Val said, "Simple, it's to maintain the illusion of this ship being a slow-ass cow."

"Oh, I almost forgot about that," Brian said with a chuckle.

Brian picked back up his fork and asked, "What about you? How did you come to find yourself to be here?"

After taking another bite of her food, Val said, "Like you said yourself, that is an interesting story."

She put her fork down, took another drink from the straw of her white bag, and began to say, "I just got out of Zesiro Yar'Adua Technical Institute...."

Brian interrupted, "That's named after the first person on Mars. It's one of the best schools anywhere! You have to maintain a B plus average just to stay there."

"Yes, that's right," replied Val.

Brian was impressed. Not only was Val beautiful, but she was also evidently extremely intelligent.

Val continued, "After school, I had several job offers. Mars needs techs with all the terraforming going on."

"So, what happened?" asked Brian.

After putting her drink bag down and sighing, Val said, "They all just disappeared. I reviewed my options a few days later and found they were all rescinded or canceled. Then, a few hours later, I was offered this job."

"Now that's odd," Brian said, rubbing his forehead with his left hand.

Val started to say, "I know, I can't believe..."

Brian interjected, "That makes three of us."

"What do you mean?" Val asked.

"My old friend Rob also ran into some employment issues," replied Brian.

Without warning, two crew members came in from the starboard door beside the food dispenser.

It was Ralph and Nutzie. They made their way over to the dispenser. Once they got their food, they headed toward them.

Once they were at the table, Nutzie asked, "Do you mind if we join you?"

"No," said Brian and Val at the same time.

Quickly, Nutzie and Ralph both went to sit next to Val.

Nutzie was a little faster and sat beside her with a soft thud. Ralph reluctantly walked back around the table to sit next to Brian.

While staring intensely at Val, Nutzie said, "I see you got a standard meal this morning."

"Yes, it's not too bad," Val replied.

Ralph focused on his meal, barely looking up at anyone.

"So, Nutzie, what's on your schedule for today?" Brian asked the stout lady.

"Huh," Nutzie mumbled.

Realizing Brian was talking to her, she looked at him and said, "Standard stuff, looking over my equipment, making sure it's ready to go." Looking back at Val, she added, "Sometimes I even help the techs when they need it."

"How nice," Val said politely as she returned to eating.

Trying to change the subject, Brian looked at Ralph and asked, "Since the ship has no name and you are in charge of communications, what does the ship's transponder say the ship's name is?"

Ralph looked up at Brian and softly declared, "There is no transponder signal coming from the ship."

Brian said with a grunt, "What are you talking about? All ships have an operational transponder. Even military ones do for friend or foe identification."

"I just know ours is not transmitting," Ralph said quietly, looking at Brian.

"I thought that was a requirement for all space vessels," said Brian with confusion.

Nutzie spoke up and said, "Military craft can turn them off to prevent tracking during special operations."

Ralph looked over at Nutzie with a blank stare.

"Considering what we are looking for. It does not surprise me." Nutzie added as she looked at her food with disappointment.

"So, Thatorn is taking this mission seriously," Val said with her eyebrows raised, looking at Nutzie.

"Then explain something to me," Brian asked, staring at Nutzie.

"What?" Nutzie asked, looking up at Brian.

"Since this ship is refit to a military vessel, why were all the windows left in? Even titanium metallic glass windows would still be a potential hazard in combat. Especially windows that big." Brian said, pointing to the ones behind Nutzie.

After taking a quick glance behind her, Nutzie replied, "Oh, that. A long time ago, all military vessels were required to have a minimum number of what they call useful windows."

"Really, why is that?" Val asked while taking a nibble at her food.

"Believe it or not, it was because of Thatorn," She replied.

Brian, Val, and Ralph were all surprised. They leaned in closer and focused their attention on Nutzie.

Nutzie smiled and said, "Back when I was an eighteen-year-old marine during the Pirate Wars. There was a space battle near the asteroid Vesta."

Ralph squinted his eyes and leaned in closer.

Nutzie continued, "Thatorn was the commander of a U.E.A. combat frigate. During the battle, a Pirate attack craft knocked out his ship's navigation and sensors. It looked like they had him when it closed in on him for a final pass. However, at the last minute, Thatorn used a window to line up a kill shot with the only thing he still had working, a dumb missile."

Everyone watched Nutzie intently as she stopped talking long enough to remove the cap on the straw of her bag and take a drink.

Nutzie resumed, saying, "It's how he got promoted to Captain of a company of U.E.A. marines and became my commanding officer for the rest of the war. That's why I know the story about the battle so well. He would never shut up about it. Not long after the war, he became obsessed with the Pirates. Going around trying to warn everyone they were still out there."

"So that's how you knew what our mission was?" asked Val.

"Yes, my dear. After seeing Thatorn was in charge, it was the only thing that made any sense," Nutzie replied.

"That was Thatorn at the battle of Vesta," Ralph said with a groan.

"Yes, why?" Nutzie asked, looking at the bald man.

"Son of a Bitch!" exclaimed Ralph.

Startled, they all stared at Ralph.

Ralph explained, "You see, I'm from Vesta. Before I was born, my parents told me a battle took place near the asteroid. Not long after, U.E.A. forces occupied our asteroid and stayed there even after the war. Well, at least until the U.E.A. finally gave the colonies

42

representation in the government. I guess they thought that might help to prevent any future uprisings."

"If you don't mind me asking, why did you take this deep space job so far from home, Ralph?" Val inquired.

With a grimace, Ralph sunk into his seat.

He then said, "I recently got divorced. My wife left me for some U.E.A. officer. I had no choice. I had to find a job that paid better so I could afford alimony and child support. This job was all I could find."

Val and Brian both looked at each other.

"I'm sorry to hear that," Nutzie said with sympathy, staring at Ralph.

Looking at Brian and Val, she said, "I'm just glad I got out of my group marriage years ago."

Then she asked, "What about you two?"

Brian and Val both shook their heads.

Ralph said, wiping a tear away, "You might be better off." After a short pause, he added," Still, I'd rather suffer through it all just so I could have my kids."

An awkward silence filled the room as they leaned back in their seats and picked at their food.

Brian finally broke the stillness, asking, "So what else does anyone know about these Pirates?"

Val replied, "I only heard some vague stories my grandparents told me about the times of the Mars uprisings."

Ralph then spoke up, "I don't know anything about Pirates. The most I remember were the U.E.A. forces occupying my home when I was a little kid."

They all turned and stared at Nutzie, causing her to laugh.

Leaning in, Nutzie said, "My unit arrived on Mars before the war. We were sent there to enforce Marshal Law on the colonists. They wanted to maintain the freedom they had enjoyed since the fall of the U.N. After some skirmishes and protests, we had the Mars colonists under control within three weeks and expected to be shipped elsewhere. Then all hell broke loose. A U.E.A. patrol ran across a previously unknown colony that decided to fight back. That, in turn, triggered several terrorist attacks and direct engagements on all U.E.A. forces on Mars. They were labeled as rogue Pirate terrorists by the U.E.A. This was when the Pirate War started. While fighting on the front lines, I started hearing interesting stories about these Pirates."

After briefly pausing to glance at her audience, Nuztie continued, "An officer told me a story about when his troops were tracking a group of Pirates near Pavonis Mons. Then, when they were almost on them, suddenly they were gone. Their scanners could no longer locate them. The field techs assumed the equipment had just failed. They swept the area on foot and managed to make a few visual sightings, but every time, they would just disappear again. He said it was like chasing ghosts."

"Come on, Nutzie, do you believe that?" asked Brian.

"Yes, the same thing happened to my squad. Once when we got lost..."

Nutzie stopped and gazed up at a lighting panel above her.

"And?" prompted Val.

Nutzie looked back down at her plate and muttered, "Um."

"Nutzie, are you ok?" asked Ralph with concern.

Slowly, Nutzie looked up at their faces and said, "Yeah, I just recalled something."

Brian laughed, saying, "Well, that was an interesting ghost story...."

Nutzie snapped, "It wasn't just a story, young man!"

Bug-eyed, Brian apologized, "Sorry."

Shaking her head, Nutzie said, "It's ok. I would be skeptical, too, if I had not been there myself."

"It is a strange story," Val said.

"Strange is not even half of it," Nutzie said, somberly staring at Val.

"What do you mean?" asked Brian, squinting at Nutzie.

Nutzie took a moment to glance at all of them and then said, "Some of us don't think they were human."

Brian and Ralph were shocked, while Val remained stolid.

"Ok, so you're telling me now that we are out looking for aliens?" asked Ralph, sour-faced.

"Back then, many of my comrades suspected they were, but I don't really know for sure myself. Come to think of it, we never caught or recovered the body of any of them," Nutzie replied, pondering over what she had just said.

"Where are these aliens from?" quizzed Brian, staring at Nutzie.

Val spoke up and coyly answered, "Why Mars, of course."

Brian was taken aback.

"What makes you say that?" Ralph leaned in and asked Val.

"It was one of the few things I remember my grandmother telling me when I was small." The young lady replied.

"I guess it makes sense considering. Who else would want an independent Mars more than a native Martian?" said Nutzie with a half-smile.

With a glazed look, Brian asked, "I'm confused. I thought when we colonized Mars, it was uninhabited?"

"Was it?" Val asked in return.

"Too much, man," expelled Ralph as he slumped back into his chair.

They all took a moment and stared at each other for a while. Some even managed to take a bite or two of breakfast.

Breaking the silence, Val spoke up, "It's been forty years, so how do we know if any of these Pirates survived and are still around, much less where they are?"

"Thatorn has had a long time to figure that out," sighed Nutzie.

"This is just great. I'm on some crazy-ass mission hunting, god knows what. Back home, I was told this was supposed to be a gravy run." Ralph exploded, scowling.

"It's hard to know who to trust anymore," Val said despondently.

Nutzie's eyes glazed over with a distant look in them, and she mumbled ever so softly, "Yes, who can you trust?"

"Excuse me." Nutzie suddenly said, jumping up from the table with her tray.

She quickly makes her way to the end of the metal box. She shoved her entire tray into the tray return with fury, causing a loud, clanking noise. She then quickly exited the room out the port side door beside the food dispenser.

Stunned, the three remaining crew members just sat there looking at the door she exited.

"What the hell was that?" Brian said, turning to look at Val and Ralph.

Ralph just shrugged his shoulder, and Val looked at Brian with a wrinkle in the left corner of her mouth.

Brian let out a deep breath in response.

"Should we check on her?" Val asked.

"I'm not. Nutzie scares me," Ralph said grimly.

"I'd rather not get involved. It's probably none of our business." Brian replied, glancing back at the door Nutzie exited.

Gradually, they all went back to eating. After a few bites, Brian felt a rumbling in his tummy.

He saw both Ralph and Val staring at him. Clearly, they heard it, too.

Brian stood up and humbly said, "Sorry, I think I should go to the head."

Ralph spoke up, "The bathroom is in the hallway. You know they are not allowed to be connected directly to the galley due to sanitation restrictions because of zero-G."

"Yes, I am aware of that. I saw one on the way in." Brian said gruffly.

Brian made his way to the starboard door beside the food dispenser. Before exiting, he saw a sign in several languages above the door about returning trays and disposing of trash.

After entering the hallway, Brian almost reached the bathroom door when he let out a long fart. It was not very loud, but it had an odor.

Waving the fumes away, he realized he felt better and started back for the galley.

Hearing a noise, he stopped. It did not come from the perpendicular hallway where the red door was. It was coming from the other direction. Where Nutzie left the galley at the other end of the hall.

Brian tiptoed down the corridor, past the central core and the square room. He passed another bathroom to his right and a galley door to his left. He stopped to listen just short of the intersection to the other perpendicular hallway. Close to the large open bulkhead door.

Brian could hear someone talking at the far end of the intersecting hallway. Slowly, he peeked to his right around the corner. He could see Nutzie at the dead-end of the hall. She was talking to someone on her C&PC, but Brian could not hear who she was talking to.

He was only able to make out some of what she was saying.

"I can't believe this! How dare you!" Nutzie exclaimed.

Brian heard a muffled reply.

"I know what you are up to," Nutzie said.

Brian heard another inaudible reply.

"You better believe this is not over!" Nutzie yelled.

Quickly, she turned off her C&PC and took off down the parallel hallway. Brian heard her in the square room and entered the circular hall through its lower door, which was adjacent to the maintenance door.

It was quiet again.

Brian shook his head, wondering what was going on. Should he even ask?

He turned around and decided to go back into the galley through the door Nutzie used.

When he entered, he saw Ralph and Val putting their trays in the return and trash in the chute.

"Finished?" he inquired.

"It's getting late, close to 7:00 hours. I have to get to the command deck. One of the consoles has some problems." Val replied.

"Yeah, I have to get there too," Ralph added.

They left the galley as Brian sat at the table beside his tray. He sighed, took his last few bites, and drank the last of his orange juice. Once finished, Brian got up and put his tray into the return. Someone entered the room just as he threw his drink bag in the trash chute.

He was a tall, thin, muscular Eastern Indian light brown-skinned man wearing the ship's standard gray jumpsuit with a dark pouch on his right side. He had a square face, thick, short brown hair, eyebrows, and a short stubbly beard. His big brown eyes made his long, sharp nose and plump lips seem much smaller than they were.

"Hello, I'm Lee Smith, the tech. I just got off from the night shift," He said with a slight British accent as he walked up to Brian, who was just a little taller than he was.

"Yeah, you missed the briefing. You were in the sickbay," Brian replied while putting his tray into its return.

"I'm still new to space travel, but the Doc's got me on something to help. Say, what are you doing?" Lee asked, smiling.

"I'm first scheduled to check the reactors on level 13, But I'm going to check the drive relays first. Starting with the lower one." Brian answered.

"Oh, that's the one near our sensor arrays and all the ship's external communication systems? " Lee asked.

"Yelp," Brian responded, heading for the door.

"Wait for a second, can't it wait. I would like to spend some time getting to know you." Lee insisted.

"Um, sorry, maybe another time," Brian explained.

"You sure?" Lee said, almost pouting.

"Yeah," replied Brian as he left the galley.

Heading for the lift, Brian thought. What was that all about? Was he coming on to me? Maybe he just didn't like to eat alone.

Brian exited elevator 1 onto level 10. He quickly looked over the ship's level layout on his C&PC to ensure he knew where he was going. Turning it off, Brian turned left and down the circular hallway. He came to the maintenance door on his left and a door to his right. He exited into a square room. This floor's layout was much like the one on the galley level. Except this one had two halls extending from the center to the ship's wings. One was going to the upper wing, and the one before Brian led to the lower wing.

Brian saw an open bulkhead door that connected the square room to the gray hall. He passed through it, then an intersecting corridor just before entering the lower wing's big open bulkhead door.

There were several more open bulkhead doors along the wing's gray hallway. Brian saw several junctions down the hall that widened, like a room, for consoles and systems controlling various functions along the wing.

Brian stopped at a console in the first widened area. This was the control point for all the power going into the lower wing from the ship's reactors, two levels below.

Brian was checking the reactor's hot waste gas output when it happened.

The ship shook as a loud rumble came from the far end of the wing. Brian could see fire and smoke for a few seconds, and then it was gone. This was the first time Brian witnessed explosive decompression firsthand.

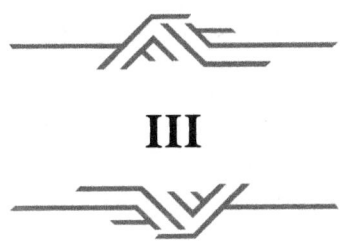

III

Brian found himself floating, surrounded by darkness. It was quiet. So quiet that he could hear his own heart beating in his ears.

Could I have been sucked out into space, He feared?

He quickly realized that assumption was impossible since he was still breathing.

He saw no stars or the ship anywhere around him. He couldn't even see his hands or any part of his body.

There was a soft, distant, mumbling noise, but he couldn't determine where it was coming from.

It grew more intense and started to sound like words.

In the distance, Brian finally saw a tiny speck of light.

Could I be dead? He thought.

The light grew brighter, and the words suddenly became a loud rambling growl.

"What the hell did you do?!" screamed Thatorn into Brian's ear.

Brian awoke with a jolt. He saw a ceiling and bright square light panels above him. Slowly, he turned his head slightly to his right and saw the wrinkled old man glaring down at him, waiting for a reply.

Brian blinked his eyes while trying to gain his bearings. He knew he was lying on a bed and was most likely in the Med Bay.

Turning to his left, Brian saw Lee standing in front of a window out into space.

"Answer me, Mr. Rush. What the hell did you do?!" screamed Thatorn again.

"Sir! I must insist you stop doing that to my patient," said Doctor Teka.

Brian looked up above his head to see the doctor leaning over him with her ample cleavage between them. Brian smiled, and she returned it.

He noticed the doctor was wearing latex gloves and holding a light in her left hand. She kept his left eye open with her right hand and shined the light into it. Repeatedly took the light away and returned it. Then, the doctor did the same to his right eye.

Once finished, the doctor turned off the light and put it into her jumpsuit pocket. She turned to stare at a large screen on the wall behind Thatorn. Brian tried to peek around Thatorn to see what she was looking at. All he could make out was a one-size-fits-all latex glove dispenser to Thatorn's right near the far corner of the gray wall.

Zala started to walk toward the screen but stopped. Looked at Thatorn and said, "Sir, if you don't mind, could you please move."

The old man snorted and grumbled as he walked to stand in front of the Med Bay door at Brian's feet.

Brian could hear the clanking of his exoskeleton legs as he went. It was nothing like the soft rhythmic noises he remembered the night before.

Once Thatorn was out of the way, the doctor walked up to the screen and inspected the readouts.

Brian could now see numerous medical data on the large display screen in the middle of the gray wall. None of which he had a clue about. He wondered how the information was being collected since he saw no scanner over him. He concluded that some kind of sensor web must be incorporated into the bed.

From a sharp pain in his head, Brian groaned. He tried to rub it and discovered there was no gravity and that his arms and torso were loosely strapped to the bed.

Brian saw the doctor remove her latex gloves and step to the left of the screen towards the other corner of the wall. She then put the gloves into a vacuum disposal chute with a biohazard symbol above the flap.

She returned to the screen and touched it, causing the display to change.

After momentarily looking at the screen, she said, "It looks like Mr. Rush will be ok. Eye checks and dilation were good, and so was everything else. I don't see any signs of a concussion. No need for any medical nanobots to do tissue repair."

Brian asks, staring at the doctor, "So what happened? How long was I out?"

Zala stepped over to the edge of the bed with her clicking boots. Looked at Brian, smiled, and replied. "We had a breach somewhere near the end of the bottom wing. As the rupture sucked you and the air out, you must have hit your head on something just before the emergency bulkhead door shut. You have been out for well over an hour now."

"I see, so there was an emergency engine shut off as well?" inquired Brian.

With a snarl, Thatorn answered, "Yes, In case of a non-combat accident, I have the ship's computer set that way to prevent any possible further damage to the ship."

"What about the power relays grounding out?" Brian asked with concern.

"The computer has also been programmed to shut down all affected areas of a breach," Thatorn replied with a snort.

Brian looked at Zala and asked, "How did you know I was hurt?"

"The C&PC's monitoring system alerted me of your location and condition, " the doctor informed Brian.

Lee said, "Since I was the closest, the Doc contacted me to get you. It was no problem moving you without gravity. "

"Enough of this!" screamed Thatorn as he walked up to the foot of the bed. "You still have not answered the question. What the hell did you do?!"

Brian looked down towards his feet at Thatorn and said, "I hardly had time to do anything. I was looking over the first set of consoles in the wing, then boom! I was out."

Thatorn glared at Brian, but before Brian could say anything, Thatorn's C&PC alerted him to an incoming call.

Thatorn raised his arm with a grunt and activated the device on his wrist.

"All Ship systems are stable. We don't seem to be having any further issues. I have a preliminary report for you about the incident, Sir," said Lieutenant Rocha over Thatorn's C&PC.

Thatorn said into his C&PC, "Go ahead, Lieutenant."

She reported, "After looking at all the data and even looking out of a few windows. It seems our communications tower has been sheared off."

"How did that happen?" asked Thatorn, glowering.

Lieutenant Rocha replied, "Unknown at the moment. Speculation at this point is that it might have been an impact from an object, but I have yet to confirm that from the sensor data."

Thatorn growled softly.

She continued, "The tower remains are trailing us at about 5 thousand kilometers, and the distance is growing. We were still at full thrust for about 37 seconds after the tower fell away, giving us a slightly higher final velocity."

"Can we retrieve the tower?" inquired Thatorn.

The lieutenant replied, "That is not possible, Sir. It's all just scattered debris."

Thatorn snapped, "Damn it!"

"What about the secondary communication system, the antenna array?" Thatorn asked.

Lieutenant Rocha started to reply, "Mr. Milsom has checked that too, Sir. He thinks it may still be intact. However..."

"WHAT?!?" interrupted Thatorn.

"Since the communications room is damaged, Sir, the antenna array is offline." The lieutenant replied.

"Shit!" yelled the old man.

Thatorn paused to compose himself, then calmly inquired, "What are our other communication options?"

Looking at Brian and Lee in the room, he added, "Anyone?"

"There is an emergency communication system in the ship's command module," Lieutenant Rocha replied.

"Limited range, low power, not designed for high data packet info," Thatorn stated.

Lee spoke up and said, "What about the Moon Hopper?"

"Not designed for long-range transmissions. Also, not good for high data packets either." Thatorn said somberly.

After a few seconds, they heard some mumbling coming from Thatorn's C&PC.

The lieutenant then clearly says, "It seems Mr. Milsom believes we might be able to fix the antenna array, Sir."

"Well then, finally, some good news." Thatorn chirped. "The antenna array will have to do. We can still transmit large amounts of data. Since it's not a focused beam, the data will take a little longer to be received."

Thatorn tapped on his C&PC, causing all the others on the ship to come to life. You could hear some feedback from those in the Med Bay room.

"This is Thatorn. Everyone is to meet in the situation room in fifteen minutes to ascertain what has happened and discuss our options. That is all."

Looking down at Brian, Thatorn calmly said, "That includes you, Mister Rush!"

Lee quickly exits the room as Doctor Tela undoes Brian's straps, which slowly retract back into the edge of the bed. While the doctor helped him sit up, she made sure he activated his magnetic boots before he tried standing.

Thatorn clanks his way over towards the door.

Brian looks at Thatorn and asks, "Why high data output?"

Thatorn stopped and replied without looking at him, "In case we find what we are looking for. I want the ability to inform U.E.A. command with as much information as possible, in case."

"In case of what?" asked Brian.

Thatorn replied, clanking out the door, "We get blown to hell."

After getting some medications, Brian and the doctor quickly made their way to the command deck.

Upon entering the command deck from the starboard entrance, Brian saw Captain Linol at his pilot seat in a tilted-up position. Ralph and Val were working at different consoles on the starboard side of the deck. He could see their holographic interactive displays but could not tell exactly what they were doing.

Brian and the doctor proceeded past the unoccupied console near the entrance and entered the situation room on their left.

The room was about a little less than a quarter of the top deck. Brian recalled the ship's layout and knew that the rest of the level included Thatorn's VIP quarters, his office, and a crew bathroom just off the circular hallway near the control room's port entrance.

After entering the room and the door closed behind him, he noticed it had the same dull, muddy gray tones as the rest of the ship's interior. It was somewhat triangularly shaped. On his left was an inwardly curved short wall part of the circular hall on its other side. To his right was an outwardly long curved one that was part of the outer hull. The remaining two walls were straight and angled outwardly from the shorter curved wall.

The far wall was slightly towards his left and ran about 40 degrees to the one behind him. Based on the layout, Brian knew the door at its center went to Thatorn's office.

In front of him, in the center of the room, was the short end of a sizeable elliptical-shaped table. A small console with a seat was just past the other short end of the table in the corner where the far wall and the outer hull met.

On top of the table at its center was a holographic projector. It was smaller than the one on the control deck.

Five chairs were on both of the long sides of the table, and a couple extra ones were in the corner to Brian's right.

A large screen took up the top half of the entire short, inwardly curved wall on Brian's left. Another same-sized screen was at the top of the outwardly curved wall to his right. The screen was not centered on that wall because the outer hull wall curved in sharper at the far end where the console was. This was designed to give those at the table a good view of the screen on the opposite wall.

Zala walked past Brian as he was examining the room. She took the first seat to Brian's left and strapped herself in.

Brian was about to sit opposite her on the other side of the table when the door behind him opened.

He turned around and saw Fa Ming enter the room. She was much thinner and taller than he was. She might even be a little older than him, but her soft-looking light tan skin and short dark hair made her look youthful. Her thin, dark eyebrows over her small, oval brown eyes seemed too long. Her square face made her pointy nose and plump lips seem tiny.

"Hello, I'm Brian Rush, the Engineer," he said, extending his hand toward the woman.

"Oh, I'm glad to finally meet you. I'm Fa Ming, IT, " she replied.

Brian noticed she had very soft hands. Being a computer specialist, that's probably to be expected.

"I'm sorry about my behavior at the briefing. I was not expecting to ever run into Thatorn," explained Fa.

Brian began to ask, "I was wondering about that. What..."

Suddenly, Rob entered the room with one of his magnetic boots, making a terrible electrical racket.

Brian turns his attention to Rob as Fa slowly makes her way past him to the seat he intended to take.

As Fa strapped herself into the seat, Rob walked gingerly towards Brian, favoring his left foot. He tried to keep it on the deck as long as possible, making short, quick steps with his right foot.

Saying to everyone, "Sorry about the noise. One of my magnetic coils blew in my right boot two days ago. I took it out and managed to get the boot to work again. It seemed to function fine until today. As you can tell, the boot's making noise and is no longer giving me much of a magnetic hold."

"I can look the boot over for you later. Do you have the blown part?" asked Brian.

"No, I tossed it into my waste chute," Rob replied, then asked. "Do you think you still could use it to get it to work?"

"Maybe. I hate to waste parts that might still be useful," replied Brian.

"Wouldn't getting a new part from stock be easier?" asked Rob.

"Yeah, I suppose so," replied Brian, disappointed.

Brian made his way to the table, strapped himself in the seat beside Fa, and Rob sat beside him.

Rob used his C&PC and turned off his boots to keep the right one from making more noise. Forgetting to strap himself in first, he quickly grabbed the table before he floated away.

Rob buckled himself down as more of the crew filed into the room.

When the captain was about to sit in the chair next to Zala, Nutzie slipped past him and took it. Forcing him to take the one beside her. Meanwhile, Val casually strolled over and sat in the chair next to Rob.

Everyone except Thatorn, Lieutenant Rocha, and Lee were in the situation room.

Brian was curious about where Lee might be since he left the Med Bay before Thatorn.

Everyone around the table stared at each other until Thatorn's office door opened.

Thatorn entered the room with Lieutenant Rocha closely behind him, who was in the middle of saying, "...think you should reconsider...."

"I have already made up my mind, Lieutenant." Thatorn insisted, glaring at her. Adding, "Take your station, please."

Lieutenant Rocha quickly went over to the small console in the corner to her left and stood behind it.

Thatorn took a few steps toward the table and stopped just behind the last empty chair on the opposite side of the table Brian was on.

Brian assumed his medications were kicking in since Thatorn's robotic legs were no longer making as much noise in his head as they were in the medical bay.

Suddenly, Lee entered the room and hastily grabbed the seat between Captain Linol and the empty one Thatorn stood behind.

Thatorn stared down at him with his thin, white right eyebrow raised.

"Good, now that we are all here," He grunted, then glanced at the lieutenant.

She activated the console before her. A virtual 3D interactive display and keyboard appeared hovering above it. After making some selections on the screen and hitting a few keys, the screens on the walls and the holographic projector on the table came to life.

The Holographic display showed a red dot over the table. Extending out from it was a white curved line heading upward toward but not intersecting a small 3D representation of Jupiter and its larger moons. The two wall screens showed the same information but in 2D.

"Captain, what is our current status?" Thatorn asked while looking at the holographic display.

Captain Linol said, "The ship is currently on autopilot. Being the pilot on duty, I'm monitoring the flight status through my C&PC."

Then, pointing up at the 3D image, he added, "The hologram above shows our ship as the red dot and its current flight path in white. As you can see, we are still heading towards Jupiter. But we will not reach our planned orbital insertion point at our current velocity."

Staring at the captain, the old man inquired, "Will that be an issue getting us to Jupiter?"

"No, Sir, once we fire up the engines again, we can plot a new intercept course. Only our arrival will be delayed unless we increase thrust to compensate," Captain Linol responded.

"Are there any known objects along our current flight path that could cause us problems?" Thatorn questioned, staring at the hologram.

"No, Sir," replied the captain. "Even without the main drives, if sensors detect something unexpected, we can still use thrusters to steer us out of its way. The ship's autopilot is programmed to handle that automatically."

"If we have already been hit by something, that's small comfort," Fa Ming said softly, glancing at Brian with a smirk.

"That Ms. Ming is what we are here to determine." Thatorn snarled, still staring at the 3D display, not bothering to look at her.

The old man then briefly glanced at Lieutenant Rocha.

In response, she tapped an icon on her console's holographic screen and followed that with a few keystrokes on the 3D keyboard. The display screens and the table hologram changed. It turned into a detailed wireframe version of the ship.

Thatorn said, "At this point, you all know something has happened to the ship. We are here to ascertain what that was and resolve any related issues. I don't plan on firing up the engines again until that happens. So we will be remaining in free fall."

Ralph let out a discernable grown.

Thatorn looked briefly at the thin, frail man, then added, "This also means the mess food dispensers will only allow zero-G friendly liquid nourishment options."

Ralph then lets out a low moan.

Ignoring him this time, Thatorn said, "Lieutenant, would you please give us a rundown of the events and what we currently know to bring the entire crew up to speed."

Lieutenant Rocha took a few steps around the console and stood on its right side.

She said, "At 7:09.07 hours, we had an incident. Ships sensors recorded a fire alarm and decompression in our communications room at the ship's bottom wing. However, sensors did not record any object approaching or impacting the ship's hull."

She pressed a button on her 3D interactive screen with her left hand. The displays and hologram zoomed in to show only the ship's bottom half and lower wing. The images revealed the ship's recorded sensor information with a few more taps.

The lieutenant continued, "In the data, you can see first a power fault in the communications room. Followed by an automatic power shutoff to the room. Then a fire alarm."

The images on the screens and in 3D showed the active communications room information winked out as debris fell away from the bottom wing.

She added, "There is a sudden decompression indication alert at the bottom of the wing."

Before them, a message on the hologram and screen informed them that a bulkhead door had closed to prevent further venting into space. A few seconds later, there is a drive shutdown notification.

"Was there any other damage to the wing?" Captain Linol asked.

"No, only the ship's communication systems were affected. Everything else seems to be working fine," Lieutenant Rocha replied.

She then hit a few more icons on the interactive display, and the 3D image and screens changed again. This time, a pulled-out 3D view of the ship showed a trail of debris spread out from the ship's bottom wing.

She said, "The fragments showing on the current sensor readings are what's left of our laser and high gain communications tower. Its scattered remains are trailing us at about seven thousand kilometers now. We were at full thrust for 37.3 seconds after the decompression, giving us a slightly higher final velocity than the wreckage."

The crew was noticeably stunned by what they saw.

Looking at the captain, Rob asks, "Since I was not on duty yet, can I assume you shut down the engines?"

Before Captain Linol could reply, Thatorn explained, "No, he did not. It is part of my emergency computer protocols. The ship's drives are placed in auto shutdown when a non-combat related breach occurs. This is to minimize and assess any damage."

"The communications tower is totally gone and in pieces?" Nutzie asked, puzzled.

"Yes, it's totally useless," The lieutenant replied.

The room became quiet after a few discernable moans and sighs.

Looking down his long crooked nose at the crew, Thatorn bluntly said, "Most of you are not aware that Mr.Rush was in the lower wing at the time and was almost sucked out into space. Fortunately for Mr. Rush, the emergency bulkhead door did its job."

Brian stared at the old man, surprised. He expected to hear more of the same accusations of being the cause of the incident he heard not less than a half-hour ago.

The crew seemed shaken by the statement and quickly stared at Brian.

"Are you alright!" Exclaimed Nutzie.

"What?!" said the captain dumbfounded.

Ralph let out a gasp.

"Oh, my God!" Shouted Rob in Brian's right ear, making it difficult for him to hear anyone else.

However, he did make out Val somberly say, "Oh, no. I'm so sorry."

Brian raised his right hand and exclaimed, "I'm fine, only a bump to the head and some bruises, according to the Doctor."

The doctor elaborated, "The C&PC monitoring system noticed Mr. Rush's vitals change and alerted me to his condition and location. From the data, his injuries did not seem life-threatening. So I asked Lee to retrieve him for me from the lower wing since he was the closest. Luckily, Mr. Rush only hit the floor or ceiling. He could have gotten cut up or even electrocuted if he had hit a control panel. If the bulkhead door had failed, he more than likely wouldn't even be here now."

"Thanks for the insight, Doctor," Brian grimaced, realizing how lucky he was.

"Mister Rush is just fine," Thatorn said with a fake smile.

"What happened exactly?" Asked Lee curiously, staring at Brian.

"There's not much to tell, really," Brian asserted. "I was just doing my job. I had not even touched a console yet. Then there was an explosion."

"There was an explosion?" Ralph nervously asked.

"That would be consistent with an object strike," Captain Linol declared.

"But we have no data to support that," Lieutenant Rocha insisted.

"Hum," the captain grunted in response, scratching his head.

Fa spoke up and asked, "What if it were something tiny and traveling very fast?"

The lieutenant started to say, "We had considered that, but the impact...."

Thatorn raised his hand toward Lieutenant Rocha, and she stopped.

"Go on," Thatorn encouraged.

"That's all. If it were going extremely fast, maybe our sensors didn't even have a chance to pick it up," Fa explained.

"Is that your professional opinion?" Thatorn asked with an awkward smile, squinting his eyes at Fa.

With some apparent apprehension, Fa replied. "Well, I'm just a computer expert. I know what some systems can and can't handle. So, I guess I would say yes, yes it is."

Thatorn nodded slightly while still squinting at her.

"Could it have been an overload?" asked Rob.

Before the lieutenant could reply, Brian spoke up. He said, "No, I was looking right at the power output readings just as it happened. I saw nothing that would have indicated that."

Thatorn looked at Lieutenant Rocha, and she nodded in agreement with the engineer.

"Is this all the data we have to go on right now?" Nutzie asks, staring at the 3D display.

Thatorn looks at LaNutza Teodoresco for a few seconds, then over at the lieutenant.

Lieutenant Rocha stares oddly at Thatorn and then the crew.

"Go on. Everyone will find out sooner or later anyway," Thatorn grunted.

The crew at the table looked at each other, confused, except for Fa.

After the lieutenant tapped several 3D icons and a few virtual keystrokes, the holographic display faded as the wall screens flickered. Two views of a gray room with control panels and a console appeared on them.

One seemed to be taken at a slight angle into the room, probably from the right side of the door that leads into it. The other showed the room from what must have been the right wall since the entrance could clearly be seen at the left. A header at the top reads communications room with camera 1 above one image and camera 2 over the other. At the bottom of both were a date and time stamp.

The crew watched what appeared to be static images. They could see the time was sped up; minutes passed in seconds. When the time got to 7:09, Lieutenant Rocha hit a key, and both pictures froze. After several keystrokes and an icon tap, the time ran second for second. When the seconds reached 7, there was a bright flash on both images, then the screen went black.

The image changed again after a few seconds of virtual tapping and typing by the lieutenant with her left hand.

The crew could see a still image of the gray wing corridor and Brian looking at a console to his left. This image was taken from above the main bulkhead door at the entrance to the lower wing. The top of the screen had the header "Lower Wing Camera 1". The time stamp was at 7:09:00.

The video began to play second for second. When the time hit 7:09:07, you could see a flash, then some smoke at the end of the corridor. The crew saw Brian turn his head towards it. Within a few more seconds, the smoke was gone, and you could just make out an opening into space at the end of the corridor.

They watched Brian struggle as he was dragged towards the opening into space. His body flopped around and bounced up to the ceiling, then onto the floor.

Brian closed his eyes briefly after seeing himself being tossed around like a helpless rag doll.

The bulkhead door closed, and Brian's limp body slowly began to float in the wing's hallway.

Lieutenant Rocha hit a key, and the screen went dark again.

So that's why the old man stopped accusing me of causing the rupture? Thought Brian.

The crew glared at Thatorn with disdain, except for Fa. She stared at the table.

"You have hidden cameras on the ship!" Growled Nutzie, banging the table with her fist.

Looking at Nuztie with a crooked grin, Thatorn replies, "It's purely a security measure."

Then, noticing Ms. Ming's behavior across the table, Nutzie asked, "You knew about this, Fa?"

Fa did not answer. Only looked at the table.

"How many of these cameras are there?" asked Ralph.

"That is classified, Mr. Milsom." Interjected the lieutenant.

"You low life...," began Nuztie as she was about to unstrap and stand up.

Placing his right hand gently on Nuztie's left shoulder, Captain Linol interrupted, "I gather you have already reviewed the footage from all the nearby cameras?"

Nutzie turned to give the captain the stink eye.

"Yes, Lieutenant Rocha and I did so before this meeting," Thatorn explained.

"And?" Rob spoke up.

"From our point of view, no details in the footage can explain what happened. Even slowing it down did not reveal the cause. That's why I thought showing you the key pieces that someone else here might glean more out of it than what we could."

The participants at the table looked at each other and shook their heads.

Captain Linol took his hand off Nutzie's shoulder and looked at her, concerned. She sighed and nodded her head, indicating that she was ok. The doctor looked over at them both and smiled.

"The critical problem we have now is that we are out of communication with the U.E.A. command. This is a crucial key to our mission, " insisted Thatorn.

"In case we find something, we can report it in before we get vaporized," Brian muttered softly, but everyone heard him.

"What!" Ralph cried.

The rest of the crew at the table looked at each other, then up at Thatorn.

Thatorn asserted, "I assure you I have no intention of sacrificing my ship just for some data. I must maintain a constant relay to prove..., I mean inform U.E.A. command of our status."

Looking directly at Brian, Thatorn added, "As you have already pointed out, this ship is far more capable than she appears. We should be able to easily escape any possible hostile actions."

"That is assuming these Pirates even exist," Rob said, sarcastically making Brian chuckle under his breath.

Thatorn looked at Rob and let out a loud snort.

Val spoke up. "As I came aboard this ship, I noticed we have a long-range probe. We could send it in to investigate from a safe distance."

"What," Thatorn said, then after looking at Val, he added. "Oh, Yes. Yes, we do."

Thatorn turned to Ralph and asked curtly, "Back to the matter at hand. Ralph, what is your assessment of the antenna array?"

Momentarily taken by surprise, Ralph replied, "Uh, well, based on what I know and have seen so far, I'm not sure."

After a short pause, he added, "I guess I might be able to get the antenna array working if there is enough left of the communications room. I'll need to bypass the damaged systems. That's assuming the explosion didn't cause any external damage to the array itself."

"I thought you said you believed the array was intact!" Thatorn barked.

"That was before I heard anything about an explosion," Ralph timidly quipped back.

Thatorn looked at Lieutenant Rocha, and she said. "Its full status is still unknown, sir."

"Maybe we could use one of the other emergency bulkhead doors as an airlock to get into the communications room to check it out," suggested the captain.

Thatorn began to reply, "Yes, that's...."

Brian interrupted, "Before we can do that, we need more information on the external damage and structural integrity. I wouldn't want anyone to get hurt in the communications room until we know what we are dealing with."

"The status and repair of the antenna array is our top priority," bellowed Thatorn.

"So, just how will we determine the array's status?" Ralph asked.

Thatorn answered. "Simple, Mr. Milsom. We will have to go out and take a look."

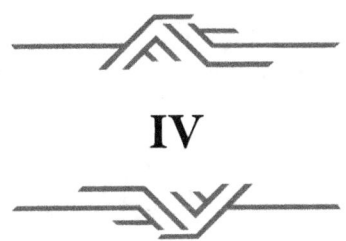

IV

Rob and Brian were the first to exit the situation room and go onto the command deck.

Brian gestured to Rob to follow him as he walked over to the console along the outer hull wall near the starboard window.

Rob took a little while to catch up to Brian with his noisy magnetic boot.

Brian saw the doctor and Lee come out and leave the command deck. While Captain Linol went to sit in the pilot seat, Valarie took up the first starboard console near the co-pilot's station.

Ralph started to head for the command deck exit as the situation room door closed behind him but stopped. He stared over at Brian and Rob. Curious, he slowly made his way towards them.

While Brian waited on Rob, he noticed that Thatorn and the lieutenant didn't leave the situation room. He assumed they must have gone through the other door into Thatorn's office.

Then he wondered to himself, *That's odd. I don't believe I saw Nutzie leave?*

"So, what's up?" Rob asked as he got to the console.

"I want to fix that boot," Brian said, pointing at his right one. He then added, "The noise is irritating as hell."

Rob said, "I didn't think you had the part."

"I don't right now, but I can assess the situation and see what's wrong. I might be able to stop it from making that much racket," Brian said as he reached into his right pocket.

"I always keep a set of tools handy." He added as he pulled out a small rolled-up belt.

He unrolled it to reveal several small tools that were in separate pockets. Most were various types of small screwdrivers, while others were more exotic-looking.

"Have they given your regular tools to you?" Rob asked.

"No, not yet," Brian replied, motioning for Rob to sit at the console.

Rob sat down and strapped himself into the seat.

Ralph approached them cautiously, stood beside Brian, and watched them with interest.

"Let's take a look at that boot," Brian said.

Rob took off his right boot and handed it to Brian.

"You'll need to hold it up for me," Brian instructed.

Rob held his boot up to about Brian's waist level.

Ralph interjected, "When I got my gear for this mission, I tried to get magnetic boots in any color other than silver. I was told they are all silver for a reason."

"That's just to make it easier to distinguish them from any kind of regular boot. To be a space traveler, you must know which are your magnetic boots." Rob explained while staring at his boot, holding it steady for Brian.

"Yeah, I was told that when I got mine. I just never knew it before," Ralph added.

Brian rolled his eyes as he took a tool from his small tool belt and left the belt floating in front of him.

Looking up at Ralph and then back at Brian, Rob asked. "You sure you guys have got time for this now?"

"We got time," explained Brian as he manually powered down the right boot.

Brian turned the boot to its side in Rob's hands, opened a side panel of the boot, and started to work on it. He then asked while working. "Did either of you see Nutzie leave?"

"No," replied Rob.

Ralph replied, "Since Thatorn only gave her, me, and you 10 minutes to be in the EVA control room. Maybe she hurried off and went on down to setup?"

"I didn't think it would take too much time to set up an RRU?" Brian asked, squinting into the boot. He grabbed another tool after placing the first one back in its proper place.

"Could you explain something to me?" Ralph questioned.

"What?" replied Rob and Brian almost at the same time.

"After Thatorn talked about going out to look at the damaged wing, he scheduled the three of us to meet with him in the EVA control room to do an RRU in 10 minutes. So what is an RRU exactly?" Ralph asked.

"You never heard of an RRU? I'm surprised the asteroid colonies don't use them. It stands for Remote Repair Unit. They are for doing remote space-based repairs and space survey work." Rob explained as he watched Brian work.

"Oh, we always called them expendables back home," replied Ralph, smiling while watching Brian with fascination.

Glancing up at Ralph, Rob said, "I guess you could look at them like that."

Brian let out a sigh and put his tool away. Rolled up the belt and tucked it back into his jumpsuit's right pocket. He closed the panel and powered up the boot.

The boot made little noise this time, only a noticeable soft hum.

"Ok. The power regulator is about shot and is causing all the noise. It's been overcompensating the other magnets to make your boot work. I made some adjustments. It won't last long but should hold you down a little better and be less noisy." Explained Brian.

Without looking away from their work, the captain and Val simultaneously exclaimed, "Thank you!"

Causing Ralph and Brian to chuckle.

Rob frowned and slipped his boot back on. He ensured it was securely on his foot before unbuckling from the console chair and standing up.

"Stop by my quarters later so I can repair it. I'll grab a new power regulator and magnet coil from the general stores in cargo bay 1 for the boot. It's on the same level as the EVA control room." Brian said.

"Sure," the co-pilot replied.

Captain Linol stood up from his seat at his station, holding something in his hand. He approached them, saying, "Hey Rob, I want to return your mini vac."

The captain stopped beside Rob and handed him a small cylinder with a telescoping tube.

"Did the job?" Rob asked.

"Oh yeah. I got my physical keyboard and keypads cleaned. They tend to collect grime due to zero-G and static charges," replied Captain Linol.

"Good idea," Ralph said, eyeing the device.

"That's why I always carry one," said Rob as he took it and stuck it into his jumpsuit's right pocket.

"Are you sure you didn't get it just to clean that crumb catcher you have there?" asked Brian with a smirk.

Rob stroked his mustache and replied, "It's handy for that as well."

"I do have one of those myself to clean up with, but mine is bigger," Brian remarked with a grin.

Looking at Ralph, Brian started to say, "Well, come on, Ralph, we only got a few minutes to get..."

Before he could finish, Ralph and Brian's C&PCs blared to life.

It was Thatorn. He said, "Due to a technical issue, the scheduled meeting at the EVA control room at 9:00 hours has been delayed. It is now set for 9:30 hours, that is all."

"That's odd," Rob said curiously.

"What's going on?" Asked Ralph, looking at Brian, confused.

"I have no clue," replied Brian, staring back at the frail man.

"I'm sure the Admiral has his reasons," the captain casually stated.

Captain Linol started to turn and head back to the pilot station. Rob grabbed him by the shoulder and exclaimed. "Just where do you think you're going!"

The captain turned back around and stared down at his co-pilot.

"It's my shift. Time for you to get some sleep," Rob insisted, looking him square in the eye.

"If..." started Captain Linol.

"Yes, Captain, I will call you ASAP if anything happens." Interrupted Rob.

With a soft sigh and a nod of his head, Captain Linol slowly left the command deck. While Rob made his way over to the co-pilot console.

Brian looked at Ralph and asked, "So, what are you going to get into before the meeting?"

"I don't know," Ralph replied, staring at Brian.

"Well, 30 minutes is not much time. I guess I could at least get my maintenance check on level 11 and the water recycling system out of the way," Brian said.

The communications specialist said nervously, "I didn't expect to run into any trouble on this contract."

"Come on. What else could go wrong?" stated Brian with a chuckle.

Brian waited patiently for the starboard lift on level 11. He looked at his C&PC for the time. It was 9:27 hours. He only had a few minutes to get to the EVA control room. Usually, this would not make him anxious, but he wanted to avoid any more of Thatorn's yelling.

The lift opened, and both Ralph and Nutzie were there.

"Going down," said Nutzie with a grin.

Brian entered the lift and stood between them.

Nutzie hit the lift controls to take them to level 13.

Brian had not been to this level yet, but he knew how different it was from his reviews of the ship's layout. He thought about this while the three of them stood there quietly as the lift descended.

A sizeable main cargo storage area was on both the port and starboard side of Level 13. Each had a separate connecting sub-storage hold towards the top of the ship.

Each of these main holds has a large door that is part of the angled-out sides of a trapezoid-shaped room at the bottom of the ship. On the shorter inside wall is a standard door near each corner with a row of storage lockers between them. The longest side is part of the outer hull with a broad access door to the outside of the vessel.

The room's primary function is an airlock. Used when cargo is needed to be loaded or unloaded in a vacuum.

At the top center of the ship are two EVA bays with their own access to the outside. A door from each bay connected them to the somewhat triangularly shaped six-walled EVA control room.

Two short, angled hallways extended toward the ship's top from the center circular hallway's top doors. Giving access to all areas on this level of the vessel.

There was an accessway from these halls to the square area around the lower half of the circular hallway. On its starboard wall of this area was an entrance to cargo bay 1, and on the port wall was one to cargo bay 2. Along the lower wall, near the corners, were the two access doors to the cargo airlock.

Brian snapped out of his thoughts as the lift doors opened. They all stepped out into the circular hallway. They proceeded straight through the door on the opposite wall from the lift and found themselves in the starboard's short gray hallway. Brian saw the opening to their left that led to the square area around the lower area of the circular hallway he was just thinking about.

They walked a few meters until they came up to two doors on both sides of them. At the end of the corridor in front of them was another door.

The door to their left was an extra-wide access door to main cargo hold number 1 on the ship's starboard side. The door before them was to hold number 1's sub-cargo area. It had a red sign with white lettering in English that read, "Authorized Personnel Only." The door to their right was to the EVA control room.

They entered the oddly shaped gray room to find both Thatorn and Lieutenant Rocha beside a tall gray locker in the corner to their right.

This corner was part of a short, slightly bulged-out wall on the other side of the circular hallway. A curved custom gray workbench with a high-tech, all-purpose gray 3D printer was placed along this wall. Just past it was another tall gray locker in the other corner.

Two angled outward walls of 35 degrees extended from the corners of the curved wall. Each had a door in its center. One was the wall behind them, and its door was the one they just used to enter the room.

At the other end of the angled-out walls were two shorter ones that angled back in at 35 degrees. A large, tall, gray space suit lockers were part of each wall.

Both of these short walls connected to the longest one. Near each of its corners was a door that led to the separate EVA bays. A large gray console with a sizable display screen and chair was at the center of the wall. On both sides of this was a generic gray control panel with a chair and window. Each was part of an EVA bay.

"Oh, you're here, good," Thatorn said as he and the lieutenant walked towards them.

"We have been busy putting Mr. Rush and Ms. Teodoresco's toolboxes in secured lockers. Lieutenant Rocha has inspected them and released them for your use." Stated Thatorn, pointing to the two lockers.

"Is that why you delayed our meeting time?" Asked Nutzie.

"You will need them to repair the ship," the lieutenant replied.

Looking at Brian, she added, "Mr. Rush, your locker is the closest," pointing at the locker she and Thatorn were just standing next to.

Nutzie and Brian quickly went to their lockers to examine the contents.

"And what about my tools?" inquired Ralph.

Lieutenant Rocha looked at Ralph and explained, "Per your request, we will be setting up a smaller secure locker with your equipment in your room. We granted this primarily because your tools are not as bulky or numerous as Mr. Rush's and Ms. Teodoresco's."

"Good," Ralph replied with a brief grin, looking at the lieutenant.

Brian walked over to his locker, but before he opened it, he saw that the nearby workbench was also equipped with holding magnetic plates with related controls and straps.

That should be helpful in zero-G, he thought.

Upon opening his locker, Brian saw that all three of his black toolboxes were securely locked on a shelf. So, he slides one of the draws from the center toolbox marked wrenches to take a look. He then maliciously goes over them to ensure they are secure in their dark gray foam inlays.

Deciding to check them all, he goes over everything in each drawer and hears Nutzie doing the same thing.

"Tools must always be in their inlays when stored," Brian stated once he was finished and closed the locker.

"It's not about being anal. It's about safety," Nutzie added, taking a final look over her tools.

Nutzie closed her locker, turned to Thatorn, and asked, "Can we lock them?"

Brian turned to look at Thatorn to hear his reply.

"If you like, we can put a passcode on the locker door," Lieutenant Rocha replied.

"Fine," said Nutzie, still staring at Thatorn.

Brian looked at the lieutenant and gave her a nod in agreement.

"In the meantime, we need to get outside and check out the damage," Thatorn said as he walked towards the large gray center console with a soft motor noise.

"I'll ready an RRU," Nutzie said as she strolled out the right door on the long wall to the port side EVA room number 2.

Brian noticed through the window the room lit up as she entered the room.

Lieutenant Rocha and Ralph walked up behind Thatorn as Brian stepped over to EVA room 2's window and console.

The gray room was bigger than he thought it would be. Four gray lockers were on the room's left wall, and along the right wall were two sizable metallic gray crates that seemed to be anchored in place. Brian could see the short side of another large secured metallic gray crate just below the window. The bay's large access door to space was at the room's far wall.

Brian noticed a sizable, odd-looking black box strapped down in the center of the room. It was rectangular, about 1.3 meters long, 1.1 meters high, and close to a third meter wide.

Before he could figure out what it might be, Nutzie distracted him when she walked over to the large gray crate on the right, nearest the outer door. She opened it, leaned over, and reached in. It appeared she pressed some buttons inside the box. She raised up and stepped away. A ball, a little larger than a human head, rose from the crate on a small, extendable pedestal. She carefully looked it over. Once satisfied, she quickly walked to the door and back into the EVA control room.

Nutzie said, "Ready," as she walked to the central control console around Brian. Quickly, Brian followed her.

Thatorn activated the console, and the screen became a wash of information as the RRU system started up.

Brian felt a little excited, having never been involved with an RRU in real-time. The few times he had been, it was only with an RRU's collected data to create a detailed 3D representation of what it examined.

The screen settled down into six blank video boxes that formed a lowercase T with several status lists along both sides of the screen. A unique interactive holographic RRU display screen and keyboard appeared above the console.

Thatorn tapped the screen and typed on the keyboard as Nutzie anxiously watched.

The right side of the console opened up to reveal a headset with a visor inside. It was held in place by a velcro strap. Next, another area at the bottom center of this console opened, and a joystick rose up from it.

It was apparent to Brian that using a physical control system with the headset was more practical.

Nutzie started to sit down at the console, and Thatorn grabbed her arm and said. "No, Ms. Teodoresco, I will pilot the RRU."

"But it is my job...." She angrily started to say with a more than usual Romanian accent.

"I'm the one in charge here!" Snapped the old man.

Nutzie reluctantly moved out of the way, grumbling softly, "Nenorocit."

Brian tried his best to compose himself because he remembered what it meant, having been called it several times many years ago.

As the old man took the console seat, Brian noticed Thatorn's mechanical legs were more flexible than he initially thought. He didn't bother to strap in since he was secured to his Exosuit's robotic legs, and its foot pads were magnetically attached to the floor.

Thatorn tapped at the holographic screen, and the lights in EVA bay 2 dimmed and went out.

Brian took a few side steps to his right for a better look into the bay through the window.

A red light on the ceiling with two strobing beams lit up the room, accompanied by a warning siren blasting in the control room. The noise stopped after a few seconds, and the outer bay door opened. Once the red strobing light stopped and went out, Brian saw an ocean of stars past the opening into space.

Thatorn unstrapped the headset with the visor and took it from the console. With the help of Lieutenant Rocha, he put it on.

Brian observed it was connected to the console via a small wire. He thought it was probably hard-wired to prevent any interactive delay.

Thatorn grabbed the joystick as the six screens flickered to life on the large display.

Brian figured the headset and visor should give him a real-time 360-degree view of the RRU's surroundings using all its cameras, along with a detailed heads-up display of the RRU's functions and status. The rest of them would have to make do with the six screens in the lowercase T formation on the big screen.

It was evident to Brian that grouping the six screens in this manner was an attempt to relate the views of the RRU's orientation. The center screen was the forward camera. The screens to the right and left were the cameras on the right and left. The one above the center was the top, and the one directly below the center was the bottom camera. The screen below that one showed the rear camera.

"Ok, here we go," announced Thatorn.

Brian watched through the bay window as the ball slowly floated off its pedestal after being released. It fired several small thrusters and flew out of the bay. Once past the doors, it took a sharp turn to the right.

Brian quickly sidestepped back towards the screen to view Thatorn piloting the RRU.

He saw the unit quickly fly over the ship's center hull. Thatorn orientated the RRU, so the ship was now below it.

It passed a couple of windows to the left. On the right were reactor vents followed by two of the ship's lower fuel tanks.

The RRU made its way over the bottom engine and headed towards the bottom of the lower wing.

Thatorn asked in a mumble, "Getting good telemetry, sensor data, and video?"

"Yes, Admiral," the lieutenant replied, looking over the giant display's status lists and the console readings.

"Good," said Thatorn.

He slowed the RRU down as it passed the small port sensor tower and its dish to the right. You could just make out the lower wing's mounted rear sensor dish at the bottom left.

After flying over the rear panel of the port's passive sensor array, the RRU slowed down even more as it closed in on the dark, barely visible long port antenna.

Brian was sure Thatorn could see everything much better with the enhanced visual options of his visor.

Lieutenant Rocha tapped Thatorn on the shoulder.

With a soft grunt, he activated the RRU's lights. Those watching the video screens were finally able to get a good look at the antenna.

The antenna stretched out on the three center video screens. You couldn't see anything on the center screen just beyond the end of the wing's bottom. That was where the communication tower used to be.

"Well, Mr. Milsom?" asked Thatorn.

Ralph leaned in and looked carefully at the antenna.

"Looks good. Let's see the other side of this antenna." He said.

Slowly, Thatorn took the RRU around the top of the antenna and rotated around it, stopping so they could get a good view of its other side.

"Good, no noticeable damage."

"Great, so we can...."

"Just a second, sir. I need to look at the starboard antenna as well." Interrupted Ralph.

"Won't one good antenna be able to send out data?" the lieutenant inquired as she bit her lower lip.

"Yes, assuming there is no massive damage to the starboard antenna that could affect the port one," Ralph responded.

Thatorn let out a grunt and took the RRU around the wing to the antenna on the starboard side.

After Thatorn had Ralph view it from each side, he asked with a grumble, "Well?"

Ralph stated, "Looks like they are in good shape. If enough of the communications room is intact, we might be in business."

Thatorn piloted the RRU down to the bottom of the lower wing. He turned the RRU around so everyone could finally see what was left of the laser and high gain communications tower.

It consisted of only a few jagged chunks of twisted metal and wiring extending from the wing's bottom.

"Hum," was all Brian could say as he stared at the tangled mess.

"We need to look and scan it from a bottom-up view to get a better idea." Explained Nutzie.

"Very well," said Thatorn as he took the RRU below the wrecked tower and turned the RRU around to look up at it.

From this view, you could see that very little of the tower remained.

The long, sharp, jagged metal pieces seemed to reach out towards the RRU. At the center was a roughly round, ripped-out opening. Only a thin splintered bar was left of a central support strut crossing near the center of the hole from the port to starboard.

"Just how big is that hole?" Ralph asked.

After hitting a few buttons on the RRU's control stick, Thatorn replied, "According to the scan data, about 1 meter, or 0.9244 meters to be exact."

"I'm afraid that support bar will need to be fixed before anyone can enter the communications room." Brian insisted.

"If you would have gotten sucked out, Brian, you might have been cut in half by that," Nutzie coldly announced.

Brian winced, thinking about it.

"Get in close, but be careful not to get tangled up in those wires. The RRU's sensors should give us enough data to build a detailed 3D image of the damage. With that, we can figure out our options." Nutzie stated.

Lieutenant Rocha added, "A spectral analysis check on the data might give us more insight into what caused the damage."

She then stepped back and wiped a bead of sweat from her brow.

Thatorn slowly guided the probe closer to the breach. A few battery backup lights were working inside, but it was difficult to see much. Once the unit got closer, its lights flooded the communications room, allowing them to see more details inside. Some of the visible instrumentation was covered with a dark coating. The rest looked utterly wrecked, just a mix of metal and wiring.

"Look at all that mess," said Thatorn.

Ralph looked at the video screens and said, "Lots of damage. An internal EVA by me probably won't be practical. From the damage, fixing it is going to take some delicate work. Something I can't do in a suit."

Nutzie looked at Ralph and asked him, "If we reinforce the strut, patch, and pressurize the room. Would you be able to work on a bypass for the array?

"I would have a much better chance, yes," Ralph replied.

"We should get as much of the structural data as possible. Can we take the probe into the communications room?" Brian asked.

"It won't fit with the remainder of that strut in the way," Thatorn replied.

"Just take it in as close as possible," Brian said.

Thatorn nodded.

After slowly approaching the opening, there was a soft shake of the images on the video screens.

"That's as far as I can go," explained Thatorn.

Nutzie grabbed Brian as she stepped back and pulled him away from the console.

"We can set up one RRU with a Z105 laser welder," Nutzie said.

Brian replied, "Yeah, then we can use some others to fairy out and hold...."

Nutzie interrupted as she sniffed the air, "Wait, that smell...."

Suddenly, several bright sparks flew out of the console. Several small bolts of electricity arced from it and struck Thatorn's Exosuit frame. Everyone standing behind him stumbled back to cover their eyes. Only their magnetic boots kept them up on their feet.

The light faded. Thatorn was still seated, shaking slightly, while the rest were stunned and blinking.

Lieutenant Rocha watched Ralph step towards the console to look at Thatorn.

Reaching for him with his right hand, he said, "Sir, are you...."

"Don't touch him!" Exclaimed the lieutenant as she grabbed Ralph's hand with her left one.

Ralph looked at her, confused.

After letting go of Ralph's hand, she quickly went to a wall panel near the big console as a few more sparks discharged from the console. After opening the panel, she pulled a small lever inside. The large screen went dark, and the holographic controls disappeared.

Thatorn slumped forward and rose slightly upward. His magnetic feet were no longer holding him to the deck.

Lieutenant Rocha quickly went over to Thatorn. Then, with her left hand, she checked for a pulse.

Raising her right arm, she activates her C&PC with her left hand and yells, "Doctor, we need you immediately in the EVA control room!"

"I already got the alert. I'm en route," the doctor replied over the lieutenant's C&PC.

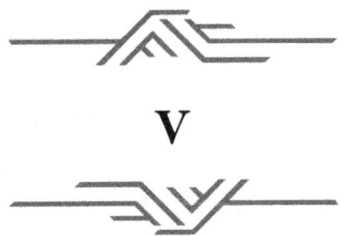

V

Brian gingerly walked out of his bathroom naked except for his magnetic boots. While rubbing his body with a towel, he remembered how much he hated using moist, no-rinse disposable cleansing cloths for zero-G hygiene. He fondly recalled his last nice, warm, relaxing shower when there was still gravity.

He tossed the towel behind his back into the bathroom. It hit the shower door and floated there.

Brian frowned as he looked over his small gray room. On the wall to his left was a small empty gray frig and a view screen over it. To the right of that was the door to the outer corridor and the room's trash chute. The wall before him had a small gray desk with a computer console and a gray chair. Along the curved outer hull wall on his right were a gray dresser, a single gray bed, a gray chair, and a window to space.

Well, at least I have a view. Brian thought as he grinned briefly.

He took a look out of his only window. Since it was the lower port window on this level, Brian could just about see the outer edge of the ship's port dock.

It was apparent to Brian that the port and starboard cabins with windows on this level are a little smaller because of the docks. He felt it was unfortunate that he was not assigned to a bigger windowed room on one of the other two cabin decks below.

He walked over to the bed and checked the webbing he had added to it earlier. It prevented him from floating around his room while he slept.

He smirked while thinking. I'd rather sleep with nothing, but I don't want my balls to get caught up in that.

Brian walked over to his dresser and carefully pulled out some dark pajama bottoms to wear to bed. He was getting the hang of zero-G by not flinging everything around when he took out items from the drawer.

Brian walked around his bed towards the chair and noticed his reflection in the window. He walked over in front of it to get a better view of himself, leaving his pajama bottoms to float above his bed.

Not too bad, he thought. I'm getting a little bit of a potbelly and starting to lose some body hair. Still wouldn't mind having a bigger dick, but I guess most men think that. I wonder if women look at their reflection and feel the same way about their tits?

Brian saw a small light just past his reflection out the window. Suddenly, it grew larger and larger until it finally struck the ship near the bottom of his window.

The ship rocked as the window cracked and splintered!

Brian ran for the door, but the window shattered before he reached the door controls.

The glass shards struck his naked body. Before he had time to react to the pain, the rush of air sucked him and his pajamas out into space. He failed in his attempt to grab onto the window frame.

He was spinning wildly out into the vacuum of space. The ship grew smaller as Brian gasped for breath.

Strangely enough, he heard a ringing. But how was it possible since there was no air out here to transmit sound?

With a loud gasp, Brian jerked himself awake. He opened his eyes and saw he was in bed. His darkened room was lit only by a dim night light from the bathroom.

The ringing happened again. It was coming from the door.

Brian maneuvered carefully out of his netting, slipped on his boots, and headed for the door.

He turned on the room light and activated the opening controls on the door. Then, frantically, he looked down and was relieved to find that he was at least wearing a pair of white shorts.

Brian looked back up and saw Rob in his doorway.

"You took a while. Are you ok? You're not still suffering from hitting your head, are you?" asked Rob, staring at Brian, concerned.

"Uh, Nah, just a bad dream," Brian dismissively replied.

"But I can see you are pale and have been sweating." Rob insisted.

"Yeah, I'll be ok," said Brian, wiping some of the perspiration off his forehead.

Rob, in turn, inquired, "Are you sure? We could ta...."

"I'll be fine." Brian gruffly interrupted.

"Ok," Rob said, then paused to look Brian over. He added. "I did not realize you were asleep."

Brian grumpily elaborated after looking at the time on his C&PC, "Ah, it's after 9 pm. Let's see, I finished my shift at 4 pm and got some liquid dinner afterward. Went to my room and cleaned up. That was about when my head started throbbing. I took some of the meds I got from the doctor and decided to go to sleep. I may have gotten around four hours of sleep at the most."

"I thought you would still be up, sorry," Rob said apologetically.

"It's ok," replied Brian with a soft sigh, then politely asked, "So what can I do for you?"

Rob said, "I stopped by to see if you got that part to fix my boot."

"Oh yeah," yawned Brian.

"It's ok, I can come back another...."

"Why?" Interrupted Brian. "I'm up. Might as well take care of it now."

Brian turned around and walked into his bathroom, gesturing for Rob to enter the room.

Rob came in and stood near the doorway, and the door automatically closed behind him.

Brian came back into the room with his most recently worn jumpsuit. After fumbling around in its pockets, he pulled his small tool belt out of the right pocket and two small objects from the left. One was a flat square, and the other a cylinder. Then, holding them in his right hand, Brian flung the jumpsuit with his left hand into the bathroom, where it floated near the shower door.

Brian said, "I'll need your confirmation of the needed part."

"What?" Rob asked, surprised.

"I have to keep track of everything I use. Thatorn's rules. It's in my contract," replied Brian.

With a laugh, Rob asked, "Will I get charged for it?"

"You might, but I could try and declare it work-related wear and tear," answered Brian with a grin.

Brian pointed at the seat near his window for Rob to sit there. Once he sat down and strapped himself in, Brian motioned with his left hand for Rob to give him his boot.

Brian released his tool belt and the small objects he collected from the jumpsuit. Leaving them floating within reach before grabbing the boot. After looking it over carefully and manually shutting it down, he handed it back to Rob, gesturing for him to hold it with the bottom of the boot upward.

"Ah yes, I see," Rob said, holding the boot as Brian instructed.

Brian unrolled his tool belt and took a tool from it before opening a compartment on the bottom of the boot.

Rob watched Brian while he worked on his boot. After a short time using a tool, Brian extracts a small, slightly burnt card-like object from inside the boot and places it in the right pocket of his shorts. He then carefully blows away any debris inside the open compartment. Using the same tool, he puts the flat object he left floating beside his tool belt inside the boot.

"Is it true?" Rob quietly asked.

"What?" Brian asked, trying to focus on his work.

"That Thatorn got fried and could have died!" Rob blurted out.

Laughing, Brian said, "That old fossil die. Nah, he just got cooked a little."

"What happened?" inquired Rob, intensely waiting for a reply.

"Overload. It fried the entire RRU system and Thatorn."

"Wow!" Rob exclaimed.

"It was odd. The old man should have seen it coming." Brian said while squinting into the opening on the bottom of the boot to ensure he had inserted the card-like object correctly.

"Really?" inquired Rob.

"The indicators on his heads-up display should have warned him. Maybe he was too busy staring at something to notice," speculated Brian.

"Or maybe it wasn't showing up on the heads-up display?" wondered Rob.

"That's possible," Brian replied as he changed his tools.

Brian stopped for a second, looked out the window into space, and said, "First me, then Thatorn. This is turning out to be an unlucky ship."

Brian started working on the boot again. He closed the panel he had opened, then opened another panel along the bottom edge of the boot. Taking the cylindrical object floating nearby, he placed it inside and swapped out another tool from his belt.

Rob inquired with curiosity. "Did you check the RRU console?"

With a grunt, Brian replied, "No, that Rocha woman wouldn't let me touch it. She told me that it was a security matter and that she would handle it."

"But you're an engineer!" Rob declared.

"I tried to remind her of that, but she informed me that she would let me know if she needed any of my assistance," Brian said mockingly.

"Did you give her an earful?" Rob asked with a grin.

"No, The Doctor showed up. As she looked over Thatorn, Rocha told the rest of us to return to our regular schedule. But as I was leaving the room, I heard the Doctor tell Rocha that Thatorn would be ok. Just be out for a while."

"Interesting," Rob mumbled.

"Done." Brian declared.

He closed the compartment on the bottom edge of the boot and placed his tool back in his belt. Then, taking the boot from Rob, Brian turned it on, held it up to his ear, and listened. It was utterly silent.

Handing the fixed boot back to Rob, Brian says. "Would you like me to sterilize it too?"

Looking up at Brian oddly, Rob asked, "What?"

Curiously, Brian started to say, "But I...."

A loud beeping from Brian's C&PC interrupts him. He looks at his wrist device, and then they hear Lieutenant Rocha say, "Calling the RRU group. Stand by. I have special instructions from Admiral Thatorn."

"Looks like the old man is up. That's my cue. It's time I got some rest myself," Rob said, taking his boot and putting it on.

Rob unstrapped himself from the chair, got up, and quickly exited the room. Telling Brian, "Thanks," as he left.

Again, the lieutenant's voice erupted from Brian's C&PC. "The Admiral and I will meet the RRU group in the Computer Core room to review all data to access repairs in 30 minutes. You all have been given temporary security access to the Computer Core for this task."

"Couldn't this have waited till morning? So much for sleep," mumbled Brian as he rolled up his tool belt.

Brian rubbed his eyes and yawned as he got off the elevator on level 5. He exited the ringed hallway and entered the square room through the starboard door.

Brian looked at this level's layout on his C&PC 3D display and noticed this deck held the same basic design as most others. In addition, he saw that the Computer Core room was in the exact location as the galley was on level 4. He also noticed there was no room marked "Restricted Officers Only" on this level.

Brian headed for the closest door to the Computer Core room on the ship's starboard side. He made a slight left turn down the gray hall, passing a bathroom at his left, and saw the door to the Computer Core room on his right.

Just before reaching it, Brian heard another door open and close. It sounded like it came from the intersecting hall that runs perpendicular to the one he was in.

Curious, he softly walked to the intersection to look.

"Ah!" exclaimed Fa Ming with a start as Brian almost ran into her in the intersection.

Brian apologized. "I'm sorry, Ms. Ming. I heard a door open and close...."

Fa interrupted. "It's ok, Mr. Rush. I just came from my office. I didn't expect there would be anyone else around, at least not yet."

After glancing at her C&PC's small 2D display, she added. "I see you came early. Almost 20 minutes."

"Yeah, I figured Thatorn would as well, so."

"Yes, you don't like the old man barking at you either, eh?" Fa asked rhetorically, looking down at Brian with her brown eyes.

Fa started walking up the corridor towards the dead-end and headed for the door to the Computer Core room on the right. Brian quickly caught up to her. They reached the door at the same time, and it opened.

"If I didn't have security access, would it still open for you?" Brian asked Fa.

Fa replied, "Oh no. If anyone who didn't have the allowed access via their C&PCs and its I.D. was near the door, it wouldn't open even if someone who did was also there. It's another security precaution. Your cabin door works the same way, except that the person assigned to the room can easily grant access to anyone else to enter through their C&PC."

"Ah," said Brian as he followed Fa into the Computer Core room.

The room was one long rectangle, about half the size of the mess hall. As expected, everything in the room was the same dull tone of gray.

Along the long starboard side of the wall on the left was a maintenance accessway, a large, complicated control panel with a console, a small screen, and a chair at its center. A mirrored version of all this was on the port side of the same wall. Between them, at the center, was a large screen with two small consoles angled outwardly on each side.

There was another holographic projector table at the center of the room, bigger than the one on the control deck, with four fixed chairs around it. Two of which were placed at the angled control consoles.

In the center of the wall to the right, opposite the large screen, was another the same size. Like in the galley, a door was near each end of this wall.

On the far, short wall was a door at its center, just like the wall behind him.

To Brian, it was evident that the center of the room was the main interface to Computer Core.

Fa made her way to the farthest angled console at the center of the room with Brian trailing behind her.

After sitting down and strapping herself in, Fa activated her console.

Like most consoles on this ship, it also had a built-in physical screen and keyboard along with holographic screens and a keyboard. However, unlike the others, this one had three 3D screens, a display screen in the center, and two interactive ones on each side.

"Is a computer A.I. part of the security system?" Brian questioned with curiosity.

She looked up at Brian and replied, "Um, no, not really. It's just military security protocols built into the ship's computer operating system."

"Ah," was all Brian could say since he didn't know exactly what she was talking about. He felt odd not knowing something, and it was a little frustrating to his ego.

Brian took the chair at the other angled console, strapped in, and swiveled around to face Fa.

By this time, Fa was focused on her console. She was tapping away on both 3D side screens and the keyboard at a frantic pace. Not only was she ambidextrous, but also fast. As a result, it was difficult for Brian to follow what she was doing.

"Loading the RRU data and all related information. We'll then be able to use it to create a detailed 3D representation to examine," said Fa before swiveling around in her chair to face the table.

Brian saw the table light up. Slowly, a holographic image began to form.

Fa explained, "The computer is now working on a detailed view of the damaged area. It may take a little while to compile all the data."

"You think it will be done before everyone ...."

Just then, both of their C&PCs went off, interrupting Brian.

It was Lieutenant Rocha saying, "To the RRU group. Thatorn and my arrival at the meeting in the Computer Core may be delayed.

The Doctor requires some final checks before releasing him. Proceed with the repair analyst even if we have not yet arrived. That is all."

"Well, that's interesting," commented Brian while staring at Fa.

Noticing Brian's gaze, Fa smiled. With her eyebrows raised, she asked, "Mr. Rush, do you have something on your mind, or are you just admiring my body?"

Taken by surprise, Brian could only stare back at her wide-eyed.

"It's ok, Mr. Rush. It's going to be a long trip. Who knows what might happen." She said, lowering her eyebrows but continuing to smile at him.

Was she flirting? Brian asked himself as he began to blush.

It quickly became apparent that Ms. Ming was taking great delight in seeing him embarrassed.

Brian thought, I'm no virgin, but I'm very inexperienced when it comes to women. She is rather attractive for an older one, though. They say mature women are better for younger men and tend to treat them better than women their own age.

Fa changed the subject to Brian's relief and asked, "Since we have time, why don't you tell me where you're from?"

"Um, I...I'm from Earth, Texas, to be exact, and you?" Brian asked, stammering.

Fa answered, "I was born and raised in the New Beijing Dome on the moon."

That accounted for her tall, slender build, Brian thought.

She elaborated, "I attended college there as well."

She then asked, "What about you?"

"I wandered from tech school to tech school back on Earth until I finally got my degree," Brian replied.

Brian thought. This might be an excellent time to ask Fa some delicate questions before anyone else arrives. I wonder if she had the same bad luck that brought others onto this ship.

He decided to find out and asked, "May I ask how you happened upon this job?"

Fa glared at Brian.

He was surprised by her reaction.

She inquired, "W... Why do you ask?"

"Mostly out of curiosity. Plus, I'm always looking for any better representation to find work." Brian lied.

Fa said wistfully, "I can't help you there, I'm afraid. My last job was on Moon Station L5. I was just getting used to the one-G on the station with the help of bone and muscle stims. Then suddenly, the company I had worked for years just went belly up out of the blue."

Brian's right eyebrow rose.

Fa continued, "After a long search, I was surprised that this was the only job I could find."

She looked down at the floor with a scowl and added, "But if I only knew."

A reference to Thatorn? Brian pondered.

Fa seemed ashamed. She couldn't look at Brian, only up at the 3D image forming over the table.

Brian thought this might be a good time to talk about something else.

Smiling, Brian asked, "Since you knew about the security cameras, have you seen any of the security feeds?"

Fa glanced over at Brian. After seeing his reassuring smile, she replied, "Ah... Well, yes."

Turning towards him, returning the smile, she explained, "I have almost the same access as Rocha, but only from here in the core room. She is one of the few that can access everything from almost anywhere on the ship. You see, part of my job is to ensure the security system stays up and running. As a result, I take the occasional look through some of the input feeds from time to time."

"In that case, have you noticed anyone acting odd when you have?" Brian inquired.

"What do you mean?" Fa replied with a question.

"I'm not really sure," Brian answered, looking slightly puzzled.

Fa stared at the ceiling momentarily, then said, "From what little I have seen, everyone has been behaving quite normally."

Brian sighed in disappointment.

Fa looked at Brian and asked, "You know about the red door on level 4 marked Restricted Officers Only on the floor plan?"

"Why yes," replied Brian with enthusiasm.

"I could not find any feeds coming from inside the room. At least none I have any access to. Because of this, I started paying a little more attention to a feed just outside the room. From it, I saw Thatorn visiting the room several times. Sometimes, Rocha would accompany him."

"Do you have any idea what's in there?" Brian questioned with some excitement.

"He is a so-called scientist. Maybe it's some kind of lab," Fa said with sarcasm.

A little taken aback, Brian inquired, "So-called?"

"He was better known as a military tyrant during the war," Fa sneered.

"Nutzie was under him at one point during the war. She never said anything about him being a Tyrant. So why are you calling him that?" asked Brian curiously.

"For what he did to my father!" Fa shouted.

Brian cautiously asked, "What was that, Ms. Ming?"

Firmly and stoically, Fa explained. "He was an honorable military man from a long line of those in my family that served. Even before there ever was a U.E.A., Thatorn disgraced my father and my family name by having him court-martialed. All because he wouldn't attack some colonists. Thatorn maintained they were outlaw Pirates during the trial. But my father told me the truth. They were mostly women and children. All of whom were unarmed."

So this is the cause of Fa's anger towards Thatorn, Brian thought.

While clenching her fists, Fa elaborated, "After the first briefing, Thatorn came to my quarters and tried to calm me down by saying that everything was all in the past and mistakes were made."

Brian started saying, "He admitted to...."

Fa interjected, "He was still implying my father was the one who made the mistakes."

"Oh...," Brian sadly said.

"Then he advised me that since we were not going back anytime soon, I should make the best of it just before he left," Fa growled.

Suddenly, the starboard door on the long wall opened. Ralph and Nutzie casually strolled in. Ralph was rubbing his eyes and yawning. However, Nuztie seemed wide awake.

Brian saw Fa quickly release her fists. After taking a deep breath, she rubbed her sweaty hands on the knees of her jumpsuit.

Nutizie walked up to the table, with Ralph following closely behind.

After glancing at her C&PC, Nutzie smirked and exclaimed, "It's just 21:52, and the old man's still not here yet? Zala must be giving him a good going over before letting him go."

Ralph stepped up to the table. While gazing at the hologram, he said, "I see you have already got the rendering started."

Nutzie looked over her colleagues one by one. Then, with a devilish smile, she asked, "I wonder how Thatorn will get around without his legs?"

"So the exoskeleton suit is not working now? I'm not surprised, considering," Brian replied, looking at the short, stout, muscular woman.

"We are still in zero-G. Rocha could just pull him around," explained Ralph.

"Thatorn has too much pride for that," Nutzie said before returning her attention back to the hologram still forming over the table.

The image began to reveal the remains of the communication tower. Shards of twisted metal and wires were sticking out from the bottom of the wing. More detail emerged, showing a roundish rupture with a thin bar of metal going from port to starboard stretch across the opening. It was all that remained of a structural support strut.

"Can the resolution be increased?" asked Nutzie as she walked over to Fa.

"Yes, Mrs. Teodoresco. Once the structure is finished, the computer will do so automatically." answered Fa, looking up at the older woman.

"Call me Nutzie, dear." She said, grinning at Fa.

"Nutzie, ok.", Fa replied, returning the grin.

"So how does..." began Nutzie as she started chit-chatting with Fa, or maybe it was flirting.

Brian was not sure. He quickly got bored listening to it, and his eyes wandered around the room. As he looked towards Ralph, he noticed a wet spot on the upper leg of his jumpsuit.

Brian whispers softly to Ralph, asking, "What happened?"

Ralph looks over at him, puzzled.

Brian subtly pointed at the wet spot on Ralph's jumpsuit.

Ralph looked down, and with a soft huff, he muttered, "Damn zero-G toilets."

Brian let out a giggle.

Nutzie stopped talking. She and Fa stared at Brian, confused.

Brian managed to distract them by pointing at the 3D image, saying, "I see we are starting to get some detail."

Nutzie frowned at Brian as she stepped closer to the table for a look.

Fortunately for Brian, details were just beginning to form on the hologram.

"I will need to clear away as much of the tower's remains as possible to get a flat area to patch," Nutzie said, pointing at the shards and wires sticking out of the wing bottom.

"That strut will need to be repaired and reinforced too." Brian insisted.

"Um, yes," agreed Nutzie.

"Any chance we can patch it all up while in flight?" Ralph asked, hoping.

"If we could do it all from the inside, maybe." Speculated Nutzie.

"That strut will need to be reinforced from the outside, I'm afraid," asserted Brian.

"You can't fix it on the outside while in flight?" asked Ralph, still optimistic.

Brian insisted, "An in-flight repair is out of the question. Even if we could fix the strut from the inside, I wouldn't trust the integrity of the wing structure under flight conditions anyway."

Ralph frowned.

"What do you think happened?" Fa asked, staring at the hologram.

"Looks like it could be a hit from below," Brian surmised.

"Lucky strike," Nutzie said with a laugh.

"Hum," was all Ralph said.

Nutzie leaned in to take a better look at the hologram. She glanced at Fa and said. "Zoom in on the interior of the communication room if you please."

Fa swiveled around in her chair, tapped, and typed away. The hologram turned into a blown-up view of the communication room within seconds. Not much could be seen of the inside wall where the hole to space was.

"I'm sorry, it's the best I can do with the data we have." Explained Fa as she swiveled back around and looked at the hologram.

Ralph leaned in, looked at everything, and said, "We'll have to rely on the backup relays by the door. Looks like almost everything else is trashed."

Nutzie then pointed at what could be seen of one of the room's side walls and exclaimed. "Look at this. There is a lot of carbon scorching."

"Can we get a spectral analysis of that wall?" Brian asked, looking at Fa.

"Sure. I'll load up the appropriate video data, and I should be able to check the light reflection off the wall. Running a full spectral comparative analysis might take a little while."

Ralph inquired, "Could that scorching have just resulted from an explosion after a collision?"

"I only heard the one explosion. There was no sound of an impact beforehand," insisted Brian.

Squinting at the hologram, Nutzie said, "Look at the hole itself. I didn't notice this when we looked at the live feed."

"What is it?" Ralph asked, trying to see what she was looking at.

Suddenly Nutzie raged, "Damn it!" slamming her clenched fist onto the table.

The rest of them were taken aback by her outburst.

After a gruff sigh, she looked at Brian and asked, "Do you see all the ripped metal all along the edges of the hull breach?"

Brian took a good look at it and replied, "You're not saying...."

Nutzie interrupted, "Yes, Mr. Rush, I am. This was the result of an outward explosion, not an inward collision. It definitely looks like sabotage!"

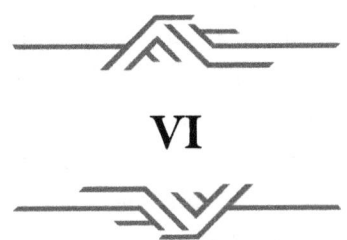

VI

"I didn't sign up for this shit! It's too much, man!" exclaimed Ralph as he sat in a nearby chair. Instead of strapping into it, he held the seat firmly with both hands and stared blankly at the floor.

"I've seen the results of internal explosions during the war," insisted Nutzie, scowling.

"You're sure of this, Ms. Teodoresco, um, Nutzie?" inquired Fa, looking at the short woman before her.

"Oh hell yes," she quickly snapped back, staring at the hologram.

Ms. Ming looked at Brian and asked, "What about you, Mr. Rush?"

"Well, honestly, I've only seen the damage caused by an internal explosion once. Nutzies right, there is an outward ripping of the hull that would indicate that's what happened," Brian replied as he rubbed the stubble on his chin.

"I have no expertise with this myself," asserted Fa.

She looked at Ralph and was about to ask him too but thought better of it.

"Who has been in the communications room!" bellowed the gruff voice of Thatorn.

They all looked over to see Thatorn and Lieutenant Rocha inside the room near the port door of the long wall. To their surprise, they saw the old man sitting in a powered wheelchair. It was small, flat black, and had not one shiny spot on it. However, there was a familiar big gray pouch attached to the right side of it.

Using his right hand, the old man grabbed a joystick on the right arm of the wheelchair. Silently, it rolled towards them while the lieutenant followed closely behind.

Brian assumed its wheels must be magnetic as he watched it roll along the deck. However, after noticing odd-looking thrusters around the chair, he realized the wheel's magnetic properties were power-activated. The old man could turn them off and use the chair's thrusters to freely navigate zero-G. Brian pondered why the old man wouldn't prefer using this freer mode of transport over his bulky mechanical exoskeleton with legs.

The admiral had looked better, thought Brian. From his pale lips, face, and sunken eyes, you could tell he must have had a rough time from the electrical shock. Yet, despite all that, his demeanor seemed ever more cantankerous by giving everyone his usual sneer.

Looking at Lieutenant Rocha, Brian wondered. She still looks the same no matter what's going on around her. Stolid, Cool, and stone-faced. Never giving away anything that went on inside her pretty tan, oval head.

"Well, Damn It! Who was in the communications room!" The old man barked once again, still rolling towards them.

"How long have you been here?" Nutzie inquired, angrily peering down at Thatorn.

"Long enough," the old man replied with a cheeky smirk.

The lieutenant and the admiral stopped just a meter from the holograph table beside the empty chair.

It seemed as if Nutzie was about to say something to Thatorn but quickly changed her mind after receiving the old man's cold, hard stare.

"Ms. Ming, check and see who had been in the communications room prior to the explosion," said Lieutenant Rocha nicely.

Fa spun around in her chair and started to tap and type away at her console, saying, "Cross-checking the C&PC tracking data with the communications room."

Thatorn stared at Ms. Ming with enthusiasm.

This was the first time Brian believed he had seen the old man show any kind of joy. Maybe he is off in the head, he thought.

The old man looked up briefly and whispered at the lieutenant, "So now we know."

Brian glanced towards Thatorn because he heard him talking to Lieutenant Rocha and noticed Nutzie looking warily at the old man.

Ms. Ming stopped tapping and typing and stared at her center screen.

"Well!" Thatorn asserted.

She taped and typed again. Then, hesitantly, she said, "The communications specialist was in the room 2 days ago."

Thatorn's neck snapped so fast to glare at Ralph that Brian was surprised he did not hear a sonic boom.

Ralph looked up at Thatorn and began to noticeably tremble.

"Anyone else?" the lieutenant calmly inquired.

After a few more seconds of tapping and typing, Fa replied, "No, as far back as the data goes."

"That would have been when I reset the system after we left the base at 433 Eros, Admiral," Lieutenant Rocha stated, looking down at Thatorn.

Thatorn grabbed his chair's joystick. Then, ever so gently, he turned his wheelchair to the left and slowly crept around the holograph table and empty chair, heading towards Ralph.

"What did you do, Mr. Milsom?" The old man asked calmly, gritting his teeth.

After a gulp, Ralph squeaked, "I was there doing my first systems check. Ensuring everything was synced up with the ship systems. Since the Earth is on the other side of the sun relevant to us, I took

103

the time to confirm the laser of the communication tower was locked onto 243 Ida's automated communications relay. "

Fa turned around in her chair to see what was going on.

"What did you do, Mr. Milsom?" The old man asked again as he closed in on the trembling man.

Franticly, Ralph exclaimed, "I just told you!"

"Did you rig the laser to overload and somehow mask the fact from the power control system!" Snarled Thatorn as he closed within a few meters of Ralph. Stretching out his free left hand towards him.

Immediately, Nutzie ran around the table, stepped in between them, and looked down at Thatorn with disdain.

The old man stopped his chair abruptly, lowered his left hand, and glared up at her.

"That's enough!" Nutzie barked.

Thatorn started to snap back, "He's the one...."

Nutzie interrupted, "We don't know that for certain." Then, she turns to look down at Ralph and adds, "Yet."

The old man started growling, "Look here, Ms. Teodoresco. This is a military ship, and I am...."

The sudden noise of several beeps from Fa's console distracts Thatorn.

"What's that!?" The old man demanded, looking over at Fa.

"I was running a spectral analysis on the inside of the communications room. My console was just letting me know it was finished," answered Fa as she looked back at her console.

Thatorn swung his wheelchair around and headed toward the I.T. specialist.

Ralph quickly collapsed in a heap in his chair. No longer holding onto it, he started to drift away.

Shaking her head, Nutzie leaned over and promptly strapped him into his seat.

"Well!" Thatorn grunted with curious excitement as he stopped within a foot of Fa.

Fa turned around, stared at her center screen, and said, "I've got the detailed elements data. The computer is saying something about...."

Fa stopped and was visibly shaken. She slowly turned around in her seat to face the rest of her crewmates in the room.

Nervously, she says, "There are traces of some kind of an explosive."

"A bomb!" Brian exclaimed.

Slowly, Ralph raised his head.

"Someone planted a bomb on my ship," Thatorn giggled.

"There is no way someone could have gotten on the ship with a bomb!" angrily insisted the lieutenant.

Thatorn takes a long look at Ralph between the tabletop and the hologram. While squinting at him, he grunts out, "Hum."

Quickly turning to Fa, Thatorn orders, "Show us all the surveillance footage of Mr. Milson while he was in the communications room."

Fa quickly turned around to her console to tap and type away. The large screen above her left shoulder flickered to life as she slightly turned her chair's seat to the left for a better look at the screen.

They all stared up at the screen intensely. It showed three images, one on top of two smaller ones.

The top one was of the wing hallway aimed towards the communications room. The bottom left was from a view of the room near the door. The last was a side view inside the room from somewhere along its right wall. Each view had a camera number above each image with a date and time stamp below.

Brian recognized these were the same camera views he had seen in the situation room earlier.

The time on each was synced together and read April 3rd at 7:15:03.

"That was just after my zero-G nutritious liquid breakfast," Ralph grumped.

Everyone stayed transfixed on the screen and ignored him.

After a few seconds, Ralph can be seen and heard in the top video by the clicking of his magnetic boots as he walks down the hallway toward the communications room.

Sound? This was the first time Brian realized that not only video was being recorded, but audio was also being recorded.

They watch him enter the communications room. The view from the entrance mainly showed his back. However, the side view revealed more.

He stood at the central wall console, logged on, and reviewed several 3D screens. After nearly ten minutes of tapping on the screen and typing on a 3D keyboard, everyone got bored except for Thatorn.

Finally, he stopped and logged off the system. He walked over to several panels in the room and looked over their 2D readout screens but never touched any of them.

They heard him sigh just before he turned and left the room. They watched him walk away from the communications room on the top video.

Fa taps on her interactive screen, and the playback stops.

Feeling vindicated, Ralph clucks, "See, I told you I didn't do anything."

Thatorn turns towards Ralph and calmly states, "Maybe not, Mr. Milson, maybe not."

Nutzie says, looking down at the old man jeering, "Seems like someone jumped to conclusions."

"We will review all the related footage later just to make sure," Thatorn sneered, looking up at the Romanian woman.

"Show us the spectral data details, Ms. Ming," Lieutenant Rocha asked curiously.

Fa turned to face her screen, and after a few taps, she replaced the 3 screens with a readout list of the spectral analysis elements. They all looked up at the screen carefully, except for Fa, since she had the same information on her center screen.

It was all gibberish to Brian. He recognized only a few things, though he would never admit it.

"But that's...." the lieutenant muttered.

Thatorn quickly gestured to Lieutenant Rocha to come closer. As soon as she leaned over him, he started whispering in her ear.

"Um, what?" Brian asked.

Once Thatorn was finished whispering to the lieutenant, he asked Fa, "You are sure Ralph was the only one in the room?"

Brian realized he was blatantly being ignored.

Looking over her right shoulder at the old man, Fa replied, "Yes, I checked it twice to make sure."

"How about near the room?" Lieutenant Rocha Inquired.

"Yes, what about that," Thatorn added.

Fa typed and tapped away again, saying. "Cross-checking C&PC tracking with the wing area before the accident, I mean sabotage."

After a moment, Fa added, "Besides Mr. Rush showing up right before, the only other person near there was Ms. Elderman. She passed the lower wing entrance on her way to the lift."

"When?" the lieutenant asked.

"Looks like she turned the corner at that intersection on April 3rd at 14:16:45," Fa replied.

Lieutenant Rocha quickly raised her right arm and consulted her C&PC by activating its holographic screen.

"Give us all available video of her passing," Thatorn ordered.

"There are several from the connecting perpendicular halls, the wing's hallway, and the corridor connecting the central core to the wing's hallway," Fa replied.

"Show them all. Pause the playback six seconds before Ms. Elderman passes the intersection," Thatorn ordered.

The large screen went dark as Fa went to work at her console. After a short time, it flickered again with several images showing the intersection from different viewpoints. Each one had a camera number above with a date and time stamp below. Val could be seen motionless in several of the views approaching the corner. She held a small tool case with her left hand while her right hand was in it. The time stamp below them all showed it was April 3rd at 2:16:39.

"Enlarge camera views 8, 11, and 16," Ordered the old man.

The three views Thatorn asked for were expanded and lined up at the top of the screen, while the rest shrank and were placed below.

Two of these camera views showed the intersection from different angles and at close range. The third view was taken from the far end of the wing hallway, somewhere above the communications room entrance.

The lieutenant stated, "She is where she should have been. After lunch that day, I had her scheduled to check several junction relays on that level. 14:15:56 was the time she logged as being finished."

Lieutenant Rocha closed the screen on her C&PC, lowered her arm, and looked at the large wall screen.

"That explains why she is heading towards the lift," Brian interjected.

Thatorn only gave him a casual glance in response.

Brian then said, "Surely you don't think...."

"We have to make sure. No one is above reproach," the lieutenant interrupted, staring at Brian deadpan.

"Proceed, Ms. Ming, at half speed and loop it from the current time to, let's say, 2:16:51," Thatorn ordered.

After a few taps, Val slowly began moving on the screens she was in.

Fa looked over her left shoulder at the screen as they all watched.

They focused on the two larger videos showing Val walking along the perpendicular hallway. Then, at 2:16:43, just before she started to turn, all the screens snowed out slightly with static.

"What's that?" bellowed the old man, annoyed.

"Glitches, I'm afraid, sir. It happens from time to time." Fa said, still watching the screen.

You could still see most of the video image and Val through the disruption. She finished her turn and closed her case just before the video looped back and started over again.

"How? This ship is heavily shielded from outside interference, like radiation and magnetic fields. Even from an EMP." The old man insisted.

Fa turned around in her seat and began to explain. "Yes, but not as much from internal interference. Some of the other ship systems can cause electromagnetic interference, especially those two H3 reactors on board."

Thatorn glances up at Lieutenant Rocha, and she shakes her head in agreement.

She says, "If you recall, sir, this was a known problem we ran into after the refit. With the scheduled launch date looming, we had insufficient time to rectify all the issues completely."

Thatorn nods his head.

Fa says, "I get a warning about any interference in the system when it occurs, and I do a quick check. The system also alerts security, even for a short glitch like this."

After glancing back at her console screen, Fa adds, "The related error log indicates this one only lasted about 21 seconds in total."

"Is that an average time for these glitches?" Brian asked, looking down at Fa.

She looked up and replied, "More or less."

Brian then muttered, "Might be related to the injector coils. Especially since we have two reactors."

"You don't remember already seeing this when it happened?" Thatorn asked with curiosity.

Fa looks at Thatorn and explains. "Sir, I don't recall this one in particular. They only happen occasionally, and I do review them. I focus on checking to see if they caused damage to any part of the system."

Thatorn tugs on his chin and mumbles for a few seconds.

He looks up at the lieutenant and gestures for her to come closer. Once she bends over, he whispers in her ear again.

She quickly rose up and said to him, "Yes, sir."

She turns and heads for the same door she and Thatorn entered earlier.

"Make sure you get to the first thing ASAP," Thatorn commanded, looking at her.

"Yes, sir, " responded Lieutenant Rocha before exiting the room.

Thatorn turns towards the others and growls. "Well then. We don't know who is responsible for this just yet."

Fa started to say, "Shouldn't we let the others know...."

Thatorn brazenly interrupted. "No! I want to keep this under wraps for the time being. Trust me, I have everything under control."

Nutzie then tries her best to hold back a laugh.

The old man replied to her with only a glare.

Looking at Brian, Thatorn says, "In the meantime, the first priority is to repair the hull breach so we can get underway ASAP."

Glancing at Ralph, he adds, "Once that is done, you can get in there and fix the array."

Ralph responds only with a timid nod.

Staring back at Nutzie, he adds, "With the RRU out, It looks like you'll have to do an EVA to do the repair."

Brian starts to reply, "I guess we...."

Nutzie interrupts, "Um, Mr. Rush, Brian, I think I can handle it from here. But, first, I'll need to download all the relevant damage data from the computer to my C&PC."

Nutzie looks at Fa, fluttering her eyes, and says, "Can you handle that, dear?"

"Sure," Fa replied.

"Good. While I wait for that, I can start getting my tools and needed materials together," Nutzie said.

"But I thought that I...." Brian started.

Interrupting him again, Nutzie says, "I've been doing this for years and prefer to do most of the work on my own. Once I have everything ready, I'll fill you in on my repair plans. Then, you can crunch the numbers and make sure it's all up to par if you like."

"If you insist, Nutzie," was all Brian could say.

"How long?" grunted the old man at Nutzie.

"I will probably take at least a day to get ready, maybe more. Also, a few hours to do the actual repair." She replied, staring at the old man.

Thatorn lets out a loud grumble.

"Best I can do. You have a very unusual hull that uses a specialized metal that...."

Thatorn interrupts with, "Fine. Just get to work."

Nutzie abruptly turned around and left through the door she had come in.

Thatorn grabs his joystick and starts his wheelchair towards the door Nutzie used. Then, he says, looking back at Brian, "Since you have the time, I have a special job for you, Mr. Rush. I will make sure to send you the details later."

Despondent, Ralph watched the old man leave. After the door closed behind him, he looked up at Brian and stated. "I better take the time to go over the backup relay schematics. I'm not sure how difficult it will be to get the array up and running until I get in there."

Slowly, he unstrapped himself and slinked off, leaving through the same door the lieutenant did.

Brian turned to look at the still-looping video on the screen

"I guess I should get to work on getting and sending Nuztie the data she requested," Fa said as she turned around to face her console.

Just as she was about to deactivate the video, she realized Brian was still watching it.

She turned around in her chair to look at him and politely asked, "Mr. Rush, uh, Brian, are you finished?"

"Um, what." He replied, realizing Fa had said something to him.

Fa said, "I was about to shut down the video."

"Oh, ok," said Brian, still watching the looping video.

"Did you see something?" Fa curiously asks.

"I thought I saw something moving down the wing hallway," Brian replied.

"Oh?" questioned Fa.

Brian reluctantly replied, "I can't really tell. Maybe it's just the glitching."

B rian had a restless night after the previous night's revelation. Still, he finally managed to get a little sleep before his C&PC alarm went off at 6:00 hours. After a quick scrub of a disposable cleansing cloth, he was off to the galley to get his liquid breakfast.

Since he has been awake, all of the recent events have been rolling around in his head.

So, someone on the ship is blowing things up. Well, to be more precise, taking out the communications system, but why? To stop us from communicating with anyone. Could the crazy old man be right? Could something be happening around Jupiter someone doesn't want us to discover?

It was also odd that the old man seemed almost gitty when he learned the supposed accident turned out to be sabotage.

Then we had the RRU crap out... Wait a second. Could that have been sabotage, too? To keep us from fixing the antenna array and communicating?

If so, might they try to stop the EVA or Ralph?

I wonder if Thatorn or Lieutenant Rocha thought about that after what we learned last night?

The lieutenant was supposed to look into the RRU malfunction. I will be curious to know what she finds out.

Brian used the port-side elevator and entered the galley from its lower port-side entrance for a change. As he made his food selection, a large bag with a built-in capped straw emerged from the machine. It read breakfast nutrition number 3.

Brian sighed and looked around the room. He noticed the doctor and the captain sitting beside each other at the port side table with the long window behind them. They seemed to be snuggling closely, whispering and softly laughing. The captain held a bag with a straw extending from it in his right hand. The doctor had one floating before her. Since their straws were uncapped, Brian assumed they had been drinking from them.

Brian was surprised to see the captain here. He was sure it was his shift to be on the control deck.

Brian thought, surely Thatorn told him about the sabotage last night. Maybe the captain's even told the doctor by now? Then again, probably not. I don't think they would be so happy and laughing if they knew.

He decided to grab a seat across from them at the same table.

They stopped talking and looked at Brian as he walked over and was about to sit down.

Brian asked, "Do you mind?"

"Well..." Captain Linol began to grumble with a frown.

"No," interrupted Doctor Teka, giving the captain a look.

Just as Brian was about to sit down, he inadvertently looked out the window behind the doctor and captain.

He felt a little dizzy and froze halfway into sitting down.

"Are you ok, Brian?" asked Zala as she looked him over.

Quickly, Brian diverted his eyes away from the window. Focusing on the doctor and captain, he was then able to sit down and strap himself in.

"Um, I'm ok, Doc," lied Brian.

She squinted at him and let out a low "Hum."

Brian looked back at her with a smile.

She followed that up with, "The mild swelling on your forehead looks to be gone. You feeling ok? Are the meds still working?"

"Uh, yeah, I'm ok. The meds are working fine. I only have some minor soreness and pain," Brian responded.

After letting out another "Hum." The doctor inquired, "Any other issues I should know about?"

"No, No," Brian lied again while smiling.

"Did you guys figure out what happened?" inquired the captain, squinting at Brian.

It was now clear to Brian that Thatorn was keeping the sabotage a secret even from the captain.

"No, not exactly. We believe it might have just been a high-velocity micrometeor strike," lied Brian.

"That's what Fa suspected," Zala stated.

"Um, yeah," Brian murmured.

"What about repairs? Have you scheduled any on the ship without a name?" The captain asked now in a more friendly tone.

"We have started to call her the Black Swan," Zala added, looking at the captain.

"Ship without a name, S W A N, and black because of its overall color. I get it," Brian replied, then he looked at Captain Linol and added. "Regarding repairs, an EVA is scheduled for early tomorrow. Thatorn wants it done ASAP so we can get the ship going. Nutzie told him she would need at least a day just to get ready."

"I see," the captain stated, looking at Brian intensely stroking his beard.

Brian elaborated, "Nutzie took charge and will do most of the work herself. I guess she knows what she's doing. She told me she would contact me to check the numbers to ensure her work will hold up."

"Oh, and where is she now?" Zala asked with a smile, glancing over at the captain.

Raising his left arm, Brian activated his C&PC with his right hand, brought up a screen, and said, "I got a message from her hours ago. She said she got up early, skipped breakfast, and gathered all the required supplies. Her message also says that she will be cutting out the needed repair plates from specialized hull repair sheets in the ship's stores."

Looking closer at his screen, he adds, "She's set up a meg shift work area in cargo hold 2. She said the EVA control room work area was a little too cramped for her."

"That sounds like a lot of work?" the captain questioned.

"I know, but she insisted on doing it all herself," Brian replied, turning off his C&PC and lowering his arm.

"Well, she is a control freak," Captain Linol mumbled.

Zala glared at the captain for a few seconds in response to his comment.

Captain Linol took that moment to raise his left arm and let go of his bag to float before him. He then tapped on his C&PC to bring up a 2D screen. Brian could see it was showing several green dots.

This." possibly indicates its connection to the ship and its status. He tapped the screen and brought up a more detailed 3D screen.

The doctor looked at Brian and politely said, "Nutzie prefers to work independently."

Zala grabbed her breakfast bag and took a sip from it. Afterward, she added, "Still, I'll be glad to finally get some real, well, more real food when the engines are finally fired up."

"Yes, and I will be glad to get some real coffee instead of this lukewarm zero-G mix they call coffee," muttered the captain, looking over his C&PC screens.

Zala glanced at him and said, "Well, Mark, if you would just use a mild stim when you needed it instead of drinking that all the time, you might be able to sleep better."

Captain Linol glanced back at Zala and mumbled, "It's this late schedule I'm not used to. The coffee helps."

Brian grinned while listening to them as he pulled the cap off the straw of his bag and took a drink. He was surprised to find that it didn't taste too bad.

"Having caffeine so close to going off duty and then trying to sleep can't be helping," Zala said before taking another sip from her breakfast bag.

The captain only silently stared at his C&PC screens.

Brian looked at Zala and said, "It's just as well Nutzie is doing the work. I need to catch up on my regular inspections and ensure everything is ok with the engines before we go to a full burn anyway."

Then he grumbled, "But before I can do that, I checked my schedule for today and discovered that I was assigned to fix Thatorn's legs."

Captain Linol laughed as he closed the status screen on his C&PC, lowered his arm, and grabbed his bag before looking at Brian.

The doctor said gravely, "When Thatorn was in the infirmary, He seemed more concerned over his mech legs than his own life. Still, he would probably be dead if they didn't ground out most of the power."

After a few moments of awkward silence, Brian decided to ask, "I'm curious. How did you guys get your job on this ship?"

"Why do you ask?" the captain grunted uncharacteristically.

"I'm always looking for a better representation," Brian lied.

Captain Linol unstrapped himself, stood up, and said, "Breaks over. I need to get back to my post."

He looked down and gleefully smiled at Zala, stroked her cheek softly, kissed her, and quickly left the galley via the port side door along the long wall.

Brian was taken aback by the captain's curt response. He looked at Zala and asked, "What's with him?"

She took a moment to glance at the door that Captain Linol exited, then looked back at Brian and said, "I'm not really sure. Mark's not been much for any serious conversation. I don't even know how or why he got back into the service."

"Back?" quizzed Brian.

"Yes, he rejoined not long ago, but that's all I know," answered the doctor.

She added, "Don't get me wrong, Mark is good for more than one thing. He can be fun. However, sometimes he gets a little jealous."

"Oh?" asked Brian curiously.

Zala elaborated, "I get rather lonely at times, especially on the medical level by myself. You see, I'm what I like to call a free spirit who enjoys themselves, and I try not to get too tied down, especially in the emotional sense. But have not been doing that too well as of late."

"Is he jealous of Nutzie?" asked Brian with his right eyebrow raised.

"Oh my, you are very observant, aren't you?" The doctor responded.

Zala leaned closer to Brian and explained, "Since most of the crew are not part of the military, Mark is free to fraternize with whoever he wants. Seems like I'm the only one he has any genuine interest in. I try my best to spend most of my free time with Mark and Nutzie as equally as possible. I don't particularly like one over the other. It's just nice to have something different. I even tried having them simultaneously once, but that didn't work out. They just got in each other's way and wouldn't take the time to enjoy themselves."

"I see," replied Brian as he pondered whether or not it was the captain who Nutize was mad at over the comms yesterday morning?

Brian asked Zala, "So how did you get this job, Doc?"

Zala suddenly turned wistful, leaned back in her chair, and said, "Well, that is a bit of a sad story. I had a great practice recently as one of the top surgeons at New Addis Ababa General on Mars. Then, after what I thought was a successful surgery, the patient suddenly died. The autopsy revealed that I missed something. I know I didn't, but I was sued and still forced to resign. Finding work after that became difficult. Even though all U.E.A. ships require a Doctor on board, I was still lucky to get this job."

She added, "When I came on board, my operations were set up in Med Bay 2 on the port side. It has an adjacent office and medication dispensary I could work out of. Being the only medical staff on the ship, I had to be ready to practice immediately. Then, all I did was hand out vitamins, especially D, mild pain medications, anti-biotic creams, and the like to the crew. Otherwise, it's been rather dull. That was until I had Lee, you, and the Admiral in my infirmary. That at least gave me something more interesting to do."

"Yeah, I can understand that myself. You're like Nutzie and even me, to an extent. We are here mostly for emergency-related issues."

"Still, it can give one some stimulating free time." The doctor said with a wink from her right eye.

Brian quickly changed the subject since he had something else to ask anyway, "What do you know about the room behind the red door on this level?"

"Red door?" Zala replied with a question.

"Yes. There is a room on this level on the lower starboard side. It has a red door, and from the ship layout I saw on my C&PC, it's labeled Restricted Officers Only."

Zala mulled over what Brian had said.

After waiting a short time, Brian added, "From the layouts, it looks like a private patient medical area is right underneath that room. Have you heard any noises, maybe some kind of machinery?"

"No, but I've had no need to use those rooms yet. Besides, there is a lot of stuff between decks that would muffle any noise," The doctor replied.

"Yes, all kinds of things." Brian realized, saying with disappointment. "I doubt you could hear much of anything from the room itself."

Zala got very quiet and looked at the tabletop.

Brian was wondering what she was doing.

She suddenly said, "Come to think of it, Mark did say something about that room to me the other day. What was it?"

She tapped on the table for a few seconds, then finally added. "Ah yes, Mark said he wasn't allowed in that room. Only Thatorn and Lieutenant Rocha were. He thought it odd to have it marked Officers Only, yet he isn't permitted access into it."

Brian replied, "Now that's interesting."

He then looked down at his breakfast juice bag and let it go. As he watched it float there. He began to deliberate on what Zala had just said.

But the doctor interrupted him before he got too far.

She asked with a friendly smile, "What about you, Brian? How did you find yourself on the Black Swan?"

"Oh, me?" Brian stammered as he was jarred away from his deep thoughts.

As Brian elaborated on the same story he had told Val the previous day, Lee Smith entered the galley yawning, got himself a breakfast bag, and walked over to them.

Brian and Zala looked up at Lee as he stood near the seat beside Brian.

Looking at them, Lee asks," You two don't mind if I join you?"

Zala said, "Oh no."

They watched Lee sit down and strap in. He had trouble using one hand, so he let go of his bag to use both.

Brian asked him, "Just getting off your night shift?"

Lee replied, "Ah yes, thought I get something to e... Um, drink before bed."

"Aren't you the only contractor doing a night shift?" Zala inquired.

"Yelp, I asked for it," Lee replied.

"Really? Isn't kinda lonely," asked Zala.

Lee stared at the Doctor and said, "Oh no, not to me. I went to several universities on Earth and the moon. I always took the latest classes I could."

"Why?" asked Brian curiously.

Staring at Brian, Lee replied, "During the day, there is always too much going on and too many people. With their chit-chat and blah blah. I feel like I can never get anything done."

Lee grabbed his bag floating before him, removed the straw's cap, and took a long swig.

"Whewww," he exclaimed, shaking his head. Then, he added, "That's one I'm not getting again."

The doctor couldn't keep herself from laughing at Lee.

Lee smiled at Zala, then looked at Brian and asked, "So what's everyone been talking about?"

"We were just talking about how we got our current positions on the ship. What about you?" Zala asked nicely.

Staring at Zala, Lee explains, "That's simple. I put in for several contracts, got a few offers, and took the best one. I was getting tired of my job at Musk Spacestation and Shipyards anyway. Didn't like the rotating work schedule and getting stuck on the day shift."

Brian looked skeptical at Lee over what he said.

"What else?" Lee insisted on knowing.

Brian and Zala looked at each other briefly, then back at Lee.

Finally, Brian said, "We were speculating about what is behind the red door on this level."

"Red Door?" asked Lee.

"The one marked on the layout for Officers Only," Brian explained.

Lee replied, "Oh yeah, I saw that on the ship maps. It's probably just an Officer's club."

Before Zala could comment, Brian quickly asked, "So, how are you feeling with your space sickness?"

"My what?" Lee asked after contemplating whether to take another sip from his bag.

The doctor said, "Your motion sickness, Mr. Smith. Remember, you were in my infirmary for it before we departed. I gave you some meds to take as needed. Not long after taking one, you fell asleep."

"Oh, that, yeah, I'm doing fine now," Lee said dismissively.

"Why would a man with space sickness take a job working in space when there was a good chance they would be weightless?" Brian asked warily.

Lee looked at Brian. After a few seconds, Lee replied, "Well I..."

Zala and Brian stared intensely at him as he paused.

"Ok, so I have a problem. I didn't expect to be weightless for so long. I just wanted a full-time night shift job that paid well," Lee frowned.

"I can understand that. Just keep the meds I gave you on hand. You should be fine." Zala said, grinning at Lee.

Lee took another long yawn.

"So, did you have a rough shift?" Brian inquired.

Lee replied, "Oh yeah. Not long after I started, the lieutenant had me take a look at the RRU."

Brian's right eyebrow raised.

Lee looked at Brian and said, "You guys really did a number on it."

"What happened to it?" Brian asked.

"Well, it's one large melted mess now. I don't know if or when I'll be able to fix it." Lee replied.

"But what happened to it?" Brian questioned with insistence.

Lee peered at Brian and then said, "I think a component gave out, and that caused a cascade failure. Fried almost everything."

Brian stared at his breakfast bag and thought, It sounds like it was just bad luck, a malfunction, and not possible sabotage after all.

Still looking at Brian, Lee asked, "So what are you into, Brian?"

Brian looked back at him and replied with the question, "What do you mean?"

With a broad smile, Lee said, "I would just like to get to know you better."

Once again, Brian found himself feeling uncomfortable. He had always assumed it was apparent to others around him that he was straight. This was the first time Brian had experienced what he believed was a come-on from another man. He was unprepared to handle something like this. He decided just to be honest and blunt.

"Look, I'm straight, and I..."

Lee interrupted, still smiling, "Mr. Rush, even if I happen to be gay or bi, you are definitely not my type. It's going to be a long trip, and I merely just wanted to engage in conversation."

Zala covered her mouth and let out a little giggle.

"Um, sorry," Brian said, embarrassed, looking at Lee.

He glanced at the doctor, still snickering at him, causing him to feel slightly insulted.

Frowning, he looked at the time on his C&PC and said, "It's time I got to work."

Brian quickly unstraps himself, walks to the recycle bin, and shoves an almost full breakfast bag into it.

He exits the room through the lower port side door, nearly running into Val and Rob, who are about to enter.

He quickly says, "Excuse me." As he bolts past them.

Rob and Val were puzzled as they watched Brian head to the lift.

VII

Before Brian got to the EVA control room to look over Thatorn's robotic legs, Lieutenant Rocha sent him a text message with additional job details. She informed him that Thatorn had a backup holding frame for his mechanical exoskeleton in cargo hold 2, just like the one in his cabin. Brian was told to take the stand to the EVA control room and put the Exosuit into it before attempting any repairs. He was also reminded that it would become a much more arduous task if not done before the drives were active again, creating gravity.

With the lieutenant's meticulous instructions, it did not take Brian long to find the dark gray holding frame in the cargo hold. He saw Nutzie working there but decided not to disturb her. She was clearly focused on laser-cutting plates for the repair job tomorrow morning.

Since Brian was coming from hold 2 on the ship's port side, he brought the frame into the EVA control room through the port side entrance. Then, using the frame's built-in powered electromagnets, he secured it between his tool cabinet and the starboard entrance. Next, he plugged the frame into a nearby power outlet and checked if the backup power packs were charging.

Getting Thatorn's mechanical exoskeleton untangled from the RRU control chair proved to be a more difficult chore. Since the accident, Lieutenant Rocha used the chair's retractable holding straps to secure the suit. However, the legs were free to float about and got tangled around the chair.

Once the exoskeleton suit was finally secured in the frame, Brian took several minutes to quickly look it over. He sighed deeply once he realized how damaged they were and that getting them to work again would not be easy. As he pondered on the situation, he glanced over at the RRU.

"Well, I guess it could be worse," he told himself.

Brian licked his lips and carefully walked over to the console.

It wouldn't take too long to check it out, he thought.

Just as he was about to open a hinged access panel on the side of the console.

He stopped and said, "Perhaps Mr. Smith is right, and it was no more than a system failure. Besides, I have enough work of my own to do. I'll just let him handle it."

Brian unlocked the electronic lock attached to his tool cabinet and got out a few sophisticated analytical tools. He spent over two hours using them to go over Thatorn's mechanical legs, only to conclude that he wasn't sure how he was going to fix them. This was when he knew he was going to need help, and it gnawed at his ego.

Brian looked at his C&PC for the time. It was 9:56, not close enough for his lunch break just yet.

"I can check on some other things on my schedule along the way to the mess," Brian told himself.

Brian took a dark cloth towel from a box in his cabinet and wiped down his tools. After stowing them neatly back in his cabinet, he locked it.

Since the starboard door was the closest, Brian exited the EVA room through it. As soon as he entered the corridor, he noticed that the door across the hallway to cargo hold 1 had an unusually dark metallic round device stuck to it. Brian looked it over and saw it was a self-powered magnetic locking clamp. It's been a while since he's seen one. Typically, they are used to secure unlockable standard sliding doors. This one was attached next to the edge that slid into the wall. Preventing the door from being able to slide open.

Brian noticed that this one didn't have the typical electronic security panel. Instead, it had only a keyhole. Some kind of physical key was needed to control it.

What's the need for that? Thought Brian. All the doors on the ship have computer security tied into our C&PCs and schedules to control access.

To his right, Brian heard someone exiting the sub-storage hold. It was the lieutenant, and she had another round magnetic clamp in her hand.

He turned to watch her attach it to the door and lock it with a key using her left hand. She promptly put the key in one of the small gray pouches on the front of her belt.

Brian just stared at her as she walked up to him.

Looking up at him, she asked, "Is there something I can help you with, Mr. Rush?"

"What's this for?" He asked, pointing at the clamp on the door beside him.

She looked at the device, then back at him, and asked, "What's your progress with the Admiral's Exoskeleton suit?"

"What?" Stammered Brian, realizing she was ignoring his question.

Lieutenant Rocha was deadpan and stated. "I had you scheduled to look it over this morning. I sent you additional instructions on how to get and use the extra frame to secure it."

Brian started to say, "Ah, yes, I got it and secured the suit in the frame...."

"What is your assessment?" she asked, interrupting.

"Most of the motor components are burnt out," Brian glumly replied.

The lieutenant began saying, "Let me know what components you need. Thatorn has stocked...."

Brian interjected, "It's not that simple. I can swap out the burned-out components, but many of the interface connections are fried. It's going to need some significant rewiring."

"I see," she replied emotionless.

"I should confer with the Doctor about the interface and probably one of the techs to go over the rewiring and electronics," Brian explained.

Lieutenant Rocha started to say, "Mr. Smith's current schedule would make it difficult for him to...."

Brian interrupted, smiling, "Ms. Elderman would be fine."

The lieutenant stared at Brian briefly, then said, "Very well then, Mr. Rush. I will check her and the Doctor's schedule and assign a time ASAP for you all to get together."

She walked past him and headed toward the lift.

Brian's brow furrowed, and he asked, demanding, "When are we going to tell the rest of the crew about the sabotage, and what are we going to do about it?"

Lieutenant Rocha stopped. Slowly and quietly, she turned back towards Brian.

With a straight face, she replied, "Mr. Rush, the matter is well in hand."

She turns back around to head for the lift again.

Brian follows her closely and decides to try a more subtle approach to get any helpful information out of her.

He asks, "I heard when that...., um, the Admiral was in the infirmary. He seemed more concerned over his mech legs than his own life."

The lieutenant only replied with a nod of her head.

"So, have you been under Admiral Thatorn long?" asked Brian, trying his best to strike up a friendlier tone with her.

"No," was her only reply as she walked.

Brian tries again and asks, "Have you been in the U.E.A. service long?"

"No," again was her reply, still walking.

Under these circumstances, Brian realizes asking her about the red door would be futile.

Before they entered the circular hallway, Brian glanced to his right. He noticed magnetic locks on the door to cargo bay 1 and the door he could see to the cargo bay airlock.

After entering the circular hallway, Lieutenant Rocha walks up to the lift door and hits the call button.

As soon as the doors open, she enters the lift, turns to face Brian, and blocks him from entering.

She says, "Mr. Rush, the Admiral, wants to make the repair to his Exosuit a top priority, second only to the ship's repairs. I will inform you when I can get Ms. Elderman, the Doctor, and you scheduled together to evaluate repairs to the Admiral's Exosuit."

She steps back, and the lift doors shut.

As they did, Brian glumly said, "Assuming it can be fixed."

Brian grinned, thinking that maybe it might be nice to see the old man continuing to use that wheelchair.

Brian found himself running down a dark corridor lit only by dim emergency lights. He was wearing a white spacesuit and holding a direct energy pistol in his right hand. He could hear himself breathing heavily in his helmet and his heartbeat pounding loudly in his ears.

He came to the end of the hall and saw it branched out into corridors on both sides. Quickly, he jumped for the corner on his right. An energy bolt followed closely behind him, missing him by centimeters. It silently hit the wall at the hall's end, leaving a blackened burn mark. Even the slightest singe from the blast could have ruptured his suit. The resulting exposure to the vacuum would have been fatal.

Slowly, he peeked around the corner and aimed his gun down the dark hall. He panted heavily, catching his breath, watching for his assailant to come after him.

The ship's thrust must be increasing. It's got to be close to 2 Gs now, thought Brian.

He was able to rest as he waited and watched. His breathing slowed, and the heartbeat in his ears began to fade.

Of course, I would have a white spacesuit. It's way too easy to see in low light, Brian complained to himself.

Brian felt a slight vibration in the deck.

Maybe they out-flanked me, panicked Brian as he tried to turn around but found himself stuck to the wall.

"Damn it!" he shouted in his helmet.

After struggling for a few seconds, he finally pulled himself free. He turned around and looked behind him down the corridor he was now in.

Nothing! Brian told himself, feeling confused.

Slowly, he crept down the hall with his gun at the ready, hoping to catch his assailant by surprise.

He stopped and waited, looking intensely down the dark corridor.

Again, he felt another vibration. It was stronger than the last, but Brian didn't see anything.

Frantically, Brian realized his error and quickly turned to see someone standing in a dark spacesuit aiming a gun at him.

Before he could react. Everything flickered, and he saw static.

Brian fired!

The flicking and static stopped.

He saw his assailant was gone, and the blast from his pistol had scorched the nearby corridor wall where he had seen them.

Before Brian knew it, he observed an energy blast explode from his chest. His blood and several vital organs spattered out and began to freeze in front of him.

As he collapsed to the floor, he turned around to see his assailant.

"How did..." was all Brian could get out as things faded.

Brian's assailant walked up and stood above him. They squatted up and down over him as the darkness engulfed him.

B rian slipped off his black virtual reality headset with built-in headphones.

His eyes focused on a small black pyramid with flickering lights about 30 centimeters tall sitting on a table before him. He placed his black game controller with his headset on the table and looked across it. Val was sitting in a chair, holding a similar headset and controller, looking at him with a big grin.

Because Val's room was on level 8 on the lower starboard side. It was slightly larger than his and had 2 additional windows into space. Her cabin had the same things as his, just arranged differently.

A large screen was on the wall with a small mini-fridge below it to Brian's right. Behind Val was the outer hull wall with 3 windows beside one another. At the center of this wall were a desk and chair. Directly on the wall behind Brian was the room's trash chute. The entrance, a drawer, and a bed were to his left along this same wall. To the far left was a wall with a closed door to the bathroom. An odd circle that looked like it was drawn with chalk was slightly more than a meter above the floor on this wall, just to the left of the bathroom door. Like his room and the rest of the ship, it had the same drab gray-colored walls, floor, ceiling, and furnishings.

After getting off duty, they both had some liquid dinner and got out of their jumpsuits. Brian wore casual wear, consisting of a baggy black shirt and some black shorts, which clashed with his shiny silver boots. However, Val's silver boots matched nicely with her tight-fitting off-white top and shorts.

Brian thought to himself. It's good to finally see her in something more interesting than a gray jumpsuit. I can tell she's not wearing a bra because of her tight blouse, and her breasts are much bigger than I thought. I don't know. A woman may not even need a bra when there is no gravity. Then again, if she had perky enough breasts or small ones, they probably wouldn't anyway.

"I beat you that time," Val said smugly as her ponytail flipped around her face in the zero-G.

Brian snapped out of his assessment relating to undergarments and replied, "Yeah, but you didn't have to teabag me, too, did ya."

"I thought you're supposed to humiliate your enemy by rubbing your crotch in their face after taking them out," she laughed as she pulled her ponytail out of her face.

Brian replied with a frown. He started to regret accepting Val's invitation to play VR games with her earlier during dinner in the mess hall and exchanging cabin locations.

"Don't be like that. You won the first two rounds," she stated.

"Yeah, that's true. You just got lucky that time. A game glitch got me stuck on the wall for a while, and then my visual display glitched out, so I couldn't see you sneak around me," Brian grumbled.

"Hum, I've had the wall problems with this game before. But never any visual glitches," Val said with a puzzling grin.

"Maybe a random reactor flare-up affected my VR headset and didn't yours," Brian speculated.

He looked at the table and asked, "Do you have a shielded wire connection for the headset. That should prevent any interference?"

"No, I've never had any wireless issues before," Val said innocently.

"It's fine. It shouldn't happen that often anyway," said Brian with a grin, then added. "I like your system anyway. It has a great built-in neural interface. The vitals simulation made me think I was feeling tired and fatigued. "

"Because of that, it wasn't cheap," Val explained.

"It's well worth it," Brian praised.

Val smiled, saying, "You know it's great to have someone on the ship I can relax and play with."

Was that a flirt? Brian hoped.

Val stated, "I heard you didn't get too far with the RRU and almost lost Thatorn."

Caught off guard for a few seconds, Brian did manage to reply, "Fortunately, the computer recorded enough data from the RRU's run for us to develop a repair plan."

"And?" inquired Val, noticing Brian's glum expression.

With a soft sigh, he replied, "The lieutenant didn't want me to look over the RRU right after it happened. I was told that she would let me know if she needed my help. Then, this morning, I found out that she assigned Lee to look it over."

"Has he come up with a diagnosis?" Val asked curiously.

"Yeah, I saw him this morning, and he told me it was an accidental system failure," Brian answered with a sneer.

Val leaned forward and said, "You don't seem convinced."

"I don't know. I can only assume Mr. Smith knows what he's talking about," mumbled Brian.

"Since I have not worked with him directly, I wouldn't know. I wonder what he does on the night shift anyway? I never have seen any signs of maintenance being done other than my own," explained Val.

"Maybe he's working on different stuff?" suggested Brian.

"I guess. I wonder what Thatorn has him doing?" pondered Val. Brian replied with a shrug of his shoulders.

Val looked at Brian wryly and said, "You know I had to fix a medical waste vacuum disposal chute on level 5 today."

"Oh, yeah, the one in Med Bay 2," stated Brian.

"No, It was the one in Med Bay 1. I noticed a system fault, and well. I just like making sure things work if they are needed," explained Val.

"Ok, am I missing something?" Brian questioned.

"It's about Mr. Smith. I found an entire bottle of what I think were space-sick meds floating in the faulty vacuum disposal chute. They had his name on them," Val stated.

"Maybe he accidentally tossed the wrong bottle or mixed it up with an empty one?" Brian speculated.

"But why did he use a medical waste chute and not the regular one in his cabin?" Val questioned.

"Perhaps he considered it medical waste and thought it should be disposed of that way," Brian replied.

"Then why did he use the chute in Med Bay 1?" Val questioned.

"Is it possible Lee didn't want to bother the doctor?" Brian speculated.

"Or did he not want her to know he was disposing of them," said Val.

"Why?" asked Brian.

Val replied, "I don't know."

Brian inquired, "So, what did you do with the meds?"

"I didn't think much about it at the time, so I just put them back in the chute. Once I fixed the vacuum, I'm sure the bottle went down and eventually got incinerated like all medical waste," Val explained.

She cocked her head and added, "It's funny. That was the first real fix I have had to do on this ship. I have a regular maintenance schedule, but I'm mostly just checking things. Most of the ship seems almost new."

"I'm doing the same thing on my rounds," Brian replied.

"Maybe the refit we speculated about was much bigger and more recent," Val surmised.

"Perhaps," Brian responded.

Then, Brian saw out of the corner of his eye the circle drawn on the wall he had seen earlier.

He stared at it for a while, trying to understand its purpose. Finally giving up, he pointed at it and asked Val, "What's that all about?"

"Oh, that's just a game I made up for zero-G. I take small objects, even wadded-up paper, to see if I can hit the target from different places and in different ways. It's a little more complicated than you might think," Val replied, staring at the circle.

Looking at Val, Brian asked, "I see. Maybe we can try playing that too."

"Later. I'm not in the mood for that right now," Val replied, looking back at Brian.

She leaned back in her seat, pursed her lips, and calmly asked, "So, what happened to the communications tower?"

Brian was caught off guard. He began to nervously bite his lip.

Before Brian could come up with a lie, Val stated, "I think Fa might be right about a small meteor high-speed impact."

"Uh, well," began Brian while looking at the floor, deciding it would be best for him to stick to a more general lie. "We have not drawn any definite conclusions yet. We decided to focus on repairing the structure to pressurize the communications room so Ralph can fix the internal systems and get the antennas operational."

Val started looking around her chair and then behind her. Her ponytail bounced around as if it had a mind of its own.

"Ah, there you are." She exclaimed, spinning her chair around and then back again with a metallic bottle that had been floating behind her.

"It got away from you again," Brian nervously chuckled, staring at Val.

"Yes, I'll be glad when you guys get the repairs done, and we can get back to flight and gravity," Val said, opening the bottle's tip and taking a drink.

"Repairs are scheduled for tomorrow morning. Nutzie and I went over everything before I came off duty. She also insisted that I spot her," said Brian.

"Spot her?" asked Val as she closed her bottle and placed it just to her right to float there.

Brian explained, "She informed me there is a safety requirement for an EVA. Someone must be suited up, in visual range, and ready to render aid if needed."

"I see," said Val, tapping her chin.

Then, Brian noticed that Val's nipples were poking out in her blouse.

Brian thought. I didn't notice any temperature change in the room.

Slowly, Brian began to get uncomfortably aroused by seeing them but couldn't stop looking.

"You seem a little distracted?" Val asked, looking at Brian inquisitively.

Brian looked past her, out the windows, and into space to take his mind off it. That was not a good idea. He got jittery and quickly looked down at the floor. Finally, after a cough, he replied, "Um, I just got a lot on my mind."

"You were acting odd this morning, too. Is something wrong?" Val asked with concern.

"Oh, No. I was just in a hurry to get to work on Thatorn's Exosuit," Brian fibbed.

"That reminds me. I got my schedule for tomorrow earlier today. I noticed you have Doctor Teka and I scheduled with you to do a repair assessment on Thatorn's legs tomorrow at 14:00."

Brian began, "His Exosuit, yes. Sorry, I did intend to bring that up earlier, but we got into play...."

"That's ok," Val interrupted, then asked, "But why so not sooner in the day?"

"To give us plenty of time to get the ship repairs done in the morning," explained Brian.

"Oh, I see," said Val.

Val's face changed and looked more serious. She seemed to be struggling with something in her head. After several seconds, she finally asked, "What's the deal with that red door on level 4?"

"Oh, that," Brian replied with a wrinkled brow.

"I think it's very odd," Val said.

Brian leaned forward and said, "Well, I won't name any names, but I found out that only Thatorn and Rocha go there."

"What about the Captain? The layout in the C&PC says Offices Only?" inquired Val.

"I also heard Captain Linol is unhappy about not being allowed in there. Someone has speculated it could be Thatorn's private lab. Which would make sense for not letting the Captain in," explained Brian.

"If that's the case, why have it labeled Officers Only?" questioned Val.

Brian replied once again with a shrug of his shoulders.

After several seconds of looking at each other, Val asked, "You want to go another round?"

Brian smirked and asked, "You got anything else we can play?"

137

Val undid her seat strap, stood up, walked to the table beside Brian, and bent over the black pyramid. She opened a small hinged compartment at its side to reveal several buttons and a small port with a thin metallic strip in it.

It was difficult for Brian to watch what she was doing because her boobs were now very close to his face.

"So, how many games do you have on that data clip?" Brian asked, trying to take his mind off what was before him.

She took out the strip, stood up before him, and said, "This clip is one of my tiny ones, only a few hundred Exabytes."

Val pulled out a small metal box shaped like a notebook from her back pocket. She opened it to reveal it had plastic-like pages with small pockets. On the first page, metal strips like the one Val took out of the game console were in all but one pocket. She placed the one she had in her hand into the empty pocket. She flipped it over to look at the other strips on the next page and said, "I've got another game on another clip I think you might like."

Trying to avoid looking at her tits and being further aroused, Brian closed his eyes, gulped, and chirped, "Fine."

Just as Val was about to take out another data clip with her right hand, she looked down at Brian. She reached down with her right hand, rubbed his stubbly face, and said, "It looks like you need a shave."

Brian opened his eyes, and his heart began to race.

He stammered, "I... It's hard to d... do without gravity."

"I like a clean face. It's much nicer on the lips," smiled Val.

What do I do now? Thought Brian, staring up at her. Do I kiss her? Should I?

Just as he was about to undo his seat strap, their C&PCs started beeping loudly.

Thatorn's booming voice followed. "This is the Admiral. The time is currently 18:22. I want all personnel to report to the main medical lab on level 5 as soon as possible and be in uniform."

"I wonder what this is about?" questioned Val as she stepped away from Brian.

Brian softly growled, "Are you fucking kidding me, damn old man."

VIII

B rian returned to his room and took off his clothes while thinking about what might have been.

He whined, "Damn, old asshole! Maybe I should make sure his Exosuit never works again."

After struggling into his jumpsuit, he suddenly exclaimed, "Fuck!"

Calmly, he elaborated, "It's really not worth my reputation."

He made his way to the medical floor on level 5 as quickly as possible.

Along the way, Brian pondered. Why did the old man have us all meeting in this lab, not the situation room? I wonder if he will finally tell everyone what is going on? Or is he still playing some kind of game? Things are serious, and they should be taken that way. We have a saboteur on the ship, and we don't know who it is or why they did it?

Brian was beginning to feel uncomfortable and worried about it.

He had been on the medical level only once, in the port side Medical Bay, where the doctor worked. He recalled on the ship layout that there is a mirrored version of this bay on the starboard side, which is currently not being used. The lower sections of this level have patient recovery rooms and a morgue. The top center area is lab space with the exact dimensions of the galley on the floor above.

He exited the starboard lift, passed through the ringed hallway into the square area, down the corridor just before him, and stopped at the first door to his right.

When the door opened, Brian stepped in. He expected to see the same ample space as the galley. However, it was one big, long, gray, rectangular room.

Along the top wall, there were 4 doors and 4 windows. The two inner doors had two windows on each side. Through them, you could see these doors went into smaller, separate labs. Both had a large console, screen, and chair along the outer hull wall. On the side walls inside were empty tables and wall cabinets.

The other two doors at each end of this wall were marked as storage rooms. There was an empty glove dispenser near each corner with a biohazard chute beside them.

The short wall at Brian's left had a console, chair, and a door. The other short wall at his far right was a mirrored duplicate.

The other long wall behind Brian had a rectangular table on his right near the door he entered. A matching table was on the left of the port entrance near the other end of the wall.

In the center of the room was a large, long rectangular table with six chairs on each side. The table was empty except for two portable computer interface systems sitting at each end.

Everything in the room had the same gray, dull colors. Some furnishings did have an ever so slight color tone variation.

He saw his fellow crewmates chit-chatting at the table, but none seemed to take notice of him.

On the side of the table near him, Fa and Ralph sat in the center two chairs, talking.

Sitting on the other side of the table, from left to right, were the captain, Zala, Nutzie, an empty seat, Val and Rob.

Brian noticed Thatorn, Lieutenant Rocha, and Lee were still not there.

He then speculated the old man was probably waiting to make a grand entrance once everyone else was present.

Captain Linol, the doctor, and Nutzie were huddled together, whispering to each other. Could Nutzie be filling them in about the sabotage? Brian pondered.

Val and Rob were sitting close together while chatting with each other.

Brian eyed the empty seat next to Val. Smiling, he started towards it.

Before getting anywhere, Lee suddenly entered the room from the port door, ran over to the other side of the table, and grabbed the seat.

Brian let out a soft sigh, looked at the table, and thought about taking the seat next to Ralph to be opposite Val. Instead, he decided to take the empty seat beside Fa, realizing this may not be a good time or place to try and engage in any romance.

Fa stopped talking to Ralph, turned towards Brian, and said, "Hello, Mr. Rush, it looks like we are all here except for the Admiral and the Lieutenant."

"Yeah," Brian casually replied, glancing at Fa.

Without any attention from Fa, Ralph just looked at the table and rubbed his hands together nervously.

Brian wondered. Maybe this meeting will be about the sabotage?

Brian looked to his right and intensely watched Rob and Val.

Fa glanced at what Brian was looking at, then back at him and said, "She made a beeline for him as soon as she got here."

"Oh," replied Brian with a furrowed brow as he stared at them.

"It's nothing new. I've seen Val and Rob together a lot. You know most of us had been waiting several days for you to arrive." Fa stated, then was distracted by Ralph and turned to him. He had a question for Fa that Brian didn't hear.

Brian gazed at Val and took in a deep breath. He was confused about her now. Was she really interested in him? Was he getting in

143

the middle of something she was having with Rob? Or was he just some handy fling?

Before he could ponder on it further, the lieutenant and Thatorn entered the room from the door of the starboard short wall. Lieutenant Rocha was carrying a small metal box with a medical insignia. This caused Doctor Tela to take notice.

Thatorn rolled up to the end of the table. The lieutenant followed and stopped to stand at his left side. She let go of the box just inches above the table, which floated there.

"What is that?" The doctor inquired.

Thatorn smiled and politely said, "That will become relevant soon."

Wow, wondered Brian. The old man seems almost friendly. Maybe it could be some meds the doctor has him because of the shock he took from the RRU?

"Why are we here in the med lab?" asked the captain, squinting at Thatorn.

"That will also become relevant. But first, several things need to be discussed before we get to that. I would like updates," Thatorn said calmly.

This drugged version of Thatorn just might be tolerable, Brian thought.

The old man turned his head slightly to his left to stare at Captain Linol. Then asked, "What is the status of the ship's flight, Captain?"

The captain looked at Rob and said, "Mr. Callen is the pilot on duty now. We should hear from him first."

Rob quickly looked at Captain Linol and then Thatorn. He cleared his throat and replied, "The ship is currently on autopilot, and I'm monitoring the flight status through my C&PC while off the flight deck. We are still on a rough course heading toward Jupiter.

Recently, a few course corrections were made using thrusters to avoid some of the innermost following Trojan asteroids."

The captain looked over at Thatorn and added. "Once ship repairs are finished, a new course can be plotted for any Jupiter orbital insert you choose, sir."

Thatorn blinked, looked at Lee, and asked, "I have not heard much about the repairs to the RRU, Mr. Smith."

Lee was caught off guard in his seat with his arms folded. He stared at Thatorn and cautiously replied, "I made my initial report to the Lieutenant."

"Good, then maybe you could inform us all about it now," Thatorn said courteously.

"Um," Lee started slowly. "Uh, well, I checked it out late last night, and like I had in my report, the entire thing is a melted mess. It's going to take a while to fix it."

"And the cause?" The old man inquired with an unusually warm smile.

"Well, um, looks like it was a cascade failure. Something blew, and it took out most of the other components with it."

"Just a malfunction?" asked Thatorn cooly.

"Y..yeah, I believe so," Lee nervously replied.

"You will inform me once you discover the exact cause, Mr. Smith." The old man said politely.

"Uh, ye... yes sir," Lee mumbled.

Thatorn looked over his crew, continuing to smile, and said, "Fortunately, we are not going to rely on the RRU."

Looking at Nutzie, he asked, "What is the status of hull repairs?"

"We are scheduled for an early morning EVA. I estimate close to four hours to have the breach completely sealed and secure." Nutzie replied, looking at the table.

"Good," The old man said just before looking at Ralph and asking, "And you?"

Ralph stared back and stuttered, "O...Once the repairs are done and the communications room pressurized, I'll then be able to make a determination on the repairs needed for the antenna array."

"Any time estimation?" Thatorn asked nicely.

"I won't be able to give you one until after I get into the communications room and make my evaluation," Ralph replied, looking curiously at the old man.

"Then that will have to do for now," Thatorn calmly said.

Looking at Brian, he asks, "And what about your status with my exoskeleton suit repair?"

Brian stared back and answered, "Tomorrow afternoon after the ship repair, I will meet with the Doctor and...."

"After the ship repair?" inquired the old man.

"Why yes. I'm going to spot for Nutzie while she does her EVA," Brian responded.

Nutzie looked at Thatorn and chimed in, "There are safety protocol regulations, sir."

Thatorn rubbed his chin and was quiet for a moment. Then, after glancing at Lieutenant Rocha, he grumbled, "Hum, very well then," looking back at Brian, he added, "Continue."

"I will meet with the Doctor and Technician Elderman to review possible repair options and then report our findings to you," explained Brian.

"The repair of the Exoskeleton is the top priority after the ship's hull and antenna array are repaired. Do you understand!" Thatorn insisted.

"Yes, of course, sir," Brian responded.

Interesting, thought Brian. That's the meanest he's been so far.

"If there are no other issues?" Thatorn asked as he glanced at everyone in turn at the table. Once they all shook their heads, the old man rolled back from the table and gestured for the lieutenant to take his place.

She casually stepped to her right to stand at the end of the table, then took a moment to look at everyone seated around it.

She said in a clear, calm, monotone voice. "At approximately 21:55 hours yesterday, it was confirmed that the loss of the communications tower was not an accident but sabotage."

And there it is, thought Brian.

The news surprised the five crew members who did not already know. Soon, they quickly noticed that the rest of their crew did not seem to respond to the news, and they began to stare at them oddly.

Lieutenant Rocha saw this and added, "Everyone involved in the realization last night was told not to reveal the facts to the rest of you."

"You mean those on the RRU team?" questioned Rob while looking at Brian, Fa, and Ralph across the table.

"Yes." The lieutenant replied and explained, "The time was used to gather more evidence. This was done to prevent alerting the culprit if the party was not one of those who already knew."

"What about those involved in the discovery?" Val asked, staring at Brian.

"They were not above suspicion. As a result, additional precautions and surveillance were placed on them while evidence was being collected," explained Lieutenant Rocha.

"That explains why my access to the security system was taken away," Fa mumbled, looking at the table.

"For now, I will handle all issues related to the security system. Including error checks," said the lieutenant, glancing at Fa.

"Who did it and why?" Ralph insistently asked, staring up at Lieutenant Rocha.

Staring at Ralph, the lieutenant began to reply, "At this point, we assume it was done to prevent us from reporting back to command. Figuring out...."

Staring at Lieutenant Rocha, Val interrupted, "Is it possible it was an attempt to prevent us from continuing our mission? Not just to stop us communicating?"

The lieutenant glanced at Val silently for a few seconds, rolled her eyes, and coldly replied, "Unlikely."

She focused on the rest of the crew and continued, "As I was saying, figuring out who is why we are gathered here now. Part of that involves resolving the how."

"Ok then, how was it done?" asked Rob as he looked smugly at Lieutenant Rocha.

"We discovered it was accomplished with explosives," the lieutenant coolly replied.

"Oh, My!" gasped the doctor out loud while everyone at the table focused on Lieutenant Rocha.

"After a spectral analysis of data from the RRU, it was discovered to be a rather unusual type, a very classified version of Octanitrocubane," elaborated the lieutenant.

"What's that?" Ralph asked.

"An all-purpose high-end explosive that can be used anywhere, even in the vacuum of space. It has its own chemically built-in oxygen, and this particular type is used only by the military, " Lieutenant Rocha answered.

"Ah, then could it..." Brian began.

The lieutenant interrupted, "To be sure, I tested residue samples from the wing hallway near the closed bulkhead door and confirmed these special explosives were used in the sabotage. Some of our own explosives, detonators, and timers are also missing from sub-storage hold 1."

How efficient, she answered my question before I could even ask it, thought Brian.

Loud chatter broke out around the table. It was difficult to make out what everyone was saying.

Brian looked around the room and pondered who was behind, almost getting him killed.

"Wait, wait, wait!" exclaimed Captain Linol, trying to quiet down the crew.

"Yes, Captain!" Lieutenant Rocha snapped, causing everyone around the table to abruptly stop talking and look at her.

Once satisfied that he could be heard, the captain asked, "Were any prints found?"

"No, but that was not unexpected. I'm sure we all have a pair or two of work gloves. Even the Doctor has latex ones that could have been taken," the lieutenant explained, gesturing towards Zala.

The doctor responded. "That's true. Almost everyone has been in Med Bay 2 for various reasons over the last few days. The glove dispenser is right on the wall. Anyone could have grabbed some while I was distracted while getting medications or other items from the back room."

"Was there any surveillance evidence of that?" asked Rob.

Lieutenant Rocha began, "No...."

"I would hope not," interrupted Zala.

"No, we have nothing because the wall in question was out of frame," finished the lieutenant.

The doctor let out a noticeable snort of disgust as she glared at Lieutenant Rocha.

"Could they have gotten some of these gloves elsewhere on the ship?" inquired Ralph.

The doctor looked at Ralph and replied, "I only put some out in Med Bay 2. The rest are locked up in my supply cabinet in my adjacent office."

"Could we get some kind of count on the gloves to see if any were taken?" Fa inquired, looking at Zala.

"Not likely. All medical waste gets incinerated. Besides, I don't keep records on how many gloves I used and had to toss Ms. Ming." The doctor stated, staring at her.

"Toss?" Fa asked curiously.

"Our so-called one-size-fits-all latex gloves were probably provided by the subcontractor that put in the lowest bid. Several have had a tendency to rip and tear," the doctor curtly stated.

Fa frowned in response.

"Even if we could get a reliable count, wouldn't it only prove that someone took some latex gloves? It would not prove they were used to commit sabotage. They are useful for other things," stated Nutzie stoically, looking at the crew.

Before Brian could ponder over what Nutzie said, Captain Linol asked the lieutenant, "Did you find any physical evidence?"

Lieutenant Rocha replied, "Unfortunately, no."

"Why are explosives even on the ship?" Val asked, staring up at the lieutenant.

"That is classified," Lieutenant Rocha sharply responded.

"Classified?" Val inquired.

"They are on board for potential optional operations," Thatorn declared from behind the lieutenant.

"What?" questioned the doctor, trying to look around Lieutenant Rocha to see the old man.

Looking at Zala, Nutzie said, "It's in case we find some Pirate station or structure on one of Jupiter's moons. It's our way of getting in."

Nutzie then stared at the lieutenant and sarcastically asked, "Could you have just gotten the munitions count wrong?"

"How dare you, Ms. Teodoresco!" exclaimed Lieutenant Rocha, glaring at Nutzie.

"The Lieutenant and I oversaw the loading of all the cargo. So No, that is not possible," butted in the old man from behind the lieutenant.

"Could this bomb have been planted before any of us contractors even came on board?" Fa asked Lieutenant Rocha.

The lieutenant angrily snapped at Fa. "Ms. Ming, The ship was under absolute military control. Only trusted officers of the U.E.A. were involved in the loading and preparation of this ship."

"Ah, ok," shouted Fa as she held her hands up briefly in surrender.

Looking at everyone at the table, Lieutenant Rocha added in a calmer tone, "Also, the only crew on the ship after leaving the military spaceport was the Admiral, the Captain, and myself. With the computer's help, we operated the ship to the rendezvous point where we collected all of you."

"I guess that answers Ms. Ming's question," Rob said, looking at Fa and then the lieutenant.

The captain then inquired, "Were you able to determine where the bomb was placed?"

The old man spoke up from behind Lieutenant Rocha once again. "I did calculate its approximate placement. It was just under the main wall console in the communications room, the same wall as the tower's base, where it would go unnoticed. The explosive was designed so the blast was directed outwardly towards the wall to take out the tower."

"How did it get there?" inquired Rob.

"That Mr. Callen is a good question," replied Thatorn, peaking around the lieutenant.

"How did the saboteur even know there were explosives on the ship and where they were?" inquired Val.

"Seems like a security breach to me," Nutzie said, glaring past Lieutenant Rocha at Thatorn.

"Even though they were obviously well informed, their intel was clearly limited," Thatorn replied with a smirk from behind the lieutenant.

Exactly what the hell does that mean? Pondered Brian.

Before Brian could voice what he was thinking. Lieutenant Rocha began saying, "Once we determined a bomb to be the cause, our preliminary check of surveillance data last night was...."

Rob interrupted, "I was just going to ask about that!"

Ignoring him, the lieutenant continued, "Inconclusive. Later, I did a much more thorough examination of surveillance along with security data and discovered a much bigger issue."

After a short pause, she elaborated, "Before the morning of the 3rd, contractors had no duties other than the doctor. Before then, you spent your time in the cabins, galley, and the occasional visit to the Med Bay. Except for Mr. Rush, who did not join us until the evening of the 4th."

"And?" impatiently asked Ralph.

The lieutenant calmly replied, "In my review, On April the 2nd, I found several unexplained data outages of the surveillance system on all levels."

Again, distressed mumblings came from several of the crew sitting at the table.

After they were finished, they quietly looked at Lieutenant Rocha.

Val asked, "Was that all you found?"

The lieutenant explained, "There were 41 minutes of missing data from the night of the 4th because of me. Since everyone was to be on the control deck for the briefing. I took advantage of this to run a full final diagnostic on the entire system."

"Could the missing surveillance system's data on the 2nd have been hacked to cover up the sabotage?" asked Nutzie.

She stared at Fa and insinuated, "Did you scramble the data to hide your covert activity of taking and planting the explosives?"

In shock, Fa replied, "You think it was me!"

"Who else! You have both the access and ability," Nutzie screeched.

Brian recalled Fa telling him of her anger towards Thatorn, so she does have a motive.

Ralph slowly looked to his left at Fa. Then inquired, "Why didn't you bring this missing 41 minutes to our attention last night when you looked up the security data on who was in and near the communications room right before the explosion?"

Fa turned sharply to her right, glared at the balding man, and snapped, "That part is simple. If the data was corrupted or missing, my searches would have missed it since that was not part of my selection criteria. I would not have found anything like that last night unless I was looking for it specifically!"

"Enough!" exclaimed Thatorn as he rolled up behind Lieutenant Rocha. Causing her to step to her left to make room for him.

Thatorn then said, "Hacking our computer system might be a method used to distort the data after the fact. However, it does not look like our saboteur put themself in such a precarious position to clean up after."

Glancing up at the lieutenant, Thatorn said, "Tell them what else you found."

Looking at the crew, she said, "At the same time of each instance on the 2nd, the ship's entire security system controlling door access based on our C&PCs was offline. Along with our C&PC's communications and its related monitoring systems."

Everyone at the table looked at each other, dumbfounded.

Ralph looked at the old man and managed to ask with a mutter, "How?"

Everyone looked to the old man for his response.

With a smirk, Thatorn looked at Ralph and explained. "I believe it was done using a sophisticated jamming device that can affect selected systems in real-time."

"Like the surveillance data, all the related C&PC information is also stored since it is part of the security system. The jamming caused gaps in all the associated data. That's how I was able to find it," Lieutenant Rocha explained, looking at Ralph.

"So, the saboteur could go anywhere on the ship and not be tracked via their C&PCs?" asked Captain Linol, tugging at his gray chin beard.

"While the jamming was occurring, Yes," replied Thatorn, staring at the captain.

"My, a very thorough device, isn't it," Nutzie grunted.

"What an interesting and powerful espionage tool," Rob said, glancing at Nutzie.

Val leaned forward on the table, looked at the lieutenant, and asked, "If the C&PC data is stored. Might you be able to find anything interesting in the location information before and after those jamming? It could give away the saboteur."

Lieutenant Rocha stared at Val and stated, "According to the C&PC data during those times. Everyone was alone and in, or very near, the same place before and after each jamming time. As a result, no one can even vouch for anyone else."

"Even the military crew?" inquired Rob, looking at the lieutenant.

"Yes," Lieutenant Rocha replied reluctantly, glancing at Rob.

Brian looked at the lieutenant and asked, "Exactly when did these jammings occur on the 2nd?"

Lieutenant Rocha raised her right arm and activated her C&PC with her left hand. She went through several holographic screens before stating, "There were four jammings times. The first started at 12:31 hours and lasted for only 2 minutes and 4 seconds."

"That may have just been a test," said Nutzie, staring at the table.

The lieutenant continued, "The second started at 13:25 hours and lasted for 11 minutes and 24 seconds. The third began at 14:05 hours and lasted for 16 minutes and 53 seconds."

"Hum, longer and longer intervals," said Val.

Lieutenant Rocha finished with, "The final one started at 15:08 hours and lasted 21 minutes and 32 seconds.

She deactivated her C&PC, lowered her arm, and looked down at Brian.

Thatorn said, looking at Nutzie, "We also speculated the first jam was probably a test."

Then, staring at everyone, he added, "We believe they took explosives on the second jam. Put the bomb together on the third. Then planted it on the last."

Lee said, "It's interesting that they did this the day before us contractors went to work with the pre-flight checks on the 3rd."

The lieutenant replied, "It was their last day to take advantage of the lull in activity on the ship to make their task less likely to be noticed."

Brian stated, "When this happened, the ship was in freefall, and the security was down. Obviously, the thief had easy access to the cargo hold and the locker cabinets with the explosives, detonators, and timers. Needing little time to actually acquire them."

"Yes, we know that. What is your point, Mr. Rush?" Thatorn asked, looking at Brian.

"Even without gravity, the thief should have been winded after these excursions? Assuming the second time was to get the bomb materials. They would still need to hurry since they only had a little over 11 minutes to get the bomb components and return to where they started," explained Brian.

Zala looked at Lieutenant Rocha and said, "We could check all the crew's recorded vitals right after the jamming times."

The old man stared at Zala and smugly replied, "We already thought of that."

"And?" Brian asked impatiently, looking at Thatorn.

"We found no noticeable variations in the stored data with anyone's vitals before and after each moment of the interference," Thatorn replied reluctantly, staring at Brian.

Zala looked at Thatorn and asked with astonishment, "How could that be possible. Even a physically fit person would have had some kind of elevation reflected in their medical data."

Everyone looked at each other in disbelief, then at Thatorn.

Thatorn simply grinned and replied only with, "Intriguing insist it."

Meds, it's got to be his meds. Brian was sure of it now.

Looking at the old man, Fa asked curiously, "Could it be the result of genetic enhancement?"

Zala looked at Fa appalled and replied, "That was outlawed over two hundred years ago."

"Still, it may not have stopped some from trying," Rob remarked, eyeing Zala.

Everyone looked at Rob, contemplating what he said.

The lieutenant interrupted them with an intentional cough.

Once gaining their attention, she said, "Since security access around the ship has been compromised. Thatorn has implemented extra security measures. As part of backup security tools, the ship has outside mechanical door locking mechanisms. Some have already been attached to critical doors that had been affected. This is to prevent further access to restricted areas and materials."

"Like explosives?" asked Nutzie rhetorically.

Lieutenant Rocha ignored her, closed her eyes, and took a breath.

Brian wondered. Do all military vessels have those kinds of things on board?

156

Zala asked, "Why didn't I receive or see any warning from the medical monitoring systems when the medical telemetry stopped?"

The lieutenant opened her eyes, looked at Zala, and stated, "It looks as if it freezes all the C&PC telemetry and the related systems, giving no warnings or alarms."

"Thought of everything, it seems," Lee mumbled.

"Wait, so no one noticed their C&PC's not working properly when this jamming occurred?" asked Ralph, puzzled.

"The only thing you might have noticed with your C&PCs would be its communications link being down," Lieutenant Rocha replied.

"Even though we all had been wearing them since we came on board, I bet none of us tried to contact anyone using them that day," Rob said.

Most of the crew members at the table shook their heads in agreement.

"Why knock out the comms?" inquired Ralph.

"Maybe to keep us from being able to talk to each other?" speculated Nutzie.

"Or, maybe to prevent arousing any suspicion if they did not take a call at the same time as the jamming," Rob said cautiously.

"It might just be a side effect of the frozen telemetry. I'm not sure at this point," the lieutenant stated coolly.

The captain asked, "What about the pilot flight monitoring systems. Were they affected by the jamming?"

"No, It doesn't seem so. Only those systems I have already mentioned were." Lieutenant Rocha replied.

Ralph anxiously said, "You mean that was all that was affected during those times. Who knows what else this jammer could do."

They all looked at each other with apprehension, wondering if Ralph might be right.

"How did this jamming device even get onboard the ship?" Val inquired, looking at the lieutenant.

"And past your security," Nutzie added, smiling at Lieutenant Rocha.

The lieutenant glared at Nutzie, obviously insulted by the remark.

The old man looked at his crew and explained, "It would not be impossible even under tight security. Components could have been smuggled in several simple devices, making them hard to detect."

Nutzie stared at Thatorn and sarcastically said, "Especially if your searches are focused only on contraband and anything considered dangerous."

Thatorn grunted as he glanced at Nutzie over her remark.

"There are a lot of electronic devices all over this ship. Could they have just built one?" Ralph asked, staring at Thatorn.

The rest of the crew at the table looked at Thatorn for a response.

"Not likely, considering the complexity of such a capable device. However, a power system for such a device would be hard to smuggle in," Thatorn said.

"There are a lot of rechargeable packs around the ship of every shape and size. Every portable device onboard the vessel uses them," Brian stated.

Rob looked at Brian and asked, "It is possible they could have tied the device directly to the power grid?"

"A power fluctuation would have been noticed by the computer," Fa stated frankly, glancing at Rob.

"Not if they knew what they were doing," Brian said, looking at Fa.

"What if it were simply plugged in, like the game system in Val's room?" Lee questioned as he turned his head to his left to stare at her.

How would he know about that? Brian wondered. Unless I'm not the only one she's been gaming with?

"It was checked when she came on board. I found nothing unusual about it," Lieutenant Rocha replied, staring at Lee.

"That explains all the scratches I found on it," mumbled Val, giving the lieutenant a dirty look.

"I don't understand. Since this is a military ship, it should be able to deal with jamming!" insisted Nutzie, staring at everyone.

"True. Military vessels are well-shielded to protect them from numerous things, including jamming. However, they are only designed to protect them from external sources," Lieutenant Rocha coldly responded, glancing at Nutzie.

"Why can't you just locate this device, track down its signal or something?" Ralph asked.

"Normally, we could. Internal systems monitor various conditions all over the ship. Unfortunately, there was nothing that indicated any kind of internal signal," the lieutenant said bluntly, staring at Ralph.

"We may be dealing with new technology working on wavelengths our monitors can't detect. I'm afraid we probably will only be able to find this jammer the hard way, by hand," said the old man with a slight sigh, staring at Ralph.

The doctor said, "Couldn't you check for a time delay on systems as they were affected by the jammer? As the jamming spreads out, the ship systems would be affected at slightly different times. You could use that information to triangulate...."

Thatorn looked at Zala and interrupted, "I'm sorry, doctor, but in this case, the time delay would be difficult to determine. Like radio waves, these jamming waves probably travel at the speed of light. Our ship's system internal chronometers are not that sensitive."

Zala smirked and nodded her head, understanding.

"I assume you found nothing on surveillance before the jamming to suggest who might be behind this?" Nutzie said smugly to Lieutenant Rocha.

"No, unfortunately, I did not," the lieutenant reluctantly admitted, staring at Nutzie.

"So they must have known about the surveillance on the ship enough to avoid it to set up their jammer?" Rob asked.

"Obviously," Lee grumpily said, staring at Rob.

"Then who could it be? We all were surprised when you revealed the survivance system on the ship to us in the situation room." The doctor said, looking around at her fellow crewmates.

"A good spy needs to also be a good actor," Thatorn replied, looking over his crew.

"Spy?" Brian asked Thatorn.

"Obviously a Pirate Spy," the old man answered with a smile after glancing at Brian.

Everyone looked at each other, contemplating what Thatorn said.

"Clearly, you missed something if someone managed to get a jammer on board," Nutzie said, gazing at Lieutenant Rocha.

The lieutenant glared at Nutzie and was about to respond until Lee suggested, "Maybe we should check everyone's rooms for this jammer?"

"I don't think they would be stupid enough to leave such a device in their room. Still, we will need to search for it," Thatorn stated, looking at Lee.

"I wonder how they activated and deactivated this jammer if everyone was under surveillance before and after each jamming?" inquired Rob, staring at the old man.

"Remote control, gone unnoticed in the surveillance footage," Lee speculated, looking at Rob.

Staring at Lee, Fa chimed in, "The Lieutenant already told us there were no unusual internal signals detected. I believe a remote transmitter would have been picked up."

"Like the jammer, the remote might use some unknown tech," Lee rebutted, looking at Fa.

Fa responded, "Maybe, but I bet this jammer was pre-programmed for select times and durations. Probably before it came on board the ship. It then could be reprogrammed for another set of times during jamming."

"I'm still going with the unknown tech remote," Lee said smugly.

Fa rolled her eyes at him.

"When things were jammed, how did they manage to get around the ship so quickly?" asked Ralph while looking at his fellow crewmates at the table.

"All the doors and lifts were still operational. Only the security control was down, so there is no record of who used them or when during the jamming times," Lieutenant Rocha replied, looking at Ralph.

"There is also the stairwell. In zero-G, you could quickly weave yourself down the center of it," said Captain Linol, staring at Ralph.

"Don't forget about the maintenance tube," said Rob, looking at Ralph.

The room fell silent once again as they looked at each other, speculating.

The captain glanced at each crew member at the table, except for Zala, and said. "So far, all we know is what was used to do the sabotage and maybe how they hid doing it. But we still don't know who or exactly how it was done."

"Not yet," replied Thatorn, giving everyone an eerie broad smile.

Brian realized something, glared at the old man, and asked, "Wait a second. All those jammings took place before I came aboard."

The lieutenant stared at Brian and replied, "Of the ones I've discovered so far, Yes."

"I came on board 2 days after. That rules me out." Brian pompously stated, looking at everyone.

Thatorn looked at Brian and said, "Does it, Mr. Rush? It's still possible there could be more than one spy on this ship. You could have had an accomplice do your dirty work before coming aboard just so we might discount you as a suspect. Then you could carry out other acts against this ship."

Before Brian could rebuke the old man's claim, Zala looked at the old man and asked, "Could we track down a chemical residue trail from the explosives themselves?"

Lieutenant Rocha stared at Zala and replied glumly, "No, They also knew what they were taking."

"What do you mean?" Zala asked, confused, staring at the lieutenant.

"We have devices sensitive enough to sniff out explosives via their chemical signature. It's part of our check on anything that comes aboard. However, our version of explosive leaves virtually no chemical trace. Its components can only be detected after detonation," Lieutenant Rocha explained.

"Huh," grunted Zala in response.

"Was all of it used?" asked Nutzie, looking troubled at the lieutenant.

"Excuse me?" Lieutenant Rocha inquired, looking at Nutzie puzzled.

"Did the amount taken equal what would have been needed in the bomb that took out the tower?" Nutzie asked in more detail.

The lieutenant began saying, "We didn't think about...."

Thatorn interrupted Lieutenant Rocha and calmly stated, "Hum, let me run some quick calculations in my head."

After several seconds, the old man added, "No, I would say they may have some left."

The lab was quiet again as everyone looked at each other stunned.

Oh great, there's another chance I can get blown out of the ship or ripped apart by an explosion. Brian fearfully contemplated.

Ralph looked around at everyone and frantically questioned, "Could they have already used some of it to take out the RRU? Maybe it's all part of keeping us from re-establishing communications?"

Lee stared at Ralph and started to reply, "There was nothing to suggest an explosive was used to ...."

Still frantic, Ralph interrupted, "My god! Don't you see! They're bound to come after Nutzie and me next!"

The communications specialist squatted down in his seat. He trembled as he repeatedly glanced around the room at all his fellow crewmates.

"Calm down, Mr. Milsom. You will see that everything is well in hand." The old man said softly, looking at the frightened man.

Got to get me some of the drugs the old man is on, thought Brian.

Ralph took a deep breath and slowly raised back up in his seat. He looked at Thatorn, still trembling slightly.

Everyone else at the table also had the old man's attention.

Thatorn pulled his chair's joystick back, causing him to back away from the table. Then, after he stopped a few meters away to get a good look at everyone, he stared smugly at them.

He said calmly, "The reason I have brought you all to the lab is to find the guilty party by testing for DNA."

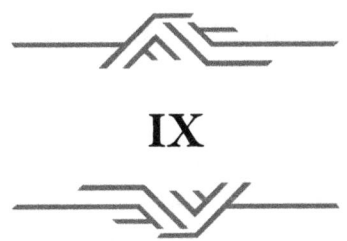

IX

It was eerily quiet in the medical lab as everyone at the table looked around at each other, contemplating what Thatorn had just told them.

So it wasn't drugs, after all. Thatorn had something up his sleeve all along. No wonder he's been so cheerful. Thought Brian as he glanced over at the old man a few meters from the table.

"If they were wearing gloves, how could they have left any significant amounts of DNA?" said Rob, interrupting the silence.

"Skin flakes. DNA can be extrapolated with modern technology with just a few of them." Zala spoke up, looking at Rob while clasping her hands together.

The crew at the table looked at her, puzzled.

Seeing this, Thatorn quickly snapped. "This ship was one of the finest science vessels in its day and still is."

Zala glanced at the old man and added, "The Admiral is right. We have devices on this ship that are still considered cutting edge."

Thatorn smugly stated, "I like to take advantage of all the available technology."

"When we are in zero-G, our dead skin cells, or dust, could float all over the ship?" Questioned Ralph, staring at the doctor.

Thatorn glared at Ralph and declared, "There are no dust issues on my ship. The forced ventilation, filtration, and carbon buffers ensure that."

In response, Ralph hid his eyes by staring down at the table.

"Couldn't they have cleaned up their DNA?" Fa asked, looking at the doctor.

Zala began, "It's not impossible, but they didn't have much time, assuming it happened during the second jamming with only 11 minutes and some seconds."

"24 seconds," interjected Lieutenant Rocha, looking at the doctor.

Suddenly, Thatorn angrily snorted. "Shall we forgo any more speculation and just find out!"

Everyone at the table got very quiet and stared at the old man.

Thatorn continued, "Shortly after the lieutenant had secured sub-storage hold 1. I had her take DNA samples from select surfaces inside the room and the explosives locker."

Thatorn looks up at Lieutenant Rocha and says. "Let us begin by checking out those samples, Lieutenant."

Lieutenant Rocha opens the box with a medical symbol she left hovering over the table earlier and pulls out a handful of small translucent tubes. Each had an odd port protruding from one of its sides. She turns, walks past Thatorn, and goes over to the console behind him. While holding the tubes in her right hand, she stands before the console and activates it. A 3D screen and keyboard appear over it. Using her left hand, she typed on the keyboard of light.

After finishing, a long rectangular metallic box rose from the top of the console to her right. Along this box were several open concaved ports. Carefully, she plugged each little tube into a separate port. Once finished, she typed into the holographic keypad again.

The console showed a holographic image with several graphs and lines of text. Unfortunately, it was too far away for Brian to make out.

The lieutenant gazed at the holographic screen for a second, then turned to see everyone at the table was looking at her.

Lieutenant Rocha said, "I have loaded all the DNA samples I took from the hold into this lab console. It has just informed me that several different DNAs have been detected."

"Several?" inquired Val, looking puzzled.

The lieutenant replied, "Since the Admiral and I supervised the loading of critical cargo, we should find the DNA of ourselves, the U.E.A. loading crew at the base, and...."

"Our thief and saboteur!" Thatorn interrupted.

Thatorn went silent and scanned each of the crew's faces for any kind of reaction.

Not seeing anything, he briefly frowned. Then, smiling, he said, "Now, we will take fresh samples of everyone's DNA to see if we find a match."

He then scoffed, "Unless you think I sabotaged my own ship?"

Brian thinks, now there is a thought. But why would he? Much less mention it.

After a brief pause, Thatorn said, "I realize we already have everyone's DNA on file, but I thought it would be better to get new ones just in case any might have changed."

"Are you suggesting someone may not be who they claim to be?" asked Nutzie, staring at the old man.

He replied, "We thought it would be a good idea to compare the DNA on file with what will be collected just to make sure."

Thatorn went silent again to scan each face of the crew at the table. Then, after staring at them for several seconds, he let out a soft sigh of disappointment.

Ralph asked, "Are you going to collect some skin cells from our skin?"

Lieutenant Rocha replied, "It would be enough DNA for testing. However, there is a chance of contamination. You could have picked up other people's skin cells on your skin, especially your hands."

"We have a better way." Thatorn boasted.

The lieutenant walks back over to the table. Then pulls out a round disk from the floating metal box.

"Doctor, if you please," said Thatorn, gesturing at what Lieutenant Rocha was holding.

Zala stood up and walked over beside the lieutenant at the end of the table. She looked in the box and said, "So, it looks like one for everybody."

Lieutenant Rocha handed her the one she had and walked back to stand beside Thatorn's right side.

"What is it?" asked Rob, curious.

"It's just a standard medical one-time-use device to draw and store a blood sample," Zala replied, looking over the device in her hand.

She noticed something about the disk and was about to comment, but Thatorn spoke up and said, "Each one has already been preset with a person's name."

"I see. This one's small readout says, Ralph Milsom."

"Does it have a needle?" inquired Ralph, seeming a little pale as he stared at the doctor.

"To just draw blood for a sample. Tell me, do the Doctors in the belt still use needles for that?" questioned the doctor.

"Yeah, why?" Ralph replied.

Zala grimaced.

Holding the disk towards Ralph, she explained, "This extracts blood through the skin from the small capillaries. No need for needles."

"The analyzer on the console will extract a few blood cells from the sample and look at the DNA for comparison," added the lieutenant.

"Oh, ok then, um, where how do you?" Ralph said, confused, looking at his disk in the doctor's hand.

The doctor replied, "The best place is to take it from your upper arm. So everyone must undo their jumpsuit just enough to expose either arm."

Everyone at the table but the captain and the doctor carefully unzipped their suits just enough to expose an arm.

"Since I already have your disk, Ralph, I will do you first," said Zala as she went over to him. She pulled a round covering strip off the side of the disk without a display and stuck that side onto Ralph's arm. She then pushed a button on its other side, activating it. Once satisfied, she stuffed the cover strip away in her pocket.

One at a time, she carefully took a disk from the box, read the name, took it over to them, pulled the cover strip, tucked it into her pocket, and attached the disk to their exposed arm.

As she was doing this, she came across one and looked oddly at the name on it. Then, staring at Thatorn, she said. "There must be a mistake. This one has Mark's name on it."

Captain Linol quickly focused his eyes on the old man.

Thatorn returned the stare and said, "Everyone is to be checked, especially if they were not part of the loading process."

The captain glared at the old man and grunted, "Sir, I am an officer of the U.E.A. Why...."

"That will be enough!" shouted Thatorn, squinting at Captain Linol. "You are an officer and will follow orders. Is that clear!"

The captain replied with a huff, undid his jumpsuit, and exposed his right arm. The doctor placed the device on it while giving him a sympathetic smile.

Everyone at the table had one on now. The doctor undid her jumpsuit enough to expose her upper left arm. She pulled out her disk she saved for last and applied it like she did all the others.

"Once finished, the device will let out a soft beep," Zala said, looking at everyone around the table.

"How long will this take?" Ralph asked, looking at the disk on his arm.

"It depends, but a few minutes should do it," the doctor replied.

"Doctor, please set up the analyst at the console. The Lieutenant can collect the blood samples to give to you for processing," Thatorn said calmly.

Lieutenant Rocha walked over to the table as the doctor proceeded to the console.

Zala sat down and strapped herself into the console seat. After typing on the 3D keypad, a small slit near the long rectangular metallic box on the console opens.

The lieutenant takes out a clear, sealed bag from the floating container over the table. From the bag, she removes a latex glove. After carefully removing the glove from the bag, she puts the glove on her left hand and places the bag in her right pocket.

Zala swivels around to face the crew and begins to say, "As I load the disks into the console, it will take some of the blood and do a DNA scan. I will then compare it to the DNA on file...."

"No, Doctor, please process all the blood samples into the system first. Once all the DNA is in, cross-check the crew's DNA on file. After that, look for a match with the collected samples."

Really Thatorn? Do you have to drag this out and make it so melodramatic? Brian asked himself.

Zala nodded, understanding Thatorn's order.

As each disk went off with a beep, Lieutenant Rocha walked over to the person, took the collection disk carefully off their arm, and took it over to the lab console.

Once the device was off, the crewmate quickly put their arm back into their jumpsuit and zipped it back up.

The lieutenant waits at the console, holding the device until the doctor signals her to place it in the slot.

Lieutenant Rocha carefully watches everything the doctor does at the console as she processes the blood samples.

Finally, the doctor's disk was the last one. The lieutenant removed it from her arm. Only after getting the ok from the doctor does she place it into the slot. Then she removes the latex glove from her left hand with her right. Then, holding the glove with her left hand, she pulls the plastic bag from her right pocket with her right hand. After placing the glove in the bag, she quickly tucks it into her left pocket.

Brian starts to feel a knot tighten in his chest. He knows it's his anxiety is building up but can't control it. His heart rate and breathing begin to rise.

He tells himself that soon, we will know who did it and maybe even why.

The doctor types away at the holographic keyboard while Lieutenant Rocha watches over her shoulder. Once finished, she slipped her arm back into her jumpsuit, zipped it up, and leaned back in the chair.

Both the doctor and lieutenant stared at the 3D screen intensely and waited.

Brian tried again to see what was happening on the console screen. Unable to see anything, he looks over his fellow crewmates at the table. Everyone was staring at each other suspiciously, except for Nutzie. She was only gazing at Thatorn.

Suddenly, there was a noticeable beep from the console. The doctor and Lieutenant Rocha leaned into the 3D screen. Everyone fixed their attention on them. That was when Brian noticed the lieutenant had her left hand in her left side pouch.

After a tense moment, Doctor Teka calmly glances at the crew to report, "First results are in, and it looks as if everyone is who they claim they are. Everyone's DNA matches what is on record."

That is somewhat comforting unless the records on file were somehow changed? Brian thought with a gulp.

"Ok, now for the matchup with the samples," stated the doctor.

She looked at the 3D screen and typed away at the console. Once done, she and Lieutenant Rocha stared intensely at the holographic screen.

Everyone at the table was nervously looking at each other. However, Nutzie was still only focused on Thatorn.

Brian glanced over at Thatorn. The old man was excitedly watching everything happening around him. He appeared to be delighted, even thrilled at what was going on.

Brian turned his attention back to his crewmates and pondered. One of you is the saboteur. Capable of destruction. For what? To stop this mission? Would you even go so far as to destroy the ship?

The knot in Brian's chest began to tighten. He was finding it more difficult to breathe.

While staring at the faces around the table, he suddenly realized. Wait, not one of them shows any signs of being the guilty party just before they are about to be found out. Why the poker face, unless....

The medical console let out a loud beep.

Everyone looked over at Zala.

Slowly, she turned and looked at the crew.

The lieutenant saw the name and quickly spun around to look at Thatorn, taking her hand from her left pouch.

"It's Lee," Zala said with hesitation.

"I knew it!" screamed Ralph, glaring at Lee across the table.

Everyone in the room stared at Lee except for Thatorn and Lieutenant Rocha. They only looked at each other.

"What? I never took any explosives!" Lee exclaimed, looking at his crewmates.

Slowly, Thatorn begins to clench his fists. He and the lieutenant then look at Lee.

Lee undid his seat strap, stood up, and slowly stepped back and away from the table.

He looks over at the old man and starts to proclaim, "Sir, you know I...."

With a snort, Thatorn interrupts, "So, Mr. Smith, what do you have to say for yourself?"

Before Lee could respond, the captain exclaimed, "We need to lock him up!"

"He's dangerous!" Ralph shouted.

Brian spoke up, glaring at Lee, and said, "Wait a minute. You tried to delay me in the mess before I went on my rounds. You knew I was going to the wing!"

"What? This saboteur tried to stop you from getting hurt or killed?" Zala asked.

Brian turned to her and replied, "Well, yeah, I guess."

"Wouldn't that be odd behavior for a Pirate spy?" asked the doctor.

Everyone started to calm down a little as they reflected on what the doctor had said.

"What's really going on here, Thatorn?" Nutzie asked, glaring at the old man.

Everyone looked at Thatorn to see a stone-cold, expressionless face.

Suddenly, the medical console came to life again and gave another beep. Everyone froze and looked at it.

The doctor glanced over her shoulder at the console screen and said, "That's odd. There's also a match for Mark as well?"

Even before Captain Linol could protest, more beeps were heard.

"What the hell!" Exclaimed Zala as she spun around in her chair to get a better look at the screen.

Lieutenant Rocha turned around to look at the console screen from behind her.

The doctor looked shocked as she swiveled back in her chair to look at the crew.

"Well, what is it? Did Lee and the Captain work together?" asked Fa, confused.

The lieutenant turned around and replied, "According to the DNA scan, it appears that everyone was in the hold except for Mr. Rush."

Looking at Thotorn, Zala says, "I'm sorry, this proves nothing. Maybe there was some cross-contamination with the samples taken from the hold."

"That's impossible!" insisted Lieutenant Rocha, looking at Thatorn with a furrowed brow.

"Or we have a clever saboteur," Captain Linol stated.

"What do you mean, Mark?" asked Zala, staring at the captain.

"Simple, they collected everyone's DNA on the ship at the time and then planted it when they stole the explosives. Brian's DNA was omitted because he came on board after the theft," Captain Linol responded.

"Yes, I see. It would be easier to leave all that DNA than to try to clean up their own." The doctor added.

"Especially if you have just over 14 minutes to do it," said Rob with some sarcasm.

"Was anyone's DNA found in a higher quantity?" Snapped the admiral, staring off into space.

The doctor typed away at the console with the lieutenant looking over her shoulder.

While still looking at the screen, Zala replies, "In each sample taken, they all varied. No one's DNA was significantly higher in all the samples."

"Dead end, I'm afraid," the doctor sighed.

It was clear to Brian that Thatorn was growing angrier as he clenched his fists even more, and his face started to turn red.

Brian thought, Wow! He's about to blow!

Suddenly, the admiral unclenched his fist, and the redness in his face quickly faded.

He looks over at Lieutenant Rocha with a smile and gleam in his eye and calmly says, "Since the hold is still secured, we will need to recheck everything. Lieutenant, gather more DNA samples and place the blood collection disks into cold storage. We'll do this again just to make sure."

Brian could firmly feel the knot start to grow again in his chest. He had hoped it would have been gone by now. Instead, he realizes it may be stuck there for quite some time.

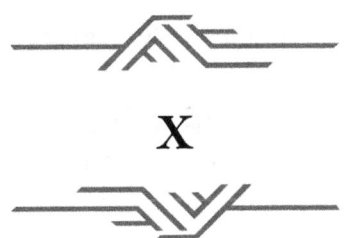

X

"That's the last one," said Brian, looking up from a dark compartment in the deck with his headlamp illuminating Nutzie as she stood above him near the edge of the opening.

Brian rose slowly up through the open floor panel. He activated his C&PC with a tap, causing it to glow for a second, briefly lighting up the compartment he was in. Once his feet were level with the floor, Brian tapped on the right edge of his wrist device, turning on his magnetic boots. He then gingerly stepped over onto the deck.

Brian and Nutzie were standing in the gloomy, lit lower wing. Most of the illumination in the hallway came from the corridor connecting to the wing entrance and some backup battery lights along the hall.

Brian turned off his headlamp and approached the glowing port side power console.

Nutzie glanced down the hallway's dark end to try to see the closed bulkhead.

She asks, "You've not been here since it happened, have you?"

After getting to the console, Brian replied. "No. I didn't need to because the computer auto cut off power to areas of the ship affected by the explosion."

"So why did you decide to manually shut down the power?" Nutzie inquired, curious.

"Purely precautionary," explained Brian, grinning as he looked back at Nutzie, lit only by the connecting corridor's light.

Brian turned his attention back to the console and went to work. Unlike most things on the ship, this control console had only a solid-state keyboard and a flat 2D screen.

The floor panel near them closed after a few taps on the screen.

After a few more taps and clicks on the keyboard, the lights in the hallway slowly came back on.

He then touched the left edge of his C&PC and said into it, "Alright, I have the power back up in the lower wing. Everything from the antenna array down is now physically disconnected. Everything else should all be up and running."

"Roger," replied Rob's voice through Brian's C&PC.

Brian let go of his C&PC and looked over the console.

Nutzie walked up behind Brian, peaking over his shoulder, and asked, "Are we ready?"

After Brian did a few more taps on the screen and keyboard strokes, he turned towards her and replied, "Wait, just a sec."

Brian pulled out two pills from his jumpsuit pocket with a water packet.

"What's that?" Nutzie asked.

"I still have a little pain," Brian lied.

Brian was glad to get some calming meds from the doctor for the EVA today. He didn't even have to tell her the truth about why he wanted them. She told Brian that several others have also asked for anxiety medications and understood why under the circumstances.

Brian considered getting someone else to spot for Nutzie. But he knew he would have to face his fear sooner or later anyway. Otherwise, he would remain forever hindered by it, letting it affect the rest of his career.

Quickly, he put the pills into his mouth, tore off the packet's corner, and sucked the water from it.

Not seeing a nearby waste chute, he jammed the empty packet in his pocket and said, "Ready."

They exited the wing and briskly headed towards the lift down the connecting corridor.

"So, who do you think is the saboteur?" Nutzie asked as they entered the square room, heading for the starboard door to the circular hallway.

"I don't know, what about you," replied Brian as he tried to keep up with her.

Instead of answering, Nutzie suddenly stopped in the square room.

Seeing this, Brian also stopped and asked, "What's wrong?"

"There are no bathrooms on the cargo level. So you better use the ones on this level before we go out," Nutizie said, gesturing to the right towards the closest bathroom down the starboard corridor.

Brian grimaced at the prospect of yet another go-around with the zero-G attachment to the toilet and lied, "I'm fine. I went right after breakfast less than an hour ago."

"Well, it will be on you, literally," she replied with a grin, then added. "At least you'll have an EVA diaper on."

"Do you need to go?" asked Brian, looking at her, confused.

She answered with a wye smile, "I've got a large blader. So I won't need to go for a while."

She stepped up to the starboard door to the circular hallway. Once it opened, she quickly made her way through, followed closely by Brian.

As soon as they entered the circular hallway, they saw the doctor exiting the starboard lift they were heading for.

"Uh oh," exclaimed Nutzie as she froze in the hallway, causing Brian to almost run into her.

"You both missed your appointment to receive your anti-radiation drug. My medical link to the C&PC tracking system told me I would find you on this floor," lectured Zala with a stern look.

Nutzie started to protest, "Those drugs can make me sick. Besides, we are far enough away from the sun...."

Zala gruffly interrupted, "You know damn good, and well, there are all kinds of other radiation out there to consider. Especially as we draw closer to Jupiter!"

"Ok, Mom," Nutzie said in a soft mumble.

"You know I care about you and want you to be safe," Zala said before grabbing Nutzie and kissing her.

Nutzie reciprocated, and the kissing became more passionate. Nutzie even began to squeeze Zala's left breast with her right hand. After watching this for several seconds, Brian finally let out a soft cough.

Zala and Nutzie quickly regained their composure. They stepped back away from each other and smiled.

"So maybe we can...." Brian prompted.

"Ah yes, let's get to it," Zala responded.

Brian looked at the doctor's hands, confused, and said, "So how will you give it to us? I don't see a laser injector."

"Oh no. I can give you longer-lasting radiation treatments with a time-release pill." Zala said, looking at Brian, reaching into her pocket and pulling out two oblong pellets with her right hand.

"Is it some kind of nanotech?" Brian asked.

"No, just a modern medication. I only use Nanos to do repair work in the body." The doctor replied.

Putting her right hand up into Nuztie's face, she says, "I'm not leaving until you take one."

Looking at Brian, she adds, "The both of you."

"What about a sip of water to help wash it down?" Brian asked.

"No need. The pills are coated slightly to help with that," said the doctor.

Nutzie grabs hers, opens her mouth, and tosses it down her throat, with Zala closely watching.

With some reluctance, Brian took the other one and swallowed his down, wishing he had another water packet.

"Ah, Good," the doctor said pleased.

She continued, "This medication is a little harsh, so if you notice any blood in your bowel movements in the next few days, it should be ok."

Then, in a more serious tone, she added, "However, you should come to see me if it's longer than that."

Before Brian could ask her about it, all of their C&PCs came to life with Thatorn's voice.

He bellowed, "I'm sure you all are aware of the schedule updates this morning. Everyone not involved in the EVA scheduled in 10 minutes at 9:00 hours must report to the command deck until repairs are completed. That includes you as well, Lieutenant Rocha. This is purely a precaution due to our situation. Since Mr. Rush and Ms. Teodoresco will not have someone controlling the EVA doors from the EVA control room. We will monitor and control everything from the command deck. Under the circumstances, lunch will be rescheduled until after the repair."

Nutzie said, "Ralph should be happy since Thatorn is taking these security measures."

It was somewhat comforting considering what was going on, Brian thought.

"I better go." The doctor said as she turned, walked over to the lift, and hit the call button to go up.

Nutzie and Brian walked up to the door behind her.

The lift door opened to reveal Lee. At first, he was a little startled when he saw them.

Lee then smiled and politely asked, "Going up?"

"I'll see you later," Zala says as she enters the elevator with a grin, staring at Nutzie the whole time.

"Later," replies Nutzie, returning a smile.

Lee presses the lift controls, and the door closes.

Brian looks at Nutzie and says, "You cougar."

She turns to face him and asks, "Jealous?"

With a grin, Brian replies, "Maybe a little."

Nutzie let out a chuckle and said, "I prefer gals myself. I realized that 30 years ago during my group marriage. They all were more interested in genetic diversity. I just wanted a nice pair of big tits in my face."

After a slight sigh, she added, "I don't mind a guy being involved occasionally, especially if it can get a hot gal in the sack."

"Like Captain Linol?" inquired Brian.

Looking at Brian, surprised, Nutzie asked, "Have you been talking to Zala?"

"Yes, and no. I gathered most of it on my own, and it just came out when we were having a conversation in the galley yesterday," Brian replied.

"You are very observant," stated Nutzie.

"That's what the doctor said," Brian replied.

"Or very nosey," Nutzie said with a cold stare.

Brian looked at her with a mixture of confusion and fear.

To Brian's relief, she let out a loud laugh.

"Yes, it is the Captain, but I think he only tolerates me so he can be with Zala, too," Nutzie said with a slight frown.

"I don't know. During the group meeting, Captain Linol seemed concerned about you when you got pissed at Thatorn," Brian explained.

With a sigh, Nutzie said, "Probably all just for show to Zala. But I don't know. I'm too damn old to be getting jealous anymore."

Brian takes a moment to ponder over what she said.

Nutzie pushes the lift call button, saying, "That should be enough time."

They both face the elevator to wait.

After a few seconds, Nutzie glances at Brian and asks, "So what about you and Val?"

Brian snapped his neck to stare at Nutzie and ask, "What do you mean?"

Nutzie turned towards Brian with a laugh and a broad grin and replied, "Ah, if I were younger, I would be all over it. Still, Val is straight, so I don't know if I would have much of a shot anyway."

"How did you know?" Brian asked intensely, looking at Nutzie.

"I see the way you look and talk to her. Unfortunately for you, I also have seen her and Rob snuggling and chit-chatting together on several occasions," replied Nutzie.

"Oh," said Brian with some disappointment.

Nutzie said, "Hey, remember, you don't get unless you ask."

Brian had no time for a reply. The lift opened, and they quickly got in. Nutzie pushed the controls for level 13, and the doors closed.

Nutzie and Brian stepped into the EVA control room through the starboard entrance.

Brian started to say, "I'll need to go over my suit...."

"No need," Nutzie interpted. "I already prechecked mine and yours. Yours is ready to go in locker 1 by EVA room 1, and mine is in locker 2 on the other side. Their oxygen and power should be good for over 6 hours, but we should only need 4."

"Thanks, but you didn't have to," Brian said.

"You see, I tend to get excited before an EVA. I've been up since 6:00 hours and thought I would get it out of the way. It took less than an hour to do them both."

Brian walked to the locker to his right while Nutzie headed for the other one across the room.

Nutzie said, "I have Micuţo all ready to go too."

"What?" asked Brian, staring at her, puzzled.

"He's my voice command space work cart," Nutzie replied.

"Is it that the box-like object strapped down near the center of EVA room 2?" Brian inquired.

"Yes," Nutzie responded.

"Not quite a little one," said Brian with a grin.

Nutzie let out a loud, jovial laugh.

With a look of nostalgia, she said, "I named it after a little dog I had when I was a child."

After Brian opened his locker and grabbed his spacesuit, he realized something. Turning around to face Nutzie, he started saying, "Maybe I should wait outside and let you...."

Brian stopped once he saw that Nutzie had already removed her jumpsuit and just slid off her panties. Now, with only her C&PC and magnetic boots on.

Brian couldn't keep from staring at her well-formed dark brown, muscular butt while she stuffed her jumpsuit and panties into a storage bag in locker 2.

Once finished, she turned to face Brian and asked, "What?"

There was not one strain of hair anywhere on her body but her head. Her naked body was far more attractive to Brian than he could have imagined.

Nutzie smiled as she allowed him to take it all in.

After several seconds, Nutzie finally asked, "So you got a banana in your pants, or are you happy to see me?"

Brian looked down to see the bulge in his jumpsuit. Quickly, he turned around in shame and said," I'm sorry."

Nutzie giggled and said, "For what? It's kinda kinky that I can turn on a straight guy. Still, if the wind blew in the right direction at your age, it would give you a hard-on as well. Come on, let's get ready."

Brian turned around and started unzipping his jumpsuit as Nutzie watched him.

"Come on, big boy, it's only fair I get to see too," said Nutzie with a devilish smile.

Brian took off his headlamp and put it into his holding bag. He undressed with reluctance and stuffed his jumpsuit and underwear into the bag.

"Hum," was all Nutzie said, staring at Brian and his rigged assets.

Brian quickly grabbed and put on his disposable extra-absorbent containment trunk. Nutzie did the same, but ever so slowly to tease him.

All Brian could do was laugh out loud to release his tension.

Nutzie followed with a laugh as well.

They took off their C&PCs and placed them in their holding bags.

After turning off their magnetic boots, they began to float. Carefully, they removed them and placed them in an empty drawer in their locker.

Nutzie and Brian gingerly slipped on their baggy spacesuits. Trying their best not to float too far away from their locker or cause themselves to start spinning.

Brian's was a generic white spacesuit, but Nutzies was a newer, soft, pale blue model.

"Nice!" Exclaimed Brian as he realized her suit was the first brightly colored thing he had seen in days.

She grinned, "Yeah, one of my favorite colors. Reminds me of home."

After activating the built-in controls in the spacesuit's sleeves, their suits slowly tightened to form fit to their bodies. This kind of spacesuit provides both counter pressure to the vacuum of space and flexibility. You could barely see the slight bulges caused by the heating and cooling mesh in the suits.

They pulled out their spacesuit's matching magnetic boots from another drawer in the locker.

As Nutzie was putting hers on, not looking at Brian, she said, "You are well versed in all emergency procedures?"

Brian paused, putting on his boots, looked at Nutzie, and then started to reply, "I have a certification in...."

"Good, then we can move on to a review of the repair," interrupts Nuztie while securing her boots to her suit.

"Brian replied, "Ok," as he focused on doing the same with his boots.

"First, I will clear away all the debris around the breach, working from the outside in," Nutzie said, putting on her second boot.

"Don't forget to get rid of all those wires too. You could get tangled up in them," added Brian, still working on his first boot.

"Right. I will then reinforce the strut. Weld my two half-circle plates inside the edge of the breach and to the strut. Once that is all secure, I'll add a slightly larger covering over it all and weld that into place. It should hold up to a pressure test and shouldn't require any reinforcement on the inside," stated Nutzie, now finished with her boots.

She activated them with the suit's sleeve controls and stood on the deck again.

"We should have some sealant foam handy on the inside, just in case," said Brian, securing his second boot.

"I'm sure it will make Ralph feel better," replied Nutzie.

Brian finished with his boots and was standing on the deck once again.

They both pulled their suit's matching backpacks out of the lockers. These will provide them with additional power, air, and a thruster system to maneuver around in space.

Once their backpacks were secured and plugged into their suits, they took out their helmets from their locker and connected them to their packs.

After putting on their helmets, they meticulously went over the connections to each other's helmets and backpacks to ensure they were secure. They gave each other the thumbs up in turn once finished.

Finally, they took the gloves to their suits from their lockers, slipped them on, and secured them to their spacesuits.

Now that they both were fully suited up, they went over the visor's heads-up display data using the suit's sleeve controls to confirm that everything was working.

Brian tapped on one of his controls and said in his suit," Test test."

"You are on the air," said Rob's voice from the radio speakers in Brian's helmet.

Brian then heard Nutzie say, "I hear you both."

"I copy you as well," responded Rob.

Brian added, "Ok, I hear you too, Nutzie."

Rob said in Brian's helmet. "You both should be good to go. Everyone else is up here on the command deck."

Nutzie grinned at him past the HUD information at the bottom through her visor. She then jesters at the EVA room 2 door close to her and says over the radio, "Ladies first."

Brian shook his head and smiled briefly as he walked to the door.

"Lieutenant, open EVA room two," said Thatorn in Brian's helmet.

After the door opened, they entered.

Once in, Brian heard Thatorn say in his helmet, "You may now close EVA room two, Lieutenant."

The door behind them slowly closed.

Nutzie walked over to the odd black box strapped down in the center of the room.

Brian got closer to take a better look.

On the back of the box was a large camera lens at its center and two smaller ones on each side of it. It had four round thrusters protruding from each corner.

A magnetic pad was on both of the box's long sides. Each had a metal repair plate attached. On the right side was a 1-meter round plate. The other had another circle plate that was less than a meter in diameter and in two parts.

Brian saw each side had a small camera lens near each corner.

On top of the box, from the rear to the center, was a shallow open compartment. There were a few long metal bars inside. A retractable wire mesh covered the opening to keep anything inside from floating away. Another small camera lens was in front of this, close to the center.

Brian thought, there's bound to be some on the bottom, too. This has way more cameras than the average RRU. They're probably needed for an AI.

Near the front of the top was a retractable white power cable wrapped around a recessed gray spindle. Its protruding cable went over the top front edge.

Now curious, Brian walked around to see where the line went.

The front was like the rear, except it had a small unlit control panel below the lens and a c-clip above them. Attached to the clip was a metallic gray Z105 laser welder. This was what was connected to the end of the power cable.

Nutzie released the straps and tapped the front panel of the box. She then said, "Micuțo trezește-l."

Then Brian heard a long beep and assumed it was transmitted from the box.

"No voice command reply?" inquired Brian, looking at Nutzie's work cart.

Nutzie replied with a snort, "If I wanted to hear constant chatter and nagging, I would have stayed married."

Brian held back a laugh, but Rob couldn't.

"Shall we proceed?" grumbled Thatorn over the radio.

"Ok, We are ready?" stated Nutzie.

"Lieutenant, depressurize the bay," said Thatorn in Brian's helmet.

Just as the bay's lights dimmed and went out, a red light on the ceiling above them lit up with two red beams strobing around the room.

While it was flashing, Brian could hear the warning siren going off, but the sound faded away as the air was vented from the room.

The red strobe stopped, and it was dark in the bay except for some light emanating from Micuţo's control panel and their spacesuits.

Then, over the radio, Brian heard Thatorn say, "Open hatchway, Lieutenant."

Here goes nothing, thought Brian as a bead of sweat rolled down his forehead.

Slowly, the main hatchway started to open. The dim light of hundreds of thousands of stars caused the bay to softly glow.

Staring into the void caused Brian to freeze. He swallowed hard and started to hyperventilate.

He thought he had prepared for this and expected the drugs to control his anxiety. Unfortunately, it didn't take it all away.

Then he heard "Brian!" in his helmet.

He recognized Nutzie's voice and snapped out of his daze.

She was now standing before him, blocking most of his view of space. Through her visor and heads-up display, he could see the concern on her face.

Nutzie turned her head to see what Brian was staring at, causing him to freeze. She quickly realized what was happening.

"What's the problem?" asked Thatorn with a grunt over the radio.

Turning to look at Brian, Nutzie said, "It's ok. I'm just checking Brian's helmet. I thought I noticed a loose connection."

Looking at Brian, she slowly mouthed out, "Deep breaths."

Brian nodded in understanding.

After taking a few, he mouthed back, "Thank you."

She mouthed, "You owe me one," followed by a wink from her left eye.

Brian managed to grin back.

"Activating night vision," declared Nutzie, tapping her left sleeve controls with her right hand to turn on her visor's enhanced optical abilities.

Brian did the same with his suit, making the bay light up through his visor.

"Ok, now activating data and video feed," said Nutzie, tapping her sleeve again.

In the left lower corner of Brian's heads-up display was a video feed from a forward camera in Nutzie's helmet, and he saw himself.

"Ok, receiving," said Thatorn in Brian's helmet.

"Me too," replied Brian.

"Mrs. Teodoresco, please let us know when you have finished the repairs. I want to start pressure testing on the room as soon as possible," announced Thatorn over the radio.

"Yes, sir," she replied, turning to face the opening.

She then walked over to the bay's edge. Brian took a deep breath and stepped over beside her.

Using her left sleeve controls, she turned off her magnetic boots and stepped out of the bay into space. Again using her controls, she fires a quick burst from her suit's thrusters and slowly drifts away.

She says, "Micuțo Veni."

Her work cart transmitted a long beep in response and fired a small blast from its thrusters to follow after her.

With her left sleeve controls, Nutzie fires her thrusters, causing her to turn right and rotate. She fires trusters again to stop her motion once she is orientated with her feet toward the ship and in the direction of the bottom wing. With another truster fire, she makes her way toward its underside.

"Come on, Brian, regulations require you to stay in visual range of me at all times," Nutzie announced over the radio.

After another deep breath, he turned off his boots and stepped out into space. After a long breath, he activated his thrusters, orientated himself just like Nutzie did, and followed her right behind Micuţo.

They passed the ship's heat vents on the port side to their right as they went around the main hull. Going down the wing, they passed two large tanks, flew over the lower wing drives, and then between the rear sensor array and port sensor dish.

Nutzie slowed down with counter thrusters after passing the long starboard antenna. Once reaching the end of the bottom of the wing, Nutzie stopped. Activated her boots and stepped onto the edge of the wing.

She turned around to see Micuţo stop behind her within a few meters, and Brian slowed down as he passed the port antenna.

"How's the view?" Nutzie asked the crew inside the ship.

"I can see Mr. Rush is taking his time," Thatorn moaned over the radio waves.

Brian could see Nutzie's view of him as he approached her in the lower left corner of his heads-up display.

"How about you roosting right here on the wing edge. That will give me plenty of room to work and for you to have a good view," said Nutzie in Brian's helmet.

Brian activated his boots and used his thrusters to stop and land beside her.

Nutzie turned back around, bent over to look at the underside of the wing, and stated, "Well, better get started."

She turned off her boots and, with a small burst, used her trusters to gently go over the edge, followed by Micuţo. She stabilized her position with her suit thrusters once she was close enough to the tower remains. Micuţo was close enough for her to take the laser welder from him and pull out enough slack for its connection to begin to cut away the metal fragments and wires. Starting on the outside, she carefully worked her way around and inward. Micuţo stayed close as she worked, ensuring the cabling to her welder was taut enough not to get in her way but loose enough so she could do her job.

Brian watched Nutzie clear everything away and start to repair the breach. She was quiet as she focused on her work.

Brian continued to make frequent checks on the status of his suit. He was still nervous but was able to maintain some self-control. He looked up into the wash of stars, and it relaxed him for the first time in a while.

He turned his head to the left to look sunward in the direction they came from. After a few seconds, he finally found a slightly bigger and brighter star than the rest. It was the sun. Over 480 million miles away.

I think I got this. Brian wondered but quickly rechecked his suit status again.

Several hours had passed, and Brian watched Nutzie as she was constantly lit by the light of her welder. The strobing effect started to make him a little nauseous.

Nutzie suddenly declares, "Ok, done and in less than 4 hours, not bad."

With relief, Brian thought, Good, now we can go back inside.

Brian could see Nutzie hovering above her repair, looking it over.

Bending over the wing edge to get a better look at Nutzie's work, Brian then says, "It looks good."

Nutzie then boasts, "I guarantee this job will hold up well on its own."

"That's fine, but I would still like to make sure," Brian replied.

Nutzie lets go of her welder and says, "Oprire, retrag sudor."

Micuțo turns off the power to the welder and pulls it and its cable in. Leaving just enough slack so the welder can be clipped back onto the front.

"Hum, that's odd," Nutzie said, surprised.

"What?" asked Brian, looking at her.

"I think I have a bad tank. The O2 level seems off, even though my gauge says the tank is good. I'm going to switch to another tank just in case," she says, touching the controls on her sleeve.

"We should head back in now that you have completed the repair," said Brian anxiously as he turned off his magnetic boots and started to float.

She suddenly says, "Yeah, I am the greatest."

"Nutzie, you ok?" asked Brian, wondering why she said that.

"Sure, I'm fine," Nutzie said with a slight slurring of her words.

"Nutzie, is something wrong?" Brian asked with concern.

Nutzie's body goes limp, and she starts drifting in the zero-G.

Over the radio, Brian thought he heard her whisper, "I didn't expect you to go this far, damn you ...."

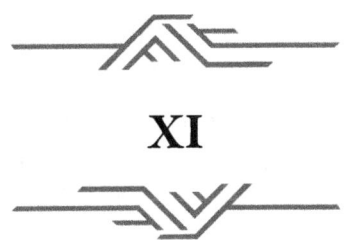

XI

Except for Rob, everyone on the ship was in the trapezoid-shaped room of the cargo bay airlock.

Val, Ralph, Fa, Lee, and the captain stood somberly in a circle around Nutzie's floating body and the doctor at the center of the room.

Zala was clutching Nutzie, weeping out loud.

Several medical devices and the doctor's medical kit floated around them.

Nutzie's spacesuit was loose on her body and partially pulled down as a result of the doctor's efforts to revive her.

Brian stood before the closed room's large hatch into space with Nutzie's work cart, Micuto floating beside him. He was still in his spacesuit, holding his and Nutzie's helmets.

The two sizeable closed cargo doors were angling in on both sides of Brian. Cargo hold 2 was on his right, and cargo hold 1 was on his left.

On the short wall opposite Brian was a row of lockers. Thatorn was sitting in his wheelchair near the starboard entrance, just in front of them, with Lieutenant Rocha at his left side.

"What happened?" Thatorn finally asked.

"Life support failure in her suit, it would seem," the lieutenant replied.

"A micrometeorite punctured her backpack?" Thatorn speculated.

Captain Linol walked over to Zala, touched her shoulder, and said, "You did everything you could, Zala."

The doctor let go of Nutzie's body, turned around, grabbed the captain, and wept aloud.

Brian said, holding back tears, "I'm sorry, Zala. I got to her as soon as I could. I tapped into her suit with O2 from my backpack while bringing her back. I thought bringing her back to this larger bay would make rendering aid easier."

Zala looked over at Brian, still crying, and said, "Don't blame yourself."

"You shouldn't blame yourself either," said Captain Linol, looking up at the doctor.

Zala leaned over and put her head on his shoulder. Clutching the captain, she started to weep.

Brian bent his head down and sighed.

Val walked over, grabbed Zala, and started to cry as well.

It was then that Brian noticed an unusual smell. He sniffed until he realized it was coming from Nutzie's helmet.

Letting go of his helmet to float in front of him. He raised up Nutzie's to look inside.

Carefully, he pulled up some of the lining inside. The smell became more noticeable now. He looked and felt around until he found the cause.

He began to feel funny. His chest felt all tied up in knots. He was convinced he could even hear his heart beating loudly in his chest.

He awoke from his daze and heard.

"What a terrible accident," said Ralph with remorse.

Brian took a long breath, stared at everyone, and said with conviction, "I don't believe it was."

B rian nervously stood in the circular hallway near Thatorn's office door on level 1. He gulped down the last of an energy bar he managed to grab from the mess on his way up and quickly stuffed its wrapper in a nearby waste chute.

He was surprised when the old man demanded to see him in his office at 13:00 hours. Especially after Thatorn ordered the doctor to do an autopsy on Nutzie right before telling everyone else to get some lunch and then return to their scheduled duties.

This would be the first time he would bear the full brunt of Thatorn alone.

Brian timidly walked up to the door and hit the door chime on the door control panel. Nothing happened. He waited for several seconds before hitting it again. Still, nothing happened. After waiting almost a minute, he was about to hit it again when the door suddenly opened.

Brian entered Thatorn's office, and the door closed silently behind him. It was not what he expected. The somewhat trapezoid-shaped room had warm, light yellow walls. Nothing like the drab gray of the rest of the ship.

The wall behind him, the entrance was part of, curved inwardly. On both sides of him, the walls angled outwardly. Halfway along the wall to his right was a door to the situation room. Another door was on the wall to the left, precisely opposite it. Brian assumed it led into Thatorn's personal quarters based on the ship's schematics. The far wall was part of the ship's hull and curved outwardly. In its center was a large bay window with a view into space.

Brian was proud of himself for having little reaction to the view.

At the center of the room were three black, overstuffed chairs. A large white desk was in front of them, towards the window. On the opposite side of the desk was Thatorn in his wheelchair. Behind him was an oversized black deck chair in the right corner. To Brian, it looked as if it was specially made just for his mechanical legs.

The old man still had not acknowledged that Brian was in the room. Instead, he worked at a computer console on the desk. Typing away on a physical keyboard and occasionally tapping on a physical display screen.

He's not using any holographic interfaces. Is it his way of keeping anyone in the room from knowing what he is doing? Or is it just a preference? Brian pondered.

Brian decided to sit down and strap into the center chair. He stared across the table at Thatorn, who continued to ignore him.

To his left, on top of the desk, Brian noticed a small transparent cylinder with a metal bottom stuck onto a magnetic plate. Leaning closer, he saw a lock of dark red hair inside the cylinder.

Suddenly, Thatorn snapped while looking down his nose at Brian, "You have gotten everyone all worked up without any real facts...."

Brian Interrupted, "Look, Thatorn, I know you don't think much of me, but being an engineer, I notice things, and in this case, I know what I'm talking about!"

Thatorn smacked his lips and ground his teeth before saying, "Unless we know for sure, we mustn't alarm the crew any more than they already are, Mr. Rush."

"I do see your point," Brian said with angst.

Calmly, Thatorn stated, "We know we have a saboteur on the ship. If Ms. Teodoresco's death was not an accident, we need to make damn sure before causing any more panic. That's why I ordered her autopsy. I also had Lieutenant Rocha seal Ms. Teodoresco's room and examine your allegations. We have to be careful, Mr. Rush."

Brian nodded in agreement.

"Because of your allegation, Mr. Milsom has openly refused to do any repairs, especially alone," explained Thatorn.

"Alert! Stand by for Engine Startup!" Captain Linol's loud voice announced over Thatorn's and Brian's C&PCs.

"Are we...," began Brian.

"Yes," interrupted Thatorn, then added, "When you came in, I was finishing my Jupiter orbit calculations and sending them to the Captain."

The ship shook slightly as the engines came to life. Brian slowly felt gravity return as the shaking calmed once the engine output stabilized. Brian could tell the force of gravity seemed higher this time.

"We must be at around a full G. Why the higher velocity?" Brian asked.

"You noticed that quickly enough," Thatorn said, squinting at the engineer.

"It could give us away," Brian remarked.

"True, but we need to accelerate our timetable and take the risk due to our situation," the old man stated.

"You should have let me check the hull repair before you fired the drives up," Brian grumbled.

"Ms. Teodoresco claimed her work would hold up," Thatorn asserted.

"She could have been suffering from apoxia at the time," Brian said, irritated.

Smugly, Thatorn replied, "Perhaps, but I ran the calculations to be sure. We will be fine."

Seeing Brian's frown, the old man added, "You are free to do any reinforcement you deem necessary."

Brian was about to get up when Thatorn snapped, "But it can wait. The array repair is paramount."

Thatorn leaned back in his chair in some discomfort and added, "That's assuming we can get Mr. Milsom to do the work."

Quietly, he rubbed his forehead, stared intensely at Brian, and inquired, "Do you know why I like living in space?"

Brian shook his head. Curious about where Thatorn was going.

"Controlled climate. No aches and pains from atmospheric pressure changes. Having higher than normal O2 levels and temperatures in my own room. It all makes me feel 20 years younger." Thatorn explained.

"And the comfort of zero-G," Brian added.

"What?" Thatorn mumbled.

Brian started to say, "Since you don't appear to have the use of your legs, I thought...."

The old man interrupted, "No! Zero-G may seem helpful under those conditions, but lose many benefits without gravity."

"I assumed with your wheelchair you could...," began Brian.

"Damn this thing!" Thatorn growled, interrupting as he looked down at his wheelchair. "You don't realize how humiliating this thing is. That's why I had my Exosuit created in the first place. It at least gives me some dignity as a man."

"I didn't realize," apologized Brian.

With a flick of the wheelchair's joystick, Thatorn spun around, faced the window, and stared out into space momentarily.

Finally, he said, "You know I was a great hero once. Right after my victory over the Pirates at the battle of Vesta, I was promoted to Captain. I was given a company of marines, which I led to glory on Mars. Of course, I had a lot to learn with the transition. Going from space combat to ground assault was challenging. The biggest thing was going from energy-based hand weapons to ballistic ones. Energy ones are safer on spacecraft since they are designed to only affect living things."

Thatorn stopped, took a deep breath, and said, "But I digress."

He continued, "Do you know how hard I worked to get anywhere! I was considered only a scientist early on in my career. I had to prove myself and my worth constantly. Finally, after many grueling years of effort, I was given a commander rank and my first ship, the Ares. It was an old, small combat frigate with a crew of seven. Armed only with two small particle cannons and only 4 missile launchers. But it was my ship. I lost two of my crew in the battle of Vesta. I ensured they were awarded medals of honor posthumously for their efforts to achieve a victory that day."

Thatorn turned around in his wheelchair and pulled it up to the desk on Brian's left side.

He smiled and said, "When I became a Captain, I realized how much more I had to prove to them. It took great resolve, but luckily, I quickly overcame any shortcomings. With a few glorious victories on the battlefield came corresponding raises in rank."

Thatorn's face soured when he said, "Until the end of the war."

Looking excitedly, he began, "However, only a few years later, I found out...."

He stopped, looked away, and said, "Let's just say things have changed."

He clenched his fists, stared wide-eyed at Brian, and added, "It's my destiny to be a great hero again!"

"But what's that got to do with Nutzie's death, and what's been happening on the ship?" asked Brian, staring curiously at the old man.

"You don't understand. This mission was laid out with great detail and planning. Nothing is going to get in my way!" Thatorn bellowed as he slammed both of his fists on the table.

The impact on the desk caused the transparent cylinder to fall over and off its magnetic plate. It started to roll away from Thatorn. Frantically, he tried to grab it, but it got out of his reach.

Brian quickly scooped it up before it fell off the desk.

Thatorn screamed, "Give me that!"

Brian quickly handed it to Thatorn. He was glassy-eyed as he held the cylinder and rubbed it against his cheek.

After doing it a few times, Thatorn gently placed it back on the magnetic plate and stared at it.

Brian was not sure what to do or even say.

Finally, Thatorn said, "You see, it was Cindy's. She and I were very close."

Still staring fondly at the lock of hair in the transparent cylinder, he continued, "We were stationed together on the research vessel Azophi over 40 years ago."

Thatorn looked around the room and said, "It was this ship. The one, the crew, has been calling the Black Swan. I had her pulled out of mothballs years ago to become my personal research vessel."

Thatorn grew suddenly quiet as he glared at the red lock of hair.

After a while, Brian grew impatient and asked, "So what happened?"

The old man wiped away a tear and said, "She died. On this ship, in fact. During one of the first Pirate attacks. It happened after an extended mission to Saturn, just as we entered Mars orbit."

"I'm sorry." Brian humbly said, now realizing that maybe Thatorn was human after all.

Thatorn wiped away another tear as he sat there looking at the lock of hair.

The more Brian thought about it, the more he became cynical. Could this mission be the latest in a never-ending quest to seek revenge?

Suddenly, the door chimed.

Thatorn reached over to his computer and activated the door.

The door opened. It was the lieutenant. Quickly, she stepped in, holding something in her left hand. She looked puzzled, seeing the state Thatorn was in.

"Am I interrupting anything?" she asked, worried.

Thatorn took a deep breath and composed himself. He looked sternly up at Lieutenant Rocha and announced, "No. Have you found anything yet?"

The lieutenant handed what she had in her left hand to Brian.

He recognized it right away as a chard circuit card.

"This is from the RRU console. Notice anything?" asked Lieutenant Rocha, staring at Brian.

After several seconds of going over the burnt card, Brian finally said, "It's a power control card."

Then he noticed something. He raised his right eyebrow and added, "Wait! There is a power regulator chip missing!"

Brian stopped, looked up at the lieutenant, then exclaimed, "You mean the RRU was running like this?"

"Yes. It allowed the system to work normally for a while before burning itself out along with the entire console," explained Lieutenant Rocha.

Brian looks at Thatorn and declares, "The RRU was definitely sabotaged!"

"I had Lee go over the system. I assumed his assessment was accurate. However, I decided to check into it myself, just to be sure," stated the lieutenant, staring smugly down at Brian.

"I guess it was a good thing you did," Brian said, looking back at the card.

"He obviously missed it," said the old man, frowning.

Looking up at Lieutenant Rocha, Thatorn asked, "Any security footage?"

She looked at the admiral and replied, "I'm looking into that next. However, if it was the work of our saboteur, I don't expect to find any."

"How much time would it have taken to do this?" Thatorn asked, looking at both the lieutenant and Brian.

Lieutenant Rocha replied, "Only minutes. All they would need was time to take out the card, pop out the chip, and return the card."

Still examining the burnt-out card, Brian said, "The power surge would have been extreme. More than enough to not only destroy the RRU but also kill the user."

The lieutenant said, looking at Brian, "That was my assessment. Fortunately, the Admiral's mechanical legs grounded off most of the charge."

Thatorn hastily asked, "Are you saying someone was trying to kill me?"

Brian bluntly stated, "No, they were after Nutzie. Remember, you took over the RRU from her."

XII

Brian stood between one end of the situation room's table and the small console in the room's corner. Lieutenant Rocha was standing to his right, and Thatorn was in his wheelchair right of her, just in front of the door to his office.

Brian looked to his right at the lieutenant and Thatorn. She was her usual emotionless ice cube self, waiting patiently in a rigged stance. While the old man appeared strange, with an uncharacteristic grin on his lips.

Brian looked down at the table before him to ensure the small gray box he had placed on the end of it earlier was still there.

Rob was sitting on the right side of the table in the chair closest to Brian. Since he was on duty, he had been staring at a hologram screen on his C&PC, checking the ship's flight status. Occasionally scratching at the stubble on his face.

Sitting next to Rob was Captain Linol, who looked puzzled as he focused on the entrance from the command deck.

Val was seated in the closest seat to Brian on the left at the table. She appeared to be bored while examining her nails.

Suddenly, it dawned on Brian that Val was not sitting beside Rob this time. He wondered if this could mean something, causing him to briefly smile.

Sitting next to Val was Ralph. He rubbed his unshaven face with his left hand while staring at the blank screen opposite him on the inner wall. Brian could see he was tired and had bags under his eyes.

Lee was in the last seat on this end of the table. He looked nervous and was constantly staring at the door to the command deck.

Brian wondered if Lee had taken that seat because he was late and just grabbed the closest one when he came in.

Glimpsing at the captain, Brian surmised that perhaps he and Lee were just waiting for the last two crew members to arrive.

Brian reached up to scratch his cheek and felt some rough growth on his face. He then realized Rob and Ralph also had not shaven in a while. Did they all prefer only using old-fashioned gravity-related means like himself?

Lee still had his short beard, but it was unclear if he had done anything to it. However, Thatorn was clean-shaven, and Captain Linol had a neatly kept goatee with no other facial hair.

Brian pondered. It must be a military thing since they are officers. Are they using one of those so-called zero-G electric razors with fancy attachments and vacuums to catch the whiskers?

Looking at the time on his C&PC, Thatorn smugly asked, "This meeting was scheduled to begin at 15:30, Mr. Rush. It is now 15:41. Why are we waiting?"

Brian knew better than to glance at his C&CP to confirm the time.

"I thought we were waiting on Fa and the doctor?" asked the captain, still staring at the entrance.

"Shouldn't they have already been here?" questioned Lee, looking over at Thatorn.

Looking around Lieutenant Rocha at Thatorn, Brian explains, "I'm sorry, but I am waiting on something important from Fa, sir. If you can just...."

Fa suddenly enters, interrupting Brian. She sits in the seat closest to the door on the right side of the table, opposite Lee. She looks up at Brian and nods her head.

Using his C&PC, Brian brings up a holographic 2D screen with a tap and reads it to himself.

"Mr. Rush, I gave you and the Lieutenant the task of looking into Ms. Teodoresco's death over 2 hours ago. We were to review your preliminary findings at this meeting."

"Ah, yes, sir, just bear with me for a second," Brian said while reading from the screen before him.

After several seconds, Brian deactivates his C&PC and says, "Ok. I got it."

Brian opens the small box before him, takes out a tiny melted bit of metal, and holds it up. Everyone except Rob looks at his hand.

"What's that?" asked Ralph, squinting to see what Brian held.

"I recovered this a little while ago from Nutzie's helmet. It is all that was left of its VOC," replied Brian.

"VOC?" inquired Lee, causing everyone, even Rob, to stare at Brian.

"Sorry, it's the variable oxygen regulator," explained Brian, surprised a tech didn't already know.

"She died because that failed?" questioned Captain Linol.

"So it was an accident?" asked Rob.

"No. It's not that simple. This was intentionally rigged to slowly cut off Nutzies O2," elaborated Brian.

Everyone at the table was shocked.

Thatorn moved his chair a little forward to get a better view of Brian. Looking at him, he calmly stated, "So you were right, Mr Rush. It wasn't a malfunction."

The lieutenant stared at Brian and coldly added, "It is consistent with other evidence. The Doctor finished her autopsy about an hour ago and confirmed she died from hypoxia."

Val suggested, "Being a long-time EVA expert. I can't believe she could have missed that someone had tampered with her suit."

Rob put his C&PC flight info into an alert-only mode, deactivated the holographic screen, and then looked at Brian and asked, "Why didn't her suit's Co2 warning system alert her?"

"Based on my suspicions, I had Fa look into some of the suit systems. That's why she was late. She relayed her findings moments ago to my C&PC and confirmed that her suit was...." Brian stopped and hesitated.

"What?" asked the captain.

"Reprogrammed," Brian said softly.

"Huh?" muttered Ralph, baffled.

Everyone else at the table just stared at Brian.

"How?" curiously inquired Rob.

"A virus was planted in the suit's computer operation system," Fa replied, looking at the ship's co-pilot.

"So, exactly what did this virus do?" Captain Linol questioned as he and the rest of the crew turned their attention to Fa.

Fa looked at the captain and explained, "It was sneaky. It reprogrammed part of Nutzie's PLSS. Um...., primary life support system. Preventing the Co2 warning system from alerting her while slowly resetting the VOC regulator to continue lowering itself."

"Then what caused the VOC to melt?" inquired Rob.

"That's the odd part. The person who created the virus didn't program the VOC to stop adjusting. It continued to do so, causing it to finally burn itself out. They seemed to make no effort to hide the virus or even what it did," answered Fa.

"Maybe they were in a hurry?" asked Ralph.

Fa looked at Ralph and replied, "Possibly, but anyone with that skill could have easily added the additional instructions needed."

"But they didn't?" Thatorn asked, squinting at Fa.

"No, sir," she replied, staring at the old man.

"So, where did this virus come from?" asked Val with raised eyebrows.

"A skilled programmer with the right software could have created it," Fa replied while looking at Val.

"Someone like yourself?" inquired Ralph, glaring at Fa.

"Ralph has a point," interjects Lee as he glimpses at Ralph but returns his gaze back to Fa.

Fa replies with only a scowl at Ralph, then Lee.

Rob starts to say, "Maybe we can check the computer system...."

Fa interrupted, "When I realized a virus was the cause, I quickly checked the logs of all the ship terminals. I couldn't find evidence of anyone using them to make such a thing."

Thatorn quietly looks up at Lieutenant Rocha.

She quickly notices him, stares back, and says, "I will make sure, Admiral."

Fa sneers upon hearing this.

"Couldn't a skilled I.T. person have covered their tracks?" implied Ralph.

Thatorn sighed and addressed the crew, "Based on what we know. I suspect they had a device for this, probably something like our C&PCs. They likely already had coded viruses ready to go that only needed some adjustments to accomplish specific tasks."

They all stared at him and considered what he said.

Rob then skeptically inquired, "So, another spy gadget?"

"Smuggled on board with the jammer?" Fa said with sarcasm.

"A device like this could be smaller than our own C&PCs. Probably not much bigger than a standard data strip. Which would make it much easier to smuggle onboard," Thatorn explained.

"Let's assume that's the case. Just how did someone get this virus downloaded into Nutzie's suit?" Val asked, tapping the table with the index finger of her left hand.

"We can check the suit for evidence, and...," started Captain Linol but stopped talking, seeing the lieutenant shaking her head.

Everyone stared at Lieutenant Rocha as she coldly stated, "No physical evidence has been found so far. However, I will take more time to examine the suit further."

"DNA?" softly whispered Ralph.

"Maybe we all did it," Rob suggested sarcastically.

Giving Rob a cold stare, the lieutenant answered, "After the autopsy, the doctor did a preliminary check. She only found her own DNA in Nutzie's suit since she tried to revive her and Brian's on the outside of the helmet because he helped her with it right before the EVA. Nutzie's DNA was all that was found inside the helmet. Brian still had his gloves on when he initially examined it, and he used latex gloves when he studied it further and found the damaged VOC."

"Then just how could they have downloaded the virus into her suit?" asked Ralph.

Fa replied, looking at Ralph, "More than likely via a wireless access link. Just about everything on the ship has one. They would only need to be near it."

"I thought links like that had access restrictions and firewalls," asked Val as she and the rest of the crew stared at Fa.

Fa explained, "We are dealing with someone who used a reprogramming virus. I'm sure they knew how to get past those. They would only need to have programmed their device to look for the wireless connection they wanted, hack in, and then download the virus."

Squinting at Fa, Ralph inquired, "Wouldn't the suit have to be on for that?"

"An inactive system like the suits could be remotely turned on with the proper commands," Lieutenant Rocha coldly stated.

"Just to download a virus?" asked Val as everyone looked at the lieutenant.

"Yes, and even turn it back off once the virus was installed," Lieutenant Rocha added, looking down her nose at Val, emotionless.

"Wow!" replied Val, wide-eyed.

"The poor thing had no idea about the danger she was in until it was too late," Thatorn stated, shaking his head.

The crew stared at the old man somberly.

Rob spoke up, "Let me get this straight. The saboteur who blew up the communications room let Nutzie fix the room so we could repair the antenna array before they killed her? Why?"

The crew stared at Rob, giving him odd expressions as they pondered over his question. While Thatorn and the lieutenant glimpsed at each other before staring at Rob.

"That is a good point," The captain said.

"Maybe they planned on making sure she was out there a little while first, then just got the timing wrong?" suggested Fa.

"Unless they took her having a spotter into account. Got her as close to death as possible before she or Brian realized it and could effectively respond," Lee proposed, looking at Brian.

Once everyone looked at Brian, he said, "Maybe. The emergency procedure calls for the person rendering aid to connect their O2 supply to the backpack of the one having trouble. Unknown to me, the VOC was cut back, so putting more O2 into her suit was useless."

"We are assuming the saboteur is also the murderer, right?" Rob blurted out.

Everyone focused their attention on Rob.

"The MO is off. Use explosives, then kill someone by rigging their spacesuit," replied Captain Linol.

"Maybe the explosives they still had were not usable?" softly asked Ralph, staring at the captain.

Captain Linol shrugged his shoulders in response.

"When could they have loaded this virus into her suit?" questioned Val, looking at everyone in the room.

Brian replied, "Well, let's see."

Everyone turned their attention to Brian except for the captain.

Brian noticed him staring at the entrance again and assumed he must still be looking for the doctor. Brian wondered where she was as well.

"And?" inquired Val.

Brian then focused on those at the table and elaborated, "Nutzie told me she did the precheck on her and my suit around 6 am. If the virus had been in the suit before then, she would have noticed something during her system check. She told me it took her less than an hour to do. If we add a little time for her to leave the control room. So it must have been a little after 7 am and shortly before 9 am when Nutzie and I got to the RRU control room."

They all then stared at Lieutenant Rocha.

After returning their stare, she responded, "I recently discovered security jamming around that time and an additional one before that."

Several of the crew let out noticeable grunts and grumbles.

The lieutenant raises her left arm and activates her C&PC. She brings up a data screen. After looking it over, she states, "It was between 8:05 and 8:11." She then abruptly turns off her C&PC and lowers her arm.

"Since the saboteur also used a jammer, it would appear the murderer and saboteur must be the same person," stated Ralph with a somewhat timid conviction.

Rob grimly declares, "It seems so," as he activates his C&PC to review the current flight data.

"Or it was just a ruse to cover for when they actually did it. Brian was with Nutzie right before the EVA. He could have planted the virus," insinuated Captain Linol, staring at Brian.

All but Fa and Rob started looking at Brian.

Staring at the captain, Fa began to say, "You are assuming he has the programming skills to...."

Glaring at Fa, Captain Linol interrupted, "No, but he could have had help from someone who does."

"What possible motivation would Fa and I have?" Brian insisted, looking at the captain.

"Yes, what?" Captain Linol asked, staring at Brian.

"These crazy implications aren't going to get us anywhere," snapped Brian.

Rob quickly deactivated his C&PC, looked at the captain, and asserted, "That's right. We need to focus on the facts at hand?"

Glancing at Rob, Captain Linol grumbled, "Very well then."

The captain stared at Lieutenant Rocha and asked, "Since you recently looked over the security data, was there anything in there before and after that might give anyone away?"

Looking back at Captain Linol, the lieutenant answered, "No, based on everyone's schedule, they were where they should have been before and after the jamming."

"Just like the other times," moaned Ralph.

Staring at Lieutenant Rocha, Fa asks, "You said there were 2 jammings. What about the other one."

Everyone then focused their attention back on the lieutenant.

She then brought up her right arm and activated her C&PC. After reviewing some data screens, she said, "The other jamming happened before the RRUs burnout on the 5th between 9:04 and 9:10."

The crew was immediately surprised by the news.

"Really?" asked Val.

"Then that was sabotage as well!" Rob snapped.

"I thought Lee said it was a malfunction!" Ralph shouted as he turned to glare at Mr. Smith.

They all looked at Lee suspiciously.

"As far as I could tell, it was," Lee said, staring back at them.

Looking at Thatorn, Lee explained, "I laid out all my findings for you in the report you requested."

The old man replied with a sneer, "Yes, and as I recall, you had no conclusions of the exact cause and that it is beyond repair with what was available on the ship."

Lee grunted, defending himself, "I simply didn't catch that a processor was missing on the power relay. What do you expect? It was a melted mess."

Gazing at Thatorn, Val said, "Maybe I can take a look at it."

Lieutenant Rocha stared at Val and firmly stated, "No, that will not be necessary, Mrs. Elderman. You already have a full schedule of critical tasks."

Fa said, looking at the lieutenant, "When I still had access to the security system on the 5th, I didn't notice any jamming."

Looking at Fa coldly, Lieutenant Rocha replied, "It's probably because you were still focused on the time before the Communication Tower's sabotage."

"Hum," Fa mumbled.

Just then, it dawned on Brian that Rocha didn't give them the exact minutes and seconds about these latest jams like she had with the others. Could she believe there is no point in doing so now?

"Still, they took a big risk, didn't they. The sabotage was done right before you two were there." Rob said, staring at Thatorn and the lieutenant.

Also staring at them, Ralph inquired, "You didn't see anyone, did you?"

"No, we were busy getting Mr. Rush and Ms. Teodoresco's tools out of cargo hold 2," responded Thatorn dryly.

"It would have only required a few minutes to accomplish anyway. More than enough time for anyone to slip in and out without our knowing," added Lieutenant Rocha.

"Tell them the rest of it," insisted Brian, staring at the lieutenant.

214

Those at the table then focused their attention on Lieutenant Rocha.

After taking a slow breath, she stated, "Evidence also suggests it was not just sabotage but an attempt on someone's life."

"The Admirals!" exclaimed Ralph.

"Nutzie was originally going to run the RRU, but I stepped in," Thatorn replied.

The crew at the table stared at each other in silence.

"So someone had been after Nutzie all along!?" asked Fa.

"Why?" asked Ralph.

"Wait. Are you saying that the person who sabotaged the ship was just out to get Nutzie?" inquired the captain.

"Was this all just some elaborate plan to kill her?" Fa speculated.

"This is not making any sense," said Captain Linol, tugging his beard.

"Maybe she did know something she shouldn't have," Lee calmly stated.

"And could have been seen as a threat to someone," Fa added.

"That's possible," said Lee in response.

"They tried to make an attempt on her life look like an accident the first time, but not this time. Why?" The captain wondered aloud.

Ralph nervously said, "Perhaps they wanted to ensure her death this time."

"Seems sloppy to me," Captain Linol grumbled, still tugging at his beard.

Fa declared, "Since we figured out the first sabotage was not an accident. Maybe they figured we would eventually discover the second and decided not to hide anything this time."

"What if they intentionally wanted us to know just to frighten us," Rob said, looking around the room at everyone to gauge their reaction.

Staring at Rob, Fa asked, "For what reason?"

Returning the look, he replied, "I'm not sure."

Glaring at them all, Thatorn insisted, "The sooner we can find them, the better it will be for the rest of us."

Brian watched everyone get quiet. Those around the table only glanced back and forth at each other with apprehension. Ralph's face grew even gloomier. On the other hand, the lieutenant was stoic as she looked around at the crew. Thatorn went back to having that odd grin on his face again.

"Was there any evidence found regarding the RRU tampering?" asked the captain, breaking the silence.

Staring at Captain Linol, Lieutenant Rocha coolly replied, "The system's interior was burnt out completely, leaving no evidence. The outside of the access panel also revealed nothing. As we suspected from previous actions, the perpetrator probably used gloves. There was no DNA either. The electrical discharge saw to that."

"Did you check into Nutzies ship communications? Maybe a clue could be found there?" Brian inquired.

The lieutenant looked at Brian oddly and said, "No. Not yet. All related digital data regarding Ms. Teodoresco still needs to be gathered for review."

In a soft whisper, Ralph asked, "Are those being recorded too?"

Frowning, Rob stated, "We're not getting anywhere."

Everyone got quiet again and started glancing at each other with suspicion.

After a short while, the old man finally spoke up. He said with a giggle, "We are definitely dealing with a very clever Pirate Spy."

Everyone in the room turned their attention to Thatorn.

That was when he added, "I must admit I've been having difficulty seeing any pattern in who is behind this based on the actions on the 2nd. In the process, something has been nagging me about the original sabotage for a while now."

The crew replied with concerned stares.

He continued, "Granted, Nutzie's murder has added some complications, but...."

He stopped.

"What?" implored Ralph.

"It has been suggested this all was just part of a plan to kill Nutzie. What if killing Nutzie was only a secondary action for reasons unknown to us at the moment. It was assumed the saboteur was only out to prevent us from reporting what we might discover. Could they have had a different motive all along? Think about it. They have not made any attempt to stop us from going to Jupiter. Why?" Thatorn asked, glancing around at the faces of his crew.

I never thought of it that way, thought Brian.

Everyone looked briefly at each other and then at the old man.

"What do you think, sir?" inquired the captain.

With a twinkle in his eye, the old man elaborated, "Even though they had explosives, they could have used them to blow up the ship and stop us."

"And kill themselves in the process," exclaimed Ralph with a squeamish look.

Thatorn looked at Ralph and calmly stated, "If they are who I think they are, why not? A good spy would gladly give their life for their cause. They could have done it in a way that would make it look like an accident to cover up the truth. Keeping the involvement of the Pirates a secret."

"Ok, so what are they after?" asked Fa gruffly.

The old man looked at Fa and coldly replied, "Perhaps someone on board the ship or even the ship itself?"

An uneasy quiet fell on everyone as they stared at each other to consider that possibility.

A somber Doctor Teka slowly entered the room. She stopped and stood by the entrance near the end of the table, taken aback by the dreariness on everyone's faces around the table.

Brian could tell she had been crying. Her eyes were bloodshot, and they had red circles around them. It must have been tough for her to do an autopsy on someone so close, but she was the only one on the ship who could. Brian was also sure she probably wouldn't have let anyone else do it, even if there was.

"What's going on?" she asked with a sniffle.

Captain Linol bolted up, walked up to her, and hugged her. Sadly, he told her, "We are now sure that Nutzie's death was not an accident."

Zala looked down at the captain in pain and exclaimed, "You mean someone killed her!"

She let out a loud scream and leaned on Captain Linol. He held her tightly and tried to comfort her.

She rose up, looked around the room, and demanded, "Who did it. Which one of you killed my Nutzie!"

Everyone in the room looked back at her with sorrow.

The captain said, "We don't know. We've been trying to determine that."

Zala looked down at Captain Linol, broke away from him, and snapped, "You, it was you. You never liked her. You were afraid she would eventually take me away from you."

"That's not true," said the captain with a painful grimace, shaking his head.

Brian noticed that the old man leaned forward in his seat and watched the doctor intensely.

Zala cried, "You just wanted to make sure I would still be sucking your cock and fucking you. I knew you were jealous of her, but to kill her!"

Captain Linol walked up to her and tried to embrace her again. She resisted violently, walked around the table, and sat in the empty chair beside Ralph. Then collapsed on the table, weeping.

Ralph looked at her and was not sure what to do. He raised his hand and hesitated if he should place it on her shoulder in an attempt to comfort her.

Val jumped up and took the empty seat between Zala and Lee. She put her right arm around her and softly whispered to her.

Ralph seemed relieved and put his hand back down.

Brian couldn't hear what she was saying, but it seemed to be helping. Zala rose off the table and into Val's arms.

Val hugged and patted her while slightly rocking, still whispering to her.

The captain was dumbfounded. He slowly crept back to his seat and sat down, staring with concern at the doctor the whole time.

The doctor's cries faded. Val let go of her, and she sat up in her seat. Looking at Val, she softly said, "Thank you."

Zala looked around the room at everyone, then with a sniffle, she stated. "I just spent the worst time in my life confirming what killed my...,"

She paused.

After wiping away a tear, she added, "Nutzie."

Several stared at her with sympathy.

Brian saw the old man lean back in his wheelchair, acting indifferent.

"Now I come to find that someone here killed her!" She exclaimed, smacking her hands on the table and glaring at Captain Linol.

The captain shook his head, gazing back at her.

She took a deep breath, looked around at the crew, and asked, "So how was it done?"

Those at the table looked at Brian. Once Zala noticed, she also looked at him.

Brian licked his lips and explained, "Someone planted a virus in her suit. We believe they did it remotely while near the suit. There was a jamming between 8:05 and 8:11 today. We suspect it was used to cover the planting of the virus. The virus was designed to lower her variable oxygen regulator and burn itself out. We're still not sure exactly how the virus was activated."

Fa looked at Zala and added, "It looks like whoever did it didn't try to cover their tracks. It was easy for us to discover that a virus was used."

"Since a jammer was used in the murder and sabotage. It is believed the same person is responsible for both," Lieutenant Rocha stated, staring at the doctor.

Zala glared at Captain Linol and said, "So someone with technical abilities probably did it."

Thatorn rolled up closer to the table near Rob.

Everyone noticed and stared at him.

Looking at Zala, he calmly said, "Look, Doctor Teka, I realize you have been under a great deal of emotion and stress in the last few hours. But we need you if we are going to get to the bottom of this. You need to focus right now. "

Zala nodded at Thatorn while trying to compose herself.

Looking around the room at his crew, Thatorn explained, "Immediately after the autopsy and DNA testing on Mrs. Teodoresco's suit. I had the Doctor finish work on a second DNA test of fresh samples from cargo hold number 1's sub-cargo area."

So that was why she was late for this meeting, thought Brian.

While staring at the doctor in a disappointed tone, Thatorn stated, "Gathering from your reaction to the news of Mrs. Teodoresco's murder and that you only leveled an accusation against the Captain. I assume the new DNA testing did not pin down who the saboteur was?"

Zala calmly answered, "That is true, sir, But...."

"Go on," insisted Thatorn as he looked away and stared at the ceiling while everyone else stared at the doctor.

The doctor stated, "I cross-checked all the DNA found with the U.E.A. database."

She stopped.

After glancing around at the crew, she added, "An unknown DNA was discovered in the new samples."

Thatorn and the lieutenant only coldly glanced at each other. While everyone else other than the doctor was noticeably stunned by the news.

The doctor then elaborated, "The only thing I can tell so far about the DNA is that it's from a female. I checked it with the female crew's DNA on the ship and at the military base several times just to make sure. There was no match."

"That DNA is probably just a fluke. One of the U.E.A. loading crew could have carried it in." Thatorn growled dismissively, staring at the doctor.

With a scowl, Zala questions, "From where? According to the records, that base has a six-month rotation and is well into its fifth now. It's unlikely anyone could have been carrying around any viable DNA from outside the base for that long."

The crew curiously stares at the old man, but Rob frowns and looks at the table.

"Could there be a stowaway on board?" Lee meekly asks.

"No one could ever get on my ship without my knowledge," snapped Thatorn, glaring at Lee.

"Like the jammer and that spy virus device?" Fa asked mockingly.

"Nonsense, a stowaway would have been spotted either by one of us or alerted through surveillance at some point. Besides, without a

C&PC and an active computer schedule, they would not have access through the ship," Lieutenant Rocha insisted.

"Until they used the jammer," coldly stated the captain as he glanced at the lieutenant.

Staring at Lieutenant Rocha, Brian said, "You even told us there were blind spots in the surveillance system."

The lieutenant only glared back at Brian in reply.

Zala spoke up, "We know if it was one of us, we could have collected everyone's DNA since we had access to each other. So how could a stowaway have gotten everyone's DNA?"

Everyone looked at each other as they considered what the doctor said.

Val looked at Thatorn and softly said, "I didn't bring this up before because I thought I might have been paranoid, but now I'm not so sure. I think my room was gone through just before we left for Jupiter."

Staring at Val, Ralph said, "Maybe it was the stowaway, and that's how they got the DNA."

"They would have had to get it before they got the explosives, built the bomb, and planted it," Brian contemplated, rubbing the stubbles on his chin with his right hand and looking at the floor.

Everyone looked at Brian.

"What? With the first jamming of two minutes that we assumed was just a test?" inquired Val.

Still eyeing the floor, Brian stated, "Right, that's not enough time to collect DNA from everyone's room. And there were no other unaccounted-for jamming times before that."

The doctor said, "Even at zero-G. It would have taken longer than the longest jamming time on that day to have gathered everyone's DNA in that manner."

"This is still assuming we have accurately determined what was done during the jamming times on the 2nd," Rob said, glancing up at Brian as the rest of the crew stared at him.

Fa started to say, "What about...."

Thatorn bellowed, interrupting, "Enough! A stowaway is just foolish speculation at best right now. Until we have more evidence, I suggest we focus on finding the spy."

The old man's sudden outburst startled the crew.

Thatorn glowered at his crew as they looked back at him silently.

Staring at Ralph, the old man asked, "I believe working in gravity best suits you, Mr. Milson?"

Ralph timidly replied, "Well, yeah I...."

Thatorn then snaps, "Good, I need you to get that antenna array up and running ASAP!"

In terror, Ralph shouts, "Oh Hell No! I not going to let them kill me too!"

The old man calmly said, "Don't worry. I will have everyone on the command deck when you do your work."

"A whole lot of fucking good that did, Nutzie!" Ralph snapped back.

Lieutenant Rocha dryly said, "Mr. Milson, I will scan the wing and communications room for anything before you enter."

"Oh, No. We need to turn this ship around and let authorities deal with it! You can just lock us up in our rooms to keep us safe. Use those mag locks if you have to," Ralph shouted.

Looking at Thatorn, Rob started to say, "He has a point. Most of us are just civilians working contracts we aren't ...."

The admiral coldly interrupted, "Not according to your contacts. If you read the fine print, you will see that during the mission, you are to follow the orders of the mission commander at all times, including in times of crisis."

"You can't hold us to that!" Ralph yelled.

223

Thatorn barked back at Ralph, "Oh, but I will, Mr. Milsom, and if you violate your contract, I will see that you won't be able to find a job anywhere. Even to clean up shit on a pig farm!"

"If we survive, you mean," spoke up Fa, who immediately got a piercing look from the old man.

Realizing he was wasting his time, Ralph let out a long, angry growl, conceded through clenched teeth, and said, "Fine, but I want to have someone with me."

"Who?" asked Thatorn curiously while squinting at the bald man.

"Brian," he replied.

Brian stared at Ralph, surprised.

"When can you get started?" inquired Thatorn in a calmer tone.

Brian stared at the old man, confused.

"Give me an hour to gather up my tools and anything else I'm going to need from my room," Ralph said grudgingly.

Brian began to say, "Wait, don't I...."

Thatorn sneered at Brian and declared, "No. No, you don't, Mr. Rush."

After looking at the time on his C&PC, Thatorn grunted, "Now that's settled, I will schedule the repair start time at the top of the next hour at 17:00. Everyone else is to meet on the command deck by that time."

At least I should have enough time for a quick hot shower, thought Brian.

Val spoke up, blinking at Thatorn, and said, "Brian, the Doctor, and I were supposed to be scheduled sometime today to review your Exosuit?"

Looking at Val with frustration, Thatorn said, "That can't be helped. Mr. Rush has to assist with the antenna repair. It has priority right now. As important as the suit is, that task must be rescheduled."

"What are we going to do about dinner?" Lee asked.

After glancing at Lee, Thatorn said, "Yes, we are in that time now. I'll have some energy bars made available on the command deck. I suggest Mr. Rush and Mr. Milsom get some before starting the job."

Brian pondered. I can't believe I will miss having that warm goo of a meal tonight.

"So now what? We still don't know who did it, why, or even if they have more in store for us," Captain Linol stated.

"We are, as they say, back at square one!" Fa announced.

The tension was thick in the room. Everyone glumly looked at each other while Thatorn and the lieutenant watched them.

"What can we do?" Rob asked softly.

"We need to take precautions," the captain stated.

"We can't rely on electronic security," Fa spoke up.

"Maybe we should consider pairing up during working hours so someone is always watching someone else?" asked Brian.

"No!" snapped Thatorn.

Then, in a calmer tone, he added, "That's not practical for several reasons. Most importantly, it would tie up too many personnel, and the work schedule is too tight as it is."

"What about keeping an eye on the live feed? It could alert us of the jamming," Ralph optimistically suggested, glancing around the crew.

"If I was given back my security access, maybe I could help with that," Fa said, looking at Lieutenant Rocha.

The lieutenant dryly replied, "No, Ms. Ming. I'd much rather you focus on the ship's computer and its security."

"How does keeping an eye on the security feed help us anyway?" asked Brian, looking around at everyone.

"Whoever is watching it could alert the crew," Ralph replied.

"If the comms are down by that point? Running around to warn everyone would take too long." Brian said, staring at Ralph oddly.

"Oh yeah, I forgot," Ralph said humbly.

Zala stated, glancing around at the crew, "Don't you see. Wouldn't it be an obvious dead giveaway when they use the jammer that they are up to something?"

Everyone focused their attention on the doctor.

"Your point?" Lee asked.

Glaring at Lee, Zala elaborated, "If they are one of us, they will know exactly whatever plan we come up with to stop them."

"Yes, I see. They would be able to adjust their strategy and stay ahead of us," Lee replied, patting his right hand on his short, stubby beard.

"Even if we had a warning system to tell when the jammer is being used to alert the crew. It wouldn't necessarily mean they were actually doing anything at that time," explained Zala.

Val asked, "What are you saying?"

"It wouldn't do us any good. They could just turn it on to scare us, throw us off if we know when they are jamming us at any given moment," Zala elaborated.

"Have us running around the ship like stuck pigs. Then strike during any of those jamming times," Lee grumbled with a frown.

Brian gloomily said, "We are not even sure if they don't have any other surprises set up from the 2nd. Maybe even one using the leftover explosives."

All eyes fell on Brian. Zala and Ralph were noticeably disturbed by what Brian said.

Looking around the crew, Captain Linol said, "We need practical ways to deal with this."

Thatorn let out a cough. All eyes in the room were on him instantly. He said, "The Lieutenant and I have been working on a few new procedures to deal with the situation."

Looking up at her, he says, "If you please, Lieutenant."

All but Thatorn then stared intensely at Lieutenant Rocha.

"Everyone will have a strict schedule, including breaks and meal times," she stated.

"Even Bathroom times?" Rob asked sarcastically.

After giving Rob a smirk, the lieutenant continued, "I think it would be best to restrict those times when you are in your cabin. Otherwise, log those times. If anything happens again, everyone must be able to account for their whereabouts at all times. Everyone is to remain in their cabins when off duty. I will be randomly spot-checking the crew on and off duty."

"Good," the captain remarked.

"That should throw them off," Ralph said, nodding.

Brian felt some relief with these measures but was not sure if they would be enough.

"What about socializing?" asked the Captian, glancing at the doctor, who angrily rolled her eyes at him.

With a smirk, Thatorn replied, "If you feel the need, make sure to contact Rocha and give her the details and the times, and when you do, stay only on the cabin levels 7, 8, and 9."

After clearing his throat, he barked, "This ship must remain operational and carry out Its mission at all costs! Is that clear!"

Everyone looked at the old man and replied, "Yes, sir," with little enthusiasm.

Like himself, Brian was sure the crew was feeling distressed about the circumstances they were all facing. Not knowing who in the room was friend or foe.

While still looking at the Thatorn, Lieutenant Rocha began to say, "In the meantime, I could look into other possible detection options. Maybe I can...."

Thatorn interrupted, looking up at her, insisting, "Wait, as the Doctor has pointed out. Giving away details here would only inform the spy. For now, Lieutenant, keep them to yourself."

"Yes, Admiral," she replied.

Looking back at the crew, Thatorn stated, "There is one other thing."

Glancing at Rob and Brian, he added, "Rob, Brian, I will have you scheduled to work on the hopper sometime tomorrow."

They looked at each other and then back at the old man curiously.

Rob spoke up, "I'm already doing a 12-hour shift."

"The Captain will cover for you during that time," Thatorn quickly said.

Causing Captain Linol to grimace.

"I have a few changes for the hopper. We need to make it a little more automatic." The old man added.

Rob asks, "Why?"

Thatorn replied, "So it will be easier for anyone to fly if we need to abandon the ship, and no pilots are still alive."

XIII

B rian moaned loudly as he ejaculated onto the shower floor as the warm water from the shower head ran down his body.

He stood there briefly, panting softly before turning off the water. He slid open the shower door and stepped into his small rectangular bathroom in a puff of steam.

Looking back into the tiny triangle-shaped shower, he checked to see that everything had washed down the drain.

Once satisfied, he took a small step to the left of the shower and stood in front of a mirror over a small sink. He glanced at his wet self before looking down to his right at a white towel on the closed toilet seat. He grabbed it and quickly dried himself, making sure his C&PC and his wrist underneath its strap were dry.

Staring back at himself in the mirror, he thinks. I needed that, plus it released some tension as well.

After letting out a relaxed sigh, he thought. So glad to have gravity again. Masturbating in zero-G can get rather messy. It's much more stimulating and cleaner to do in a shower.

Placing the towel on the sink, Brian looked in the mirror. He wanted to make sure he had removed all his facial hair when he shaved just before getting into the shower.

The jumpsuit he had just taken off was on the back of the toilet. He grabbed it and was about to put it back on, then noticed an odor. He held it close to his nose, sniffed it, and reacted with a sour look.

Brian thought, Even though these high-tech jumpsuits are resistant to stains and have special micro self-sterilizing fibers, they still require an occasional wash. I'll add it to some other things I've got to clean when I take a trip to the laundry room.

Beside the sink was a half-full laundry bag velcroed to the wall and floor. Leaning over, Brian opened the bag's velcroed flap, jammed the jumpsuit inside, and velcroed the flap closed.

Brian walked over to the closet door on the opposite wall of the sink and opened it. After rummaging through a few drawers, he finds his last unused clean jumpsuit still neatly folded in a bag.

A soft chime emanates from Brian's C&PC. Quickly, he looks at the time.

Brian exclaims, "Crap, I only got 10 minutes before the repair time, and I still have to meet up with Ralph at his cabin and get to the communications room."

Frantically, he pulls the jumpsuit from the bag and puts it on, saying, "I wonder, is Ralph paranoid, or am I not being enough of one?"

Brian swiftly made his way to level 9 to meet Ralph at his quarters. He didn't know where Ralph's quarters were until he got the information this morning from an updated schedule over his C&PC. It was on the lower port side, just like Brian's room two decks above.

When Brian looked up the layout data on the cabin levels, he noticed it was minimal. It only revealed that Ralph's room had two windows and was slightly larger than Brian's since that level had no docking ports to take up space.

Brian assumed the secrecy of who had what cabin was done to maintain some privacy. If anyone wanted you to know which cabin was theirs, they could just tell you.

Brian smiled, thinking. Like Val did when she asked me to play games with her.

He then frowned, remembering. It might have turned into something even better if not for the old man.

Brian arrived at Ralph's door and rang the doorbell. To his surprise, Ralph contacted him over his C&PC. Only after having a detailed conversation to confirm that Brian was, in fact, in the hall did Ralph finally open his door.

Ralph popped out of his room so fast Brian didn't even get a peek inside. Ralph was holding two toolboxes and immediately handed the heaviest one to Brian.

Brian saw that Ralph was shaven, wearing a clean uniform, and smelled of aftershave.

Seeing this, Brian thought. It's been since the morning of the 5th that we've had gravity. I wonder if Ralph exaggerated the time he needed to prepare just so he could clean up, maybe even use the toilet without vacuum hoses? That's fine by me since I was able to take advantage of it myself. With our meeting and the work schedule, I bet nobody else has been able to yet.

Based on the Admiral's suggestion, they went down to level 10 only after going up to level 4 to pick up some energy bars.

Once on the wing level, they walked down the corridor towards the lower wing. Ralph nervously followed closely behind, finishing up one of his bars. After not finding a nearby disposal trash chute, he just jammed the wrapper into his right pocket.

They entered the wing section just past the first open bulkhead door. Brian stopped, causing Ralph to do as well. The power control consoles were now on both sides of them. Brian looked briefly at them before looking down the long hall before him. It was partially lit by the light from the hall behind them and a few battery emergency lights along the hall. The communications room at the end was barely illuminated by those backup lights that survived the explosion.

"It's dark down there," said Ralph, looking around Brian.

Brian replied, "Yeah. I manually shut off all the power to that section so we wouldn't have any issues. When the bypass is set up, I'll power it up with any needed related circuits."

"I brought a couple of battery-powered illuminators in my box with magnets we can put on the walls. I also have my headlamp," Ralph explained.

"I got mine in my pocket," stated Brian.

Ralph asks, "What time is it?"

With a quick glance at his C&PC, Brian replied, "16:58 hours. Everyone should be on the command deck by now."

"Call in and check," insisted Ralph.

Before Brian could reply, a soft clank interrupted him from the dark end of the wing hallway.

They both froze and stared down into the darkness.

Ralph whispered softly. "What was that?"

"I don't know," replied Brian softly.

Brian slowly started to walk toward the end of the hall and stopped when Ralph grabbed him.

Ralph quietly exclaimed, "What the hell are you doing!"

"Seeing what caused that noise," Brian replied in a hushed voice.

"Let's call it in," whispered Ralph.

"If it's the saboteur, they probably have the comms jammed anyway," softly stated Brian.

"I don't want to end up like Nutzie. Let's leave!" Ralph franticly demanded in as quiet a voice as he could.

Brian looked back at Ralph and said, "No, I want to know who is behind all this! You can leave if you want, but we would have a better chance of catching them together."

With a gulp, Ralph looked at Brian nervously, then reluctantly nodded.

Gingerly, they put down Ralph's toolboxes, trying their best not to make a sound.

Ralph silently pulled out his headlamp from the smaller toolbox and started to put it on.

Brian stopped him and whispered, "The light could give us away."

Ralph nodded and carefully put this headlamp back in the small toolbox.

Brian opened the heavier toolbox he had been carrying and pulled out the biggest tools inside. Two large pliers.

He handed one to Ralph.

"What do you expect me to do with this?" Ralph asked in a heated whisper

"They are the only weapons we have," Brian said sternly, staring at Ralph.

Ralph grimaced and took the tool.

Slowly, Brian let out a breath and started down the left side of the hallway, with Ralph closely following behind. Each holding a pair of pliers in their right hand.

They passed 3 powerless recessed consoles, each with an open bulkhead door. Then, 2 recessed windows, one forward and the other aft. Finally, they passed the last open bulkhead door and drew close to the opening of the communications room. Due to the dim emergency lights, they couldn't see much in the room.

Then they heard a sigh inside the dark room, causing them to freeze. Brian gripped his pliers firmly. Ralph trembled as he tried to do the same.

Suddenly, a dark figure appeared in the doorway, blocking out the dim light inside the room.

Brian swung as hard as he could only to find his hand was instantly immobilized, and his wrist was being held by the figure.

Ralph let out a cry and stumbled to the floor.

The figure stepped out of the room and demanded, "Just what the hell are you two doing?"

They could see that it was Lieutenant Rocha from the faint light emanating from the hall behind them.

She looked at them both with contempt, still holding Brian's right wrist in her left hand and an odd device in her right.

Ralph stood up, looked at her, and said, "We thought everyone was on the command deck."

"And why didn't you check?" the lieutenant asked as she let go of Brian's wrist.

Looking at her, Brian explained, "I was about to when we heard someone in the communications room."

Lieutenant Rocha replied, "I accidentally kicked something on the floor. It's a mess in there."

She stared at them oddly for a second, then asked, "Wait, you assumed I was the saboteur?"

"Well, yeah," replied Brian reluctantly.

"And you both were coming to get me?" the lieutenant asked with a curl on her lips.

"Sure," replied Ralph.

Lieutenant Rocha laughed out loud.

Brian and Ralph glanced at each other, feeling insulted.

After over thirty seconds of laughing, the lieutenant finally stopped and reassumed her professional deadpan look.

"Why are you here?" Ralph asked Lieutenant Rocha.

"I was running a final security sweep for you as I told you I would," she replied, holding out the odd device in her right hand.

"I forgot about that," said Ralph humbly.

The lieutenant said, "Let me know when you are finished. I want to lock the room down."

"How are you going to do that?" asked Ralph with interest.

"Simple. I'll lower the bulkhead back down and secure it with keyed mag locks," Lieutenant Rocha said curtly.

"That sounds like a good idea," Brian said.

"Well, I won't keep you. I'll let you get to it then," The lieutenant coldly said as she strolled past them and headed down the hallway.

After ensuring everyone else was now on the command deck. Brian and Ralph approached the communications room again. Brian carried the large toolbox while Ralph had the smaller one.

They stood in the doorway with their headlamps shining in the room. They could see the mess of loose chard debris littering the small square room.

Brian saw the repair Nutizie did of the hole in the outer hull of the room. The explosion shattered the electronics that were once part of this wall. Only the chard remains that did not get sucked out into space were now covering the floor. Panels on the side walls closest to the outer wall were burned and fried. Those closest to the entrance seemed likely to still be intact.

Brian entered the room and found walking around the debris difficult. He looked more closely at Nutzie's work and was amazed at how well she reinforced the support strut and sealed the breach.

He thought Thatorn might be right. It doesn't look like any reinforcement is needed. However, I think I will do some later just to make sure.

Ralph stood in the doorway and sat down his small toolbox, just inside the room near Brian. After a quick look around the room, he stated, "They're crazy if they think I'm going to clean up this mess!"

Brian replied with a soft giggle.

After examining the room further, Ralph pointed to the panel on the right wall closest to the door. It was the only one on that wall that still appeared intact.

He told Brian, "We can use that one to reroute everything we'll need."

Brian sat down the large toolbox he had and removed several lights from it. He set them up high on the communication room's right wall, brightening the entire room.

Ralph stepped back from the entrance, turned off his headlamp, and pulled up some schematic information on his C&PC.

After several minutes of being told what to do, it became clear to Brian that he was going to be doing all the work.

While looking at and in the panel he was going to be rewiring, Brian inquired, "By the way, why did you pick me for this in the first place?"

While still looking at a holographic 2D screen of specs, Ralph replied, "I don't think if you were the saboteur, you would put yourself in danger. Plus, if you were who you claimed to be, you would have enough knowledge to understand how to do the job with my supervision. I can be close enough to do so and be at a somewhat safe distance."

"I see," frowned Brian while staring at the panel.

Brian sighed after about an hour and a half of rewiring and reconfiguring the panel. He looked at Ralph, illuminating him in his headlamp, making sure not to shine the light into his eyes.

Brian said, "Ok, what's next?"

"What?" replied Ralph.

"What's the next step?" Brian asked.

Ralph dropped down his left arm, causing the schematics he had been using to disappear. He rubbed his eyes with his right hand and said, "Oh, huh, sorry. I'm feeling somewhat drained."

He looked at Brian and timidly asked, "The power is off in this section, so all the surveillance should be off here as well, right?"

Surprised by the question, it took Brian a moment to reply, "Even if any of it survived the explosion, none would be active without power."

"Do you think the surveillance down the hall can pick us up?" Ralph asked before taking a brief look over his shoulder.

"Might be able to see us a little, I guess. Well, at least your backside," answered Brian.

"Can they hear us?" asked Ralph in a whisper.

"I don't think the mics are that sensitive," Brian replied, then asked, "Why?"

In a normal tone, Ralph said, "There was a reason I had you do the work in the communication room by yourself."

Brian started to say, "I assumed you were afraid...."

"That was a factor, but it wasn't just that," interrupted Ralph.

"Oh," said Brian.

"Promise me you won't tell anyone," insisted Ralph.

"Ok," said Brian curiously.

Ralph explained, "You see, I'm having issues with the gravity. Especially now, since we just went from zero-G to at least a full G. Most inhabited asteroids like Vesta were spun up to achieve some gravity. My home has only a third of a G, and that's all I've ever been used to."

"But I thought everyone on this mission was rated for one G. It was in my contract. Thatorn brought that up during our first briefing," Brian stated.

Ralph elaborated, "After getting and reading the contract I got for this job, I realized I wasn't qualified because of the 1 G requirement. When the recruiter came to collect a signed contract, I told him I was not rated for that high a G and would have to decline. He told me it was no big deal. The ship was scheduled to do only half a G at most. He suggested that since they are not illegal, I should get some muscle stims before coming on board to help. They do, but I still can get worn out."

Brian asked, "Why say there was a 1 G requirement and then dismiss it? Especially since it turns out this is a military vessel?"

Ralph shrugged and replied, "I don't know, but this sudden change in gravity has really hit me hard."

"Did Rocha even ask you about the stims when she checked your stuff?" inquired Brian.

"No," replied Ralph, then asked, "Should she have?"

"You would think she would have been at least curious about them," replied Brian.

Ralph pondered it momentarily and then said, "I suppose so."

Brian asked, "Your weakness with gravity is why you needed me to do the physical work?"

Ralph somberly replied, "Yes. I'm sorry."

Brian replied, "Now that I understand, it's ok."

Ralph said, "Working in this kind of gravity has been weird. Things fall straight down. I have lived in rotational gravity all my life. I am used to the Coriolis effect of items falling in a curve. I thought zero-G would be the hardest thing to deal with here."

Brian asked, "Shouldn't we return to work before Thatorn calls to complain that we are taking too long?"

Ralph raised his arm, and the 2D specs from his C&PC 2D reappeared. After staring at them momentarily, he said, "It looks like we are almost done. Only one last major task to do."

"Ah, good," smiled Brian.

Ralph stated, "We just need to pull the auxiliary relay lines from the antennas and connect them to the rewired panel."

"Where are they?" Brian asked, turning back to the panel.

"The condition of the panel we used was not the only reason I selected it to rewire. You'll find a thick green cable behind the damaged panel to the left with the needed lines."

Brian gingerly stepped carefully to his left, stopped in front of the badly damaged panel, and opened it.

"It should be easy to pull free. There is not much of that panel left for it to be connected to now," explained Ralph.

Brian leaned over. Using his headlamp, he looked into the panel. "I see it. It looks like it's dangling free," said Brian as he reached in to grab it.

After struggling to get the cable, Brian grunted, "Damn, I can't reach it."

"We need to patch into that line, or nothing will work. Try harder," Ralph insisted.

Laboring to reach, Brian snapped, "Damn you, come here!"

Suddenly, Brian exclaimed, "Oh, I got it, but I don't...."

Ralph interrupted, "Great, now pull it out and feed it through. There should be enough slack."

Brian pulled out the cable and made sure there was enough slack to reach and patch into the rewired panel. After retrieving the proper tool from Ralph's small toolbox, he stripped away some of the outer green casing to reveal two thick blue and yellow wires.

As he started stripping away part of each wire's coating to connect them to the panel, Brian said, "I just need you to tell me exactly where each wire connects to the panel. Once that's done, we can do a low power test. With luck, we should be ready to transmit shortly after."

Ralph turned off his C&PC, stared at Brian, and said, "Before we do that, I want to ask you something."

Brian paused his work, turned off his headlamp before looking at Ralph, and asked, "What?"

"Who do you think our Sabatour is, and why did they kill Nutzie?" Ralph asked with anticipation.

Brian shook his head and replied, "I don't know. We all have spent a lot of time trying to figure it out."

"So you have no guesses?" Ralph shyly asked.

"At this point, that's all they would be, just guesses," Brian replied.

Ralph reached up with both hands, angrily grabbed what little hair he had, and let out a low growl.

Seeing this, Brian started to say, "Uh, what's...."

Ralph let go of his hair, glared at Brian, and snapped, "Damn it! It's just one big fucking puzzle that can't be put together. There aren't enough pieces and the ones we have just don't fit! Do they! Do they!"

XIV

Lieutenant Rocha was sitting at the unusual console along the inside curved wall of the command deck. Thatorn was in his wheelchair, just on her right. Both were staring intently at one of the console's small 2D display screens.

Val sat quietly in the starboard seat beside the center holographic console, watching them.

Brian stood behind her, looking down at the back of her head, wondering if she was getting as tired of waiting as he was.

Fa stood beside Brian on his right, diligently observing those at the inner console.

Just to Brian's left, he saw three others.

An exhausted Ralph slumped back in the starboard's first console seat, facing away from the console. Intently watching the lieutenant and the old man while gently rubbing his fingers with his thumps.

Rob was in the co-pilot console's tilted-up position, rubbing his eyes. Brian speculated that Rob was probably getting tired since it was almost time for his piloting shift to end.

Captain Linol stood in front of his level pilot console while gazing longingly at the doctor seated on the port side chair of the holographic table.

She sadly stared at the deck.

Brian wondered if Zala still believed the captain was behind Nutzie's murder? Clearly, he still feels for her, but she does not seem to care about him. At least not anymore. Then again, did she ever? Was it just sex for her when it came to him, while there was more with Nutzie?

241

Ralph glanced at the time on his C&PC and blurted out, "It's 20:47. We should have received a reply from U.E.A. Command through the communication relay on 243 Ida by now.

Captain Linol glanced at Ralph. He then looked at Thatorn and said, "It's important for us to know what command thinks about our predicament and what we should do."

Fa looked at the captain and cooly stated, "Yeah, It's going to be interesting to find out what they've got to say."

"I'm just glad our precautions have paid off and given us the ability to regain outside communications again," said Rob, focusing on his controls.

Brian closed his eyes, sighed, and softly stated, "This waiting is nerve-racking."

Thatorn and Lieutenant Rocha ignored the conversation behind them as they stared at the small display on the control console before them.

Then, the console suddenly beeped several times.

The Lieutenant and Thatorn leaned forward to read the information on the console's 2D screen. The rest of the crew stared impatiently at them.

Brian squinted and tried his best to see what was on the screen. It was too far away for him to make out, but he did spot Thatorn clench his right fist.

"What did they say, sir?" asked Captain Linol.

Thatorn takes a quick breath, turns his wheelchair around to face the crew, and says, "Turn back, abandon the mission."

Val softly says, "Good."

Ralph lets out a loud sigh of relief.

Rob lowered his tilted seat as the captain asked, "So, we are to turn around then?"

Lieutenant Rocha swivels her chair around to look at Thatorn.

Unclenching his fist, Thatorn replied, "But they only suggest we consider it. Command also informed me how important it was to continue the mission."

Brian found himself letting out a snort in protest as others expressed their frustrations in grumbles and grunts.

Ralph even muttered, "This is ridiculous."

"We must finish the mission!" exclaimed Thatorn, staring down his crew.

In response, the crew just glanced silently around at each other.

Thatorn looked at Captain Linol and asked, "Can we increase speed?"

"Yes, but it would require pushing us past 1 G," the captain replied with concern.

Ralph let out a noticeable moan.

Thatorn started to say, "It can't be helped we...."

Interrupting, Captain Linol explained, "We must also consider we will need to do a flip and burn sometime tomorrow evening to start deceleration. Some final calculations still need to be done for an exact time. Any increase at this point won't significantly affect our projected arrival time. Sir, it is my opinion it would not be worth the extra stress on the crew."

Thatorn closed his eyes and was quiet for a moment.

After opening his eyes, he looked at the captain and said, "You are right, Captain. It would not."

Turning his attention towards the rest of the crew, Thatorn says, "Mr. Rush, Ms. Elderman, and Doctor Teka. I had the Lieutenant reschedule you to work on my Exosuit first thing in the morning on the 8th at 7:00 hours."

Brian sighed, realizing he would not get much sleep with this late night and the early rise.

Thatorn glared at Brian and growled, "That suit has priority now, Mr. Rush!"

Looking at Rob, the old man stated, "Also, Mr. Callen, you and Mr. Rush have been scheduled to start the upgrades on the hopper at 14:00 tomorrow. I will set up access to all the related details and documentation on the main computer system for your use. Both of you can review them beforehand."

Then, looking around at the rest of the crew, he snapped, "That is all! Everyone get back to work if you are scheduled for duty. Otherwise, retire to your quarters!"

The crew didn't move, only stared at each other.

Glaring at the crew, the lieutenant barked, "You heard the Admiral!"

Rob tilted his seat back up and focused on his console.

Captain Linol strolled over, sat in his pilot console, and said, "I might as well just wait for my shift."

Thatorn and Lieutenant Rocha watched as the rest of the crew exited the command deck.

—⊬⊬⑂⊬—

Brian and Val were standing near the EVA control room's starboard entrance beside the Exosuit and the framework in which it was placed.

"What's keeping the Doctor?" asked Brian, checking the time on his C&PC.

"I don't know," replied Val as she stared at the burnt-out RRU console.

"I hope we're not delayed too long. I have to go over documents before working on the hopper later," Brian grumbled, glancing at the entrance.

"Maybe the Doctor had something she had to do," stated Val, looking at Brian.

"I guess we should wait," Brian replied, staring at Val. That was when he noticed her eyes were a little bloodshot.

Val looked around the room. She quickly sat down at the starboard EVA bay 1 console and took a deep breath.

"You ok?" inquired Brian, staring at her with concern as he walked over to her.

"Well, not entirely," Val said with some reluctance.

"What do you mean?" asked Brian.

Staring up at him, she replied, "It's the full G. I couldn't get comfortable last night, and I only got maybe 3 or so hours of sleep."

That would explain the red eyes, thought Brian.

"I'm not used to gravity this high being from Mars," she added.

"Interesting. You make the second person that can't handle 1 G. Even though Thatorn mentioned we were all supposed to be rated for it at the first briefing," Brian stated.

"Second? Who else?" Val asked.

Brian replied, "Ralph. He claimed the recruiter told him it was no big deal and said the ship would be doing only half a G anyway. He was advised to get some muscle stims to help."

Staring inquisitively at Val, Brian asked, "What about you?"

"I saw the requirement and thought it was just for emergencies. When I asked about it before I signed my contract, the employment agent told me the same thing about the ship only doing a half G at most. I figured I could handle that increase in gravity, at least temporarily. I didn't expect to be doing a full G for quite this long," Val explained.

"It seems the requirement for 1 G was ignored on the hiring end. I wonder if Thatorn is aware of that?" Brian deliberated out loud.

"I don't think it really matters. Thatorn is determined to find his Pirates at any cost, even if it continues to put us all at risk," Val scoffed.

Brian sighed and nodded.

Val frowned and said, "It's all becoming too much for me."

Brian tried to smile before replying, "It's getting to most of us. All we can do is follow all the precautions, stay alert, and be cautious."

Val said, "I guess we don't have much choice."

Brian said, "Nope."

He glances at the time on his C&PC and asks, "It's 7:18 hours. Maybe we should review the hardware-related issues until the Doctor arrives?"

"That sounds good," replies Val.

Brian heads towards the Exosuit.

As Val rose off her seat, she lost her balance and fell to the deck.

Hearing this, Brian quickly turned and made his way over to her.

"You ok?" He asked as he leaned over her and offered his right hand to help her up.

After taking it with her right one, she stood up, faced him, and replied, "Yeah, I just got a little dizzy."

"Maybe the gravity?" inquired Brian.

"Combined with getting up too fast, perhaps," Val replied.

"Perhaps you should talk to the doctor about it when she gets here," Brian suggested.

"I'm fine. I'd rather not involve the doctor with my health more than necessary," Val insisted.

Her attitude surprised Brian. Curiously, Brian asked, "Are you sure? She could...."

"No," Val interrupted staunchly.

Just then, Zala entered the room, panting slightly.

Startled, Brian and Val snapped their heads to look at her.

The Doctor started to explain, "Sorry, I'm late. I...."

She stopped and stared at them for a moment.

What was she staring at, Brian wondered.

He realized the doctor was not looking at their faces but at something lower down.

Together, they looked down and saw they were still holding each other's hands. Embarrassed, they slowly let go, turned, and faced the doctor.

The doctor explained, "Ralph was waiting at the Med Bay for me early this morning, so I had to care for his needs."

"What is going on with him?" asked Brian.

Frowning, Zala said, "You know I can't talk about that. If Ralph wants you to know, he can inform you himself."

"Understood," Brian said before pursing his lips.

Zala looked at the Exosuit and said, "Ok, we better get to work."

Brian glanced at Val, then looked at the doctor. Hesitantly, he said, "Before we get started, I think the Doctor should know Val had a dizzy spell and fell. She has been having grav...."

"I'm fine!" Val interrupted, glaring at Brian.

"Are you? Have you been experiencing more symptoms?" Zala asked, looking at her oddly.

"Symptoms?" asked Brian, looking curiously at the doctor.

Staring at Brian, Zala insisted, "I'm sorry, Brian. This is something Val and I should only discuss in private."

"It's ok, Zala," said Val, looking at the doctor.

Looking at Brian, Zala replied, "Very well."

Staring at Val intensely, she asked, "Was this dizzy spell accompanied by a migraine, like before?"

"No," Val replied bluntly.

"Any more nose bleeds?" Zala frankly asked.

"No, I only had one of those. Besides, that all happened days ago," Val grumbled.

Zala curtly told her, "Yes, that was 6 days ago. I think you use that gaming system too much. It could be the cause of your migraines and might even trigger dizzy spells. I'm uncertain if it could be responsible for a nosebleed."

Val started to say, "I really don't think...."

The doctor interrupted, "Who else has been playing with you? They could develop similar symptoms if it is the cause."

"Well, Brian has," Val said, gesturing towards him.

Brian tells the doctor, "I've not had any headaches or dizzy spells, but we have not played together that much."

Looking at Val, he asked, "What about Lee? He's been gaming with you, too, hasn't he?"

"No!" snapped Val, looking at Brian with disgust.

Brian started to say, "Since he knew about your game system, I just thought...."

Glaring at Brian, Val angrily interrupted, "No, Lee has not partaken in any gameplay with me. Only you, Mr. Rush."

Zala was taken aback and stared wide-eyed at Val and Brian.

Brian apologetically said, "Sorry, I assumed he did since he knew you had one."

After snorting at Brian, Val looked at the doctor and asked, "Since we are on the subject of Lee, did he get new meds from you?"

Staring somberly at Val, Zala replies, "Once again, You know I can't tell you those things."

Val explained, "It's just that I found some unused meds with his name on them in the medical disposal shoot I repaired in Med Bay 1."

Grabbing her chin with her right hand, Zala said, "Hum, well, it's not unheard of for someone to get over space sickness."

"Maybe so," Val said, unconvinced.

Zala looked at the Exosuit in the framework. She pointed at it with her right hand and declared, "Shouldn't we get started on Thatorn's suit. I would like to get him off my back about this as soon as possible. I'm sure you two do as well."

At the same time, Brian and Val nodded in agreement.

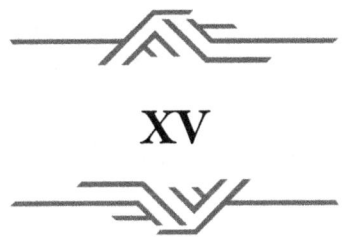

XV

Brian entered his cabin and made his way to his desk. He flopped down in the desk chair, closed his eyes, and let out a loud belch.

"Must have been that stuff called broccoli and cheese soup I had for lunch," Brian told himself.

After opening his eyes, he glanced at the time on his C&PC and said, "Let's see, it's 11:47 now. I've got a few hours before meeting up with Rob in the lander. That will give me time to finally review the Moon Hopper's specs."

The 2D screen on his desk computer came to life after he touched its 2D keyboard. He typed away and started to access data from the ship's computer system.

He looked up the documentation section and saw a new folder labeled as accessible. No doubt put there by Rocha. The files in it were likely only the documents she felt he needed to have.

He saw a folder named Moon Hopper Modifications with a file of instructions for the changes and one detailed digital document about the ship's hangar and the Moon Hopper.

Brian had been around the hangar doing maintenance but nothing directly related to the Moon Hopper. In fact, up until now, he's not been inside either the hangar or the Moon Hopper.

Before reviewing the changes, he decided to first look over the Moon Hopper and hangar details.

After opening the file, he read the opening summary page to himself.

The model X495 Moon Hopper is made up of two separate vessels.

The bottom section is cylindrical with landing gear, a surface hatchway, a small control deck, and the hopper's main H3 reactor.

The top section is a flattened cone-shaped command module with a much smaller secondary reactor, the main control deck, and a few small cabins.

The hull material is classified.

Brian stopped reading and asked out loud, "Classified? I bet it's the same unusual dark armor material as the Swans?"

He continued reading.

While in the hangar, the ship is docked in a custom resting bed. Secured in place by two large clamps. One on each side. While docked, its landing gear is extended and rests on the hangar's heavily reinforced floor. This is level 17, the lowest floor of the main ship. When in flight, it bears most of the Moon Hopper's weight.

The Moon Hopper's replenishment arm is on the hangar's starboard side wall. Fuel, O2, and other related storage tanks for this are located in the extra large spacing under levels 14 and 15.

Brian stops, looks up, and then proclaims, "I believe I looked into that area at least once during a maintenance check."

Returning to the document, he continued reading.

On the port side wall of the hangar is an extendable grappling arm. Used to assist in docking or repairing the hopper.

Level 16 has a platform that gives access to the lander section's surface hatch.

Part of level 15 has a corridor that has a hatch to the hopper's command section's main dock.

The primary control room for the hangar is on level 14. Operations can also be handled from the ship's control deck.

Brian changed the page and saw the first of several detailed diagrams of what had just been described.

He poured over all the nuances of the hangar and the Moon Hopper in the elaborate document. He was very impressed with the little ship's level of sophistication.

Before continuing, Brian decided he should check the instructions.

In it were two separate lists. One was for Rob, and the other one was for him. After reviewing his list, Brian realized he wouldn't need any tools. Making it one less thing he had to get beforehand.

He returned back to the details in the Moon Hopper and hangar document.

It was later before he noticed the time on his computer console.

"Crap, I'm late!" he yelled, jumping from his chair and running for the door.

———————

While Brian impatiently waited in the Moon Hopper's oval two-man lift, he recalled the specs he had just gone over about the central circular core. It housed the elevator and its mechanics and was the central hub for all the craft's wiring and plumbing. Similar to the design of the Swan's core.

Once the door finally slid open, Brian stepped onto the lower section of the command module's circular control deck. At first, he was slightly disoriented, facing a dull gray hull wall with a window and bright light emanating from a square panel in the ceiling just above him.

He glanced out the window to see only a dimly lit hangar floor. He remembered from the hangar specs that the clamps and cradle the ship was docked to were well below this window and out of view.

To his right, he saw part of a control station facing a gray wall. He could also see part of another one to his left. According to the ship documents, these consoles are like those on the Swan's command deck.

Quickly, he zipped to his right around the central core just past the starboard control station and stopped before the pilot stations. Rob was in the starboard co-pliot's console in the tilted-up position.

Brian noticed that pilot consoles looked similar to the ones on the Swan's control deck. Only a little smaller.

When Rob noticed Brian, he lowered his co-pilot console and smugly said, "So we finally showed up." Then, after glancing at the time on his C&PC, he added, "It's 14:13. You're 13 minutes late."

Brian humbly stated, "Sorry, I was looking over the related specs, and the time got away from me."

Brian turns around, sits at the console on the ship's starboard side, and activates it.

While waiting for it to power up, he looked at Rob and said, "I saw in the documents that this Moon Hopper doesn't have an official name, just like the ship."

Rob looked back at Brian and started to reply, "The Captian did tell me he gave our ship the nickname, the Black Swan, because...."

Brian interrupted, "Ship without a name that is dark in color. Yeah, I already heard it from him and the Doctor."

"Ah," Rob replied, sounding slightly disappointed, having been beaten to the punch.

Then he added, "As far as the Moon Hopper goes, it has no official name either. However, I did hear the Captain call it Moon Zero Two a few times. Not sure what he meant by it. Since he's from the Moon, maybe it's some kind of a moon joke?"

Brian shrugged and said, "Don't know. I've never heard it before. It is an odd name."

"Maybe we should call it something like the ugly duckling after its mother ship. That might be more apt," said Rob with a grin.

Brian giggled in response.

After Brian's console came to life, he quickly went to work. With his C&PC, he brought up a 2D image of the instructions for his assigned tasks.

Not long after he started, he glanced at Rob and noticed he had returned to work.

As he started his tasks, Brian told Rob, "I bet it's nice you're getting a chance to do something different for a change."

Rob replied while working, "Yeah, my 12-hour piloting shift can get somewhat monotonous, especially since we are out this far in the solar system. There's not much to do on long flights. Just keep an eye on everything and be ready when needed."

"Your work day is longer than mine. Is it because we only have two pilots, and it's a 24/7 job?" inquired Brian as he reviewed his task list.

Rob replied, staring at his console, "Yelp, for the most part. I'm on a special contract with a more extended shift, for which I'm supposed to be paid more."

Brian glanced at Rob and chuckled, "Probably not enough."

Before Brian returned to his tasks, Rob looked at him and stated, "This is a very high-end Moon Hopper. Don't you think it odd that it wasn't already more like the Swan?"

"What do you mean?" Brian asked, staring at Rob.

"The Black Swan can already practically fly itself," answered Rob.

"We are uploading new programming from Thatorn that will switch several systems to automatic and change some of the hoppers configuration settings. It seems to me it was not far from having the ability all along," explained Brian.

"I guess so," replied Rob, twisting his mustache.

Brian said, "I find it interesting that a craft this small has an ion drive."

"Yeah, I noticed that, but according to the specs, the command module doesn't. It only has a simple plasma-chemical drive," Rob declared, then asked, "I wonder why?"

Brian replied, "Each part of the ship has its own H3 reactor, so they can operate independently. The reactor in the command module is smaller than the one in the lander. According to the specs, it's not powerful enough to run an ion drive. Anything bigger wouldn't fit."

Rob stated, "That makes sense."

Brian asked, "Did you notice in the ship's specs that the lander has its own pilot console on its main deck."

Rob replied, "Yes, I did. I also saw it could be controlled remotely from the command module. That cuts down on the need for pilots."

"That might be why that model was chosen for this mission since we only have two," said Brian.

Rob sneered, "It just makes more work for the Hopper pilot."

"In the documentation, I found that this Moon Hopper was designed to allow the pilot to turn off its telemetry and transponder at any time. Why?" Brian asked.

Rob replied, "It's more than likely that they can be disabled if it is discovered that the Pirates are using them to track the ship."

Brian said, "On day one, when I was in the mess hall, Ralph told me that the Swan wasn't transmitting transponder data."

"I noticed that rather quickly on my first shift. But it was not surprising since we are a military craft pretending to be an innocent research vessel. Creeping around the solar system, not trying to draw too much attention to ourselves," Rob said with a grin.

"What if we get spotted and are asked to I.D. ourselves?" questioned Brian.

Rob responded, "That's simple. We can just say we are a poor research vessel having trouble with our transponder. I'm sure Thatorn has several fake transponder I.D.s ready just for that."

"I guess I am a little naive about those things," Brian frowned.

Rob said, "Being a pilot for as long as I have, you learn a lot that most people don't even have a clue about."

Brian nodded as they slowly returned to work and picked up where they left off.

After only a few minutes, Brian stared at Rob and inquired, "If you don't mind me asking, just how did you lose that great job you had?"

Looking at Brian, Rob replied, "Not much to tell. I was railroaded. The company simply wanted to replace me with a cheaper pilot."

Frowning, Brian said, "Seems like that's how they do it everywhere nowadays."

Rob asked, "By the way, how are Thatorn's leg repairs going?"

Brian replied, "Not bad. Val took on the biggest burden of the re-wiring. I'm helping as much as possible, and the Doctor is reviewing the interface. We are hoping to be done in a day or so."

"Thatorn will be clanking around again soon enough," laughed Rob as he returned to work.

"Yeah," giggled Brian.

Instead of resuming his work, Brian slowly swiveled his chair to face Rob. After taking a deep breath, he casually tries to ask, "So, what do you think of Val?"

While still working at his console, Rob replied, "She's alright."

Alright? What the hell does he mean by that? Brian asked himself.

Rob stops, looks at Brian, and inquires, "Why do you ask?"

After a dry gulp, Brian thought. So, do you ask him what his intent is? Are they a thing?

Brian then stammered, "Well, I uh. Since she and I. Um, I was wondering what you thought about her.... abilities."

Rob asked curiously, "Abilities?"

"Yeah, her tech ones," Brian quickly replied, knowing it was not what he really wanted to ask.

Rob cooly replied, "She is a great gal, but I don't know much about her technical skills."

"I see. Is that all?" inquired Brian, fishing for more.

"Yeah," was all Rob said before returning to his work.

Brian swiveled his seat back around and returned to his own tasks.

As he worked, Brian thought. It sounds like nothing is happening between them. Could I have been wrong about them? Maybe I should ask him directly to be sure.

Suddenly, his console screen started to flash a red warning message.

Irritated, Brian hits the console with his fist in frustration.

Startled, Rob gazed at Brian wide-eyed and asked, "What's wrong?"

Once Brian calmed himself down, he sighed, looked at Rob, and explained, "I keep running into system access denial problems."

"Oh?" asked Rob curiously.

Brian elaborated, "When I disconnected the lower wing's power before working on fixing the antenna array. I noticed extra extensive power cabling. It's way more than everything on the wing actually needs. After Ralph and I finished, I reconnected the power. Then I decided to inquire about these extra cables on the computer system. I was denied access to any of the related data."

"Could the extra cabling be due to the Swan having two reactors?" Rob speculated.

"Oddly enough, one reactor that size should be plenty for this ship, even to fully power the DEW," Brian responded.

"Maybe the extra reactor is for backup?" asked Rob.

"I suppose that's possible, but if it were that simple, why was the information denied to me?" Brian inquired.

"That's a good point," replied Rob.

"Not long after, I managed to ask Rosha about it," said Brian.

"And what did she tell you?" asked Rob.

Frowning, Brian answered, "The only thing she told me was that my denial was due to military-related data restrictions."

With a smirk, Rob said, "Sounds like crap to me. I've not run into it myself, but the Captain told me about having similar problems."

"What! But he's the Captian!" exclaimed Brian, baffled.

Rob explained, "He feels the Admiral and Lieutenant resent him and are keeping things from him. Even placing unusual restrictions on him."

Rob leaned in towards Brian and added, "The Captain thinks it's because he is not a lifer like them since he had retired from the force once already. He also told me Thatorn has a food dispenser system in his VIP cabin on level 1 but has never been invited to a meal there."

"Maybe the old man wants to eat alone," presumed Brian.

"From what the Captain said, Thatorn regularly invites and has meals with Rocha in his cabin," explained Rob.

Puzzled, Brian said, "That's Funny. At lunch today, I saw Rocha taking a tray of food out of the mess when I was going in."

"That must have been before I got there," Rob stated, sitting back in his chair.

"Maybe she just didn't want to eat with Thatorn today," Brian surmised.

"Perhaps," Rob said, stroking his mustache.

Brian then stated, "Since you are more familiar with the Captain. I've been wondering something."

"What is it?" asked Rob.

Brian responded by asking. "Do you know what got the Captain back into the service?"

Rob replied, "He only told me the story once and ignores me whenever I try to bring it up again."

"So what happened?" impatiently inquired Brian.

"He was in the service for twenty years, several as an electronic expert, before becoming a pilot and finally a commanding officer."

Brian quickly thought. Wait a second. Did the doctor already know about the captain being an electronic expert? Is that why she suspected him of causing Nutzie's death?

Rob continued, "After that, he retired and got a job in command of a fancy high-end moon fairy. He had it made with that cushy job. It would easily slide him into final retirement after only a few years. Then, Captain Linol had an accident with his ship. Fortunately, no one was hurt. He said some new technician caused instrumentation failure, But he was blamed. He became a liability, and with that black mark on his record, he found his only option was to return to service."

"That's interesting. That makes another one," Brian whispered.

"Another what?" asked Rob

"Nothing," Brian responded as he squirmed in his seat and returned to work.

Rob watched Brian for a few seconds, noticing his discomfort. Then said, "Well, we better get to work. Enough chit-chatting."

Brian nodded as he focused on his tasks.

Rob leaned over his console and typed on his keyboard. After selecting a few options on his 2D screen, he activated the ship's com system. There is a noticeable low hiss coming from some hidden speakers.

Brian looked up and said, "What's that noise?"

Looking at Brian, Rob explained, "The Hopper has an internal communication system. The Swan does, too, but Thatorns forces us all to wear our C&PCs to make us dependent on them. The sound you hear is white noise and will prevent mics from picking up audio. We can talk without Thatorn hearing us, even though he still might be able to see us.

Staring at Rob, Brian asks, "Do you think the Hopper is rigged with the same surveillance system as the Swan?"

"Of course I do. The white noise should be loud enough to prevent all the mics from picking us up. Even the ones in our C&PCs."

Brian raised his arm and looked at his saying. "You think it's always on, and he listens to everything?"

Smirking, Rob stated, "Just because Thatorn told us about the surveillance system doesn't mean he told us about everything. Like never telling us about the cameras and mics in our rooms."

Brian gazed at Rob, shocked.

Rob added, "It would not surprise me if he's even got a camera in our C&PCs."

"What!" exclaimed Brian.

Puzzled, Rob said, "I'm surprised for such an intelligent guy that you didn't consider that?"

Brian felt slightly embarrassed thinking about what might have been heard and possibly seen. Especially with his activity in the shower yesterday.

He asks Rob, "Where did you pick that trick up?"

Rob explained, "Someone I worked with years ago showed me. They were somewhat paranoid and thought the boss was always listening in. I guess he felt better if he could vent freely when he had it on."

"Won't they get suspicious if they can't hear us?" asked Brian.

Rob said, "Perhaps. Since we are free to discuss things openly, we should continue to work and act as if we are not saying anything."

Brian and Rob lowered their heads, looked at their consoles, and started working.

It wasn't long before Rob asked, "You were saying something about another, another what?"

"It looks like almost all of us are here due to what seems to be bad luck," Brian replied.

"Because of what I told you about the Captain and myself?" asked Rob.

Brian responded, "Yes. So far, not counting the old man and Rocha, only Lee has claimed that he picked the best job he was offered."

"Odd man out," Rob speculated.

"Or a liar," Brian insisted.

Rob reasoned, "If so, maybe he's embarrassed or ashamed over what really happened."

After glancing at Rob, Brian elaborated, "I can't believe it was a coincidence that everyone Thatorn picked just happened to be down on their luck."

"Hum," mumbled Rob.

Brian began to say, "I don't know about you, but with everything going on...."

Brian stopped and thought a moment about what he was about to say. He decided he didn't want Rob to know the truth about how scared he really was. Instead, he only said, "I'm worried."

Rob humbly said, "I hate to admit it, but I'm a little rattled by it myself."

Was that Rob's way of saying he was scared to? Thought Brian.

"No one is above suspicion," Rob added glumly after glancing at Brian.

With discomfort, Brian said, "Or to be trusted."

It was quiet for a while.

Finally, Rob said, "We have gotten entangled in a mess and have to make the best of it."

Brian grumbled, "Clearly, we are in over our heads here. Why not just turn the ship around?"

Rob looked away from his screen at Brian and said, "I'll tell you why not. It's clear to me that Thatorn cares only about his mission. He's after these Pirates or whatever they are at any cost."

Brian stared back at Rob and stated, "If we could figure out why Nutzie was murdered, we might be able to piece together what's happening."

They realized they were looking at each other and quickly returned their focus to their screens and tasks.

"Her death makes no sense to me either," said Rob.

"Could something so important be going on at Jupiter to kill for?" Speculated Brian.

"That I could not say," replied Rob.

Brian raised his right eyebrow and said, "I wonder."

Rob glanced at Brian out of the corner of his eye and inquired. "What?"

After glancing back, Brian replied, "There was something that happened that I've not told anyone."

"You have my attention," said Rob, focusing intensely on his console.

"It happened the first morning I was on the ship. I overheard part of a discussion Nutzie was having in private with someone over her C&PC," stated Brian.

Ignoring trying to look busy, Rob leans towards Brian. Stares at him and says, "This has something to do with you asking Rocha about Nutzie's communications?"

Looking back at Rob, Brian explains, "Yeah, it does. Val, Ralph, Nutzie, and I were in the mess hall. Nutzie was telling us about her days as a marine. Without warning, she just left abruptly. None of us knew why. Right after that, I had to go to the bathroom, and when I went out into the hallway, I heard Nutzie talking to someone on her C&PC. I couldn't hear too well since she was on the port side of the level, down an intersecting corridor."

After briefly pausing to lick his lips, Brian continued, "I got closer to try and hear. She had no idea I was there."

"What exactly did she say that made you think it could have anything to do with her death?" inquired Rob.

Brian replied, "She seemed angry. I didn't pick up everything she said, only a few sentences. Uh, I can't believe this. How dare you. I know what you're up to, and I think something about it not being over."

Curiously, Rob asked, "Who was she talking to?"

Brian answered, "Even though I was closer, I still couldn't determine who she was talking to."

"Do you suspect it could have been her murder?" pondered Rob.

"If it was, then they couldn't have been a stowaway. They won't have had access to the communications system without a C&PC. Plus, It was evident to me she contacted them," explained Brian.

Rob rubbed his temple with his left hand before saying, "From what you said, it still could have just been a lover's quarrel."

Brian responded, "Hum, I did hear there was some friction between her and the Captain over Zala."

Rob asked, "Don't you think if it was more, Rocha would have said something after going over Nutzie's communications?"

"Yeah, I guess you're right," replied Brian.

Then Brian asked, "Do you remember Nutzie's last words?"

"She was woozy and blathering something, but I didn't catch it," replied Rob.

"I did. She said I didn't expect you to go this far, damn you," said Brian.

"Maybe she did know who killed her after all?" reasoned Rob.

Brian said, "There was something else. Before the repair, Nutzie also asked me who I thought was the saboteur. I told her I didn't know and asked her what she thought."

"And?" impatiently asked Rob.

"Well, she never said. She changed the subject," replied Brian.

"Odd," said Rob, then asked, "Who do you think it is?"

"I don't have a clue. And you?" Brian inquired.

"Nope," responded Rob.

Brian sighed and said, "Puzzle pieces that don't fit."

"That sounds about right," Rob said.

"It was something Ralph said about our situation while fixing the array," Brian elaborated.

"We may be safe from the killer as long as we don't discover whatever Nutzie did," asserted Rob.

"I hope you're right," Brian said, unconvinced.

Brian and Rob returned to work and went silent.

It wasn't long before Rob asked, "Since we are free to talk. What's with that damn red door on the starboard side of level 4?"

Brian replied, still focused on his task, "Yes, I saw it was labeled Restricted Officers Only on the deck plans. At the time, I assumed it might have been an officers club."

"But the Captain is not allowed in there. That was another one of the restrictions he told me about," said Rob.

"The Doctor was telling me about that, too," Brian said.

"I've seen Thatorn go in it, but only once," stated Rob.

Brian explained, "I heard from Fa that Thatorn has regularly visited the red door room on level 4. Sometimes with Rocha. She noticed it on the security footage before her access was restricted."

"Maybe we should ask Thatorn about it," Rob said.

Both of them let out a loud laugh.

Rob wondered, "I've been thinking about that door lately. What could Thatorn be up to in there? Why keep the Captain out?"

Brian said, "I checked that door once and heard a groan from inside."

"I heard noises too. I'm not sure what they were," Rob declared.

"Fa speculated it's probably some kind of lab. Maybe it could be some kind of machinery inside making noises," Brian guessed.

"I considered that possibility as well until recently," Rob said.

Rob stopped working, gazed at Brian, and said, "I've been thinking."

While still working, Brian asked, "About what?"

Rob softly replied, "Since we are relevantly sure there is no stowaway. What if the unknown DNA came from that room.

Brian quit working, stared at Rob, and asked, "And that would mean?"

"A prisoner," replied Rob gravely.

XVI

R ob's loud voice blared over Brian's C&PC, waking him up.
Rob said, "Just a friendly warning. The drive shutdown flip and deceleration burn should occur in 15 minutes. I will issue a five-minute warning and a final 30-second countdown. We will be weightless for several minutes as this maneuver is being done. Make sure all loose items are stowed away."

Brian shakes his head and rubs his eyes as he rises from the small couch in his cabin. He sees a message on the large wall screen saying the movie is over.

Brian uses his C&PC to turn off the screen. He notices the time on it, which reads 19:21 hours.

"Man, that old flick must have put me to sleep," he muttered.

A ring came from the door.

It's probably just Rocha doing a spot check, Brian thought to himself.

Slowly, he gets up and walks over to the door.

He hits the open button on the control panel by the door and is stunned to see no one in the hall when the door opens.

Brian backs away from the door to his desk while watching the open door. After carefully opening the desk's right side drawer, he undoes a couple of velcro stripes around a large pipe wrench and takes it out.

Nervously, he raised the wrench above his head and carefully tiptoed back to the door.

Suddenly, Val appears in the doorway, staring at Brian.

Brian stopped himself from swinging it once he realized who it was.

"Oh my God, what are you doing! I could have hurt you!" exclaimed Brian as he lowered the wrench, glaring at her.

"Sorry, after I rang, I noticed a bag I thought I had in my pocket fell out and was down the hall. I thought I could retrieve it and return to the door before you opened it," Val explained, holding up a small dark bag in her right hand.

"Bag, what's...," began Brian.

"I didn't scare you, did I?" Val asked, interrupting.

"No," lied Brian.

"Then what's with the wrench?" She curiously inquired.

"Not long after Nutzie was murdered, I got it from my tools and decided to keep it handy in my cabin, just in case," explained Brian.

"Aren't you afraid it could cause issues due to another unexpected gravity change?" pondered Val.

"No, let me show you," said Brian as he walked over to the desk. Val followed.

Brian placed the wrench back in the drawer and strapped it back into place.

Seeing this, she said, "Oh, I see."

Concerned, Brian asked, "What are you doing here? We are supposed to stay in our rooms when off duty. Unless you informed Rocha? That's the protocol now."

Ignoring him, she said, "Didn't you hear we are close enough to Jupiter to get a good view now. Since Jupiter is on the Port side, and so is your room, I thought I could get a good look at it from here. I've never seen it in person before."

"Well, ah, ok, I guess," Brian replied.

Brian and Val stepped over to the window and looked out. Looking upward, they could see the gas giant.

With a few taps on his C&PC, Brian turned off his room lights so they could get a better view.

They could distinguish several colors and details as their eyes adjusted to the dim light.

The multi-colored strips of cloud layers appeared to be vertical from their point of view and stood out in the inky dark background of space. You could make out many of the colors. Red, orange, brown, yellow, white, and even some blues. There were numerous white vortices all over the planet. However, the most prominent one was still the centuries-old raging storm known as the Red Spot.

Seeing so many colors was calming to Brian. He never thought he would have missed them so much.

"The colors seem a little washed out to me," Brian stated.

"You're probably used to seeing the images of Jupiter that were exposed longer or enhanced. Jupiter is over 520 million kilometers from the sun. So it will be about 10 times dimmer looking than the Earth would be from its orbit," elaborated Val, clutching the dark bag in her right hand.

Brian was impressed with Val's knowledge.

Val added, "I never realized how much you could miss some colors until you haven't seen them for a while."

Brian smiled hearing that, then said, "Me too."

Val said, "I spent most of my life on Mars. Through every outside window, you mainly only saw red. Now that I've been away this long, I didn't realize how much I missed it."

"Did you know Thatorns's office was a pale yellow?" asked Brian, glancing at Val.

"No, but I've not been bad and gone to the principal's office like you have," she giggled.

Brian snickered with her before asking, "I wonder why he chose that color?"

"Maybe it has some meaning to him," Val replied.

"You know there is something else I miss," said Brian.

"What's that?" inquired Val, glancing at Brian.

"Rain. I never thought I would ever miss it," Brian replied.

Val looked at Brian and asked, "What's that like?"

Brian stared back at Val, grinning, and replied, "Well, it's kinda like the shower, but outside."

With disappointment, Val asked, "Is that all?"

Brian responded, "No, not exactly. It usually comes with dreary days, clouds, and sounds the rain would make. Sometimes, it would come as storms with lightning and thunder."

"Sounds like that could be scary," Val said.

Brian elaborated, "Some can be, but with modern weather control methods, they are not as devastating as they were in the past. After a lightning storm ionizes the atmosphere, it can give you such a relaxed feeling. It was always best when there was a cool breeze afterward."

Val humbly said, "I have been aware of those things since my early school days. However, I've never experienced it for myself."

"If you ever make it to Earth, you might get the chance to," Brian said.

"Yes, if," Val mumbled as she walked away from the window.

Brian activated his room lights with a few taps on his C&PC as he turned around and looked at Val curiously.

He wondered if the unknown threat and stress were wearing on her as much as they were on him. Would it be a good time to bring it up and talk about it with her?

"Are you feeling well tonight?" Val asked out of the blue, staring at him.

Caught off guard and unsure how to respond, Brian finally said, "Uh, sure."

"Good. The 1 G tires me out. But I took a nap before coming over. I hope to get a better night's sleep tonight, though." She replied with a sinister grin, still clutching her dark bag close to her.

"Oh, did you get something from the doctor?" asked Brian, glancing at the dark bag in her right hand.

Val did not reply. Only continued to smile oddly at him.

Brian was confused by her response. He waited for a few seconds, hoping she might elaborate.

Getting only a weird smile, he walked from the window up to her.

He wasn't sure what to say. Finally coming up with something, he awkwardly asked, "So how are the repairs coming to Thatorn's Exosuit?"

Still smiling, she replied, "I've got most of it done. I should be able to finish up tomorrow."

"I figured it would take longer. It would if I were doing it," Brian said, staring curiously at Val.

"Since you brought it up. I contacted Rocha earlier to schedule a time for you and the Doctor to join me and finalize the repairs," Val stated while continuing to smile.

Brian raised his arm, looked at his C&PC, brought up a 2D image, and said, "I don't think I got that update on my schedule yet."

"I'm sure it will be soon, knowing Rocha," said Val now with a broader smile.

Brian lowered his arm, deactivated his C&PC, and replied, "That's true."

Suddenly, from Brian's and Val's C&PC, Rob's voice announced, "Shutdown flip and burn will take place in 5 minutes. Make sure to stow away all loose items. Final 30-second countdown in less than 4 and a half minutes."

Once hearing Rob, Brian realized something. He glared at Val and declared, "You could have seen Jupiter from your room if you just waited until after the flip."

"Well, Brian, you found me out." She said, biting her lower lip as she started to creep closer toward him.

Brian froze, staring at her wide-eyed.

"How long will we have no gravity?" She asked softly.

Brian nervously replied, "Uh, I don't know. Rob said earlier it would be several minutes."

"We better get started then," she whispered.

"With what?" asked Brian, with a touch of panic in his voice.

"You see, I got this just for you," she said, reaching inside the bag.

Brian franticly thinks, Oh god, what is it? Could she be...

Before finishing his thought, Val takes out several condoms from the bag.

Brian was confused.

"I know it's old school, and the burden has to be on you. It was all the Doc had on short notice. I got a couple of different sizes, just in case," she giggled.

"What?" asked Brian, puzzled.

Val replied, "You see, Mr. Rush, I never have had zero-G sex before."

"But what about Ro..." was all he could say before she kicked off her boots and was out of her jumpsuit. She stood there naked before him. While holding the condoms, she dropped the empty black bag to the floor.

Brian quickly rose to the occasion.

XVII

Brian walked into the galley through the lower starboard side entrance. He sees Val emptying her tray into the recycle bin. With a broad smile, he quickly walks up to her.

While placing her tray into the return slot, she sees him and returns the smile.

With a cheerful chip, Brian said, "I see we left early."

"I didn't want to wake you. You seemed so cute and peaceful in bed," Val replied.

"It would have been nice to have had breakfast with you," said Brian disappointed.

"Sorry, I just wanted to ensure I'll have the Exosuit finished and ready to go over with you and the doctor before our scheduled meeting time," Val explained.

"When is that? I haven't looked at my schedule for today yet," asked Brian.

"Rocha set it up at 9:00 am," Val replied before snuggling up close to Brian. She embraced him, leaned down slightly, and softly kissed him on the lips.

Slowly, she let go of him and headed to the same door Brian entered.

Before reaching the door, she stops. Looks at Brian, winks, and says, "Don't worry, I'll make it up to you."

Brian stared silently, watching her exit the room.

After taking a deep breath, Brian slowly went to the food dispenser to get himself something. Walking towards the tables, he felt slightly uncomfortable looking out the large window. He sits at the end of the far starboard table with his back to the wall.

Instead of eating, he stared at the door Val had exited. As he thought about her, he let out a relaxed sigh.

"Brian," said a familiar voice.

He looked up to his left and saw the Doctor and Fa with their trays standing on the other side of the table.

Brian was surprised. He hadn't noticed them at all until now.

"Are you alright?" asked Zala, looking at Brian, concerned.

Brian managed to chirp back, "Fine, just fine."

"May we join you?" asked Fa.

"Sure," Brian replied.

As they sat down opposite him, Brian saw Captain Linol enter the same door he had and go to the food dispenser. Shortly after ordering, he pulled out a tray with only a cup on it. Grabbing the cup, the captain put the tray in the return slot. He glanced at the doctor momentarily before quickly leaving through the same door he had entered.

Before Brian could say anything, Rob entered the room from the lower port side entrance.

Brian started to feel his stomach churn as he watched Rob get his food and head toward them.

Rob sat next to Brian and took a drink of hot coffee from a metal cup on his tray.

He looked at Brian and said, "You look chipper this morning."

"Yes, he got lucky last night," said the Doctor, grinning.

"Oh," said Rob, looking at the Doctor, then Fa, assuming it might have been one of them.

Brian bit his lip and stared at Rob.

Just as Brian was about to talk to Rob about Val, Ralph rushed into the room through the lower starboard entrance. He ran up to the end of their table, carrying something small and shiny.

Surprised, everyone at the table looked up at the brooding bald man.

He was panting as he stood over them, looking run down and tired. His eyes were bloodshot with dark bags under them, and his face was sweaty.

Brian thought I bet he's not been sleeping due to the 1G.

Ralph then gingerly placed what he was carrying on the table.

It was a small metallic box with several small holes with something that looked like tiny audio speakers inside and a red button on top.

"What is that?" Zala asked.

After pressing the button on the top of the box, Ralph replied, wheezing, "An Ultrasonic audio jammer."

"A what?" inquired Fa.

Gasping, Ralph replied, "It's so we can finally have a private conversation without Thatorn or Rocha hearing us!"

Brian and Rob glanced at each other for a moment.

Ralph continued, "Even if he can still see us, he won't be able to hear, even from our C&PC mics."

Zala and Fa looked at their C&PCs at the same time.

"Where did you get that?" inquired Rob curiously.

Ralph puffed out dismissively, "I made it with some spare parts."

Everyone looked over the box as Ralph took a few deep inhales to catch his breath.

Ralph then said with assertion, "Look, we all need to talk about what we are going to do!"

"Do?" questioned Zala inquisitively.

"It's blatantly obvious to me that Thatorn only cares about the mission and not any of us," snapped Ralph.

Again, Brian and Rob glanced at each other.

"We have no idea of the saboteur and the killer's true motives," Ralph nervously added.

Fa began saying, "True, only speculation. We went over that..."

Interrupting, Ralph frantically said, "We have no idea who or what their next target might be."

Everyone at the table looked at each other for a moment.

Zala looked back at Ralph and asked, "Clearly, you've gone to a lot of trouble to talk to us in private, Mr. Milsom. Why so secretive?"

The others at the table stared up at Ralph for his answer.

After looking around the room, Ralph took a dry gulp. He softly said, "We must take over the ship, return to a commercial port, and have the authorities handle this."

"Are you suggesting mutiny?" Fa inquired.

Ralph whispered, "Is it? We are only contractors, not members of the military."

"Mr. Milsom, did you take the medications I gave you to help calm you down?" the doctor asked.

Ralph sneered at Zala and declared, "No, they only fog my mind. I need to be able to think clearly. "

The doctor glared at Ralph, but before she could reply, Rob asked, "What if Ralph has a point?"

This caused them all to stare at him and Ralph to grin.

"Do you mean we should take over the ship?" questioned Brian.

"I'm not sure what's going on anymore. I don't even know if we can trust Thatorn." Rob replied.

"Ok, even if we thought we should, how could we?" Zala asked with a scowl.

Ralph began to explain, "Easy, Rob could pilot us back to...."

Interrupting, Rob declared, "Wait a second. That won't be possible without full access to the computer system. Otherwise, I would be flying blind."

"What if we could get the Captain to join us?" inquired Fa.

Looking at Zala, Ralph states, "I don't know. One of us thinks he was behind Nutzie's death.

Can we trust him?"

Zala looks at Ralph and glumly says, "I may have overreacted. I'm not as convinced he had anything to do with it now."

After taking a breath, she adds, "Besides, it's irrelevant anyway. Mark told me he had limits on the system, too. "

Fa interjects, "It's true. Only Thatorn and Rocha have full access."

Slowly, they all looked at Fa.

After letting out a puff of air, she says, "Well, I might be able to give you some access related to navigation. Since it's on a slightly lower access level."

She paused, thinking briefly before adding, "Still, it would take time."

Brian questioned, "Are we not forgetting the obvious. How are we going to handle Thatorn and Rocha? We don't even know if they have access to weapons?"

"Then there is Lee and the Captain to consider. We don't know if they would even side with us?" Rob pondered.

"What about Val?" asked Fa.

"Oh yeah, her too," replied Rob.

Brian said, "There is one other person we must consider."

Everyone looked at Brian.

"Who?" Zala curiously asked.

"Our murderer and saboteur, the spy," Brian replied.

"Yeah, if one of us is this spy, they will have a heads up," Rob said.

"I hadn't considered that," stated Ralph, concerned as he glanced around at everyone at the table.

They all started to look around at each other.

"Who's to say this spy would even allow us to do it?" asked Brian.

"Unless they think they would have a better chance of escape if we reached a nonmilitary port before authorities showed up," speculated Rob.

"What if they would rather we meet up with their friends at Jupiter," Fa glumly stated.

With frustration, Ralph exclaimed, "We must turn this ship around for no reason other than that!"

Zala's C&PC let out a loud wine. Quickly, she tapped at it and brought up a 2D image. Staring at it, she exclaimed, "It's an alert for you, Mr. Milsom. Your heart rate is way up, and so are your adrenal levels. You need to calm down."

The side starboard galley door opened, and Lieutenant Rocha entered the room.

They all got quiet as they watched the lieutenant head toward them.

She stopped near the table and asked them, "Am I interrupting?"

Ralph says, "Too much, man," grabs his box, and franticly exits the room through the lower starboard door.

Zala turns off the screen of her C&PC and runs after him.

After watching them leave, Lieutenant Rocha looks at the remaining three at the table and asks, "Was it something I said?"

B rian enters the EVA control room from the starboard entrance, explaining, "Sorry, I'm a little late. I...."

Brian stopped talking when he saw Val holding the Doctor in the center of the room near the RRU's burnt-out control system.

Zala mumbles to Val, "It's not knowing that is the hardest thing."

Brian saw that the doctor had been crying. Her eyes were red, and she had dark rings around them.

The Doctor sniffed loudly and said to Val, "Thank you, I needed that."

"No problem," replied Val with a warm smile.

Zala said, "Oh, I need to sit down."

She walked over and sat down in the seat to the remains of the RRU control system.

"You ok?" inquired Brian, staring at the Doctor with concern.

"Yeah, I needed to... I just need some rest." Zala replied, slumping in her seat.

"Did chasing down Ralph earlier wear you down?" inquired Brian.

Zala responded, "I managed to get him to sick bay and gave him a shot to calm him and some more meds. I also told him to go to his cabin and rest and that I would be checking on him to ensure he was taking his meds."

"What happened to Ralph?" asked Val, looking at Brian.

Brian looked at Val and began, "He came in and...."

Zala let out a cough. Brian looked to see her giving him a stern stare.

Oh yeah, big brother, thought Brian. There is no need to give Thatorn any reason to lock them all up just for listening to Ralph. It might be best to keep it under wraps with only those involved, at least for now.

Zala looked at Val and replied. "He had a little breakdown."

"Oh, dear," said Val as she looked at Zala.

"He should be ok. I'm not sure what else to do that can help. I'm not a shrink," Zala explained.

Staring at Zala, Brian asked with curiosity, "Did Rocha ask you about him?"

"No, but I did inform her of his status and that he needed to be taken off duty for the time being due to stress and fatigue," said the doctor, looking at Brian.

"What did she say?" Brian asked.

Zala replied, "I only got an acknowledgment that she got my message and will take him off the schedule."

"I hope he'll be ok," said Val seeming concerned.

"I plan on looking in on him after this," informed the doctor.

Val looked at Brian. He smiled in return.

"You're late, Mr. Rush," she scolded him.

Surprised, he replied, "Uh, Sorry. I had a tricky emergency bypass repair on deck 3. Thatorn wants to ensure all backup systems are 100 percent. I almost dropped one of the few 27 L5 switches we had when I got it from the package. They're pretty small and can be tricky to find if you drop one. Anyway, I managed to grab it as it fell."

Val's features softened as she stared at Brian, then said, "That's interesting."

"What is?" Inquired Brian.

Val smiled and replied, "Oh, just that you have more cat-like reflexes than I've seen so far."

With that, Zala looked at Brian with her eyebrows raised.

With some embarrassment, Brian said, "Well, Uh, don't you think we should get to the suit?"

Looking at the suit in the frame, Val declared, "I'm finished with it. I just need you to review everything for the engineer's final approval. After that, we can get Thatorn in it to finalize all the settings."

Val and Brian walked over to the suit in its harness. Zala got up and joined them.

Brian bent down and looked over Val's work.

Val picked up a 2D pad off the nearby workbench, handed it to Zala, and said, "I've tied into the suit diagnostics. These are the default bio settings. Since the entire system was fried, I had nothing to go on to set them."

Zala took the pad, looked over the information, and said, "Thatorn gave me his biometric data. I'm sure I can set it up close enough to get us started, then adjust them once Thatorn is in the suit."

"Wow," exclaimed Brian.

Val looked down at him, troubled, and asked, "Something wrong?"

Brian stood up, looked at Val, and replied, "Oh no. I'm very impressed with your work."

"Ah," said Val with a subtle prideful grin.

"Have you tried any load testing?" asked Brian.

Val replied, "Some, along with motion testing, to ensure all the servos are operational. I plan on doing more load testing with Thatorn to make any needed final adjustments."

"That makes sense," stated Brian.

From the port side entrance, Thatorn and Lieutenant Rocha come in unexpectedly. They all looked at them, surprised.

Thatorn excitedly asked, "Finished?"

"Not quite, Sir," Val replied.

"We were just talking about needing you to fine-tune the system and calibrate the bio interface," Zala said warily.

"Then it's good that I'm here," smiled Thatorn.

Looking at Brian and Val, the lieutenant sternly said, "I noticed you left your cabin at 19:15 hours last night, Mrs. Elderman, and stayed in Mr. Rush's cabin all night."

Brian and Val looked back at Lieutenant Rocha with apprehension.

"I received no text message from you, as I advised everyone to do when they found the need to fraternize," the lieutenant snapped with disgust.

Zala glances at Brian and then Val.

"Sorry, Sir, I got caught up in the moment," Val timidly explained.

"With everything the way it is, you need to follow protocol. We must remain vigilant if we want to catch the spy," Lieutenant Rocha insisted.

Brian asked, "By the way, Lieutenant, did you find anything in Nutzie's communication data?"

Caught off guard momentarily, the lieutenant stared at Brian and replied, "No, Nothing revealing. I only found her yelling sometimes, but that seemed normal for her."

Zala glared at the lieutenant.

Suddenly, the doctor's C&PC let out a loud wine.

She exclaimed, "Medical Alert! Someone must be in distress!"

Before she could even check her C&PC to find out who it was, another alert came from everyone's C&PC.

Fa franticly exclaimed, "We have a power fluctuation in the power controls in the upper wing. Backup systems have been engaged. The computer readings show the system is currently suffering from internal damage."

"Doctor, who's in distress?" asked the lieutenant, staring at the doctor.

Quickly, she pulled up a 2D data screen. After checking it, she looked at Lieutenant Rocha and said, "It's Mr. Milsom."

XVIII

Brian and Lee were carrying an unconscious Ralph, following the doctor. They turned down the short hall and headed for medial bay 2. Trailing closely behind them were Val, Thatorn in his wheelchair, and Lieutenant Rocha.

The doctor stopped at the medial bay door.

Once it automatically opened, she stepped to the side and said. "Put Mr. Milsom on the table. I'll use the retractable restraints in the table to secure him."

Brian and Lee entered the room with Ralph's limp body, followed by the doctor.

Just after entering the room, the doctor stopped at the threshold and raised her right hand to prevent the rest from entering.

Brian and Lee placed Ralph on the medical bed. The doctor walked over to the bed, pulled out the hidden restaurants, and strapped Ralph down.

"Alright, get out," insisted the Doctor, glancing at Brian and Lee as she stepped over to the bed's interfacing wall screen and activated it.

Val, Thatorn, and the lieutenant had to back up to give Brian and Lee room to exit.

Once in the hall, Brian tried to glimpse the data on the wall screen, but the door closed before he could make anything out.

Val looked at Lee sternly and exclaimed, "Why did you have to come charging in just as we arrived?"

Lee glared at Val and declared, "He was using his hammer to destroy the power control panel. He had to be stopped."

"You didn't have to hit him so hard and knock him out!" Val snapped back.

Lieutenant Rocha stared at Lee and stated, "I'm surprised you responded to the alert?"

Looking up at Lee, Thatorn asked, "Yes, why did you?

Surprised by the question, Lee replied, "I uh, I just thought you could use help catching the spy."

Just then, Zala exited the Med Bay, and everyone in the hall focused on her.

"Well?" Inquired Thatorn.

After ensuring the door closed behind her, Zala looked at Thatorn, and cooly replied, "Patient confidentiality prevents...."

Thatorn interrupted, demanding, "Look at your damn contract, Doctor. In case of threats to the ship or its crew, all medical information shall be provided to those in command."

The Doctor looks at the others in the hallway and asks, "Does that include everyone else who is present?"

"Yes, damn it, we will all need to know sooner or later anyway!" snapped back Thatorn.

With a loud snort, Zala replied, "Fine. Mr. Milsom is suffering from severe stress and fatigue. I have him sedated and restrained."

Lee said, "Good, we don't want him escaping."

"The restraints are to prevent him from hurting himself, Mr. Smith," said Zala, giving Lee a dirty look.

"Where the hell could he go anyway?" asked Brian, glaring at Lee.

Zala elaborated, "I'm not a shrink, but I believe he may be suffering from a mental breakdown. I'll need time to evaluate that with the help of the medical database. The shot I gave him early after his outburst wore off much quicker than I expected. I had planned on checking on him after finishing the Exosuit and...."

"Outburst?" Loudly interrupted Thatorn, glaring at the doctor.

Looking back at Thatorn, Zala explained, "Most of the crew have been under a great deal of stress. Despite the facade of trying to appear unaffected, most of the non-military crew are fearful of the situation we are in. As such, I have them on various forms of medication to help them cope, just short of being dangerous or addictive. This morning, Ralph said he had stopped taking his meds before telling everyone in the galley that we should take over the ship. He even had some kind of box that he claimed would allow us to talk in private."

Looking troubled, Thatorn asked, "What did he say?"

Zala replied, "After taking over the ship, we should turn around and let the authorities handle what was happening."

"Exactly where did he plan on taking the ship?" Thatorn inquired.

"I believe he said something about going to a commercial port," replied Brian

"Did anyone entertain this idea of mutiny?" inquired the lieutenant, squinting at Brian.

Taking only a few seconds, Brian contemplated how he should reply and thought. So if the box worked, he didn't hear anything. Unless the old man did and is now testing our loyalty. But would he let Ralph run around after talking about mutiny? If he wanted to catch him red-handed and anyone working with him, he might. With Ralph in his hands now, the old man might extract what was said this morning anyway. So either he knows or will find out. Brian realized it might be a good idea to get ahead of it.

"Rob did," said Brian bluntly, getting a surprised look from Zala.

Both Thatorn and Lieutenant Rocha glared at him through narrow eyes.

Before they could say anything, Brian added, "Obviously, to find out what Ralph was up to."

Nodding, Zala said, "Well, I must admit I was curious too. Considering what he was saying, it did allow me to evaluate his mental state."

Thatorn and the lieutenant glanced at each other. Then looked at Brian, intrigued.

Looking back at them, Brian said, "Ralph was hoping to get us all to join him with this plan."

"I don't think he thought it through. I believe he expected us to help him figure out the details," Zala elaborated, staring at Thatorn.

Thatorn and Lieutenant Rocha glanced at each other and then looked at Zala.

"If Ralph is the spy and wanted us to turn around, isn't it most likely there are no Pirates at Jupiter waiting for us?" elaborated Val.

Thatorn glanced at Val and puckered his lips.

"What about this box he had?" the lieutenant asked.

"He claimed it was an ultrasonic audio jammer and would prevent the security system from picking our audio up," Brian explained.

"Maybe he rigged that up because his spy jammer was no longer working," Lee guessed.

"That is possible," admitted Thatorn.

"So if Ralph was behind it all, why did he kill Nutzie?" Val asked, looking around at all of them.

Lee shrugged his shoulders.

Brian stared at Val and replied, "I don't know."

Zala looked at Brian and sadly stated, "I would like to."

"When will Mr. Milsom be able to answer questions?" Thatorn asked.

Zala replied, "Not for a while. Ralph will need some rest if you want to get any useful information out of him."

Glancing at everyone in the hall, Thatorn says, "It looks like we'll have to wait before we can get to the bottom of it."

"I think we should put a guard on him," Lee mumbled.

Ignoring Lee, Thatorn asked the Doctor. "Please inform me when Mr. Milsom is ready to talk."

"Yes, sir," said Zala.

Anxiously, Thatorn asked, "Incidentally, can you leave Mr. Milsom long enough to finish work on my Exosuit, Doctor?"

"I believe so. Ralph will be out for several hours. I can keep an eye on him through my C&PC while I do that."

Relieved, Thatorn said, "Good. Then I suggest we get back to work.

Staring at Val and Brian, Thatorn added, "Mr. Rush and Ms. Elderman, after we finish with my Exosuit, I will need you two to fix all the damage Mr. Milsom has caused ASAP."

Val and Brian nodded, staring back at the old man.

Looking at Lee, Thatorn said gruffly, "And Mr. Smith, you should return to your room."

"You'll need your rest for your shift tonight," interjected Lieutenant Rocha.

Lee oddly stares at Thatorn and the lieutenant, then says, "Uh, Yes, sir." Then quickly jogs off down the hallway.

As Brian, Val, and Zala walk down the corridor, Brian realizes Thatorn and Lieutenant Rocha are not following them. They were still near the entrance of the medical bay.

He turned his head and was about to inquire just as Thatorn said, "You three go on. We will join you shortly."

Before Brian turned the corner, he noticed Thatorn and the lieutenant staring strangely at each other.

Brian finished checking a power relay panel in the circular hallway on deck 1 before looking at his C&PC. He saw it was

9:40 on the 10th of April and realized, Wow, so much has happened in just the last 6 days.

After closing the panel, he let out a long yawn and rubbed his eyes.

Brian thought. It took Val and me most of yesterday to repair the damage caused by Ralph, and it made for a long workday.

With a broad smile, he then thought. It didn't help that neither of us slept much. Val definitely made it up to me like she said she would.

Brian was glad they had time to get more modern birth control so he wouldn't have to wear a condom. It's way more enjoyable without it.

With a satisfied sigh, he thought, It's been great spending our free time together yesterday for lunch and then off duty in her cabin. Stopping by the mess only to get something to go. I wonder if she'll be interested in the same thing for today?

Rubbing his chin, he thought. I guess there must not have been anything between Rob and her after all.

Brian quickly looked around the hall and remembered Thatorn was always recording everything. It made him a little queasy, thinking Thatorn and Rocha might have been watching all his exploits with Val if Rob was right about surveillance being in the cabins, too.

He stopped and focused on the control deck's nearby starboard entrance.

"I wonder if Rob's heard anything new since breakfast," Brian mumbled as he headed for the door to the control deck.

After entering, he looked around, and Rob was at his co-pilot console in the down position. They were the only ones there.

Brian quickly sat at the first starboard console beside Rob's station.

Rob glanced at him while working and politely greeted him with, "Hello."

Brian looked at Rob and asked, "Did you learn anything new about Ralph from the Captain this morning?"

Rob stared at Brian and replied, "He asked me if I heard anything new before I could even ask him. I told him I compared notes with you, Fa, and Val at the mess this morning during breakfast. It turns out it wasn't anything different from what he already knew and had told me last night after my shift."

Concerned, Brian asked, "So Thatorn's not even keeping the Captain up to date?"

"It does not look that way," Rob replied.

"If the Captain came down and got coffee this morning, we could all have compared notes together."

"He told me he was trying to stop drinking it before going off duty because he had trouble sleeping."

Brian pondered to himself. So he finally took the doctor's advice. Or is he just trying to avoid running into Zala?

"Hum, Lee wasn't at breakfast this morning. I wonder if he might know anything?" wondered Rob.

Brian said, "I've not seen Lee since Ralph freaked out. Come to think of it, I believe the only time I saw him before that was on the 6th."

"Well, he is working a night shift," stated Rob.

"I hadn't seen the Doctor at all this morning. Maybe she's keeping a close eye on Ralph?" Brian speculated.

"Why, Thatorn's got us all under surveillance," said Rob.

Suddenly, Brian looked at Rob wide-eyed since he had forgotten to tell Rob what he had said about him and Ralph the previous day to Thatorn. He realizes the information might seem incriminating.

Brian decided to inform Rob to prevent him from getting caught off guard by Thatorn. If he hasn't already.

Thanks to Big Brother, Brian also knew he had to do it in a way that avoided suspicion and hoped that Rob would catch on.

"What?" Rob curiously asked, looking at Brian's odd expression.

Smiling, Brian said, "I told Thatorn you acted interested in what Ralph said yesterday morning. About the mutiny, but only to find out what he was up to."

Rob stared at Brian blankly for a few seconds before saying, "Ah, yeah."

"Zala told him about that box Ralph had that supposedly gave us privacy," Brian added.

Brian breathed a sigh of relief as Rob nodded, seeming to understand what Brian was inferring.

Rob squinted at Brian and asked, "So, is Ralph the spy? Is he responsible for Nutzie's murder?"

Looking at the deck, Brian thought quietly about it for a moment before replying, "I'm not sure."

Then Brian stared at Rob and asked, "What do you think?"

Rob replied, "No, I don't think so."

"Really? Why?" inquired Brian.

Rob responded, "Frankly, I don't think he could kill anyone."

Brian asked, "What about the sabotage then?"

Rob replied, "Uh, Well, I guess he's shown he is at least capable of trying to do that."

After a short pause, Rob added, "It's funny. He was the one that seemed so afraid and scared of what was going on."

Brian inquired, "Could it all have been a show?"

Rob replied by asking, "Do you believe that?"

Brian answered, "I'm not sure, but since he was recruiting for a mutiny and caught in the act of sabotage, it makes him the most likely suspect."

Staring at the deck, Brian added, "Still, there are way too many things that don't add up."

"No, they don't," said Rob.

Looking at Rob, Brian asked, "Let's assume he is the spy. Why would he try to enlist the crew for help?"

"Maybe a gambit to turn us against Thatorn," replied Rob.

"So when that failed, he resorted to more sabotage," Brian said.

"At least a very sloppy attempt at it," Rob stated.

"Is it possible even a well-trained spy could have a mental breakdown?" wondered Brian.

"I never heard of that," replied Rob.

"Unless it is an attempt to make himself seem so pathetic that he couldn't possibly be the spy," proposed Brian.

Rob responded, nodding, "Possibly."

"You know. Considering everything, it might be safe for us all now," Brian declared.

"Why do you believe that?" curiously inquired Rob.

Brian explained, "Simple. If it is Ralph, he is confined. If not, then the real saboteur and murderer would be foolish to do anything else as long as Ralph is being blamed."

With a dreadful look, Rob says, "Unless there is more going on we don't know about."

Brian stares at Rob strangely and asks, "What do you mean?"

Rob shakes off his look of dread and says, "I don't know. Ignore me, just overthinking it, I guess."

Rob got quiet and returned his attention back to his station.

Brian sat there wondering. It's upsetting to think that if it's not Ralph, who could it be?

Just as Brian was about to leave, he thought of something else he wanted to ask.

Looking at Rob, he inquired, "What was with that course correction we had around 9:15 this morning?"

Rob stared at Brian and replied, "I'm glad Thatorn informed the crew over our C&PCs beforehand. Especially about the thrust reduction to about .9 G. With everyone on edge, the ship shuddering from the maneuver might have caused some panic."

Brian thought. The reduction in gravity might give Val some relief. Maybe even Ralph as well.

Brian asked, "I thought we were already set for a Jupiter orbital insert?"

"We were," replied Rob bluntly.

"Are changes like that normal?" Brian questioned.

Rob replied, "Minor adjustments are, and most would go unnoticed. However, this was not a typical correction. It was a rather radical one."

Brian reiterated, "Radical?"

Rob explained, "To say the least. We were bound for an orbit close to the one of Callisto. Now we are going further in for one just outside the orbit of Ganymede."

"That seems odd, isn't it?" asked Brian.

Rob grimaced and said, "Unless Thatorn already worked over the spy and got some viable intelligence from them, like a base's location."

Brian began to say, "Spy? Are you talking about..."

He was interrupted when he heard Thatorn entering the control deck from the port door, followed by Rocha. Brian turned to see Thatorn in his repaired exoskeleton with many new shiny parts that clashed with the dull, dark original ones.

With a soft clanking, Thatorn quickly approached Rob's co-pilot station. Lieutenant Rocha made her way to the large console along the inside wall, immediately activating and using it.

Looking down at Rob, Thatorn ordered, "We need to change course again."

Rob looked up at Thatorn curiously.

With a smile, Thatorn said, "We need to plot a new orbit. The Lieutenant is now placing the new coordinates in the flight computer along with the thrust reduction needed. You, Mr. Callen, will need to verify them and lay them in. Let me know when you are ready. But only execute them when I give you the order."

Rob began to protest, "But we just did one...."

"Carry out your orders," interrupted Thatorn.

"Yes, sir," said Rob, looking down at his screen. After seeing the new course in question show up on his console, he added with suspicion, "But that will put us into an orbit between the orbits of Europa and Io."

"Exactly," Thatorn happily snored.

Rob focused his attention on his co-pilot console to wait for the new course to be confirmed by the navigational computer.

Why another course change so soon, thought Brian.

Thatorn raised his left arm up and activated his C&PC.

Suddenly, all the other C&PCs on the command deck came to life, and then Thatorn said, "We are closing in on Jupiter. To remain inconspicuous, we will refrain from going into an alert status. The ship systems can quickly become combat-ready when needed."

Getting involved in a possible conflict disturbed Brian. He was sure his fellow contractors would feel the same way.

Thatorn continued, "Our sensor array should warn us well in advance if something important is detected. So far, none of our instruments have detected anything unusual."

Thank god for that, thought Brian.

Thatorn added, "We need to do a new course correction. Stand by for some more bumps. Our velocity will also be further reduced, resulting in the ship's gravity going to .843 Gs. You will be informed once a final orbit is about to be established."

Thatorn deactivated his C&PC, turned around to the holographic table, and activated it.

The table displayed a 3D representation of Jupiter and the moons nearby with their orbital plots around Jupiter, including the projected trajectory of the ship.

Thatorn evidently wanted to watch the course change happening in real-time.

"The new course has been verified, Sir," Rob declared.

Thatorn smiled at Rob and said, "You may proceed, Mr. Callen."

After Rob hit a few keys, the ship jerked and shook as the thrusters fired.

Thatorn watched the 3D image of the ship's projected flight path alter, taking the vessel into a new orbital insertion.

The lieutenant turned from the console to look at the 3D image and then saw Brian.

"Don't you have other tasks you must finish before lunch?" inquired Lieutenant Rocha as she gave Brian a stern look.

Looking at her, he responded, "Yes, Lieutenant, I was just about to go and handle them."

Brian stood up, but before he headed for the exit, he looked at Thatorn.

Thatorn was still fixated on the changing flight data of the holographic image before him.

Brian wondered if Rob was right.

He asks Thatorn, "Excuse me, um, Sir. Have you found out anything regarding Ralph yet?"

Being interrupted, Thatorn grunted, glared at Brian, and coldly said, "The crew will be informed once we have finished our evaluation of Mr. Milsom."

"I see," stated Brian.

Rob took notice of what Thatorn said.

Brian sees Rocha's cold stare and quickly heads to the control deck's starboard door.

As he exits, he notices Thatorn appears to be almost gleeful.

Now, what's that all about? Thought Brian.

XIX

Brian entered the computer core room and saw Fa sitting at the port side angled out console. It was the same one she used the last time he was here.

Brian looked at Fa and asked, "My schedule has a request from you that only says you needed me to check some decking."

Glancing at his C&PC, he adds, "It's 10:15, and I've got another task I need to do before lunch. If it's too big of an issue, I'll have to schedule a time to do it."

She stood up, quickly approached Brian, looked at him, and said, "I think some decking might have buckled. It feels odd underfoot. I was concerned it might be serious."

Brian asked, "Where is it?"

"In the starboard maintenance corridor. I noticed it the last time I was in there," Fa replied.

She and Brian walk over to the starboard maintenance access door, which opens.

Brian looks at Fa, and she explains, "I requested entry access for you today to look at the decking."

Nodding his head, Brian entered the cramped maintenance corridor between the outer hull and the computer core.

Once Fa was inside behind him, the door closed behind her. She then said, "It's further along. Down by the servers maintenance access."

They went down the tight corridor until they came to the location Fa specified. Brian stopped to look at the deck plating.

Brian turns to ask Fa exactly where the problem is, only to see her looking intently at her C&PC. He noticed a red light emanating from it and saw his C&PC was lit up, too. He raised it closer to see the red display telling him it was offline.

Fa then whispered to Brian. "Good, we are close enough to the computer servers, so the electromagnetic interference jams the link to our C&PC."

Brian looked at her and asked, "What?"

In a hushed tone, Fa said, "Shhhh, lower your voice. I'm pretty sure there are no bugs or cameras in here, but keep it down in case any external mics in the computer core room might be able to pick us up."

Confused, Brian inquired, whispering, "I don't understand."

Fa held up her left arm, pointed at her C&PC with her right hand, and said, "If Ralph is right about Thatorn using these to keep tabs on all of us, I, we have to be careful. That's also why I picked a vague issue you could easily dismiss as my imagination. That way, we shouldn't stir up any unwanted attention."

"Ok, but if our C&PCs go offline, won't that trigger an alert?" Brian asked.

Fa stated, "No, I took care of that. We will be fine for a while."

Brian raised his right eyebrow and asked, "What's the need for the secrecy?"

"I have to talk to someone about what I've uncovered, and I'm not sure who I can trust," Fa responded.

Intrigued, Brian asked, "So you trust me?"

"Let's just say I trust you more than the others, and I don't trust Thatorn at all," she replied.

Brian inquired, "Alright then, what do you have to tell me?"

"You recall, Rocha took away some of my ship system access since the sabotage. Mostly the access to the security data and footage, including system checks when errors were detected." Fa replied.

"Yes, but at that point, everyone was a suspect to her," Brian interjected.

Fa explained, "She came to me early on the 8th and told me she had re-established my access to the error-checking system and that I would be responsible for it again. She also told me to inform her immediately if I found a bigger issue I could not handle due to my restricted access."

"Why?" Brian asked.

"She said it was because her workload was getting out of hand," Fa replied.

"I didn't think she had any limits," grinned Brian.

Fa continued, "As a result, I also got limited access to security footage but only of the area affected at the time."

"And," pushed Brian.

Fa said, "From one error check, though it was far down the corridor, I could tell Rocha was headed towards the room with the red door carrying a food tray."

"When was that?" questioned Brian.

"Around 11:12 hours on the 8th," replied Fa.

"Interesting. I saw Rocha leaving the galley with a tray that day," stated Brian.

Fa said, "I think Rocha was taking food to someone in the room."

"Who?" asked Brian.

Fa responded, "I believe there is a prisoner inside the room, and that is who the unknown DNA was from."

Brian thought. Now that's interesting. Rob mentioned the possibility of a prisoner as well. Should I tell Fa about that?

Fa added, "Remember I told you before I lost my access that I saw Thatorn sometimes with Rocha going to and coming from the room behind the red door."

Brian replied by nodding his head.

Fa explained, "In some related security footage from an error check I did this morning, I saw Thatorn coming out of that room alone. It was right before our first course correction. I believe Thatorn is milking intel from whoever he has behind the door."

Brian thought. Wait! Was Rob referring to them as the spy and not Ralph earlier?

"I believe it's more than a coincidence," Fa added.

Brian said, "It would explain a few things."

Fa nodded and said, "I've also been trying to access the entire message U.E.A. command sent us, with little luck so far. I even tried to check the buffer on the antenna array. I still had access to that system but found its data had been wiped."

"Do you think Thatorn is deceiving us?" asked Brian

"Like I said, I don't trust him," grunted Fa.

After a brief pause, Fa added, "While checking through some of the stuff I have access to, I came across a subroutine that was part of a relay system."

"And?" inquired Brian.

Fa answered, "It had a section that referenced self-destruct."

With a gulp, Brian replied, "Well, now. He didn't tell any of us about that!"

Fa got quiet and started to fidget.

Noticing this, Brian asked her, "Is that all?"

"There is one other thing. I've been doing some thinking. Do you remember Val thought someone was in her room, and Rocha told us of a diagnostic she ran during our first briefing?" asked Fa.

"Yeah," Brian replied.

Fa explained, "The spy seemed to know a lot about the ship. I bet they were even aware of the diagnostic going on. With the security down, it might have been how they got everyone's DNA and maybe even took some time to spy on the crew."

Brian pondered what she said briefly before saying, "But we were all on the command deck."

Fa said, "Not all of us."

Brian backed away slightly, glaring at Fa, and said, "That's right. You left before the briefing started."

With cold, steely eyes, Fa said harshly, "That's true, but since I know, I didn't do it. That leaves only one other person who was not there."

B rian finally arrived on level 4 a little later than he had planned. He was troubled going over the things in his mind Fa had just talked about.

As he walked to the starboard galley door, these concerns faded as his thoughts turned to Val. He became chipper and started to smile. Almost dancing along the corridor.

Brian was expecting Val to be waiting for him in the galley. She hadn't talked to him since this morning. He did consider messaging her but decided better of it. He feared it might make her feel he was bothering her too much.

Just as Brian approached the galley door, it suddenly opened. Zala exited in a huff, with the captain following closely behind her. Brian managed to get out of their way as they barreled past him.

What was that all about? He pondered as he stepped up to the open door.

Inside, he saw Rob eating at a nearby table. Just as Brian was about to enter, Val walked into view carrying a tray she must have just gotten from the dispenser. She sat next to Rob, snuggled up to him closely, and began to hug him, smiling.

Slowly, Brian stepped back away from the door. As it closed, he was sure they had not noticed him.

He stood there contemplating. Was I expecting too much? She never did say anything about being my girlfriend. Is she done or board with me now? Has she decided to hook up with Rob now? Is it because he is better than me in bed? I guess there was something between them after all. Well, if she wants to play the field, then....

Brian felt a small tear in the corner of his right eye. He gingerly wiped it away with his right hand.

He looked at the tear on his fingers and whispered, "Get a hold of yourself, damn it, man. It was just sex. Besides, it's too soon for you to get tied down anyway. There is plenty of time to find the right woman. I'm sure I'll find an even better one."

He looked at the closed door and asked out loud, "But what if I don't?"

XX

Slowly, Brian crept out of his room, looking rather grim. He shuffled along the corridor, heading for the circular hallway. Lifting his left arm, he looked at his C&PC and saw the time was 11:56. With the forefinger of his right hand, he activated the device. After scrolling through a 3D menu of options, he brought up a 2D image of his schedule.

From it, he sees that his first scheduled task after lunch is at 12:00 hours, which reads: The doctor insists that a ceiling panel needs to be fixed immediately in Med Bay 2. You are to assess the situation and make any necessary repairs.

Brian softly grumbled, "Sounds trivial, probably just a loose fitting. I'm an engineer, not a damn janitor."

After sighing, Brian deactivates his C&PC and stares vacantly at the floor as he lumbers his way to the lower door of the circular hallway. He turns right after passing through, then comes to the port side elevator.

With reluctance, Brian pushes the call button for the lift. When the door opened, he meandered in. With another sigh, he looks at the control panel and selects the elevator to take him up to level 5.

After the short journey, the lift opened. As Brian stepped out into the circular hallway, his C&PC chimed.

He stopped and raised his left arm to activate his C&PC. A holographic 2D image showed him that he had just received a message from Val.

Brian softly gulped as he selected the option to open the message.

A 2D image of the message appeared.

Brian nervously read it. It said, "Sorry I missed you for lunch. I have a busy day, so I'll be going to bed early. See you later."

Brian's heart sank.

He thought. Is this Val's way of brushing me off? Is she planning on hooking up with Rob after he gets off duty tonight?

Brian gets angry and hits the nearby wall. Just missing the lift's hallway control panel.

He looks at it and then at his hand and says out loud, "Well, that was stupid."

He closed his eyes and shook his head.

After taking a deep breath, he tells himself, It looks like it was not meant to be.

Realizing his eyes teared up, he quickly wiped them away. He stood erect and walked into the square room through the port side circular hallway door.

Just as the door closed behind him, he stopped when he heard talking to his right. Curious, he slowly starts to walk in that direction.

Brian cautiously crept around the curved wall, listening but could not understand what was being said.

Around the edge of the wall, he finally spots Captain Linol and Doctor Teka standing between the lower circular hall's entrance and the door to the ship's morgue.

Brian could now clearly hear them whispering to each other.

"You know I could never hurt you in any way," said the captain, gazing lovingly at Zala.

Staring at the deck, she replies, "I've heard that many times before from so many different people."

Captain Linol muttered, "I knew you cared about her. I thought maybe you did me as well."

Still staring at the floor, Zala declared, "I can't deny I had feelings for you, but that was before...."

The captain interrupted, "I had nothing to do with her death. It's obvious Ralph was behind it all."

With tears in her eyes, the doctor looks up at Captain Linol and asks, "Was he?"

Suddenly, the captain noticed Brian out of the corner of his eye.

Captain Linol grunted loudly and abruptly left through the nearby lower circular hallway entrance.

Brian stares at Zala and asks, "Is everything ok?"

Zala looked at Brian with a tear rolling down her cheek and said, "Yes, I'm fine."

Looking at the closed door the captain used, she adds, "I believe he's thinking with the wrong head and is having trouble understanding."

Brian began to apologize, "I'm sorry to have...."

The doctor interrupted, "It's ok."

Zala stares oddly at Brian and asks, "What's wrong with you?"

"Nothing," Brian lied.

"Ah, I can see it in your eyes, too," explained Zala.

"What are you talking about?" Brian asked, confused.

"Is it love or lust?" the doctor inquired.

"Love? What are you talking about," Brian stammered.

Zala began to say, "Never mind, She's out of your league anyway. You are better ...."

Angerly, Brian interrupted, saying, "No, I'm not. I...."

He stopped.

The doctor said, "You see, you are also in a state of confusion. We all go through it, especially when we are young."

Looking back at the door Captain Linol took, she added, "and at other times in our life."

"You miss Nutzie?" Brian asked timidly.

Zala looked back at Brian and snapped, "Of course I do!"

Stuttering with a soft sob, she added, "I can't seem to get her off my mind."

Brian asked, "So it was love?"

Zala looks at Brian and says, "I clearly had strong feelings... It's ironic. After all these years of not wanting to get tied down, maybe deep down I really wanted it all along?"

The doctor abruptly wipes away her tears, coughs, and declares, "Now to business. I have a noisy ceiling panel in my Med Bay. It started not long after that first course correction.

Zala quickly leads Brian to the Med Bay. Once there, she points to the ceiling above the window.

Brian walks over to the window, aims his right ear upward, and listens. He soon notices a subtle squeaking coming from it.

Brian says, "It's not that loud."

"Try putting up with it for a couple of hours!" Zala shouted.

Brian holds his hands up, exclaiming, "Ok, doc, It's probably just a loose fitting."

Brian drops his hands, approaches the window, and looks up at the ceiling.

Brian turns, looks back at Zala, and explains, "I don't think we have any replacement fittings. I'll have to make some new ones with the 3D printer in the RRU control room. It shouldn't take too long. While there, I'll get some specialty tools for the job and grab the small step stool in cargo room 2."

"Thank you," the doctor politely says.

Brian walks up to the door to leave, then stops. He knows the old man can hear everything he says on the ship. But Brian decides he will have to throw caution to the wind if he's ever going to figure anything out.

Looking at Zala, he says, "I see Ralph is no longer in here. Do you mind telling me how he is doing? I asked Thatorn, but he just told me he would inform the crew after evaluating him."

She pursed her lips together and said, "That's interesting."

Intrigued, Brian asked, "Why do you say that?"

Zala replied, "I've been given orders not to relay any further information about Mr. Milsom's medical condition."

She walks up to the med bed, not looking at Brian, and says, "However, what Thatorn said to you puzzles me. He ordered me and Rocha to lock up, restrain, and keep Ralph sedated in one of the patient rooms. Since then, he's not said anything about questioning him. You think he and Rocha would have wanted to start interrogating him as soon as possible."

"At least they've not wanted to yet," Brian said.

Zala turned, stared at Brian, and said, "Still, it seems odd."

Everything seems odd with Thatorn, thought Brian.

After sitting on the med bed, Zala closed her eyes and said, "How long will it take you to get back to fix that noise."

"Not too long," Brian replied.

Brian examined the doctor more closely. He notices darkness under her eyes and then asks, "Let me guess. You are not rated for 1 G, either."

Zala opens her eyes, stares at Brian, and says, "Is it that obvious."

"That makes 3," mumbles Brian, shifting his eyes away from Zala.

"3?" inquired the doctor.

Brian glanced back at the Doctor and then looked around the room.

Zala said, "We're all in too deep at this point. Who gives a crap about what Thatorn hears us saying."

Brian nodded, then explained, "Ralph told me about his situation before we repaired the communication antenna. In fact, that's why he wanted me to help him, so I could do most of the work."

Zala looked at the floor and started tapping the fingers of her right hand on the table.

"That would explain his extreme fatigue," she murmured.

She stopped tapping, looked at Brian, and asked, "And who is the third?"

Brian hesitantly replied, "It's Val, but she didn't want me to tell you."

Zala said, "She's from Mars, like me. Being younger, she has probably been able to handle the extra Gs better than I have."

Brian asked, "Let me guess, the job recruiter told you that you wouldn't need to worry about more than half a G like they did Val and Ralph?"

Zala replied, "No, there was no mention of it at all. If so, I probably would not have taken the job. After it came up in our first briefing, I checked my copy of the digital contract. Needless to say, I was surprised to see the requirement was there. I'm sure it wasn't there before. I didn't think a digital contract copy could be changed after the fact."

"Neither did I," Brian said as he thought reviewing his contract might be a good idea. Just in case there was something he didn't see when he signed it.

Brian starts heading for the exit, saying, "Look, I need to get started on the repair if I'm going to make my rounds. I'll be back as soon...."

Zala interrupted him, asking, "Do you think Ralph is responsible for everything?"

Brian stopped, turned, and looked at the doctor.

After rubbing his chin, he finally said, "Let me ask you this. How could a spy use such skill and cleverness on one sabotage and then be so crude and clumsy trying to do another?

"You don't think he did it?" Zala asked.

Brian replied, "I don't know for sure, but it seems unlikely the more I mull it over."

Zala confessed, "I've been thinking about it a lot, too, and I don't believe he has it in him to hurt anyone."

Interesting, thought Brian, neither did Rob.

Curious, Brian asked, "Ok, If it's not him, why did he try to get the crew to take over the ship to turn us around? "

Zala replied, "I believe he was just afraid. But not of getting caught. I think he snapped because he kept constantly worrying about our situation. Causing him to be scared out of his mind and finally triggering a mental breakdown."

"You don't think it's just an act, a clever ploy?" inquired Brian.

The doctor replied, "I'm not a shrink, so I can't say it's not for sure."

"If it's not Ralph, who do you think the real saboteur and murderer is then?" Brian asked.

"I thought I did," Zala said sadly.

Brian coldly stated, "Maybe we won't know until after we get to Jupiter and meet their Pirate friends?"

B rian enters the circular hall from the upper port side door and calls the lift.

While waiting, he hears a soft mumbling coming from his left.

He strolls around the curved wall. Just as he passed the waste chute on his right, he found the captain leaning on the wall near the door where he entered the circular hallway earlier.

Brian thought it might be best to leave, but Captain Linol saw him before he could.

He raised up off the wall, looked at Brian, and softly asked, "Can I help you, Mr. Rush?"

Brian replied, "No, sir, I was just waiting for the lift."

The captain slumped and explained, "I'm sorry about my behavior. You see, I just thought things would be different now since...."

"You mean with Zala?" Brian asked, interrupting.

Captain Linol replied, "Yes."

The captain rubbed his head with his left hand and said, "Maybe I shouldn't expect much from her since she is still grieving over Nutzie. Maybe I'm just being selfish."

Unsure what to say, Brian admitted, "Honestly, I couldn't say."

Captain Linol sighed loudly, then said, "I can't seem to get anything right anymore. After retiring from the U.E.A., I had a cushy job as moon ferry Captain."

He smiled briefly and added, "Got lots of tail back then too."

Then frowning, he said, "Everything went to shit after I lost that job, and it wasn't even my fault. After that, no commercial operation wanted anything to do with me. That's what forced me back into the service."

He smiled again, continuing, "Then I met Zala, and it all seemed good again."

With some hesitation, Brian asked, "Except for Nutzie?"

The captain looked down at the floor and replied, "Yeah, Zala said she didn't want to be tied down to anyone, which was good enough for me at the time. Then Nutzie got involved with her. I didn't like the idea of sharing Zala. At least not at first. With Zala's encouragement, I tried getting used to the idea and did my best to get along with Nutzie."

"So now, what is it you want from the Doctor?" Brian asked.

"I'm not sure if I want her or just the sex. Still, I would like to find out if more could be between us," softly admitted Captain Linol.

"Maybe you should just be patient and give her some time," Brian said.

The captain looked at Brian and said, "I wonder just how much time we have left?"

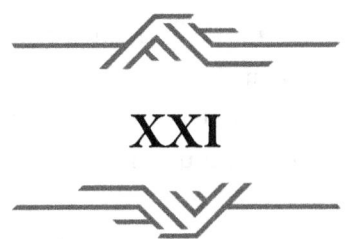

XXI

Brian steps out of the shower and looks back into it, wondering if he should have jerked off one last time before the ship goes into orbit and free fall. It might be some time before there is gravity again.

Frowning, he then thinks about Val and realizes that no matter what, it could never be as good as it was when he was with her.

He sighs, grabs a towel, and starts to dry himself off.

In an attempt to not think about her, he begins to ponder about other matters.

What is with all these course changes Thatorn has made since we got close to Jupiter? We've got to be close to going into a final orbit soon. Why has he not told us when we will. Is there something the old man knows that he's not telling us?

Once dry, Brian shoves his towel into the hamper, walks into his room, and goes to his dresser. Before grabbing anything out of it, he looks at his bed and then glances at the time on his C&PC. It was almost 21:00 hours.

He thought. There is too much going on right now. I don't think I'll be able to sleep anyway.

Brian lets out a nervous breath and looks at his video screen. He considers what he might watch to take his mind off all his woes.

He then thinks. I wasn't hungry for any dinner earlier. I should take the opportunity to get a hot meal while I still can.

After putting on a jumpsuit, per Lieutenant Rocha's new protocol, he texted her his intention to go to the galley over his C&PC.

As Brian left his cabin and headed for the lift. His thoughts returned to the predicament they all were in.

We've been close to the Jovian system for a while, and no Pirates so far. Still, they might lie low and wait to see how things play out on the ship with their spy on board.

If the spy is Ralph, and since we have him neutralized, what might they do?

Then again, what if there are no Pirates? This might be some kind of nightmare that Thatorn has dragged us into with him.

Still, someone caused sabotage and murder for some reason.

Brian entered the circular hallway and called the lift. Once it arrived, he entered it, selected level 4, and continued contemplating.

There is that jammer that keeps the culprit hidden. How did that get on the ship?

Who could the guilty party be, Pirate or not? Assuming it's only one person. When Thatorn suspected me, he thought I had an accomplice on board.

Fa has a possible revenge motive towards Thatorn, but I can't see why she would kill Nutzie?

Then there is Lee. He has so many unusual behaviors. Could he have been in everyone's room when the security was down while Rocha ran that diagnostic during our first briefing? Giving him a chance to collect everyone's DNA.

The lift door opened. Brian walked through the circular hallway and exited the upper starboard door. As he walked towards the lower starboard galley entrance, Brian deliberated more.

Rocha? She's Thatorn's right hand and has all the needed access to do it, but why? I think she's too devoted to the military to be responsible. Unless Thatorn put her up to it?

Speaking of the old man, there is no reason for him to cripple his own ship. Unless he wants us all to think there are real Pirates out there?

Nutzie's death complicates it all. Who killed her and why? Did she see or know something?

Sure, the Captain might have had issues with her and wanted Zala all to himself. Could he have murdered for it? It seemed Zala thought so at one point. But sabotage the ship just to set up the attempt to kill her in the RRU control room. Only to then have to try it again before finally succeeding?

What about the Doctor. I can't tie anything to her, especially Nutzies death. Can I?

Then there is Rob? I knew him from years ago. He's not changed. Well, not too much.

Can't forget Val. Is there anything that could tie her to what's been going on?

Thinking about Val, Brian sighed and rubbed his forehead as he reached the galley entrance.

Just before Brian enters, he hears a door open. It sounded like it came from the connecting hallway just to his left.

Slowly, he creeps up to the corner. After taking a quick peek to his right down the shorter end of the corridor, he sees nothing. He then turns to his left to look down at the other end of the hall.

Brian sees Thatorn coming out of the room with the red door. Hearing only the door close behind him and nothing else.

Brian thought. It didn't sound like anyone was in the room.

Brian watched Thatorn take the parallel corridor. He stood silent, listening until he heard Thatorn enter one of the doors to the circular hallway.

As Brian walked back to the mess door, he thought. That was odd.

Brian entered the galley and, to no surprise, found it was empty.

After selecting a meal, he headed for the starboard table by the large window. Just before sitting down with his back to the window, Brian glanced out into space and was thankful it didn't affect him as much as it used to. Thanks to some meds and the encouragement he got from Nutzie.

Suddenly, Brian was caught off guard by Thatorn's loud voice over his C&PC.

Thatorn announced, "We have one more slight course adjustment to make. Final orbital insertion will follow in approximately 5 minutes and 12 seconds. It will take us close to the orbit and the moon of Io. I want all personnel to report to the command deck before then. Once in orbit, we will assess our situation."

Brian thought. Now that's interesting. A course change after he was just in the room behind the red door? Fa said he did the same thing this morning before the first course change. Maybe she could be right, and the old man is getting information from someone he's got locked up in there.

The ship shook slightly from the maneuvers of the course adjustment.

When Brian was confident it was over, he started eating his food and thinking again.

Maybe I should try to focus on the start of it all for a change. The sabotage itself.

How did anyone place the bomb when no one but Ralph was in the room? There is no evidence that he planted anything while in the room. If the data had been faked, Fa or even Rocha would have spotted it.

If it happened during the last jam on the 4th, that would not leave much time in the previous jammings to steal everything and make the bomb.

With gravity coming and going, how could you keep a bomb in one place? What would prevent it from bouncing around? The ship was still in free fall until the night of the 4th.

How would I have done it?

Brian stopped eating and thought, Of course, a magnet, but where...

When I checked the inventory, nothing was missing when I got a powered magnet from storage for Rob. He claimed he tossed a bad coil when it failed two days before I looked at it. That would have been on the 3rd, a day after the bomb items were stolen and planted. It doesn't fit. Unless we got it all wrong. What if the bomb wasn't planted on the 2ND after all.

If so, how could the bomb have been planted?

Brian's eyes lit up as he thought, Oh, of course! Why didn't I think of that before!

Brian raised his left arm and activated his C&PC. After selecting the call list and Rob's name, nothing happened. The communication system was down.

"Shit!" He exclaimed and ran to the galley door he came in.

Brian bolted out once it opened, nearly running over Val. She was close to the door, not facing it but looking towards the starboard intersection.

Seeing her caused Brian to feel awkward at first, but he still felt the need to apologize for almost slamming into her.

He started to say, "Uh, I'm sorry, Val, I...."

Brian stopped when he realized she was not paying any attention to him.

He walked around to face her. She stared past him with glazed over eyes and an expressionless face.

Before Brian could say anything else to her, he heard footsteps behind him. He turned and could tell they were coming from the left down the intersecting hallway.

Brian peaked around the corner to see it was Rob. He had stopped and was standing in front of the red door.

Rob took a deep breath and walked up to the door.

Once it opened, he cautiously entered the room.

Just before the door closed, he heard yelling.

Quickly, Brian ran down the hall and up to the door.

Once it was open, he saw Rob standing along the outer hull wall near a table with an odd device on top of it.

Then he saw Lee several meters before him, standing slightly left of the door facing Rob.

Lee was clearly focused on Rob and did not notice that the door behind him to the hall had reopened and that Brian was standing there.

Rob was in the middle of explaining, "You have it all wrong. I thought I heard someone in here needing...."

Lee snapped. "Don't give me that crap. I know the jammer is active and is the only way anyone without access could enter this room."

"Why are you in here?" Rob asked bluntly.

"Isn't that obvious? I work for the Admiral," Lee replied while reaching into the pouch on his right side, pulling out an energy pistol and aiming it at Rob.

With a smirk, Lee added, "The Admiral had me stake out the room to catch the spy. He has outsmarted you, Pirates. With your capture, he has all the proof he needs."

Suddenly, Brian started to feel lighter. He realized the drives just shut down as the ship entered orbit. There was no warning because the coms were being jammed.

Lee quickly tries to activate his boots using his C&PC, but Rob takes advantage of the distraction. Using his legs and the lack of gravity, he pushes off the hull wall and launches himself at Lee.

Before Lee can activate his boots, he sees Rob flying towards him and tries to fire his weapon, but nothing happens.

Rob impacts Lee, causing Lee to fly into the wall beside the doorway, hitting his head.

Lee drops his weapon, and he and it begin to float motionless. Rob activates his boots and stands beside him, looking him over.

Brian quickly activates his boots and enters the room. He looks at Lee to see any signs of life.

"He's only knocked out," Rob insisted.

Brian then saw to his left a console, a chair, and a large screen on the wall.

The screen displayed several snowed-out images. From the information at the bottom of each one, they were obviously security camera feeds on this level.

Rob said, "The room was a trap with Mr. Smith waiting. He was using the security feed to warn of jamming and a possible intrusion into the room."

Pointing at the device on the table, Rob added, "The trap even had a machine to generate fake groaning noises."

Rob was not looking at Brian but at the door behind him. Brian turned to see Val standing in the open doorway. She still had a dead expression and glazed eyes, staring off into space. Her magnetic boots were on, so she must be aware enough of the loss of gravity to have turned them on.

Looking at Rob, Brian snapped, "Just what the fuck is going on?"

Staring curiously at Brian, Rob asked, "Why are you here?"

"I was getting something to eat and.... Hell, what's going on, damn it!" Brian barked.

Rob grins and says, "Just before you came aboard, we realized Thatorn was trying to flush one of us out."

"Us?" asked Brian.

Looking back at Val, Rob complained, "I told you to stay in your cabin. We can't afford for you to blow your cover. If something happens to me, it's up to you to report what we found out."

"I thought you might need help," mumbled Val in a slow, monotone voice.

After glancing at the snowed-out screens, Rob asked Val, "How much longer do we have?"

"Sixteen minutes more or less, " she coldly replies, not looking at either of them.

"We won't be able to cover this up with Lee being involved. We'll have to proceed as planned and use the Moon Hopper," Rob said, scratching his cheek.

Staring at Brian, Rob said, "You see, Thatorn manipulated the lives of those he suspected of being a Pirate operative. Just so he could get them on this ship. He was the cause of everyone's lousy luck. Val and I realized this was a common aspect early on. Until now, we were not sure why Lee was the only one that didn't seem to fit this pattern."

"That explains a few things," Brian said, nodding. Then asked, "So who are you then, Pirates?"

Frowning, Rob explained, "We prefer to call ourselves Solarians. You see, it all started 40 years ago when the colonists on Mars only wanted to keep their independence and freedom from the U.E.A. Not long after they were suppressed, the U.E.A. discovered and attacked one of our hidden colonies. Unfortunately, there were groups of us that retaliated, triggering a war. The U.E.A. thought they were fighting rogue elements of the Mars colonists. They were declared Pirates and called The Pirates of Sol."

Before Brian could say anything, Rob elaborated, "Since we were steered into working on this ship, we were tasked with finding out what Thatorn was really up to. We were given what intel there was, like data on the ship's surveillance, bugs, and even the explosives and where they were. However, there was nothing in our intel about this room. Only how zealous Thatorn was towards what he called Pirates."

Brian blurted out, "Then why did you blow up the communications tower? I almost got killed."

With a sigh, Rob said somberly, "I'm sorry about that. When I set the timer, no one was supposed to be anywhere near there based on the work schedule."

"I changed it up at the last minute," muttered Brian.

Rob explained, "Once we realized Thatorn was out to find us, I had to come up with something. I had hoped the damage would be seen as an accident. Dismissed as a micrometeorite like Fa suggested. Forcing Thatorn to turn back to a port and giving us a chance to be long gone before the truth was discovered. Alas, I underestimated how determined Thatorn was to find a Pirate. The truth came out sooner than expected when it was determined to be sabotage. This only confirmed for him that he had a Pirate on board. At that point, we were sure no matter what we did, it wouldn't get him to turn the ship around."

Brian said, "So that's why you didn't try any further attempts to disable the ship with the rest of the explosives. What did you do with the rest of the explosives, detonators, and timers anyway?"

Rob replied, "When I took them, I kept what I needed and hid the rest in an emergency rations storage locker in the cargo airlock in case I might need them. I knew if they were found, everyone's DNA at the time of the theft was all over them and wouldn't point to anyone.

Brian bragged, "I did figure out how you managed to keep the bomb in place."

"Really?" inquired Rob.

"You took a shaped charge, detonator, and timer, then attached it to the low-powered magnet you got from your boot. Put a small battery cell on each side for power and balance. You ensured the explosion's direction was toward the magnet and the wall it would be attached to. The magnet made sure the bomb stayed in place even when there was gravity. With all the other systems running in the communications room, its low power would never be noticed, even with a scan."

"Very Good," praised Rob.

"I assumed you planted it during one of the jamming times," asked Brian.

"Ah, but we never went into the communications room," replied Rob.

Brian glanced at Val to see she was still in a daze. Then stares back at Rob, confused.

Rob explained, "The device was thrown down the hall in zero-G. It was aimed for and stuck to the wall under the standing console. Which was opposite the entrance to the communications room. Exactly where Thatorn calculated it was planted."

Brian inquired, "What if you missed?"

Rob stated, "It only required a toss with your hand just below your waist. Plus, the throw was well-practiced beforehand."

Turning to look at Val, Brian said, "Of course, it was in the camera footage from the 3rd. You took the bomb from your case while putting a tool away. You threw it toward the communications room behind you as you turned down the hall heading to the lift. Since you were aware of the surveillance in our rooms, you disguised your practice throwing with a made-up wall game."

Val did not reply. She continued to stare off into space.

Rob added, "We added a little jammer glitching to help cover it up in the security footage."

Brian said, "I thought I saw something on the surveillance playback, but it wasn't clear."

He then asked, "I assume you did it with the same jammer you used on the 2nd?"

Rob replied, "You could say that. The only thing I did on the 2nd was to take the explosives on the last and longest jam. Doing

320

everything the way we did helped cause confusion. Since everyone thought it all took place on the 2nd, the data on the next day with Val wasn't scrutinized more."

Rob elaborated, "Since I also knew about the security camera frame limit in Med Bay 2. I took some latex gloves without detection during a doctor's visit."

"So not to leave any prints," said Brian.

Rob explained, "Not just for that. I pretended to be a germaphobe, and after shaking someone's hand, I used my little mini-vac to collect DNA from my hands once out of sight. When I was ready on the 2nd, I used the electrostatic nature of the gloves to hold all the DNA. After statically charging the glove of my left hand, I used its fingers to dig into the mini-vac to collect its contents. I kept it closed until I got to the hold. Once there, I strategically spread the DNA from the glove before taking the explosives, detonators, and timers. I disposed of the gloves in the medical waste chute during another visit to the doctor. I slipped them in as I walked by it with my body obscuring the act from surveillance."

Rob added, "The germophobe angle worked on everyone. To keep up appearances, I even continued to do it when I shook your hand when you came aboard. I admit you threw me off with that boot sterilization remark. It was a good thing we were interrupted."

"You knew Thatorn had us all bugged. Tell me, how did you keep him from overhearing you two give yourselves away?" Brian asked, holding up his left arm and showing Rob his C&PC.

"As field agents, we can use our limited telepathy," replied Rob.

"You can read minds?" asked Brian stunned.

Rob clarified, "No, we can only read thoughts sent by those of us who can transmit them, but only from a short range. Since we must be so close, it would look odd if we were together and didn't say anything to each other, so we covered it up."

"By flirting?" asked Brian.

Rob replied, "Yes, we maintained the appearance that we were interested in each other."

"That's also how you gave her the bomb," said Brian.

"Since it was small and we were so close together, it was not difficult to slip it into her pocket at breakfast on the morning of the 3rd without being noticed," stated Rob.

Brian inquired, "But how did you make the bomb without being caught?"

"I knew there was a nice blind spot in my room from our intel. Part of my desk was in it, so I worked on it the night of the second while pretending to watch videos," Rob explained.

Brian asked, "Why did you decide to act now?"

"Remember what we talked about in the hopper? The unknown DNA and sounds behind the red door convinced me there was a prisoner," replied Rob.

"Well, yeah," said Brian.

Rob said, "I believed the prisoner Thatorn had was one of our own."

"So when we were on the control deck, you said Thatorn may have gotten intel from the spy. It wasn't Ralph you were refereeing to?" questioned Brian.

Rob responded, "Right. After the first 2 course changes, it was the only thing that made sense. I knew I had to rescue them and escape in the Moon Hopper. Lunch was coming up, so I knew I could get close to Val and have a chance to communicate with her about it.

"I saw her sit beside you and snuggle up to you," admitted Brian.

"You came into the galley?" asked Rob.

Brian answered, "No, I was at the open door briefly after Zala and the Captain exited."

Rob said, "I'm sorry about that. From your point of view, it must have been hurtful."

Brian nodded silently.

Rob continued, "After talking about the rescue plan, Val asked me if it would be ok if she stayed on the ship to be with you. That was when I informed her I had already planned for her to stay anyway in case I could not return. That way, she could report back what we learned."

Brian looked at Val and still saw her expressionless face staring at the outer hull wall, and she began to tear up.

Val says in a low, monotone voice, "We are running out of time."

Looking at Brian, Rob insists, "Better get to the control deck. Everyone was supposed to be there before orbital insertion."

Val walks over to Brian and kisses him on the cheek without closing her eyes. Quickly, she turned and left the room.

"She really cares about you, Brian," Rob said, watching her go.

After wiping the tears away, Brian looked at Rob and said, "Tell me something. After Ralph attempted mutiny and sabotage, several of us assumed he was behind everything. However, you didn't pile on. You could have used him as a scapegoat to cover your tracks, but you didn't."

Rob replied, "I had my reasons."

"What reasons?" questioned Brian.

As Rob leaves the room, he says, "You better get to the control deck. I need to leave!"

Brian quickly follows him and exclaims, "I still have questions!"

Rob did not reply as he turned the corner and headed for the square room at the center of the level. Brian was on his heels and followed him through the lower door to the circular hallway.

Rob stood at the maintenance door, waiting for it to open when Brian entered the hallway.

Brian asked harshly, "Look, I know you have reasons for what you did, but why did you kill Nutzie?"

Looking back at Brian, Rob sadly said, "Neither of us killed her or even made an attempt to. We only sabotaged the communications tower, that was all. You have to believe me. I'm not sure who did it or even why."

Shocked, Brian gazed at Rob.

"We did not create those two jammings related to Nutzie's death either," Rob sincerely stated.

Rob added, "I suspect there might be another operative I'm unaware of onboard who is responsible. I have no idea why they went after her?"

"Operative?" curiously asked Brian.

Rob explained, "They could be from one of our other groups."

"Groups?" Brian asked with confusion.

"It's complicated. And I don't have time to explain." Rob insisted, looking at the open maintenance door.

Brian asked, "There is something I still don't understand. Even with the jamming coving your movements, you should have had an accelerated heart rate and breathing after you were back where you started, even in zero-G. How did you fool the C&PC medical readings with no unusual vitals?"

Rob chuckles and smiles at Brian before saying, "The less you know, the better off you'll be."

After deactivating his boots with his C&PC, he quickly dives down the maintenance shaft.

Brian stepped up to the open door to look for Rob, who was already out of sight.

XXII

Brian rushes onto the command deck through the starboard entrance. Once inside, he saw Val and Zala standing a few meters from the door.

Captain Linol was in the pilot console in the tilted-up position. Fa was sitting at the console near the co-pilot console.

Brian could only see the backs of Thatorn and Lieutenant Rocha to his left as they stood at the holographic table.

Brian walks gingerly over to the doctor and Val and stands beside Val.

Looking at the Zala and Val, Brian asks, "What's going on?"

The doctor replied, "Thatorn and Rocha have been hovering over the holo table since I arrived. I don't think anyone realized we were being jammed until Thatorn tried to give the final drive shutdown warning. So everyone would be prepared for free fall."

"I wondered why I didn't hear the drive shutdown warning," Val lied, grinning at Brian.

Brian sees Thatorn pointing at something in the 3D image before him and the lieutenant.

"The Moon Hopper is clear of the ship and on full burn," said the captain, peering out the window.

"Ship status?" asked Thatorn, looking over at Captain Linol.

"All flight systems normal. We are in a stable orbit around Jupiter, not far from Io," the captain replied, looking over his large display screen. Once he seemed happy with what he saw, he lowered his tilted console.

Thatorn looks at Lieutenant Rocha and asks, "Has the jamming stopped?"

The lieutenant walked over to the console along the inside wall. After looking over some of its screens, she replied. "Yes, sir, according to the data, it stopped just a few seconds ago. Security, surveillance, and comms are coming back online."

"As I expected," said Thatorn with a smirk. Using the holographic controls, he changed the view of the image to show a red dot moving away from a larger blue dot at the center of the 3D image before him.

They all heard the port side entrance open, and Lee stumbles onto the control deck. He was holding his head with his right hand, moaning slightly.

Everyone's attention was on him as he shuffled to the back of the holographic table's port side seat.

"It was Mr. Callen, sir. I'm afraid he has escaped," mumbled Lee, looking at Thatorn through the 3D image of a red and blue dot hovering over the table.

Lieutenant Rocha looked at Lee coolly and stated, "The jamming started several minutes before the orbital insertion. You should have been aware of a possible intruder since you were monitoring the security feed."

Embarrassed, Lee explained, "I was and had the drop on him. But when the drives shut off and sent us into zero-G. He used the opportunity to jump me. I had time to react, but my gun failed to fire. Mr. Callen slammed me against the wall, knocking me out."

Thatorn ignored him while the lieutenant just blinked at him.

Lee stared back at them, puzzled.

After Lee glances at Brian and Val, he exclaims to Thatorn, "What will we do about Mr. Callen's accomplices. His girlfriend, Mrs. Elderman, and friend, Mr. Rush!"

Val glares at Lee and snaps back, "His girlfriend? Then why was I fucking Brian!"

Brian looks at Val, feeling a little embarrassed but proud as well.

Lee coldly replied, "I don't know. Maybe you're just a slut!"

Val starts toward him, screaming, "You fucking bastard!"

She stops suddenly when she sees Thatorn turn to face her, pull out an energy pistol from his right belt pouch using his right hand, and aim it at her.

Lieutenant Rocha quickly walks behind Thatorn to stand on his left side and face Val. Using her left hand, she pulls an energy pistol out of her left belt pouch and aims it at Val.

"That will be enough, Ms. Elderman," snapped the lieutenant.

Thatorn and Lieutenant Rocha were now being stared at with shock and confusion by everyone but Lee.

"What the hell, Thatorn!" exclaimed Fa, gazing at the man with disgust from her seat.

Thatorn asks Lee while looking at Val, "Do you have any proof of their involvement with the spy?"

Staring at Thatorn, Lee replied, "From the security feed, I saw Brian in the galley before the jamming started."

"Did you see him or Ms. Elederman with Mr. Callen?" asked Thatorn calmly.

"Well, no," Lee admitted.

"If they were working with Mr. Callen, I'm sure he would not have left them on the ship, at least not alive," Thatorn explained with a smirk.

Lee lowered his head.

"What the hell is going on?" Zala asks, glaring at Thatorn.

Captain Linol slowly stood up from his console, looked at Thatorn, and inquired, "Admiral, I don't understand?"

"Is it not obvious. Lee is one of Thatorn's goons," Fa growled, glaring at Lee.

Staring at Fa, Thatorn explains, "I prefer to call him an undercover security officer."

"That explains why you and the Lieutenant were surprised with the DNA results when they first pointed to Lee," Zala said.

Still staring at Lee, Fa said, "During the diagnostic, the Lieutenant was running during our first briefing. I thought Lee was out collecting DNA. I assumed he was our Pirate spy."

Brian glanced at Fa and said, "You were right about him being a spy. You only missed that he was working for Thatorn."

Staring at Fa, the lieutenant explained, "The Admiral thought it would be best if I covered Lee's exploration of your cabins with the excuse of a diagnostic. In that way, there would be no data you might stumble upon later."

Looking at Lieutenant Rocha, Val said, "That explains why he disposed of his space sickness meds. He didn't really need any! He pretended to be ill just to spy on us."

Lee raises his head and looks at Val.

She stared back at him and said, "The vacuum in the disposal of Med Bay 1 was not working. I found them before I fixed it while we were still in free fall."

Lee shouts, "Damn it! I wanted to ensure the evidence would be destroyed. Since I couldn't dispose of them in front of the doctor, I used the other because everyone had unrestricted access to them. If I had used any other medical room chute, it might have alerted Fa that I had gained access to areas outside my working schedule and hours."

Looking at Lee smugly, the lieutenant ridiculed, "I assumed you made sure the chute was working when they were disposed of. Otherwise, I would not have scheduled Val to do the repair without checking for myself first."

Brian grins, being amused by Lee's anger and embarrassment.

Lee notices, sneers at Brian, and says, "What's so funny. You thought I had a thing for you. All I was trying to do was get intel on you."

Looking over the crew, Lee adds. "My job was to find out everything I could about all of you. That's why I was on the night shift to make it easier to collect evidence."

"Evidence?" asks the doctor, staring at Lee.

"Is that why you were spying on us?" Fa scornfully asked, glaring at Lee.

"Exactly what's going on here, Admiral?" the captain insisted, looking at Thatorn.

With disdain, Thatorn said, "Fine, since we are almost at the end of this little charade anyway."

"Charade?" asked Brian, staring at Thatorn, puzzled.

After a long groan, Thatorn explained, "For you to understand, We need to go back 40 years. During the war, I heard many fascinating tales about our enemy, the Pirates. Most were put down as over-imaginative storytelling. Just some ghost stories, the grunts told each other to entertain themselves."

"Many years later, after the war, I was promoted to U.E.A. command and assigned to an old office not used since the war. When I had it upgraded and remodeled, the workmen came across some old physical reports that had fallen behind a cabinet."

"When I looked through them, I found some of them had the same fantastic Pirate stories I heard during the war. At first, I took these reports as just stories of fiction. Maybe even some propaganda the Pirates tried to use against us. The problem was I could never find any digital version of them in the U.E.A. Database. I even couldn't find any physical copies of these reports in the archives."

"Several of these reports came from highly decorated U.E.A. officers. A few I knew personally. They were not the kind to make up these kinds of stories."

"It was not long after this that I happened to run into an officer who wrote one of those reports. After talking about the war days with them for a while, I asked them if they could recall creating the report I had."

"They claimed to have no idea of what I was talking about. I even sent them a copy of their report, and they thought I was playing a joke. When I pressed them about it, they just chalked it up to being one of their fellow officers trying to pull a prank all those years ago. Creating a fake paper report and putting their name on it."

"I then checked with the other officers who supposedly wrote these mysterious reports. Not one of them knew what I was talking about. It all could not be a coincidence. That's when I started fitting it together."

"Someone covered up those reports. Taking them from the archives and deleting all the digital versions. Hell, they even went out of their way to erase personal memories. This was when I realized the Pirates were not just some thugs or rouge colonists. The only conclusion that made sense was that they were aliens, possibly even native Martians, who managed to remain hidden all this time."

The command deck was silent as the crew, including Lee, stared at Thorton in disbelief.

Lieutenant Rocha, on the other hand, had no reaction.

Brian wondered why the revelation was not a surprise or mattered to her. Then again, she probably already knew about it.

Thatorn continued, "I then asked myself, how did all those people lose their memories? The aliens or Pirates clearly wanted us to forget about these reports. Why? The information in them seemed to be trivial at best. So then I wondered what else they had hidden since they had gone out of their way to erase what seemed to be such insignificant data. What were they up to back then? If they are still around, what are they up to now?"

"They could be a grave threat to humanity. Who knows what they ultimately have in store for us?"

"Since then, I've been researching and digging to discover who they are and what they are up to. As a result, I'm convinced they are still out there. I don't yet know their true intent, but I'm sure we may never be able to if we don't stop them soon."

Everyone except for the lieutenant stared at each other in stunned silence over what Thatorn said.

Their attention was grabbed by Thatorn again when he said, "In an attempt to find these aliens, I did secret testing on the population of Mars. But to no avail. Either I didn't manage to collect any in my sampling, or the aliens could have some adaptive ability that lets them hide among us."

"These aliens or Martians might have deliberately changed some of their own kind to be more human to infiltrate us. That's why I was not surprised when they managed to fool the metabolic C&PC sensors that helped hide their activity when they jammed our security system."

A frightening thought suddenly occurred to Brian. Wait, if Val and Rob are aliens, I fucked one!

Brian's thoughts were broken when Thatorn started up again, "For the last few years, I looked over countless records and data. Looking for anything that might help me locate any of them. In the end, I had a list of suspects. I took the ones I considered most likely...."

Thatorn paused a second before adding, "You see, you all were my prime suspects. I arranged to have you on this mission so I could find a Pirate and interrogate them for information."

"What!" exclaimed Zala.

With a smirk, Thatorn elaborated, "You see, I coordinated events in your lives, so you would have little choice other than to take this job, assuming you wanted to eat."

"But I thought I got this job only because it was all I could get," Fa explained.

"You destroyed Ralph's marriage and family and manipulated my career for this?" Val snapped.

"That explains why you let some on this mission that didn't even have a 1 G gravity tolerance," Brian angrily declared.

Fa raged, "Because of my father, you thought I was involved with these Pirates?"

"My practice was destroyed because of you!" growled the doctor.

"Was I part of this too?" Captain Linol asked gruffly.

Thatorn looked at the captain and replied, "Yes, even you."

"You were behind the accident that ruined my civilian career!" snarled Captain Linol, glaring at Thatorn.

"I'm sure you all can see disturbing your lives was a small price to pay for the safety and security of humanity," Thatorn proudly boasted.

Captian Linol growls and starts toward Thatorn. He stops cold when Thatorn and Lieutenant Rocha aim their weapons at him.

Thatorn smugly says, "I wouldn't if I were you."

"I suggest you move over beside Ms. Ming, Captain," says Thatorn, waving his gun toward her.

The captain walked over and stood beside Fa while the lieutenant aimed her weapon at the rest of the crew.

"Mr. Smith, if you please," says Thatorn, motioning for Lee to approach him.

Once there, the admiral carefully hands his weapon over to Lee. Lee quickly aims it toward Captain Linol and Fa.

Thatorn stands beside the holo table between Lee and Lieutenant Rocha, then declares, "It's ironic that Mr. Callen was the easiest to get on board. He was the only one of you already down on his luck for corporate espionage. He was even jailed for a little while for it."

Surprised, Brian blurted out, "What!"

Thatorn added, "That was why he was placed high on my list."

Perplexed, the captain stated, "It's hard to believe that about him."

"It makes sense now that we know he is a Pirate. He's probably been stealing secrets for them for years," Thatorn elaborated.

"What about me?" Inquired Brian, glaring at the old man.

"Dropping your rating was not difficult," Thatorn replied.

Brian snapped, "Not that. I mean, what's all this got to do with me? I have nothing to do with any Pirates!"

Thatorn looked at Brian curiously and said, "You really don't know. Do you."

"Know what?" Brian asked.

Thatorn replied smugly, "Your Pirate spy parents were killed when you were less than a year old in an attempt to leave Mars. You got lost in the bureaucracy back then and adopted out, but I eventually uncovered the truth."

Brian was shocked. He stared at the deck, shaking his head.

He asked himself out loud, "Why didn't the people I thought were my parents ever tell me I was adopted? Why did they keep it a secret all these years? All along, I, I was...."

"A Pirate brat," interrupts Thatorn, taunting.

Brian glares back at the old man.

"So, how exactly did Nutzie fall into your group of suspects?" the doctor asked, glaring at Thatorn.

Thatorn stared at Zala and replied, "During the war's final days, she went missing for a few hours and supposedly got lost. At the time, I thought nothing of it. It happens in the fog of war. However, after years of research, I realized she might have been compromised. Worse yet, what if the Martians copied and replaced her?"

Zala stares at Thatorn, shocked.

Thatorn looked over his suspects and stated, "As for the rest of you. I placed you at the top of my list for various reasons, but that doesn't matter now."

"I can't believe the U.E.A. would condone any of this," Captain Linol sneered.

Fa spoke up, "I don't think they did. Remember, at the beginning of this mission, Thatorn let it slip that he had to prove, not just report, the presence of Pirates."

The captain asked, "What about that communication we got from the U.E.A. after we fixed the antenna array!"

Thatorn cleared his throat, looked at Captain Linol, and said, "The part about turning back and abandoning the mission was the only real part of it. I added the rest about the importance of continuing anyway."

"You lied to us!" Fa barked.

Thatorn growled, "Those fools at U.E.A. command are too stupid to see the truth."

Then, with a giggle, he added, "They even threatened to dispatch a ship to retrieve us if necessary."

"That's why you were in such a hurry to get us to Jupiter," the captain said, nodding.

Turning his attention back to the crew, Thatorn said, "Getting you all here was the easy part. Determining who the Pirate spy was and capturing them alive would be the real challenge."

"After the destruction of the communications tower, Lee, Lieutenant Rocha, and I got together right away before the meeting with the rest of you to review what happened."

Brian then realizes that was why Lee came in the door from the control deck shortly after Thatorn and Rocha did. He went around through the circular hallway from Thatorns office to avoid suspicion.

Thatorn continued, "In my office, Lieutenant Rocha pulled up the related security data of everything before the incident. The same data we later presented to you at the briefing. We, like you, could not identify exactly what had happened. At this point, we only had some speculation that sabotage might have been involved, but there was no evidence."

"Lieutenant Rocha was impatient and wanted to start interrogating you all."

"I told her no."

"She tried to get me to reconsider even as we entered the meeting."

"I thought it would be best to take our time and investigate the incident properly. If we discovered it was sabotage, chances were high that it was the work of a Pirate spy and be revealed during the investigation."

"We finally knew it was sabotage during the computer core meeting. It was then I knew my plan had worked, and we had at least one Pirate on board."

Fa asked, "Just how did Rob accomplish the sabotage?"

Thatorn grumbled, "Since the who has finally revealed themselves, the how is now irrelevant!"

Gloating, he adds, "All that matters is my carefully orchestrated plan has finally come to fruition."

Brian smugly says, "Then why didn't you see the RRU overload coming, which turned out to be the first attempt on Nutzies Life? She intended to run the RRU, but you stepped in."

Thatorn stares at Brian and laughs aloud, then says, "You see, my boy, I set that up myself."

Everyone other than the lieutenant, Lee, and Thatorn looked at each other, confused.

Thatorn explained, "I rigged the system to operate for a limited time and then burn itself out. Giving me enough time to gather all the needed repair data before it overloaded."

Smirking, Brian asked, "And fry your legs too?"

Smiling at Brian, Thatorn stated, "I ran all the calculations. They told me that 97 percent of the power would be ground out on the frame of my exoskeleton. The surge would likely knock me out, and there was a good chance my legs would be damaged. I was not too concerned about that since I had a capable engineer and a tech on board that could fix them for me."

With a snort, Brian said, "So the RRU meeting delay was to give yourself enough time to rig the RRU control," Brian said.

"I took that power regulator chip from the power control card. At the same time, Lieutenant Rocha moved your tools into the RRU control room. It was not difficult for her to do alone in zero-G. We had more than enough time before you joined us there," Thatorn explained.

Brian said, "That's why the Lieutenant didn't want me to look over the RRU and why she had Lee do it. I bet he didn't even look at it since he knew what really happened. It was all just a cover to hide the truth."

Thatorn said, "I wanted everyone to think it was just an accident before it looked like more sabotage. Lee did a good job pretending to have worked on the RRU and took the heat for missing the obvious sabotage."

Staring at Brian, Thatorn added, "You were the first to come up with the theory that it was the first attempt on Ms. Teodoresco's life. I expected someone would eventually. You see, taking her place on the RRU would relieve me of any suspicion later."

"Suspicion?" asked Brian.

With a curl on his lips, Thatorn coldly stated, "Since I knew I had to kill her."

XXIII

Horrified, Thatorn's suspects glared and screamed at him. The doctor raged, "Damn you!" as she lunged toward Thatorn.

Captain Linol grabbed her and pulled her back to him as Lee and Lieutenant Rocha aimed their weapons at her.

Zala leans on the captain and breaks down, sobbing.

Once everyone had settled, Thatorn then calmly stated, "Mr. Rush discovered it was a murder a little sooner than I would have liked. But I managed to make the best of it."

"But why did you kill her?" Zala wailed with her face buried in Captain Linol's shoulder.

Thatorn stared at the doctor and said, "Honestly, it was never part of my original plan."

Looking back at his suspects, he continued, "I became concerned about Mrs. Teodoresco not long after we started out for Jupiter. She called me on her C&PC, telling me she figured it all out and knew what I was up to."

Brian grimaced as he thought, So what I heard was related to her murder after all. It also explains why Rocha claimed to not find anything significant when reviewing her communications. It makes sense now.

Brian's scowling face caught Thatorn's eye.

Thatorn looked at Brian and said, "Ah yes, Mr. Rush. During our surveillance review, we noticed you were listening in on part of that conversation."

Brian stared at Thatorn wide-eyed.

Thatorn added, "Fortunately for you, we determined you did not pick up anything significant."

Turning his attention back to the rest of his suspects, Thatorn said, "Right after the crew meeting on the tower's destruction, Mrs. Teodoresco came to me complaining."

So that's where she went, Brian realized.

"Mrs. Teodoresco suspected it might be sabotage right away as we did. She didn't want me to put her and her girlfriend in danger," said Thatorn, glancing at Zala.

He added, "Fortunately, she said she did not tell her anything to avoid worrying her."

Frowning, he continued, "I did not like being placed in such a vulnerable situation. That was when I realized Mrs. Teodoresco left me with no choice. If she had told any of you of my plans, years of hard work and effort would have been wasted. That's when I decided I had to shut her up. So, I had to improvise and set up my subterfuge with the RRU. You see, not only did I want to avoid future suspicion of her death, but I also needed to get her outside ...."

Fa interrupted, snapping, "To kill her during an EVA."

"Exactly," Thatorn replied, grinning at Fa.

Recalling Nutzies last words, Brian thought. So, it was Thatorn she was cursing right before she died.

Thatorn said, "She came close to blowing it when we were in the computer room, examining the RRU data when the sabotage was confirmed. I didn't know how much longer she would remain silent. That's why I pushed to get the EVA going right away."

Brian speculated. If she had told anyone else, I wonder what the old man would have done to them.

"You made the virus and put it into her suit?" asked Val.

"Yes. I created it and had Lee load it into her suit. Since our spy saboteur made for the perfect pasty, I had no need to hide it. That's why I allowed for the cause of her death to become so apparent," admitted Thatorn.

"You made sure you cleaned up your tracks on the main computer so I would not be able to link the virus to you," remarked Fa as she got up and stood beside the captain and Zala.

"My activities creating the virus needed to be hidden. I also had to sell the idea that the spy could have a device on them that could do it. That was not too difficult since they somehow managed to get a jammer onto my ship.

"The tricky part was ensuring she finished fixing the communications room first and couldn't get any real help at the last minute. Otherwise, she would have ruined it all if she had survived."

"She was an old soldier and had a lot of experience working in the vacuum of space. I knew I had to be sneaky about it. A sudden cut-off would have alerted her."

"So I just appealed to her pride and vanity in her work. I had the virus monitor the suit's radio. It was keyed to activate and slowly reduce Mrs. Teodoresco's O2 once it heard her declare she was finished."

Brian said, "That was why you asked her to tell you exactly when she was done. Not because you wanted to know when to start a pressure test in the communications room. You just wanted the virus to be triggered."

"I actually wanted both, Mr. Rush," replied Thatorn.

"What were you planning to do if we needed more repairs without Nutzie?" Captain Linol asked.

Thatorn replied, "I considered that too. Mr. Smith has a good EVA rating, and Mr. Rush seems to have overcome his fear of space. He could have suited up as well."

The old man knew about that too, thought Brian.

Fa inquired, "So you created those last two jams to cover up the RRU and Nutzies suit sabotages?"

"We didn't need to since no one but ourselves had access to the security data at that time. So we just claimed there were," responded Thatorn.

"That explains why Rocha didn't give us exact times on those occasions like she did with the real jammings," Fa stated.

Brian proclaimed, "Lee was on the lift right before the EVA when Zala got on. It never occurred to me at the time that he was coming up from the cargo level."

Lee looked at Brian and explained, "Lieutenant Rocha was monitoring where the crew was the entire time and informed me over the C&PC while I was rigging the suit. We were caught off guard when Zala hit the call button when I was on my way up to the control deck."

"I came up with a quick story. I was going to claim the lift control was merely handling things as efficiently as possible, and it took me down from my cabin's level to collect the Doctor before going up. However, no one seemed to notice."

Brian glumly said, "Since we were later told the jamming took place well before that, I never put it together."

"Why wait so close to the EVA time to load the virus?" Val inquired curiously.

Thatorn elaborated, "The actual time the virus was planted ensured everyone would be out of the way for Lee to do his work. Most of the crew started heading for the control deck at that time. We knew Mrs. Teodoresco and Mr. Rush were still on the wing deck and were not heading to the EVA control room yet."

"We couldn't claim the time closer to when it happened because the Doctor used the tracking system to find Mr. Rush and Mrs. Teodoresco. That would have caused issues with how we believed the Jammer worked. We knew Mrs. Teodoresco already checked her and Mr. Rush's suits before 7:08 hours. So we just claimed the jamming to cover up the planting of the virus took place after that."

The Doctor let out a sob upon hearing this.

Val said, "We all wondered why the saboteur killed her after she fixed the hull. Especially since we thought they didn't want us to be able to re-establish communication."

Fa said, "Then the first sabotage had nothing to do with everything else. That's why nothing was making any sense."

"You still took a chance letting me spot her," declared Brian.

Thatorn responded, "Mr. Rush, Mrs. Teodoresco's insistence on regulations of a spotter only required someone to be ready to assist her. When I found this out in the meeting at the lab, I did a rough calculation to determine all the factors. They indicated it would still be too late when she realized what was wrong, and you could get her to the airlock. I knew the emergency procedure to add air through her backpack port would be useless."

Brian gritted his teeth.

Thatorn elaborated, "I knew trying to hide Mrs. Teodoresco's murder would be impossible. So I used it to my advantage to place extra pressure on the rest of you to help me find the spy. That was why I also intentionally suggested the Pirates might be out for someone on the ship or the ship itself.

With a broad smile, Thatorn added, "There is no better motivator than fear."

"Not only did you suspect all of us, but you used us too!" Fa exclaimed.

Thatorn ignored Fa and said, "It became evident that I was dealing with a high-level agent. One that cut off our communication to command using our own explosives. Concealed it from us with a sophisticated jammer, they managed to get on my ship. Then, they used our DNA against us to help hide their identity. I knew capturing them was going to be difficult."

After a short pause, Thatorn added, "I realized that I would have to add more cheese to my trap to make it irresistible."

"Cheese?" inquired the captain as Zala stopped crying and looked at Thatorn.

"Trap?" asked Fa.

Thatorn replied, "It was the room with the red door on level 4. My surveillance showed that everyone did check it out at some point early on. The fake sounds and groans from a random noise generator in the room proved too subtle. I hoped the spy would react if they thought I was holding one of their own in the room. If they tried, I had a gas trap waiting for them."

Thatorn took a breath and continued, "However, after we discovered the jammings, I wasn't sure if I could trust this trap to work. That's why I assigned Mr. Smith to be stationed and ready in the room to capture them."

"That's why we never saw much of him after the 6th," Val said.

"Since he was on the night shift, no one noticed," said Brian.

Thatorn said, "I had Lieutenant Rocha take him food and cover for him part of the day so he could shower and sleep in his cabin."

Fa sarcastically said, "And handle special errands. Like killing Nutzie?"

Thatorn only smiled in response.

"Wait, why didn't you just have the lieutenant load the virus so Lee would not have had to leave the room?" asked Fa.

"I'm a U.E.A. officer, not a spy like Mr. Smith," the lieutenant snapped.

"We might have been able to avoid it all if the DNA testing pointed out the spy. But its failure gave me an idea," said Thatorn.

"I ordered the DND rechecked for a reason. There was a slight chance a retest might find something. I did hold out some hope for that. In any case, I used the opportunity for another purpose. You see, I added the unknown DNA myself."

"Where did you get the DNA from?" asked Zala as she composed herself, left Captain Linol's shoulder, and stood erect, staring at Thatorn.

Before Thatorn could reply, Brian said, "It was from a lock of hair he has in his office."

Thatorn looked at Brian, briefly grinned, and nodded his head.

Confused, Fa asked, "Then why did you try to dismiss this DNA?"

Thatorn looked at her and said, "It was to make the cheese more appealing. To push the idea that I secretly had a Pirate being held captive onboard behind the room with the red door."

Brian stated, "That's why you and the Lieutenant never tried to hide your comings and goings to the room."

"Yes, it was intended to help draw the spy in," Thatorn explained.

Lieutenant Rocha said, "In order to hide Lee's coming and going from the room behind the red door, the Admiral had me take Fa's security access away. Later, he had me give her back limited access to the security data for a special reason. While ensuring she knew nothing about Lee or the trap."

Intrigued, Fa inquired, "What are you talking about?"

"I wanted to feed you information and see how you would react," said Thatorn.

The lieutenant said, "That's why we allowed you to see me taking food to the room."

"We thought you might be our spy if you didn't share this information with your fellow crewmates. On the other hand, if you shared your information with the rest of the crew, it could also help to lure the spy in," said Thatorn.

Lieutenant Rocha said, "We know you told Brian about it. Just after he came to you this morning to check a problem you claimed to be having in the computer core's maintenance corridor."

"Since the ship's refit, we have been aware of a few areas on this ship that can cause interference to the C&PCs. That is why I had special sensitive microphones placed just out of the range of these areas of interference," Thatorn said smugly.

Brian looked at Fa, realizing Fa's precautions for privacy turned out to be useless.

"Why?" asked Zala.

Smirking, Fa said, "It was a backup in case the constant monitoring of us through our C&PCs microphone didn't work."

"You are listening to everything we say!" exclaimed the captain.

Brian added, "Not only that. I believe Thatorn even has cameras and mics in our cabins."

Zala, the Captain, and Fa were shocked by what Brian said.

Thatorn glanced at Brian before he said, "When looking for a spy. You need to take advantage of all your opportunities."

Looking at Fa, Thatorn added, "I commend you, Ms. Ming. You also managed to do a rather good job hiding your C&PCs offline status from triggering an alarm as well."

Fa only snarled at Thatorn in response.

Brian thought. Little seems to have escaped the old man. Well, except maybe my private conversation with Rob in the hopper.

"Since you were testing Fa, does that mean you never thought Ralph was the spy?" questioned Captain Linol.

"Correct. There were just too many things that didn't add up for it to be Mr. Milsom," said Thatorn.

Brian thought. Funny, I assumed the same thing.

"But you allowed us to believe that he was?" Fa asked.

"Yes," replied Thatorn.

Zala said, "That was why you had me keep Ralph locked up and sedated."

Thatorn explained, "I wanted our real spy to feel safe and free to act. Everyone's insistence on freedom over security early on also helped with that."

The lieutenant said, "Interestingly enough, Rob was the primary advocate for this freedom."

Brian said, "That's why you didn't want us teaming up to keep an eye on each other. It would hinder the spy."

"Exactly," said the old man.

He then boasted, "My master stroke was coming up with all the course corrections. I had no real idea where the Pirates were, but I wanted the spy to think a Pirate captive was giving me information. Finally, the last course correction sprung the trap."

"Mr. Callen still managed to escape," the captain mocked.

Thatorn replied, "Oh, has he?"

Then he followed it with a loud belly laugh.

The suspects looked around at each other, bewildered by the old man's behavior.

Once Thatorn was finished, he elaborated, "I thought that whoever this trained spy was could easily subdue Lee. But I had to be sure of that. Under the guize of checking Lee's weapon, I had Lieutenant Rocha disable it so he would not be aware it was no longer functioning."

Stunned, Lee gazed at Thatorn and asked, "What? Why?"

"All part of my new plan," Thatorn replied, smirking.

"Part of the new plan? I don't understand," Lee questioned, glancing at the suspects, trying to keep his weapon aimed at them.

Boasting, Thatorn replied, "You see, Mr. Smith, I had your gun rigged to fail because I wanted our spy to escape."

"Escape?" Lee asked.

"Why let him escape?" curiously asked Val.

Thatorn explained, "If the spy felt that valuable information was being extracted, they would have little choice but to commit to a

345

rescue and try to escape. I was sure that even after they discovered there was no one to rescue, they would have little choice but to flee."

Thatorn looked at Lee and added, "I knew there was a chance that Mr. Smith might get killed in the process, but I thought it would be worth it."

Dismayed, Lee started to stare at Thatorn and lower his gun.

Lieutenant Rocha saw him out of the corner of her eye and said, "Mr. Smith, focus."

Lee slowly turned his attention and weapon back onto the suspects.

Smiling briefly, Thatorn said, "Once they escaped, I plan to use them to lead me to their Pirate compatriots."

Captain Linol asked, "How could you have known they would be able to fly the hopper? Rob just happened to be a pilot."

Thatorn replied, "I assumed there was a good chance this spy already knew how to. But just to make sure I...."

Brian interjected, "That's why you made changes to the hopper to make it more automatic. It wasn't for us, but the spy."

Thatorn said, "To give them confidence that they could pilot it even if they were unsure how to, yes."

"How can you be sure Rob knows where a Pirate base is out here?" asked Val.

Sneering, Thatorn replied, "Even if he doesn't, I'm sure he will try to contact them for assistance. Then, he will lead me right to them. U.E.A. Command were idiots for not taking me seriously! But I'll show them. I will finally have my glory at last!"

"You are mad, Thatorn!" growled Fa.

Thatorn only grins at Fa before looking at the lieutenant and asks, "See if we are getting any flight telemetry or transponder data from the hopper?"

Lieutenant Rocha handed her gun to Thatorn, who quickly aimed it toward Val and Brian as Lee pointed his at the rest of the suspects.

The lieutenant sat at the console on the inner wall and examined its 2D displays.

Looking back at Thatorn, she said, "No, neither appears to be active."

"I didn't think they would be," said Thatorn, staring at Val and Brian.

"Are sensors tracking the hopper?" Thatorn asked, glancing at Lieutenant Rocha.

The lieutenant brought up a 3D keyboard and typed away on it. Within a few seconds, another 3D display appeared in front of her.

She then told the admiral, "Yes, sir."

"Power up the DEW," ordered Thatorn.

He added, looking at all his suspects, "I'm surprised Rob didn't use the rest of his explosives to try and take out the ship's Directional Energy Weapon."

He tilted his head, smirking, and added, "No matter. Even if he did, it wouldn't have mattered that much."

Thatorn swiftly and softly clanked around the Holographic table and stood on its port side. After aiming at Val and Brian again through the 3D image, he ordered, "Activate full combat systems."

Lieutenant Rocha typed on her keyboard of light, bringing up several more 3D displays, which she quickly tapped on.

A 3D real-time computer image of the ship appears over the table between Thatorn and his crew. They watched as the four unusual boxy raised areas on the ship's wing opened. From inside each, a weapon platform emerged. The holographic image showed each had a missile bay and a Gatling gun.

Thatorn proudly stated, "This is a fully armed combat vessel."

Brian thought. This would explain the need for two reactors, extra extensive power cabling, and why access to some systems was denied to me.

The captain asked coldly, "That's all impressive, but how will you take on a Pirate base with just this ship?"

Thatorn stared through the holograph at him and replied, "Not just this ship. I came prepared." Then, looking at the lieutenant, he nodded.

She then brings up an unusual 3D screen on her console and taps on it.

The center holographic table view zooms in on the Probe attached to the upper wing on the opposite side of the DEW. Numerous displays of data on the device also appear.

"I had this specially made so everyone, especially the Pirates, would believe it was only a Probe. I expect they will go out of their way to ignore it and not scan it to remain hidden. When they discover its true nature, it will be too late." Thatorn giggled.

"True nature?" asked Brian.

"It's really a very special kind of missile. It took me a long time to collect enough anti-matter for its warhead," leered Thatorn.

Shocked, Val screamed, "Oh My God!"

Fa and Captain Linol looked at each other, terrified.

"He is mad!" yelled Zala, glaring at Thatorn.

"We would have never thought he would go that far," Val whispered to Brian.

Thatorn explained, "I knew the Pirates didn't know everything. Otherwise, if they did, they would have destroyed this ship. Even if they had, it still wouldn't have saved them. The ship's destruction would have given the Pirates or, should I say, Aliens away."

"If anything unusual happened to us, I instructed my colleagues to give the U.E.A. all my suspect information on the Pirates, along with all my transmitted updates and reports. So even if they erased all our memories, it would do them no good. That's why getting communications back up was so important."

Thatorn shifted slightly to get a better aim at Val and Brian while ensuring Lee still had his weapon squarely aimed at Fa, Zala, and the captain.

"Now that we know much more. Lieutenant Rocha, transmit an update on our situation. Start a continuous live data feed as well," ordered Thatorn, not taking his eye off Val and Brian.

Lieutenant Rocha quickly obeyed his orders as she typed and tapped away on her screens of light.

Fa asked, "What if the Pirates jam you?"

Thatorn replied, "It won't matter. By the time they discover what I'm sending and do, enough data will have already been sent to vindicate me by then. Besides, I plan on returning with a ship full of data to prove my crushing blow over the Pirates!"

Fa arrogantly suggested, "But what if the spy or spies managed to take over your ship?"

Thatorn sighed, then bragged, "I had a contingency plan for that, just in case. Since my disappearance would alert my colleagues, they would take the collected evidence to U.E.A. command. This would leave me free to strike. Simple to say, I had a Trojan horse ready for the Pirates."

"A what?" inquired Zala.

"I have a failsafe set on the ship's reactors and are linked to the anti-matter missile," replied Thatorn.

He elaborated, "The computer checks me at night in my quarters every 24 hours. Confirms my identity and my life signs. If I miss this, the computer will go into a 5-day self-destruct countdown. It should be plenty of time for the Pirates who captured the ship to have it docked at one of their bases by then."

Lee glanced at Thatorn as if it was the first time he had heard this.

With a happy sigh, Thatorn said, "No nobler a death than to die a glorious hero!"

"You're crazy, Thatorn," Captain Linol says, stepping towards the Admiral only to have Lee shove his gun into his side. Causing him to back away.

Val closes her eyes. Suddenly, the table's 3D image started to break up and fade.

"Is it that jammer again!" Barked Thatorn as he went to the lieutenant's console, still keeping his weapon aimed at Val and Brian.

"It's only affecting sensors and the weapon systems now," replied Lieutenant Rocha as she tried to work on 3D screens as they faded in and out.

Thatorn calmly said, "He must have re-programmed that Jammer on the ship before he left."

The lieutenant tries using her console's physical keyboard and 2D screens to keep the ship's sensors and weapons systems up and running.

Brian sees Val starting to sweat and shake slightly.

The more Lieutenant Rosha worked frantically at her station, the more Brian saw Val struggling.

Finally, Val lets out a gasp and collapses backward. Her body floated while her magnetic boots kept her feet on the deck.

Brian leans over to check on Val as the doctor rushes over to examine her. Brian sees she is out cold and notices a little blood coming from the top of her left nostril.

Brian thought. Val was using her mind somehow to cause the jamming, interfering with the ship's systems. I bet she even used this ability to cheat when we played on her gaming system.

The lieutenant declared, "Interference is clearing."

Thatorn gloated, "I thought as much. Based on its previous uses, it always seemed to need a cool-down time. I knew it would give out quickly this time since it was used only a short time ago."

He softly clanked back to the Holographic table to see the ship's 3D image return.

"Tracking target again," Lieutenant Rocha said, staring intently at a 3D console screen.

"Any communications to or from the hopper?" Thatorn asked, glancing at the lieutenant.

"Not at the moment," Lieutenant Rocha stated.

"Unless it happened while we were being jammed," Thatorn contemplated out loud.

The lieutenant declared, "It appears that the hopper has changed course and is now heading for Io."

"Ah, maybe he knows where he's going to after all, or he got instructions on where to go," speculated Thatorn.

"It looks like he's about to attempt a landing on Io," said Lieutenant Rocha.

"Give me tactical display," ordered Thatorn.

Within seconds, the lieutenant changed the image before him to show a 3D representation of Io with a red dot heading for it.

"Sensors still tracking him?" Thatorn asked.

"Yes, sir," replied Lieutenant Rocha.

"I want our missile to hit whatever he lands on. I want to take them all out," Thatorn chuckled.

Then, the red dot on the hologram before Thatorn began to blur.

Thatorn snapped, "What is it!"

The lieutenant explained, "We are losing our sensor lock. We are getting interference from Io."

Thatorn stared briefly at the fuzzy red blob before saying, "What about the ion trail?"

"Yes, we are picking that up," Lieutenant Rocha replied.

"Set the missile to follow that trail!" exclaimed Thatorn.

"Yes, sir!" the lieutenant answered.

"Stand by," said Thatorn, glaring at a red haze near Io on the 3D display before him.

Brian runs up to the table and yells, "No!"

Thatorn aims his pistol at Brian, smiles, and barks, "Fire!"

Epilogue

Several months later

The small room was dimly lit from overhead, with no windows and only one entrance. A large empty desk was in the center of the room. A fancy chair was on the side of the desk that faced the closed door. On the other side were two chairs occupied by a young woman and a man dressed in casual, brightly colored attire.

They were looking at a thin woman wearing a drab all-black suit sitting near the man on the desk's left corner. It was hard to see her narrow tan face in the low light. However, you could make out that she had short black hair, thin black eyebrows, small blue eyes, a long nose, and a small, thin-lipped mouth.

The woman in black stares at them and asks, "Ok, Mr. and Mrs. Rush, what happened after that? "

Brian said, "Well, Ms. Gizem, along with everyone else on the control deck, Val and I watched the missile follow the ion tail until it impacted Io."

Val said, "The explosion took out a few chunks of Io, and the Captain had to do some quick maneuvering to dodge the debris. Once we were out of harm's way, Thatorn had the area scanned."

Brian explained, "The radiation and debris from Io made it difficult to get accurate readings. Even though the ship was well shielded, the doctor insisted we all take radiation treatments due to our proximity to the explosion."

After a short pause, Brian continued, "After many hours of searching, Thatorn was convinced he had taken out Rob and the Pirate base he was heading for. Then he ordered the ship to return to the military base at 433 Eros ASAP. Even though the old man was wary of his suspects, he still needed us to maintain and operate the ship. He spent the rest of the trip in his room, eager to proclaim his mission's success, compiling a detailed report. Mr. Smith and Lieutenant Rocha took turns guarding him and spent the rest of their time looking for the Pirate jammer."

"I bet the doctor might have tried to take Thatorn out if she had the chance," Val added.

Brian stated, "The authorities debriefed us as soon as we arrived. Then sent us on our way."

Val said, "Except for Ralph. He was hospitalized as soon as we got back. After the doctor woke Ralph up and told him what had happened, he lost it. The doctor thought it best to keep him in the patient room she had him in to keep an eye on him. At least until he could get the care he needed."

The woman in black said, "Yes, he is still under medical care."

She leaned forward and said, "I see that his ex-wife and all the real contractors, including yourselves and the Captain, have lodged a formal complaint against Admiral Thatorn, Mr. Smith, and Lieutenant Rocha. You all are demanding a full investigation into the matter. Ralph's ex-wife seems more interested in suing for financial gain."

The thin woman stood up and said, "I know I have both of your sworn statements on file from the original debriefing months ago. I also realize we have just reviewed everything again, but there are a few things I would like to get more details about."

She then sits in the elaborate chair on the opposite side of the desk and says, "First, we will ask and test you, Mr. Rush."

Brian and Val watch her wave her hand over the desk. Several holographic screens and a keyboard appear above the desk. A small area opens up at the center of the desk on the side of Brian and Val. A metallic arm extends out about half a meter from inside the desk.

On top of it seems to be some kind of a camera with two small dishes on each side.

"What is that?" inquired Brian.

"In layman's terms, it is a truth detector. It scans you for several variations, like pupil dilation, temperature, and heart rate," Ms. Gizem replied.

Brian looks at it oddly.

"It's standard procedure when handling any legal issues. This stipulation is laid out in your contracts," The thin lady said.

She stared at Brian and Val, then asked, "Were you not tested in this manner during your debriefing?"

Val said, "They had trouble with the equipment, so we never saw one before."

"I assure you this one is in top working order. I just tested it myself earlier. It can even show you the results instantly," says Ms. Gizem with a smile.

Brian nods, and the thin woman taps on her 3D screens and brings the device to life. It glows slightly, and a small holographic 2D screen beside it, visible from both sides, flickers into existence. Slowly, the device is aimed at Brian.

Ms. Gizem asks, "Based on your testimony and to your knowledge, was Mr. Callen the only Pirate aboard the ship?"

Looking at Val and then back at the woman in black across the desk through several 3D screens, Brian said, "Yes, he acted alone."

"Was he responsible for the sabotage but not the murder of Mrs. Teodoresco?" asked Ms. Gizem.

"As I have already stated. What we thought was an attempted murder, then the actual murder of Nutzie, um, Ms. Teodoresco, was arranged by Thatorn," stated Brian.

"Yes, several of you did testify to that. I just wanted you to clarify it from your position," the woman in black said.

After tapping on one of her screens, the small screen beside the arm showed several green lines.

She points at it and says, "All indicators are green. You are being truthful. If you were lying, they would show up as red."

Insulted, Brian said, "Why wouldn't I tell the truth!"

Ignoring Brian, Ms. Gizem looked at him and asked, "What about the room with the red door?"

Brian replied, "I never knew what was in it until Thatorn told us he set it up as a trap using his undercover spy, Mr. Smith."

They all briefly looked at the screen again to only see green lines.

"In your own words, tell me exactly what happened with this trap?" Ms. Gizem asked.

Brian replied, "Based on what Mr. Smith said, his weapon failed to fire, and Rob got the jump on him and knocked him out. Then Rob escaped in the Moon Hopper."

"So Rob managed to get away?" the woman in black asked, watching Brian intently through the translucent screens.

Looking back at her, Brian said, "Yeah, But I never became aware of it until after I got to the command deck for the orbital insertion."

They all glanced at the small screen again, showing green lines.

"Look, I told you all this already," grumpily stated Brian.

Ms. Gizem said, "Yes, I know, but I just want to ensure the accuracy of your original statement."

After leaning back in her chair, she asks Brian, "Did Mr. Callen ever tell you anything that might have made you believe he was a Pirate?"

"No," stated Brian.

She glanced at the display, not seeing any red lines.

"At any point, did Mr. Callen ever tell you he was one of these so-called Pirates?" she asks, staring intensely at Brian.

Brian replied, "No."

Again, the display still shows only green.

She asks Brian, "Do you believe Admiral Thatorn was right and Mr. Callen was a Pirate?"

Brian thought about it before saying, "To be honest, I don't really know. He left the ship for some reason."

Green lines only showed on the display.

Ms. Gizem leaned forward and stated, "We just finished with a deep analysis of this case and concluded that the Admiral orchestrated a hoax. He wanted to convince everyone on board of these Pirates, including Ms. Rocha and Mr. Smith. Even that he managed to destroy some of them."

"Admiral Thatorn was aware of Mr. Callen's previous espionage convictions. He set out to use him in his ruse once he was sure he could get him aboard. He wanted Mr. Callen to believe he had some things of value on the ship worth stealing. The Admiral probably enticed Mr. Callen with scraps of information that led him to believe there was something of value in the room behind the red door. The trap set there was only intended for Mr. Callen, which the Admiral would later claim was for the Pirate spy."

"The Admiral was sure that once Mr. Callen found nothing in the room, he would flee rather than be locked up again. That was why he ensured his trap failed by rigging Mr. Smith's gun to malfunction. Admiral Thatorn made sure Mr. Callen could steal the Moon Hopper. All the theatrics were designed to create the impression that Mr. Callen was a fleeing Pirate the Admiral used to find the rest of them. Then appear to destroy the Priates and claim victory."

"That's sick!" Brian exclaimed.

"As far as we have been able to determine. The Admiral wanted one last taste of glory, even if he had to make it all up and even take Mr. Callen's life in the process."

"He was also responsible for Nutzie's death," Brian grumbled.

Ms. Gizem replied, "Yes. Admiral Thatorn at least told the truth about killing Ms. Teodoresco. He felt threatened by her because she must have seen through his ruse. He simply adjusted his plans to include taking her out of the picture."

Brian asked, "So if Rob did not sabotage the communications tower, who did?"

After leaning back in her chair and taking a deep breath, Ms. Gizem said, "The Admiral did. It was his way of creating suspicion among the crew and that there was a Pirate amongst you. He erased some security data. Then blamed a jammer for covering up Pirate activity, which led to the bombing of the tower."

Brian looked at Val and said, "So no one actually smuggled a jammer onto the ship."

Mrs. Gizem said, "One of the things the Admiral claimed in his debriefing was that Mr. Callen left this mysterious jammer on the ship to aid in his escape. Insisting the entire crew witnessed its effects on the ship's systems as proof."

"We did see some kind of interference on the control deck when Rob fled," Brian declared.

The lady in black said, "Yes, everyone testified to that. However, after a complete inspection of the ship, taking weeks of looking through every possible hiding spot, no jammer was ever recovered."

"The Admiral insisted the reason for that was obvious. The device was set up to self-destruct."

"After further inspections, no residue or scorched surfaces that would have resulted from this were found either."

"He explained that since it was alien technology, it was designed to leave none."

Brian asked, "What about us being suspects and Thatorn causing our misfortunes?"

"All part of the illusion. Admiral Thatorn just signed up a group of convenient contractors who needed jobs at the time to be his crew and audience." Gizem replied.

"And what Thatorn said about my parents?" inquired Brian.

She replied, "No data suggests that Linda and Randy are not your parents. Maybe he just wanted to get at you, or it was part of his theatrics."

Brian asks, "So what's going to happen to Thatorn?"

The woman in black says, "He acted without authority, committed fraud, conspiracy, and murder. His sanity has been questioned before. It must be re-evaluated before he is brought up on any formal charges."

"His cohorts in command will also be investigated. We will need to determine if they were willing participants in the scam or were just conned."

"What about Rocha and Smith?" asked Brian.

Ms. Gizem reluctantly said, "There will be a full tribunal for them. Since they were following orders and were tricked like the rest of you, there might be some leniency. However, Mr. Smith is complicit in Ms. Teodoresco's death. Regardless, it will be up to the military court to decide."

"How did a madman like Thatorn get an anti-matter weapon? " Brian asked.

"A full-blown investigation is going on into just how he acquired it. I assure you it is not standard U.E.A. ordnance," explained the woman in black.

"Why did Thatorn need to use such a destructive weapon if it was all just a hoax?" Brian asked.

The woman in black smirked and said, "That's simple. What better way to end up with no physical evidence if there was none, to begin with."

Brian's eyes opened wide, and he softly said, "Huh."

Ms. Gizem looked at Brian and Val and inquired, "Is there anything else you would like to go over, Mr. and Mrs. Rush?"

Brian snapped out of his gaze and replied, "No, I think that's all I have, Ms. Gizem."

Val said, "I think my husband covered everything."

The woman in black stood up and looked sternly at the couple. She stated, "I want to remind you that you are bound by a non-discloser agreement according to your military contracts. You are not to discuss the incident or any related details with anyone other than select U.E.A. officials. If you do, you will be subject to arrest. Is that clear?"

Brian and Val looked at each other, then at Ms. Gizem, and nodded.

She said, pointing at the door, "Very well. Mr. Rush, Someone will be waiting to take you to another room for a blood screening. It's to confirm you are not on any drugs that might have interfered with your responses to the machine."

Curiously, Brian stared at her and asked, "Why did you not check that first?"

She replied humbly, "The military has its set procedures, Mr. Rush."

After looking at Val, she stated, "I have some questions to ask Mrs. Rush. After that, she will join you to be screened as well."

Brian stood up, leaned over, and kissed Val on the lips. He then makes his way to the door. Once it opens automatically, Brian stops and sees someone in a white lab coat waiting for him on the other side of the door. He looks back at Val.

She says, "I'll be along shortly, dear."

Brian nods and walks through the door.

After the door closed, Ms. Gizem walked around the desk and took Brian's seat.

She stared at the readout screen of green lines before saying, "It seems he no longer knows the details about who you and Rob really are."

Val cautiously looks around the room.

Looking at Val, Ms. Gizem says, "Don't worry, agent Elderman. We are quite safe. This room has electronic barriers in the walls, ceiling, floor, and even the door."

After a sigh of relief, Val looked at the woman in black and said, "I'm sorry, Agent Gizem. I was just concerned the room might be bugged."

"Understandable, considering your last assignment." Ms. Gizem said.

Val explained, "During our trip back, I got Brian to play several of my games. It was easy to use the memory alteration part of the system to remove all the dangerous memories about us."

The lady in black asked, "If you did that, why did you disable the U.E.A.'s truth detector after you got to 433 Eros? You can easily lie and fool those machines."

Val slumped in her seat and said, "I was not sure if I completely succeeded in the memory alteration of Brian until now."

Ms. Gizem said, "Yes, that's why they sent me, your contact, in to take control of this interview so that it could be verified. I can now turn Brian's truth detection data over to the human's U.E.A. military. Along with some fabricated results for you. It should prevent any further follow-ups."

Val asked, "And if I had not succeeded?"

The woman in blank bluntly began to say, "Well, data can get lost and changed, but as for Brian, we would have had to..."

Val interrupted, nodding, "Yes, I know."

Ms. Gizem said, "Letting you and Rob go on this mission was a risk, but it was our only way to learn what Admiral Thatorn knew and was up to. Unfortunately, our intel was not perfect. We could only give you what we had. The Admiral was very good about keeping secrets and knowing who to trust."

"He's been very clever all these years, hiding his investigation into us and building up a secret network of others like himself."

"If we erased his memories about us once we realized what he was doing years ago, it would only have alerted the others in his network. Causing them to go underground and become a potentially greater threat to us later. At the time, it was believed best to let everyone think he was just a crackpot."

"Changing the memories of everyone on the ship would have just made it worse. Even the Admiral knew that."

"That's why we devised an alternate truth to discredit the Admiral. Making him a madman and part of a corrupt military conspiracy. It also allows us to investigate everyone involved through our secret U.E.A. contacts and agents."

"Eventually, all Admiral Thatorns conspirators will be found and discredited, too. Finally, putting an end to this threat."

"What about the anti-matter? Surely, that's a threat to us as well." Val asked.

The lady in black replied, "Yes, we will find where it is being created and stop the humans."

Then Val sadly asked, "Have you found out what happened to Rob?"

"No, nothing so far!"

A tear slowly cascades down Val's cheek.

Ms. Gizem changed the subject and asked, "What are your plans? You know we need those like yourself more than ever."

"I don't know yet. I'm sure you already have something in mind," Val replied, wiping away the tear.

"I believe we do," the woman in black said after pulling out a data chip from her pocket and handing it to Val.

She added, "Everything is encoded and can only be read from your unique game system with your agent passcode."

Val takes the clip and slips it into her pocket.

Just as Val gets up and starts to leave, the lady in black asks, "I'm curious. Why did you leave Brian knowing what Thatorn told him about his parents?"

Looking at Ms. Gizem, Val replies, "I had to. There were too many witnesses. When we were debriefed, it might have caused some red flags."

Ms. Gizem nodded and said, "It was wise of Rob to have you remain on the ship and ensure your cover was not blown so you would make it back to report everything to us in case he didn't."

Val stared at her and said, "I also wanted to be with Brian."`

Val then tilted her head and asked, "Is that going to be a problem?"

The woman in black replied, "In Brian's case, no. It's funny. Until we recently discovered the truth, it was assumed he was killed with his parents on Mars."

To be continued.

Don't miss out!

Visit the website below and you can sign up to receive emails whenever Lee Crystal publishes a new book. There's no charge and no obligation.

https://books2read.com/r/B-A-ZNPTB-YUASD

BOOKS 2 READ

Connecting independent readers to independent writers.

www.ingramcontent.com/pod-product-compliance
Lightning Source LLC
Chambersburg PA
CBHW070753280626
47162CB00016B/266